OPERATION PEREGRINE

Deceit • Espionage • Seduction

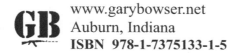
www.garybowser.net
Auburn, Indiana
ISBN 978-1-7375133-1-5

TABLE OF CONTENTS

ACKNOWLEDGEMENTS

After writing intelligence reports and academic papers for many decades, shifting to a fiction-style of writing was a serious challenge for me. With Operation Peregrine, I came to understand that writing a book is indeed a team effort.

Thus, I deeply appreciate the support my family provided in the months it took to produce "Operation Peregrine". My wife, Lisa, and daughters Amanda, Emily, and Rebecca went above and beyond giving understanding and support; they all became active participants in creating and editing the various drafts of this book. Without their support and assistance, this book could not have happened.

Nikki Craig has made a great contribution to the book with her professionalism in reviewing and formatting the text. Along with her husband, Duanne, their enthusiasm to move the project forward has been a positive factor for all involved in Operation Peregrine.

Thanks to Bob, Dave, John, and Todd - a group of friends who have shared a weekly morning coffee session for several years. They each made constructive suggestions and inputs to the first draft which I appreciated.

Thanks to the Vietnam veterans who faithfully answered when the country called on them. Their patriotism, dedication, courage, and bravery were exemplary in a conflict which over time became controversial. They stood firm in their patriotic commitment – our Country owes them respect and thanks. They are the prototypical heroes for the characters in the story.

This book is dedicated to Colonel Richard C. Husemann (USAF, Retired). He was my friend for over 45-years. He passed before the manuscript was finished. Before that, Dick contributed to the story line, editing, and every phase of the book right up to the time our Lord carried him home. We shared many 'adventures' together over those 45-years. I appreciate Dick's wife Brenda's sufferance and patience with Dick and me during our many adventures over all those decades. God bless you Dick and bless your family.

INTRODUCTION

I made a dedicated effort to keep the strategic facts consistent with the realities of the 1962-1964 time frame. The book is not a political book, though the politics of the day during 1962-1964 are part of the "Operation Peregrine" story. The book is about 'people living the Vietnam War'– some heroes, some villains, some victims. It is about personal commitments, fidelity and loyalty, courage, love, and hatred – the things that make us real people.

'The story' is a twisted complex of espionage, deceit, treachery, interwoven with two romances, and face-to-face confrontations with 'certain enemy sons-a-bitches'. While the story is fiction and the core characters are fictional – they are fictional only in the sense the story could have happened; maybe it did happen. It was a secret operation, wasn't it? Though the story is fiction, I tried to ensure that the setting for the 1962-1964 tale is historically accurate. I could not rely solely on my memories, so I have extensively researched events, people, street names, restaurants, 1962-1964 technologies, and other details.

When Vietnam veterans read this book, and I hope they all do – I want them to nod their heads with a – "I remember that": the heat and humidity, the dust and dirt of the cities, Mimi's bar, the Rex Hotel rooftop restaurant, the Saigon traffic, the pungent smells of the Orient, the rock & roll and country music of that time, and so on and so on –providing chords of credibility for all who have experience or familiarity with the 1962-1964 times and places .

The core fictional characters are realistic in the sense that the US military, the KGB, NSA, North Vietnamese moles in the South Vietnamese government, all represent surrogates for the real-people who actually did things like the actions presented in 'the book'.

This story cannot be told without incorporating the military vernacular of that day some language used by the American GI in Vietnam (a little rough at points but cleaned-up enough to not offend, I hope). Slang in Vietnam, and military people talked back then, had a certain, earthy- -quality to their military-tribal dialects. There is a Glossary section to help the reader who is unfamiliar with certain terms ingrained in the dialog from 'back in the day'. I recommend each reader take a few moments to scan the Glossary.

My perspective for the book is to give the reader a 'tour de force' through the enigmatic 'world of smoke and mirrors'; depicting realistic espionage operations by inserting selected factual information about deceit, deception, tradecraft, and the brutality of the 'secret wars' in that time period- the Operation Peregrine "secret war" as described in 'the book' includes all the great emotions of the people who were 'doers' in the front lines for the defense of our values and country.

CHAPTER 1 THEY KNEW WE WERE COMING

The South Vietnamese Colonel exhales a cloud of American Marlboro cigarette smoke and smiles, "It will be an easy victory"!

An intelligence report shows a Viet Cong radio site in the village of Ap Bac is vulnerable to attack. The Army of the Republic of Vietnam (ARVN) 7th Division staff and their American Advisors plan a multi-pronged attack for January 2, 1963.

A South Vietnamese Army unit was being slaughtered by a well-planned and expertly executed Viet Cong and North Vietnamese Army ambush in the Battle of Ap Bac, Wednesday, January 2, 1963. The cries of the ARVN wounded and dying were co-mingled with the staccato drumming of AK-47 assault rifles on full-automatic, deafening explosions from enemy mortar shells, and sharp blasts of the lethal rocket propelled grenades.

Amidst the carnage and tumult, a US Army Special Forces Captain, an advisor to the ARVN 7th Division, transmitted a sitrep to the US Military Assistance Command Vietnam in Saigon. The Captain's radio was shattered by an AK-47 bullet, so he switched to an ARVN 7th Division radio using the Vietnamese tactical net to make his final report. The US officer was calm and professional, though the stress in the US Army advisor's voice is obvious as he describes the ongoing massacre of US Advisors and the ARVN soldiers – he detailed the tactical situation, including a crucial piece of intelligence, as he uttered – "they knew we were coming." Ominously, the radio went silent immediately after the Captain transmitted the crucial information, a comment which would have strategic consequences for the US, the Soviet Union, and South Vietnam. The bodies of the four American advisors were never recovered, leaving grieving families and critical questions for US intelligence and counterintelligence agencies.

Annie Hoffman is shaken as she reads the Captain's message describing the ambush and massacre. She is a novice intelligence analyst, learning her trade at NSA headquarters. Annie is deeply patriotic and strongly influenced by the death of her brother, a US Marine killed

1

on Iwo Jima, and the other World War II sacrifices made by so many Indiana families in rural communities. The Gold Star mothers' flags in the windows of their homes served as constant reminders of fallen husbands, fathers, brothers, and sons. Annie holds poignant indelible memories of her mother's tears as her mother placed a Silver Star medal and a Purple Heart award on the mantle and then hung the Gold Star flag in their front window. Her older brother, Robert Hoffman, Private, US Marine Corps was awarded that Silver Star medal posthumously for heroism saving fellow Marines in the battle for Iwo Jima.

Annie grew up on a farm in central Indiana, graduating from a small rural high school as Valedictorian. The pastor from her small church noted that Annie had the great work-ethic Indiana farm kids exemplified, and she had a brilliant intellect.

The pastor contacted a friend at Indiana University who arranged a full-ride scholarship for Annie based on her academic excellence during high school. While at Indiana University, Annie studied international relations with a minor in Southeast Asia history. Unknown to Annie, one of her professors was a talent-spotter for CIA and NSA. The Professor saw Annie had great promise to serve the country as part of the Intelligence Community, which insiders called 'the IC'. After consulting his CIA and NSA contacts, the Professor found both agencies had an interest to hire Annie after her Summa Cum Laude graduation in 1961. The talent-spotter Professor approached Annie with a proposal that she send an employment application to the National Security Agency (NSA). Annie had no idea who or what NSA was – few people outside the IC were aware of the NSA. NSA often was referred to, in the Washington arena, as the No-Such-Agency. NSA was the most secretive organization in the IC; NSA performed the highly-secretive mission of collecting and analyzing signals intelligence (SIGINT), enemy radio transmissions and other modes of communication. The Professor talent-spotter, sensitive to the NSA extreme-security mantra, could not and would not tell Annie much substantive about the secretive agency located at Fort Meade, Maryland. The professor instead, simply told her, she had the natural talent and work-ethic to contribute to the security of the United States of America. The 'proposal' to apply to NSA resonated with the pride Annie had for her country and her intense patriotism. Annie applied to NSA and began to worry when no response was immediately forthcoming. The professor told her that the NSA security standards and the Top Secret security clearance required an in-depth background check for all applicants which took a lengthy time to process. If the background investigation identified no adverse information, the applicant would be invited for an interview and a polygraph examination.

Annie Hoffman was selected as a NSA 1962 new-hire, civil service grade, GS-7. For her first assignment, NSA sent her to Defense Language School, Monterey, California to study the Vietnamese language. Returning to NSA headquarters at Fort Meade in October 1962, Annie, as the office newbie low-ranking GS-7, was assigned a boring job of cataloging military and civil communications intercepts from South Vietnam. Little did anyone expect that Annie quickly would soon be catapulted into being a major player in the Vietnam War, dealing with engulfing the enemy deceptions and dark clandestine operations. Annie soon would become a full-fledged participant in the world of 'smoke and mirrors'.

Annie's office in one of the sub-basements of NSA Headquarters was relatively large, though definitely dreary. Grey concrete walls, a grey government issue metal desk, a grey metal desk chair, and many grey file cabinets, and a low-bidder brown tile floor. Her duties were as dreary as the lack of ambiance. Although NSA was on the cutting edge of electronic systems for analysis of signals intelligence and used advanced computers. The information storage and retrieval process is based on labor intensive work using tape drives and computer punch cards. Annie's daily task was to sort through a large volume of message traffic from Vietnam, categorize by subject, organize in time sequence, and give each message a recovery code for entry onto tape or a punch card.

The cataloging work was tedious, demanding, and never ending as the flow of collected communications never stopped. NSA communications collection operations were ongoing, day and night, 365 days a year, using aircraft, ships, planted 'bugs', and clandestine penetration of enemy facilities to capture enemy signals for NSA intelligence analysis. Each day was drudgery for Annie, at times discouraging given the dreams Annie previously had about serving the country as an NSA analyst. She wanted to be making significant contributions to national security. She wanted to be a lead-analyst immersed in the secret 'smoke and mirrors' world, not the filing drudgery she faced as a low-level file-clerk for classified SIGINT information.

All changed for Annie, January 4, 1963, resulting in profound consequences for Annie's future. All a result of Annie reading a message from a US Army advisor hotly engaged in the battle of Ap Bac.

The early US involvement was a combination of sending US Army military advisors for the South Vietnamese Army (ARVN) and conducting a wide range of clandestine CIA operations in South Vietnam, North Vietnam, Laos, and Cambodia. The US early deployments, 1955 through 1963, were closely held secrets by the US government. The flow of US advisors to the ARVN seemed open-ended as the Viet Cong and North Vietnam Army were gradually gaining ascendancy in the South Vietnamese countryside

Annie sat in her dreary basement office, January 4, 1963, laboriously sorting and cataloging the 'daily take' of incoming communication intercepts from Vietnamese military and political transmissions. These electronic intercepts were classified Top Secret/Special Compartmented Information (TS/SCI), and these intercepts were known as communications intelligence (COMINT).

One COMINT message caught her eye; the January 2, 1963 message content hit her emotionally recreating powerful visions of WW II gold-star flags in the windows of too many grieving Indiana homes.

US communications were not part of the collected NSA 'daily take' from Vietnam, the NSA was to collect and analyze 'foreign communications' from foe and foreign-friend. However, this particular US message was sent by a US Army Advisor embedded with the ARVN 7th Division and the Captain was using the Vietnamese radio net. Thus, the US message was intermeshed with the Vietnamese military communications, a target for NSA collection.

Tears began to flow down Annie's face as she read the intercepted message. The deaths of the four American advisors devastated her. She read and reread the message, focusing on the US soldier's calm rendering of the reality - the devastating massacre of the ARVN force and the deaths of the American advisors – one simple phrase took on a clarity beyond the despair of defeat, resonating toward a broader crisis – that poignant phrase *they knew we were coming*" became the foundation of a clarion vision for Annie. She sensed there was much more to understand beyond these soldier's dying words. She made a sacred commitment at that point to find the 'what, why, and when' for the calamity at Ap Bac.

She was committed to determine how the US could avoid a repetition of the American soldiers' deaths in the battle of Ap Bac.

Nonetheless, the daily flow of incoming intercepts would not wait for Annie to begin her quest. Reluctantly, Annie returned to the drudgery of sorting and cataloging, even as she began to plan an approach to understand the meaning and context to the poignant phrase "they knew we were coming". As the regular workday ended, Annie set out on her 'mission' to avenge the US Army advisor's deaths. First, she had to understand the context behind the battle. Trekking to the vending machines, Annie purchased food to provide nutrition that evening in her mission to find the reasons behind the NVA/VC ambush of the ARVN forces in the battle of Ap Bac. Then she would identify a way to counter the enemy in the future – how did this ambush happen?

The initial step was to become knowledgeable on all facets of the January 2, 1963 Ap Bac debacle. She benefitted that NSA was the greatest single reservoir of information in the world. By January 4, the Vietnamese and American after-action reports were arriving in Washington through various channels. Annie decided to work the early timeline with initial emphasis on what happened prior to the Ap Bac engagement and follow with an expansion of the timeline through the battle and aftermath.

The South Vietnamese battle plan was predicated on an unverified intelligence report which stated there was a VC radio transmitter in a hamlet near Ap Bac defended by 120 poorly trained VC in the same area. The ARVN 7th Division had responsibility for this region and would overrun the target destroying the small VC force. The attack plan, classified Secret, was a professional effort and, when executed, would crush the expected VC presence in Ap Bac. The date for the ARVN attack, was January 2, 1963. Annie read the after-action reports which documented the catastrophic results, the expected small poorly-trained VC unit was actually a combat-hardened NVA/VC force in prepared positions to ambush the ARVN. But how did the NVA and VC know exactly when and where to wait?

The US missed connecting the dots from its intelligence sources which indicated the local VC had been reinforced by a large number of experienced NVA combat troops. The combined NVA/VC force proceeded to construct sophisticated defensive positions that matched the 7th Division attack corridors. The NVA/VC needed several weeks for logistics preparation and building the Ap Bac fortifications – fortifications set in the exact positions to provide 'kill zones' in all three ARVN attack routes. Additional defensive fortifications and slit trenches were built to mitigate the ARVN artillery and US air firepower, which had been effective for the ARVN successes in many prior ARVN/VC engagements.

The NVA/VC were waiting in bunkers providing interlocking fields-of-fire in near-perfect ambush positions – waiting, just as the message of the dying US advisor had memorialized in his final message – "they knew we were coming" – a message which would later echo up the chain-of-command to the President of the United States.

The Ap Bac battle was likely a harbinger of the clever NVA deceptions which would lure American advisors and ARVN troops to their deaths in future ambushes. Annie sadly shook her head as she reaffirmed her commitment to determine how the ambush disaster happened and determine how to identify such VC deception plans in the future.

Annie understood a commitment alone had no meaning unless there were positive results from subsequent actions on the battlefield. Momentarily, she was beset with self-doubts. Annie was relatively inexperienced as an analyst and she certainly was not authorized by her boss to spend any time on this 'they knew we were coming' project. Could she get in trouble or even be fired for delving into an area she might not have a 'need-to-know' or authority to investigate? She decided to proceed in a careful 'under-the-office-radar' manner, while she concurrently tested the political waters. Annie's intuitive sense registered she was opening an 'analytic door' that had been missed in the past by US intelligence, missed at a peril and risk to US troops. Annie understood, she was a file-clerk, so she needed to know if she was ready for the task. Annie decided to contact Dr. Charles Smyth, a legendary NSA analyst, to solicit his advice and counsel.

When Annie requested an appointment, Dr. Smyth said he could only spare a few moments of his time late that Friday afternoon. Annie thanked him and was allotted 15 minutes at 4 PM that Friday afternoon. Annie put her thoughts together to discuss a hypothetical scenario and how to approach the analysis of such a scenario. This scenario would mask her 'unauthorized excursion' into an ongoing security compromise in the Vietnam War. She would ask Dr. Smyth what analytic methods should be used when you have incomplete data.

6

Charles Smyth was a legitimate-genius at solving complex SIGINT problems. He sat in his office unbothered by any humility, basking in his importance. Charles accepted his professional history was legendary, as were his peccadillos chasing young females working at NSA. Charles' ego left him in denial that he was aging, which is not a good thing for a lothario. His hair was thinning, a stomach-paunch was now prominent, and he was on the downward-side of middle-age. Even so, Charles still saw himself as an iconic type, a Romeo with eccentricities which made him even more desirable to young women. One eccentricity was his disdain for the conservative dress-code for senior NSA officials.

Exactly on the 4 PM time-hack, Annie knocked on Charles Smyth's office door, the response was a gruff "Enter!" Mildly intimidated, Annie entered Charles' office, large by NSA standards. As Annie stepped into Dr. Charles Smyth's office, she was mildly shocked and amused by the man sitting behind a large wooden desk. Instead of the usual suit and tie, Dr. Smyth was attired in a white silk-shirt with a broad collar, unbuttoned down to the third button, a thick gold chain adorned his neck hanging down to the third button, a pair of tight grey-linen slacks that unintentionally drew attention to his paunch, and a pair of light-tan western-style boots. Completing this cartoonish-combination, Charles had tried to comb his grey-streaked thinning hair in the style of Elvis Presley. Apparently, SIGINT analytical genius did not necessarily extend to wardrobe wisdom.

Smythe looked up with an initial stern-visage of 'why are you bothering me', the grim visage immediately turned into a smile as he saw a buxom, attractive young woman in the doorway. Annie dressed modestly at work and off work. She buttoned up her blouses, avoided tight sweaters, and wore dresses with a hem line below her knees. Even so, there was no disguising her voluptuous figure.

Charles stared at the statuesque, five-feet, eight-inch tall curvaceous figure, sculptured by hard-physical work helping her father with the family-farm chores, Annie was a beautiful young woman.

Instantly regretting the 15-minute time limit, he invited Annie to take the chair in front of his desk; Charles followed with a solicitous question,

"How may I help you?

"Dr. Smythe, thank..." (Charles interrupted rudely before she could complete her first sentence, he glanced quickly at his appointment calendar to check her name, he had not remembered her name, nor was interested until he saw her)

"So, Miss Hoffman, it is Miss, isn't it? May I call you Annie? Why haven't I seen you before? When were you assigned to the Soviet Division?"

"Dr. Smythe, it is Miss, you may call me Annie, and I am not assigned to the Soviet Division."

Charles was now slightly off his game, wondering why was she there, what did she want?

"You are not assigned to the Soviet Division, why are you here?"

"I am assigned to the Vietnamese Division. I just returned from Vietnamese language training and have only been here at the headquarters for a few months."

Interrupting yet again, Charles tried to recover and employ his usual approach to attractive new-hire females.

"I am pleased to see you, even if, you are not in the Soviet Division, may I ask why you are here?"

"Sir, I want to be an analyst. I asked my friends in the Vietnamese Division who was the top analyst in NSA who might be willing to give me some guidance how to improve my analyst skills. All my friends said you were the person to go to for help."

His ego stroked and sensing a vulnerable target, Charles rolled out his obsequious smile, more a leer.

"Well, Annie, that is great. How can I help you and let's see just what we can do together?"

Annie returned a pleasant smile to cover her disgust with this aging-abuser. She focused on her goal and gave 'leering Charles' her cover story about needing advice and guidance for complex-analysis challenges. In particular, what analytic methods and techniques should be used for situations where 'an answer' is suggested, but the data is incomplete including a high degree of ambiguity. Annie ignored Charles gazing at her breasts as he paused to respond to her question. The reply for this type challenge was elemental for an experienced analyst. Normally, Charles would dispense with such an intrusion on his time by recommending three different books, then, summarily dismissing the intruder. Now he wanted to extend the contact with the attractive young women with blue-eyes who sported a long-blond ponytail.

With an ingratiating smile, Charles launched into a lecture on analytic methods citing specific techniques like 'timeline analysis', 'hypothesis testing', 'alternate competing hypotheses', 'divergent/convergent thinking', 'the scenario tree', among many potentially applicable analytic tools for her to use. Annie remembered the cliché, 'drinking from the fire hose', as she was overwhelmed by the cascade of rhetoric Charles delivered, all the while he was continuing to do his 'personal-analysis' of her body.

Annie noted the clock on the wall and saw she had been there 45 minutes. She graciously thanked him and apologized for taking time over the allotted 15-minute limit. Charles composed himself to preserve his mental-image of his legendary status as a top analyst and a person who attracted young women. In reality, an image where the former was true and the latter failing with the passing of the years. Dr. Smyth rather lamely noted he had mentored many new NSA analysts. (concealing the fact that almost all were attractive young women). He welcomed Annie to return after she had thought about the various choices of analytic methods to apply to the problem she was working on. Charles suggested they could reconvene on the following Friday. Annie thanked him profusely and made her exit.

Annie reflected she had gained some useful knowledge from the encounter. Charles was a lecher, but he also was a brilliant analyst. Second, the timeline analysis technique appeared promising to find the answers in her quest to find the reality behind the ominous last statement of a brave US soldier. Before Annie departed, Charles provided three more pieces of 'analytic wisdom', principles which would serve Annie well for the rest of her intelligence analyst career. Charles offered as insights:

"When things are too perfect, there is a back-story that holds the real truth – find the back-story!"

"The evidence is always there, always! The analyst must persevere to find the evidence, identify the context and determine the meaning of the evidential data."

"Always look for patterns in the data! Patterns show the way to answers!"

Now, she would go home and prepare some food, for what will be a long weekend at the office, pursuing clarity for a "they knew we were coming' revelation. She mused as she traveled home, Charles had validated her original decision to start with a timeline analysis; in addition, she had pulled Charles into the fledgling unauthorized project as an unwitting co-conspirator. She was learning the games of political survival in the DC bureaucracy. The food for Saturday and Sunday was prepared and packed for Annie's research and deliberations in her basement office. She settled in for the Friday evening with a glass of wine and worried, if she should initiate this 'unauthorized project'?

After a large breakfast of scrambled eggs, bacon, toast, orange juice, and a banana, Annie was revved-up and on the way to the office. Saturday was a workday at NSA, but the staff on the weekends was numerically-fewer than the regular five-day work week – unless there was a crisis ongoing, which was 'often' for NSA intelligence collection and analyses. Having a personal coffee maker (an unauthorized personal coffee maker) was one of the few advantages of her bleak sequestered basement office. A cup of 'illegal' coffee in-hand, she resumed her unauthorized project, giving a shy smile while thinking that she was on the verge of being a 'rebel'.

She reviewed all the existing material and considered the next step. The timeline technique presented a challenge as she only had three data points: the date when the Ap Bac deceptive intelligence report was received by the ARVN 7th Division; the time frame the 7th Division staff and American advisors used to plan the January 2, 1963 attack, and the after-action reports detailing the battle. These after-action reports exposed a fact previously ignored by the US analysts. That fact was, the necessary preparation-time the enemy needed to be ready for this dramatically successful ambush.

The NVA/VC ambush was the result of a 'deception operation' which laid the foundation for a well-prepared ambush plan executed by veteran NVA combat troops. Annie's initial analytic move would be to reconstruct the various obligatory activities necessary for the events to transpire as the NVA intended. Two 'red flag' observations set the perspective. This clearly was a sophisticated deception operation triggered by the false intelligence report the NVA used as a deception ploy to lure the

10

ARVN into the trap. Second, the overall operational preparation by the NVA/VC was professional, beginning with the deception plan, followed by the logistics phase, and the final combat phase to ambush the ARVN force. Annie wondered, was this a one-of incident or was it a part of a sophisticated continuum of past NVA/VC successful deception operations? Was this an NVA/VC strategy which the US and South Vietnamese intelligence services had not yet recognized? She understood that organization and discipline would be her path to find the "patterns" and discover the answers.

Start with the known data. The VC needed several weeks to prepare for an operation on the scale of the Ap Bac ambush. Approximately how much time did these preparations take? The VC faced a constant challenge when moving men and materials securely and covertly within South Vietnam. All the NVA/VC necessities for war were moved by foot transport using thousands of porters and was time consuming. The logistics buildup for the Ap Bac battle would have taken four to six weeks, at a minimum. Construction of the hidden ambush fortifications would take about the same amount of time as the logistics effort; of course, with enough manpower, the two efforts could be done in parallel. Most of the preparatory work had to be done at night to avoid US and South Vietnamese aerial reconnaissance.

The VC would withhold their 'deceptive intelligence report' until all their preparations were complete. This was necessary to avoid a preemptive ARVN strike. Once the NVA deceptive intelligence report was in the ARVN hands, the big question emerged, how did the NVA know when and how the ARVN would respond? Annie smiled as she had an epiphany – it is clear! – "North Vietnam had a high-level "mole" inside the ARVN!"

Now, Annie could develop a conceptual timeline for the ambush based on NSA archived data. She would go back in the files to September 1961. She intuitively knew there would be patterns and evidence in these files. After pouring over stacks of files, Annie built a timeline for Ap Bac:

June 1962: SIGINT indicated the Ap Bac ambush operation is conceived. Orders were issued to begin the logistics buildup and movement of supplies; begin construction of the ambush positions; finish the planning, train the troops to execute the joint NVA/VC ambush attack.

December 14, 1962: The VC would use 'double agents' to deliver false information about the situation in Ap Bac

December 24, 1962: The ARVN and US advisors plan their attack and assemble the attacking force. According to the ARVN plan, the ARVN force with US advisors would attack January 2, 1963 at 0700 hours: The ARVN would engage the small VC unit in the Ap Bac village.

However, the details of the ARVN plan were betrayed by a North Vietnamese 'mole', or 'moles'. The North Vietnamese spies provided the NVA all the 'timing' information needed to be waiting in ambush. Leveraging the knowledge from the 'mole', the entrenched NVA/VC troops decimated the ARVN attackers. The VC anti-aircraft weapons shot down five helicopters damaged all the other incoming helicopters.

Annie stared at her expanded, assumed, timeline; she shook her head, how do you find a wider-pattern with so little data? Needing a brief break, she went to her illegal 4-cup percolator to pour a fresh cup of coffee. As she returned to ponder the meager information she had organized, Annie thought back to the analytic guidance Charles had given her – 'when something is too perfect, look for the back story; the evidence is always there, identify the evidence; patterns tell the story'.

So, how to characterize the overwhelmingly successful Ap Bac ambush? If not 'too perfect', the ambush was very close to perfect – what is a plausible back story? The attack was the product of a superb VC deception plan that integrated long-term objectives, logistics, training, and most important, a detailed knowledge how to deceive and manipulate the ARVN enemy. The ambush plan held many risks and costs for the VC. The VC would have to allocate significant resources of manpower, material, and political-capital to support the ambush of a major ARVN force. A VC failure at Ap Bac would generate negative consequences for the VC across the totality of South Vietnam. Why would the NVA and VC accept these risks in the complex Ap Bac ambush plan?

Annie believed she had made an analytic breakthrough as she thought about the last question, she smiled, she had uncovered and identified a basic fact – this was not the 'first rodeo' for the NVA/VC deception ambush technique – Ap Bac was likely a scaled-up version of previous smaller deception-based ambushes.

Annie determined she must pursue a new thread to detect the evidence of a NVA strategic plan based on a "mole' in the ARVN. Are there similar NVA ambushes in the archives? Why didn't US analysts previously connect-the-dots? She moved back to the archived intelligence to search for possible related events, working backwards from January 2, 1963. The first shock in this new research thread was the large number of successful ambushes the NVA/VC had carried out in the past eight months. Furthermore, there was one obvious commonality between all these ambushes. In every one of the NVA ambushes, there were one or more US Advisors in the ARVN force the VC ambushed.

As Annie delved deeper into the COMINT records, she found 'patterns' in the VC communications. There was an azimuth-directed encrypted message sent from somewhere in the Saigon region prior to every ambush. The signal azimuth direction was always towards the A Shau valley, a NVA stronghold in northwest South Vietnam, bordering Laos. These Saigon signals were sent two-five days prior to each ambush. The encrypted signals all used the same frequency and repeated the call signs, bad tradecraft and bad radio traffic security by the VC. Immediately after a Saigon signal was received by a site somewhere in the A Shau valley, three encrypted signals were transmitted from the A Shau site: a high-level encryption signal used only by the KGB, high-power, and directional toward Moscow; a second signal, using the same encryption as the original message from Saigon was azimuth-directed toward Hanoi; the third signal was not azimuth directed and seemed to be generally broadcast for various VC radio receivers in South Vietnam. Annie gave a silent shout of joy – here is a pattern! Furthermore, this pattern had a definite beginning date, March 1962. The signal pattern matched the COMINT 'take' for the Ap Bac ambush. Everything Charles Smyth had told her was validated: evidence there, patterns there, the 'too perfect' back story there.

How had the NSA, CIA, and military analysts missed what now was obvious? There were major NVA/VC deception operations ongoing for about a year, specifically targeting US advisors embedded in ARVN combat units. The most reasonable explanations why the US analysts missed the correlation of all these events were twofold. First, up to the Ap Bac ambush, the proceeding ambushes were against relatively small ARVN units with US advisors. Secondly, the series of 1962 ambushes were distributed throughout South Vietnam giving no consistent geographic patterns. Annie looked at her notes. It was absolutely clear, 'there was a high-level "mole" in the ARVN betraying operations of ARVN units with US advisors'. She had made an astounding discovery in her unauthorized research and analysis effort.

Now, what does she do with the strategic and political implications of her 'profound results'? The standard procedure would be to take her work to her immediate boss, Kyle Menninger. Kyle was a premier example why bureaucrats are mocked and disliked. He used every situation to promote his career, usually at the expense of others and the mission. If she took her work to him, there were two likely results, neither good. Kyle had a bad reputation for taking credit for others' work, when that work was good and could advance his career. Or, he could fault her for working behind his back, doing an unauthorized project, an unsanctioned action which could have negative career consequences for Annie. Going to her boss for guidance appeared to be a lose-lose choice.

She thought about going to the Vietnamese Division Chief, Dr. David Slade. Dr Slade had a positive reputation inside the Agency. He was recognized as brilliant on the professional side and reputed as 'one of the good guys' as a person and boss.

Dr. David Slade was a talented man, a sophisticated gentleman, a top-level NSA player, an exceptional technical analyst, and a savvy man in the Washington political jungle. In personal appearance, Dr. Slade appeared as a dapper spy-type Cary Grant, well-tailored suits, pleasant to all subordinates, an engaging sense of humor, and handsome. These personal qualities did not mask his intensity to serve the national security interests of the US. David Slade was one of the 'go-to' guys the NSA Director depended on for critical projects. One of his strongest characteristics was his respectfulness toward all NSA employees. David Slade understood national security was a team effort from the humblest gate-guard or janitor flowing up to the President of the United States.

Annie decided, Dr. Slade would be the person she would contact for guidance on 'her unauthorized project'. Even if the contact with Dr. Slade went badly, she still had her Top Secret/Sensitive Compartmentalized Information clearance and would be able to find another job in the Intelligence Community. Annie would present her case as a request for advice based on remarks Dr. Slade made at a recent 'greet new NSA employees' morning coffee. This generic reason would excuse her from the need to contact her boss 'in the chain of command'. She would tell Dr. Slade that she conducted some research based on a personal interest and found 'unexpected results' which might be significant. Since her work was personal and not a task from NSA, Annie is requesting Dr. Slade's advice.

Annie called Dr. Slade's secretary, Mrs. Martha Sellers, to request five minutes of Dr. Slade's time related to the recent new employees' coffee. Martha Sellers saw one of her major responsibilities as the gate-keeper for Dr. Slade's' schedule, Martha would protect the busy PhD NSA Division Chief from frivolous time wasting requests. Martha was put-off by Annie's request, from a GS-7 no less, related to a meet-and-greet coffee. Who does she think she is, this Hoffman girl? Regardless, Martha said she would check with Dr. Slade. About 30 minutes later, the secretary called back in a huffy voice telling Annie that Dr. Slade would see her that afternoon at 5 PM for five minutes. Annie immediately began to rehearse what she would say.

Annie arrived at Dr. Slade's office at 4:45, to be greeted coolly, almost rudely, by the secretary. Martha said Dr. Slade would see Annie for the five-minute contact now, as he needed to leave work as soon as possible today. The secretary used the intercom to tell Dr. Slade that Annie was there for her 'five-minute meeting'. Dr. Slade told the secretary to show Annie into his office. Dr. David Slade's demeanor was the opposite to his secretary. He greeted Annie warmly, offered a chair in front of his desk, and asked what he could do for her.

Annie sat down and went directly to her rehearsed remarks to initiate their dialog:

"I am sorry to take up your time, but I have a personal situation that requires me to better understand NSA procedural practices. I have been doing personal research after regular work hours regarding an ongoing situation in Vietnam."

"Please let me interrupt, what section are you assigned to?"

"I am assigned to the Vietnam Branch cataloging military and civil communications intercepts from South Vietnam."

"To be honest, that sounds a little boring."

"Yes sir, it is boring, but I realize it needs to be done."

"How long have you been working at NSA?"

"I have been at the Headquarters since last October. My first assignment was to the Defense Language School to study Vietnamese."

"So, what is this personal situation research about done after work hours?"

"During sorting of incoming cables, I read a message from a US Army advisor to the ARVN 7th Division. This Special Forces captain was giving a real-time account of the Ap Bac battle, actually the Ap Bac disaster. That message impacted me, and I wanted to know more. So, I began the off-duty personal research. I found information that led me to conclusions which I think may be important – however, this was not an approved NSA task assigned to me. My dilemma is what to do with the results from this 'unapproved task'."

"OK, you have my attention, what were the results from your unapproved task?"

"I found, what I believe to be significant evidence, of a high-level NVA mole in the Vietnamese defense establishment. This individual has been betraying ARVN operations since March 1962. Furthermore, the mole is only betraying operations that include American advisors."

"Now you really have my attention! I want to hear the details right now! Would you like a cup of coffee?"

Dr. Slade buzzed the secretary to ask for two fresh coffees and asked that he not be disturbed unless it was the President or NSA Director.

Dr. Slade listened intently, occasionally sipping his coffee, as Annie briefly described what she found in the course of her research

"Have you told anyone else about your unauthorized project?"

"No sir, you are the only person besides me who is aware of this 'work'."

"Good, you are not to discuss your work with anyone! No one! I want you to prepare a two-page summary of your work and your conclusions. I want the document on my desk by 8 AM tomorrow, deliver the document to me personally by your hand. Better get started, I do not want you worn-out in the morning."

Annie thanked Dr. Slade for his interest and help. As she departed his office, she noted the raised-eyebrows of the secretary who had waited while the 5-minute meeting turned into a 45-minute closed-door discussion.

Annie went first to the vending machines and then to her office, excited, but anxious for what tomorrow will bring after this meeting with Dr. Slade.

Dr. Slade buzzed his secretary and asked her to reach out forthwith to the NSA Director, Lieutenant-General Gordon Blake. Five minutes later, the secretary notified Dr. Slade, General Blake was on the phone, General Blake responded even as Dr. Slade picked up the secure-line phone:

"David, I am listening, what's up."

"General, I just learned of a situation that has political ramifications as well as being a hot security problem. I need 30 minutes of your time tomorrow morning. I will bring the young analyst who"

(General Blake interrupted)

"Just a second, how about 0930. I will figure out the rest of my schedule after our session."

"Thank you General, we will be there, I think you will find all the aspects of this issue quite intriguing and disturbing."

General Blake hung up and switched his attention to the ever present 'other pressing-issues' for an NSA Director.

Annie took extra care with her makeup and her hair as she prepared for the meeting with Dr. Slade and 'somebody'. She had worked until midnight last evening, editing and re-editing the TS/SCI memo; the document was two-pages of text, as directed, and a two-page annex of supporting data. Annie arrived at Dr. Slade's office 15 minutes early and was surprised to be warmly greeted by the secretary, Martha offered Annie coffee before showing her into the inner office.

After nominal pleasantries, Dr. Slade explained that they would meet with General Blake at 0930 to brief him on 'the unauthorized project'. Annie's anxiety from the last evening was transformed into serious trepidation. Dr. Slade recognized the dire concern on Annie's face and set out to both comfort her and prepare her for what would be a momentous meeting for NSA and Annie. Dr. Slade gave Annie a brief background on General Blake and emphasized that General Blake was 'one of the good-guys'.

"I can see you are anxious about the meeting with General Blake, let me tell you a little about him to try to put you more at ease. General Blake graduated from the US Military Academy in 1931. He is a pilot and received many medals for his service during World War II. The two things which are most important to you are his technical credentials and who he is as a man, this latter being the most important. General Blake is expert in the areas of electronics, communications, plus the research and development process. As I mentioned, the most important is General Blake, the person. He is a leader. A man who cares about and takes care of 'his people'. You will find him most interested in what you have to say and appreciative of your initiative in this matter. Your background memo is excellent."

"Just relax and be yourself, as you were when you brought this issue to me."

Annie smiled and nodded, not commenting on her extreme nervousness at the meeting with Dr. Slade yesterday. Dr. Slade reread the short document, nodding several times and making notes in the margins, he called the secretary to make two copies after marking the original TS/SCI security caveat as "limited-distribution". Slade reviewed the meeting protocols and procedure. He would introduce Annie, give a short precis, and Annie would take about ten minutes to give the background on her findings. They would depart at 0910 for the meeting.

Annie's head was swimming after the meeting with the NSA Director. General Blake was pleasant and personable – he gave earnest attention to her every word. He asked a few questions about the report and asked questions about her: where are you from? What is your job and civil service rank at NSA – when she said GS-7, General Blake looked at Dr. Slade and raised his eyebrows. At the end of the discussion, which had lasted some 50 minutes, General Blake thanked Annie for her initiative and the solid-work she had done. He told her to not discuss this issue with anyone except Dr. Slade. Smiling, General Blake shook her hand and said, "we will meet again, soon." The Director asked Dr. Slade to stay to discuss some other issues. Dr. Slade gathered up all three copies of the document and put them in his briefcase. Dr. Slade asked Annie if she had any other copies, she replied 'no other copies', but she did have her notes. He advised her to secure those notes in a separate locked filing cabinet.

After Annie departed, General Blake made three comments: one, promote her today to GS-11; two, as we say in Washington politics, we have an opportunity here, of course in DC, every opportunity can be a problem; three, I need to call "Bull".

General Blake asked his secretary to reach out to General Wojcik forthwith requesting General Wojcik to call him. The intercom buzzed seven minutes later,

"General Blake, I have Major-General Wojcik on the line:"

"Good morning Bull"

"Good morning General – what do you have on your mind this morning?"

"I am hurt Bull; can't an old friend call the JCS Chairman's Deputy for Special Projects – and invite that person to lunch at NSA?"

"I am already checking my wallet for the cost of that lunch – when do you want to see me?"

"Can you be here tomorrow around 1100? I will arrange lunch and even pay for lunch. As I remember, grilled salmon is one of your favorites. On the work side, I have an issue, I mean an opportunity, to discuss with you. It is an 'eyes-only' thing. I would prefer your aide not participate in this meeting. Does that work for you?"

"I will be there – always up for 'an opportunity'."

"Sounds like a plan. Give my regards to Mary."

Lt General Blake met fellow West Pointer Bull Wojcik in the mid-1930s. The two hit it off, starting with their shared values from their US Military Academy days at West Point. The two wives, Mary and JoAnne had become fast friends.

The lunch, in the Director's private dining room, was grilled salmon complemented with grilled asparagus and American-style fried potatoes with onions (another favorite of Major-General Wojcik), a green salad with balsamic vinegar dressing, hard crust dinner rolls with butter, and complemented with an excellent Rhein River white wine. The piece-de-resistance was a cherry-covered vanilla cheesecake, cognac and coffee. Bull commented,

"General, you may be paying for this exquisite meal now, but I know, I will have to pay later. Thanks anyway for the excellent repast".

After the table was cleared and the room secured, General Blake, General Wojcik, and Dr. Slade got down to the business at hand. General Blake noted the 'new situation' was indeed an opportunity, an opportunity in the middle of political minefields. The 'new situation' presented a security problem of a serious magnitude, politically and militarily, and the problem had to be resolved as soon as possible. General Wojcik nodded his head making no comment. Dr. Slade proceeded to give General Wojcik a detailed briefing of what they knew at this point.

General Wojcik turned to the NSA Director and asked simply, "what do you want me to do?"

General Blake replied, "I think we must do two things, sooner than later. First, we build a draft plan to solve this multi-dimensional security problem. Second, we take the plan and the problem to the JCS Chairman for approval and guidance."

General Wojcik asked, "how long do I have to develop the plan?"

"Bull, you have three days to create a draft plan. That plan would be TS/SCI Limited Distribution to the three of us in this room, for now."

General Wojcik asked,

"Who discovered this mess?"

Smiling, General Blake looked at Dr. Slade, who responded, "she is a young woman, new hire, who has a bright future with NSA. She will be at our next meeting."

General Wojcik firmly shook hands with General Blake and Dr. Slade and departed. Bull Wojcik heard an ominous ticking from the 'political disaster' clock – Project Safeguard security was about to be breached. Project Safeguard was a Top Secret Restricted Access JCS study that was investigating security beaches behind a series of unusual ambushes of Top Secret US SOG operations in Vietnam.

Dr. Slade returned to his office to deal with the many administrative actions involving Annie and creating an internal organization for a new restricted access TS/SCI program. When these tasks were done, he called

Annie. She answered and recognized Dr. Slade's voice. He proceeded to give her a series of inputs which momentarily overwhelmed her; she would be promoted to GS-11 today; she would move to a new office tomorrow. She could hear Dr. Slade chuckle, when he told her to bring her unauthorized coffee-maker – compulsively, she interrupted, asking how Dr. Slade knew about the coffeemaker. Dr. Slade's response was, "Welcome to NSA. Security swept and searched your office last night. And you can keep the coffeemaker as long as it is not obvious to visitors. Your boss was advised you are reassigned effective today. You will be 'read-in' to the new special access program tomorrow. Get packed to move to your new office and congratulations on the promotion."

After hanging up, Dr. Slade mused, now we wait for the plan and the mission for the Peregrine operation.

Annie hung up, momentarily dazed by the fast-moving events – an unbelievable promotion, jumping several civil service grades, a new assignment, and security taking stock of her basement office in her absence, finding the hidden coffee percolator. She quickly recovered and began the various actions for the next steps in 'the unauthorized', now authorized, project. First, pack her personal items in the basement office, including the illegal coffee percolator.

CHAPTER 2 PEREGRINE MISSION APPROVED

Cadet Stanislaw Wojcik graduated with the US Military Academy Class of 1923. On graduation Second Lieutenant Wojcik joined the Infantry branch of the Army combat arms (Infantry, Artillery, Armor). Second Lieutenant Wojcik was physically imposing at six feet tall, 230 pounds, and an 18-inch neck, hence, "Bull" Wojcik. Bull Wojcik had been the NCAA national champion heavyweight wrestler three years in a row while at West Point. More important, Bull Wojcik had an exceptional intellect and was prescient as regards the future role of irregular units operating behind enemy lines. In 1933, a senior Army officer assigned to the White House commended Captain Wojcik to President Roosevelt as a man suitable to do 'special work' for the President as the storm clouds of war gathered in the Pacific and in Europe. Captain Wojcik performed a number of secret missions in Germany, France, and China for President Roosevelt. As the war clouds broke into a cataclysmic storm of World War II, Captain Wojcik was transferred to the Office of Strategic Services (OSS). The OSS would become the forerunner of CIA and American Special Forces. Captain Wojcik served with distinction for over two-years behind German lines in France and made a major strategic contribution to the success of the Normandy invasion.

Despite his distinctive service and bravery, the hide-bound Army leadership had little patience for West Point, 'deviants', those individuals who served outside the traditional three branches of the traditional combat arms. By early 1944, his classmates had been promoted to Colonel and General Officer ranks, 'Bull' Wojcik remained a Captain, the old-line leadership determined to make an example of him for West Point graduates. Those who chose career paths outside the traditional combat arms were considered as heretics. However, General Eisenhower appreciated the critical role Captain Wojcik played before and during D-Day. General Eisenhower directed that Captain Wojcik be promoted to the rank of full Colonel in November 1944. In January 1945, before his death April 12, 1945, President Franklin Delano Roosevelt used an Executive Order to promote Colonel Wojcik to the rank of a one-star General, Brigadier-General Wojcik.

Brigadier-General Wojcik served as one of the drafters of the National Security Act of 1947 which established the Central Intelligence Agency. President Truman assigned Brigadier-General Wojcik to the fledgling CIA to guide the new organization in the 'smoke and mirrors' 'intelligence-war aspect of the Cold War conflict with the Soviet Union. None of his career moves and promotions set well with the Army traditionalists. In a final rebuff by President Eisenhower, as a former five-star General and now President, President Eisenhower promoted Bull again, to the two-star rank of Major-General..

The foresight of the young Wojcik during the 1930s was proven during the next three decades, including WWII and the Communist Wars of National Liberation. Small highly-professional units could achieve strategic goals. Plus, the small units offered deniability that a particular operation even happened. Now, Major-General Wojcik was the Pentagon 'go to' guy for 'smoke and mirrors' Cold War clandestine engagements.

Bull was contemplative as his US Army captain military aide drove him back to the Pentagon. He briefly smirked at the thought how often he had been tasked by the JCS Chairman for dirty jobs. Now, he was going to ask the Chairman to approve his participation in one of those 'dirty' jobs. This was a situation where, if you succeed, no one can know. If you fail, everyone will know, and the backlash will be severe from many directions.

Bull began to mentally outline the many actions that would make this new operation a success. This was not his first rodeo for a complicated sensitive clandestine operation. He knew each mission was unique and nuanced, nonetheless, the enduring principles always reigned to plan every operation. He had a mental template for the essential elements: what is the Mission; what are the Mission Objectives; how do we pay for the operation; the timeline for execution; overall security considerations; the personnel to execute; and of singular importance, who approves the operation and gives the 'go ahead'.

Bull grabbed the car-radio handset to call Colonel Clifford Steward who was Bull's 'go to guy' when he needed a plan done fast and done right the first time. When Colonel Steward answered, Bull ordered him to meet in the JCS SCIF in 45 minutes – and, by the way, tell Janice, Colonel Steward's wife, that he would not be home this evening. As soon as Bull disconnected with Colonel Steward, he dialed the Office of the Chairman of the Joint Chiefs of Staff

"Hi Kathy, this is Bull Wojcik, I have an urgent matter for the Chairman. Does he have about two minutes for me?"

"Good morning Bull, the Chairman has folks in his office, but, let me buzz him and see when he can talk to you."

The JCS Chairman excused himself and picked-up the phone as soon as his secretary told him who was on the line.

"Good morning Bull, how urgent is this?"

"General, we have a serious political issue, I would like to have about 15 minutes of your time in "That Room"."

Laughing, General Lemnitzer replied: "In "That Room"! – well this is serious. How about 1530, you know where."

"Thank you General, see you at 1530"

"That Room" was spook-insider slang for a room constructed to be the most secure place on the planet. "That Room" was essentially a large plexiglass box set on pedestals to raise the room above the floor to allow security checks under the floor; all power to "That Room" was filtered to run the dedicated-internal heat-and-cool system; heavy curtains blocked any view into "That Room"; a 24-hour guard station monitored the room and controlled all accesses. The Pentagon had two of these 'super-secure rooms', one for the JCS and one for DIA. Several US Embassies around the world had a "That Room" installed within the CIA Station office spaces.

Bull had every confidence Colonel Steward would produce an excellent plan on time – hell, Steward crosses more t's and dots more i's than anyone Bull had known during his many years in the Army. Steward was the quintessential planner, when Steward was done, he would try to find more t's and i's to fix. At the same time, Bull had learned that no matter how good the plan is, in the end, it always came down to the people who executed the plan in the field, people who made decisions under pressure, decisions forced by circumstances, decisions made with incomplete information. Depending on circumstances in-the-field, these operators would trash the plan to go with their gut, as the field guys do when they believe it is necessary to 'do the mission'. Bull had to pick the "right" people who would do the job and accomplish the Peregrine Mission.

Steward saw the people in the field 'doing the job' as his nemesis when they deviated from the plan and began to improvise – to do the mission their way. The operators had a saying, the plan be damned. We are going forward, doing whatever it takes. After Steward completed his part drafting the plan, the next step was to deal with the bureaucracy. 'The Plan' was what you needed to get approval, money, and resources – after that it was in the hands of the 'operators'.

Colonel Steward was waiting in the SCIF with a notepad and pen, plus the look, 'I am ready Boss, what do you need?' Major-General Wojcik briefed his planner on all he had learned at NSA. They discussed a Mission Statement to launch the drafting process. Bull approved the Mission Statement as: Identify and Negate Enemy Agents who have Penetrated the South Vietnamese Government and the ARVN. These agents, moles, are actively compromising certain ARVN operations with the intent to kill the embedded US advisors. Looking at Steward, Bull ordered him to have a draft ready by 1200 tomorrow and departed the SCIF to set criteria for the type of men needed to do this Mission.

From Bull's experience conducting clandestine missions, he knew the type of 'hard men' needed. Hell, he was one of those hard-men. He understood who could and would do this type 'dirty job'. Bull had to smile when he thought of the many times in the OSS during WW II when he reverted to the motto – 'it is better to ask forgiveness than request permission'. Describing the 'operatives' needed for Peregrine was a straightforward task, these men had to be True Believers that the mission was sacred. Now to identify this group of men for the Peregrine team.

Bull saw the team as a composite of highly experienced Special Forces NCOs and two-three high-performing junior-officers. Each man had to hold the stance, 'my country, right or wrong, my country'. If selected, the officers would have to subordinate personal interests to those of the team and The Mission. Each man needed to have the physical, intellectual, and emotional make-up to overcome stresses, mental and physical. Every man selected for the Peregrine team has to have the capacity to be totally ruthless, as needed, for the mission. The bottom line was simple – each man must be a "True Believer" for God and Country – and The Mission!

When Colonel Steward was buzzed into Bull's office at 1145 the following morning, he carried a completed draft plan. Steward was freshly shaved wearing an impeccable uniform. Beyond that, his face was

26

drawn from 30 straight-hours work to build the draft plan, plus the many cups of coffee fueling the creation of a complicated clandestine operation. Colonel Steward described the plan in detail. Bull thought, damned straight, Steward has done it again. Steward is a treasure for the Army. The two began to critique and evaluate each paragraph and each sentence in the draft plan.

Bull thought how he would put 75-minutes of information into a 15-minute bag for the JCS Chairman. He reflected on Project Safeguard, a restricted Top Secret program, compartmented for security access to fewer than ten of the top Generals and Admirals in the JCS. Project Safeguard is an analysis as why the MACV/SOG operations were being consistently compromised, a security and political problem. Political considerations were unavoidable as the four-star Flag Officers developed military policies. Current political problems were further complicated by the ongoing political backlash from the ill-conceived CIA Bay of Pigs fiasco. Now, the inadvertent NSA discovery of compromised ARVN operations threatened potentially horrendous political fallout and negative consequences raining-down on the Chairman and the JCS – this could be a damned disaster if we do not get our arms around this mess and fix this problem, now!

The operational team will work under an organizational cover that avoids any indication of the actual mission (the field team will function under a cover organization as the "DoD Adjunct Inspector General Team #4"). The commander of the unit will use a personal cover name in Vietnam when dealing with individuals outside the team. False personnel files will be constructed to provide a cover for each team member for the time the team members are assigned to Peregrine. The actual true-name personnel files will be sealed. All funding shall be drawn from a Presidential restricted black-money account with the oversight and expenditure of the black money done by the program manager. The operation is to be totally clandestine, start to finish.

Based on the sensitivity and scope of the operation, the approval authority should be the President. Approval action should be requested for the earliest possible date. The project-team is headed by Major-General Wojcik, JCS Deputy for Special Projects; the project senior members of the team shall include Major-General Wojcik, the NSA Director, the CIA Director, and the President's National Security Advisor.

At 1520 hours, Major-General Bull Wojcik was talking to the guard outside "That Room". General Lemnitzer and his aide arrived at 1525. Motioning for his aide to wait outside, the two generals entered "That Room". Once inside, curtains closed, the two old-friends shook hands and sat down at the conference table.

"Bull, I have a hell of a budgetary fight going on with Congress – is what you are about to tell me going to make things worse?"

"General, if we do not get this situation under control, Project Safeguard will blow-up in our faces and we will have a shit storm to deal with."

"For now, give me the short version."

"NSA stumbled onto information about the ambushes and assassinations of US Advisors in Nam. The 'cat-is-out-of-the bag'. General Blake knows about the problem targeting American advisors, as do several NSA analysts, but only from this limited NSA first look. I have a proposal for you to consider which will bring this mess under control, but we have to move beyond the 'Speed of Dark'."

"NSA is not supposed to intercept US communications, how the hell did NSA 'stumble' onto this information?"

"The intercept was a Vietnamese message, but a US Advisor was sending the message. A very sharp young NSA analyst ran the issue to ground – and – here we are."

"Damn Murphy and his Law! When can you have your 'how to fix it' proposal to me?"

"Tomorrow at 1600"

"Sounds good, I will meet you here, tomorrow, at 1600, give my regards to Mary. Have to get back to this budget shit – I would rather be in a good old-fashion fire-fight with non-weasel enemies than dealing with weasel politicians."

The generals shook hands before exiting "That Room", each to engage in the political problems that go with the Washington DC territory.

The following day, Major-General Wojcik congratulated Colonel Steward on a job well done and assigned him administrative and security responsibility for the plan and the operation.

General Lemnitzer and Major-General Wojcik entered "That Room" exactly at 1600 hours the following day.

"What do you have Bull?"

"The plan is called Operation Peregrine. It should solve the Project Safeguard political dilemma and at the same time, give us a path to fix this problem of attacks on US advisors. Here is the Executive summary for your consideration and approval."

Bull handed the Chairman a one-page summary.

General Lemnitzer, read the one-page executive summary twice before looking Major-General Bull Wojcik in the eye.

"Good plan! Make it happen! You will speak for me as this is a JCS priority initiative – you will get whatever you need. Will I see you and Mary at the White House clambake next week?"

"General, may I remind you, 'two-stars' are like furniture at the White House. I won't be there unless they need more waiters."

After firm handshakes – two warriors left "That Room" to move to other battlefields, political and military.

Bull tasked his secretary to arrange meetings with CIA Director John McCone and National Security Advisor, McGeorge Bundy for as soon as possible. He met with the former the following day at 1015.

Major-General Wojcik was ushered into the CIA Director's personal office and warmly greeted by the Director, John McCone, a former businessman, known as a 'friend of Presidents', Republican and Democrat. He was Washington-savvy having served in many capacities including the 1948 organizing of the CIA, head of the Atomic Energy Commission, Under Secretary of the Air Force, and now, the CIA Director replacing Allen Dulles after the Bay of Pigs fiasco. McCone was working to restore a positive image for the Agency and restore morale within the CIA ranks. Director McCone listened carefully as Bull laid out the problem, the risks, and the proposed solution, Operation Peregrine.

Bull told the Director he was seeking a Presidential level approval for Peregrine and he was meeting McGeorge Bundy tomorrow. Bull bluntly asked if CIA would support Peregrine. McCone answered carefully, as his priority was rebuilding the Agency after the Bay of Pigs debacle and strengthening the Congressional political support for CIA.

"CIA will support you, but as a silent partner, acting at the operational level versus a prominent role in the Washington politics which Peregrine will inevitably face."

Major-General Wojcik smiled as he thanked Director McCone, each man gave the other a knowing-glint in his eye and a firm handshake, signifying that each man had achieved his respective goal from this meeting. General Wojcik had received affirmation for Peregrine to have in the field support from CIA and tacit support in DC – and both men understood, if anything goes wrong – it is solely on "Bull".

Riding back to the Pentagon on the George Washington Parkway, Bull used the time to call his secretary. He asked her if she could arrange a meeting with the Chief of Naval Operations and the Army Chief of Staff today, together if possible and that he needed 15 minutes of their time for a sensitive matter. Although the CNO, Admiral Frank Kelso, and the Army Chief of Staff, General Earl Wheeler, were each four-star flag officers, outranking the two-star Wojcik, they knew Wojcik was in tight with the JCS Chairman. Politically, it was expedient for the four-stars to get the meeting done and move-on. Both gave Bull his requested 15-minutes that afternoon. Bull asked each four-star for confidentiality in providing information to match the personnel criteria he cited for Peregrine team officer candidates:

Names of USMA and USNA graduates from the respective classes of 1958-1961 who:

Graduated in the top 10% of their class

Had a conduct record in the bottom 20 % of their class

Current assignment and service records to include their respective times at the USMA and USNA

Later that afternoon, Admiral Kelso called General Wheeler, a bit amused and curious; the request from Bull Wojcik, both generals thought the personnel criteria were borderline bizarre, even for Bull.

An armed courier arrived before Bull left his office that evening, the courier gave General Wojcik a sealed envelope; General Wojcik signed the delivery receipt and opened the envelope after the courier departed.

Top Secret Project Safeguard

Immediate

EYES ONLY: Major-General Stanislaw Wojcik

To: JCS Deputy for Special Projects

From: Project Safeguard

(TS) A combined ARVN/US Advisor training patrol was ambushed 12 April 1963, Bến Tre Province, Vietnam.

The patrol consisted of 23 newly arrived American advisors and 90 South Vietnamese Rangers.

Assumed: 22 American advisors KIA and 90 South Vietnamese Rangers KIA. No bodies recovered at this time.

ARVN Paratrooper battalion with US advisors in route to recover bodies.

Captain Basil Watkins, US Army Special Forces, only known survivor. Captain Watkins debriefing continues.

Captain Watkins dropped out of formation temporally to deal with a severe dysentery issue. Before Captain Watkins could rejoin the patrol, the patrol entered the ambush' kill zone'. Captain Watkins identified incoming fire to include

AK-47, RPG, and mortar fire, all zeroed-in on the 'kill zone'; Captain Watkins believes was fire from several 12.7 mm heavy-machine guns in addition.

Captain Watkins states, "this was no hasty ambush" – adding – "they knew we were coming".

Incoming fire ended after about seven minutes. Occasional single shots followed, likely executions of ARVN and US wounded.

Captain Watkins conducted his E&E to a clearing about 3 klicks south of the ambush site. He contacted a passing US helicopter using a PRC-90 and was rescued.

Oliver Brown, Colonel

US Army, MACV-SOG

'Bull' Wojcik reread the message and concluded two points: we have gone from a big problem to a super-crisis, a political and military super-crisis; we need to get Operation Peregrine underway immediately.

The next morning, Bull received the 'candidate personnel' information he requested from the CNO and Army Chief of Staff. Bull was looking for individuals who were intelligent plus having a native characteristic as risk-takers, men who were willing to break rules and regulations, that is, ideal clandestine operatives. Not surprising, the list was rather short. Top 10% academically of your Academy class and low conduct-grades were a rare combination. Bull directed Colonel Steward to bring five candidates from the Smart-boy/Bad-boy list to report to him forthwith at the Pentagon.

After interviewing the five officer candidates for the Peregrine Vietnam deployment team, Bull selected two who qualified as "True Believers" in every respect. Captain Robert Williams, US Military Academy, Class of 1959 to lead the team and LT Gary Baumgartner, US Naval Academy, Class of 1961 as his deputy. When asked to volunteer for an unspecified dangerous mission, both men did so without hesitation or questions.

McGeorge Bundy was not happy with the call from Bull Wojcik. The Administration was still stinging politically from the Bay of Pigs disaster. Political criticism and recriminations were being used for political gain over the young President, and foreign enemies used the Bay of Pigs to mock President Kennedy. Bundy, in no way, wanted another risky adventure, the risky-type that Bull Wojcik was famous for. Bundy deliberately stalled providing an answer to the request for a call back to 'Bull'. At the same time, Bundy knew Bull was close to the JCS Chairman and Bull would be speaking for the Chairman, all the while giving political cover to the Chairman. The pecking order in Washington was well understood by the insiders; you do not indefinitely ignore the JCS Chairman. Bundy decided he had to give Bull some time, but Bundy would have to find some rationale to avoid any new operations that could result in blow-back for the President. McGeorge Bundy's executive secretary called Bull's office to say the National Security Advisor could give Major-General Wojcik 15 minutes the following day at 5 PM.

Major-General Wojcik arrived 15 minutes early, unaccompanied by any other senior officials from the Intelligence Community. While not without precedent, it was somewhat unusual, given the rank of Major-General was rather unimpressive in the lofty halls of the White House senior bureaucracy. McGeorge Bundy had given his executive-secretary instructions to show Major-General Wojcik in as soon as he arrived, she should buzz Bundy on the intercom exactly 15 minutes later, in a rather rude and clumsy way to show Bull the door.

Bull entered Bundy's office, took the seat as offered and launched directly into the reason he was there. The US faced a serious security breach in Vietnam; this enemy-threat had been specifically targeting and killing US Army advisors for about a year. The threat was identified by a low-ranking NSA analyst just a few weeks ago. The 'new threat' knowledge was contained 'for now' to a very few individuals. The Pentagon had taken the lead to find a solution to identify and neutralize the threat. Bundy checked his watch to see how long it would be until the 15-minutes were up.

Bull caught this crude gesture as the epitome of why Bull despised certain senior bureaucrats. The reality of young American soldiers being killed in ambushes in a faraway land tended to be an inconvenience and imposition on a bureaucrat's time. So, Major-General Wojcik went to a point he knew would at least stop Bundy from yawning. Bull stated the fact, if this threat was allowed to persist, the political rancor and backlash would make the political nightmare problems of the Bay of Pigs fiasco a minor memory.

McGeorge Bundy saw the implied political threat, most of all he wanted to avoid another political scandal to engulf the new Administration. Bundy asked Bull to expand and clarify the seemingly gratuitous-comment why this threat was such a serious political risk for the President. Bull went into detail how the threat had evolved during the last ten months and the dire consequences this threat portended going forward. As Bull began to describe Operation Peregrine, the intercom buzzed, 15-minutes had expired. By now Bundy had realized this was no 'wild man' Wojcik high-risk proposal, it was an approach to save the President, and McGeorge Bundy, from another political embarrassment. Bundy summarily told the secretary he was not to be bothered unless it was the President; the secretary looked at the phone in her hand, grimaced and replied, "yes sir!"

As Bull described Operation Peregrine in detail, Bundy was relieved that Peregrine was a very modest effort in size, cost, and political liability. If Peregrine succeeded, a potential major problem was resolved and eliminated. If Peregrine failed, the opposition blow-back would be on the Pentagon in the same magnitude as the size and visibility of Peregrine, minimal risk for the White House. Besides the obvious "fall guy" was sitting across the desk from Bundy, in the event of failure.

Bundy asked what Wojcik wanted? Bull replied with a succinct response, throwing a political curve-ball at the National Security Advisor. Bull said the Chairman of the JCS, the CIA Director, and the NSA Director would like to meet with the President face-to-face to gain President Kennedy's personal seal of approval for the mission and receive any guidance the President may have. Bundy gave a loud sigh of relief; such a meeting would allow Bundy to avoid any personal responsibility to approve Peregrine and avoid all political liability for himself.

McGeorge smiled for the first time since Bull entered his office, he shook Bull's hand and said he would reach-out to the President to get Peregrine on the executive calendar. Bull thanked Bundy for his time and stated the Chairman would be on standby for Bundy's call for the schedule to meet with President Kennedy.

The meeting with President Kennedy happened two days later; the attendees were greeted warmly by JFK and seated in the Oval Office with coffee and breakfast rolls for this early Saturday morning contact. In addition to the President and his National Security Advisor, attendees included the Chairman Joint Chiefs of Staff, the NSA Director, CIA Deputy Director for Special Projects, and Major-General Wojcik. All silently noted, CIA Director McCone was avoiding any of his personal-fingerprints on the Peregrine operation. McCone had sent his Deputy to avoid showing personal involvement by the CIA Director. As savvy DC insider-politicians, all made the foregone conclusion, Bull would take any blame if Peregrine went awry.

The meeting lasted for an hour, 45 minutes over the allotted 15 minutes. President Kennedy relished his special forces and clandestine operations discussions. JFK had many questions and offered suggestions. One matter of high-concern for all was the security of this project. At the conclusion, President Kennedy gave not only his approval but his endorsement, Presidential Authority for a close-hold clandestine operation. The President promised whatever Peregrine needed – money, resources, and protection from various bureaucrats' or field commanders' interference. Peregrine was a go!

The Peregrine team members were standing-by at the Pentagon, waiting for orders from Major-General Wojcik. The initial order was given by phone to Colonel Steward as Major-General Wojcik departed the White House – assemble the team in the SCIF in 15 minutes.

Major-General 'Bull' Wojcik walked into the SCIF conference room exactly on the 15-minute time-hack. Colonel Steward and eleven tough-looking men were waiting for him, they snapped to attention as the General entered the room, all presenting a professional curiosity about the status of their mission. Bull looked around the room, there was no question, these were the right hard-men for the job, the "True Believers", the elite warriors of the elite, ready for a fight.

Team Commander – US Army Captain Robert Williams, USMA Class of 1959; 6 feet 2 inches, 215 pounds, brown hair cut short, classic features, played linebacker for the West Point football team, effective in negotiations and coordinating with other organizations such as CIA. One tour in Vietnam as an advisor to an ARVN paratroop battalion

Deputy Commander – US Navy Lieutenant Gary Baumgartner, USNA Class of 1961; 6 feet 2 inches, 205 pounds, light brown hair cut short, ruggedly handsome, expert in Krav Maga (hand-to-hand combat taught to Israeli special forces), tour in Vietnam with CIA to find and assassinate senior Viet Cong leaders (a prelude to the CIA Phoenix Program), relaxed with a sense of humor and a sailor's interest in 'the girls'.

Ops Officer – US Army Captain Reginald Denning, Special Forces; 6 feet 1 inch, 195 pounds,, dark brown hair combed straight back in the European style, handsome aristocratic face, continental mannerisms, a quiet but forceful leader; a former French Foreign Legionnaire with two tours in Vietnam as commander of a French Foreign Legion paratroop company, led his men in the A Shau valley on missions to find and kill Viet Minh; speaks Vietnamese, German, French; believed to be an ethnic German and possibly is in the US Army under a false name

Operations Lead NCO: US Army Master Sergeant George Washington Jones; Special Forces. 6 feet 4 inches, 235 pounds. 82nd Airborne Division heavyweight boxing champ before he transitioned to Special Forces. Married with three children. Devout Christian. One previous tour in Vietnam with SOG

Operations NCO: Woodrow Clayton: US Army Master Sergeant, Special Forces. 6 feet 1 inch, 185 pounds, tall, lean, and wiry, craggy face. Part-Cherokee Indian, master woodsman and tracker. Devout Christian. Expert in jujitsu and hand-to-hand combat. Superb marksman with a variety of weapons. Taciturn, but speaks with authority when he talks. Married with two children.

Intelligence: Jacob Risner: USMC, Gunnery Sergeant, Force Recon. 6 feet 3 inches, 220 pounds, brown close cropped brown hair, good-looking and a smooth talker. Powerfully built. Master of Muay Thai hand-to-hand combat (kicking and striking with the hands). Tour in Vietnam with SOG. Drinks and likes the ladies. Divorced, no children. A very earthy guy.

Intelligence: US Army Warrant Officer Carl Renner; 6 feet 1 inch, 200 pounds, short brown hair, studious in manner and appearance. A brilliant intelligence analyst, meticulous, works the details, enjoys reading and drinking with friends – and is known to be 'a bit wild' at times

Weapons: Jacob Podowski: US Army Master Sergeant, Special Forces. 6 feet 5 inches, 250 pounds, toughened as a young man working in the coal mines of West Virginia. Intimidating but had a good sense of humor. Expert in explosives and various foreign weapons. Expert in Defendu, a method of "quick kill" hand-to-hand combat developed by William Fairbairn (co-developer of the Fairbairn-Sykes commando fighting knife). Two deployments to Vietnam, one as an advisor to a Vietnamese Special Forces company and one with SOG. Built like a bulldozer and probably the toughest man in a team of tough men.

Communications: James Arthur Wilson: USAF Special Operations, Technical Sergeant; 6 feet tall, 190 pounds, teen-champion surfer, short blond hair, handsome, the youngest member of the team. Naturally gifted in the operation and maintenance of communications equipment and electronics gear. From California. Happy go lucky, reliable friend, drinks, chases women.

Supply & Logistics: Wilber James, US Army Master Sergeant, known as a world-class scrounger, 'I can get that for you', and all around wheeler-and-dealer, known to have 'liberated' any and all equipment from other units to support his unit's mission (and comforts). 6 feet 1 inch, 200 pounds, light brown hair, handsome. Black Belt in Karate. One tour in Vietnam as an advisor to a Vietnamese Ranger battalion. Fast talking and glib – enjoys a few drinks and romances the ladies

Medical Corpsman: US Army Master Sergeant Karl von Eisenberg, "Doc" von Eisenberg. Five feet ten inches, 185 pounds, light-brown hair close cropped, studious face, friendly demeanor. Expert in a wide range of medical matters, treatment, medications, and even has performed major surgeries in the field during his previous Vietnam tour as a Special Forces A-Team medic. Trained in trauma care at the John Hopkins School of Medicine.

Major-General Wojcik stood at attention, briefly looking at each man, before he announced:

"We are going to do what we do best – find um; fix um; kill um. Peregrine is a go!"

Eleven men responded with a – HOOYAH – that rocked the SCIF.

CHAPTER 3 THE EAGLE AND THE BEAR

Three senior US intelligence officers, Lt General Blake, NSA Director; Major-General Wojcik, Advisor to the JCS Chairman; and, Christopher Watkins, CIA Deputy Director for Special Projects raised glasses of vintage Kentucky bourbon to celebrate the President's approval of Operation Peregrine. Not only did President Kennedy approve the operation, JFK admonished the Peregrine team to move forward 'with all due prudence' – Washington speak for 'get it done yesterday but smartly'. Normally, a Presidential Directive would generate a flurry of activity by the White House staff and any government agencies affected by the directive. In the case of the security blackout for Peregrine, there was only one White House Staff action. The National Security Adviser sent a memo to the White House Budget Director, set up a black-money account with a revolving fund maintained at a $20 million dollar level. The only person authorized to access the revolving fund will be Major-General Wojcik, JCS Special Projects. Major-General Wojcik will account directly to the National Security Advisor for expenditures from this account.

Five thousand miles to the East and eight hours earlier, KGB Chairman Semichastny and KGB First Main Directorate Head General Sakharovsky shook hands and drank an ice-cold vodka toast to the initiation of Operation Red (Операция Красный), a deception operation against the US and North Vietnam. They are the only two individuals in the Soviet Union with full access to Operation Red details including the ultimate objective for the mission.

Operation Red was originally conceived by Captain Aleksandr Petrov as a strategic deception plan directed at the US and the Soviet 'ally', North Vietnam. General Sakharovsky immediately recognized the plan was brilliant and could advance his career so he claimed authorship and ownership from his protégé Captain Petrov. Sakharovsky understood the new generation of KGB officers like Petrov were the future of the KGB. Gone were the days of uneducated thugs in ill-fitting suits. The new generation of KGB officers were well-educated and had an urbane sophistication. When Sakharovsky hijacked his idea, Petrov was pleased, as this was an endorsement by Sakharovsky.

General Aleksandr Michael Sakharovsky was a living-legend in the KGB. He was renowned for his personal courage in clandestine operations including the collection of political, scientific and technical intelligence, plus the control of deep cover moles in foreign governments. He was held in awe for his mercilessness during counterespionage operations during the Great Patriotic War and later for his brutal role in suppressing the 1956 anti-Russian uprising in Hungary. Sakharovsky was second only to the KGB Chairman in the Soviet Union as influential for intelligence matters and operations.

The Chairman of the KGB was the second-most powerful man in the Soviet Union, superseded only by the General Secretary of the Communist Party of the Soviet Union (CPSU). In 1962 Vladimir Semichastny was the Chairman of the KGB. Vladimir Semichastny was a lifetime politician with no experience in intelligence; Semichastny's loyal political servitude had accrued powerful friends, including Nikita Khrushchev and Alexander Shelepin, a former Chairman of the KGB. Semichastny's appointment was primarily to protect the political interests of an inner-circle of the CPSU. Semichastny was totally dependent on KGB senior intelligence professionals to conduct the devious "smoke and mirrors" business of the KGB.

In the slang of the West, Semichastny was a servile 'suck-up' constantly cultivating powerful friends seeking their patronage. Semichastny rose through the ranks of the Communist Youth League (Komsomol) working in the fields of propaganda and administration. In 1950 he moved to Moscow where he was befriended by Alexander Shelepin. who brought Semichastny to the attention of Nikita Khrushchev. In 1961, Khrushchev appointed him as Chairman of the KGB. At the age of 37 he was the youngest Soviet security and intelligence chief of the Cold War era. Surprised when Khrushchev appointed him as KGB Chairman, commenting that he did not have any experience in intelligence and counterintelligence; Khrushchev, bluntly told Semichastny that the KGB needed, above all, a deft political hand.

Semichastny's young age and his lack of professional experience in intelligence and counterintelligence matters forced him to rely on the KGB Chief Directorate department heads, particularly General Aleksandr Sakharovsky.

Aleksandr Michael Sakharovsky ruthlessly climbed the KGB promotion ladder to the powerful position as head of the First Chief

Directorate (foreign intelligence). Early in his KGB career, he understood that just being an effective intelligence operative was only part of the path to the top of KGB power. Political alliances with powerful individuals inside and outside of the KGB were even more important than his legendary work in the field. KGB General Sakharovsky held great influence over the Chairman of the KGB. Sakharovsky and Semichastny formed a co-dependent relationship where General Sakharovsky was the intelligence brains and Chairman Semichastny delivered the pollical clout.

The KGB First Chief Directorate under General Sakharovsky effectively controlled the Warsaw Pact intelligence organizations in East Germany, Czechoslovakia, Poland, and Hungary. General Sakharovsky approached Chairman Semichastny with a proposal for a deception operation to give the KGB control of the three North Vietnamese intelligence services: the Ministry of Defense Intelligence Department, the Public Security Directorate, and the super-secret Liaison Directorate. In addition, the operation has a strategic hidden purpose beyond the penetration of the North Vietnamese intelligence services. That purpose was to recruit a high-level mole in the US State Department.

Operation Red – the primary objective is to recruit a high-level target in the US State Department. This target will be recruited to serve as a KGB mole in the top echelon of the US State Department intelligence organization, the INR. The KGB deception plot will use North Vietnamese military forces to assassinate US advisors in South Vietnam, misdirecting the US from the objective to recruit the high-level mole. KGB Chairman Semichastny bought into the plan as a chance to further his political influence within the CPSU.

Sakharovsky gave the Chairman a further update:

"Chairman Semichastny, Operation Red can be a great success for you and the KGB. We will use the "Vostok" agreement you signed with North Vietnam as leverage for North Vietnamese cooperation".

"As I remember, Vostok was to supply North Vietnam with radios and electronic equipment for signal intercepts. The North Vietnamese were glad to receive modern electronic gear and dependence on the Chinese for equipment".

"That is correct. The North Vietnamese even chose the name Vostok to insult the Chinese at the same time. Vostok gets us inside sensitive

North Vietnamese operations and gives the KGB excellent cover for Operation Red. Assassinating the American advisors is a powerful tool to misdirect the American from our real objective".

"Excellent, I will advise comrade Khrushchev that Operation Red is moving forward".

General Sakharovsky directed Captain Petrov to prepare a precis of Operation Red. Petrov was to make only one copy and hand-carry that copy to the General.

Petrov went to work to meet the challenge of condensing a complex project into a few persuasive paragraphs, including a two-paragraph Executive Summary. The objectives for Operation Red were clear and easily stated but the 'devil lay in the details'. Petrov was aware KGB Chairman Semichastny had no background in intelligence matters and Semichastny would read the Executive summary but leave the execution of the operation to General Sakharovsky. Petrov went to work understanding this document, and Executive Summary, was more a political instrument than a description of a working Ops Plan. Chairman Semichastny and General Sakharovsky would use the executive summary for a private eyes-only meeting with the General Secretary of the Communist Party, Nikita Khrushchev.

During the respective celebrations, neither side realized nor accepted that the other side was following a false premise.

The Americans believed they had uncovered a major threat from the North Vietnamese; oblivious to the reality they had taken the Russian bait. The Americans were confident the Peregrine Operation would effectively negate the North Vietnam operation assassination US Army advisors to the ARVN.

The Soviets believed the Americans were unaware of the KGB shadow role in the 'North Vietnamese mole operation' assassinating US Army officers. The Soviets were supremely confident that, in any event, the Americans would be victims of the Russian Maskirovka (deception). The KGB officers poured another round of vodka and laughed – when will the Americas discover the KGB 'planted' encryption messages? Of course, that encryption protocol is obsolete, and we only use it now to mislead the Americans.

Captain Alexandr Petrov is a rising star in the KGB and a graduate of the Red Banner Institute, the most prestigious KGB espionage school. Aleksandr Petrov was an imposing man at six feet, one inch tall and 210 pounds and moved with a smooth grace of an athlete. Petrov was trained in the harsh Spetsnaz (KGB special forces) regimen of the hand-to hand combat techniques of Sambo and ARB, techniques which incorporated grappling, knife fighting, and firearms. Petrov is brilliant, well-connected to high-level KGB power-brokers, and an experienced field operative. Petrov accepted that the fates took joy in creating risks in every clandestine operation, some risks anticipated and some unexpected. Petrov was supremely confident he could conquer each risk as it surfaced.

Operation Red, was Captain Petrov's creation, though KGB General Sakharovsky took the credit with the KGB Chairman for the innovative plan. Petrov and Sakharovsky recognized two risks as existential for Operation Red. The two fault lines in the operation, together or independently, might lead to a failure of the mission. In the event of failure, Sakharovsky, without hesitation, would throw Captain Petrov to the wolves as the fall-guy. The two failure modes centered on the future encounter between the KGB case officer for Operation Red, and the recruitment target. Could the case officer carry-off the actual recruitment under the guidance of Captain Petrov acting as the Operations Officer? Was the target capable of 'bringing home the goods' for the KGB, after being recruited as a mole? What actions did 'Sasha' Petrov need to take to mitigate the risks?

Thinking back to the genesis of Operation Red, Captain Petrov determined that a "Swallow" would be the keystone to his long-term objective to insert a mole in a high-level intelligence job in the US government. The 'Swallow' is a KGB-trained enchantress who approaches a recruitment target, seduces and compromises him, setting a trap for recruitment as a spy for the KGB. Swallows fall into two classes. The run-of -the-mill Swallow who was essentially a prostitute who had the KGB as her pimp. There were a few Swallows who were sophisticated courtesans based on their physical attributes and higher intellect than the typical 'Swallow'. These KGB courtesans were successful in sexual compromising many high-level Western politicians in sensitive political, military, and intelligence security positions.

Sasha reviewed the files of current operational Swallows and selected three for interviews. The Swallow training facility, "State School 4", was outside the Moscow Ring Road in a secluded birch-forest. The Swallow training center was commanded by KGB Colonel Svetlana Ivanovna Sokolova, one of the few female colonels in the KGB. Sokolova was extremely arrogant and self-assured based on her KGB patron, therefore she was thoroughly disliked and despised by most of her KGB officer colleagues.

Sokolova was a former Swallow who realized she could use her sexual wiles to leverage advantages for her career; she targeted senior KGB officers who would trade sex with Sokolova for her promotions through the KGB ranks. One might say her career had several twists and turns as she screwed her way to the rank of Colonel. Now, she ran a brutal training program for the young women candidates on the treacherous demeaning path to become a KGB "Swallow".

Captain Petrov called the State School #4 to set up interviews with the three swallows of interest to him for Operation Red. Colonel Sokolova greeted Captain Petrov with a disdainful welcome, condescending and smug. She had to give Captain Petrov access for the interviews given his First Chief Directorate priority orders, but she did so under-protest to her KGB senior-officer patron. After a terse greeting, she dismissed Captain Petrov with a wave of her hand aa part of the rude welcome.

A female Sergeant ushered Captain Petrov into a small dirty windowless room with two filthy wooden chairs. He carefully placed two candidate personnel files on one of the chairs. He reexamined the personnel file of "Nyugen Kie^", primarily of interest because of her language skills, including Vietnamese. There was no photo in the file. A different female sergeant brought Nyugen Kie^ in for the interview. Captain Petrov did not sit down on the filthy chair to avoid soiling his impeccably appointed KGB uniform. He mentally noted that the Vietnamese used a different naming process than the Russians. In Russia, the individual's personal name was listed first followed by the patronymic and then the family name. In Vietnam, as in many Asian countries, the family name was listed first follow-by the individual's personal name. Thus, Nyugen was the family name and Kie^ was her first name.

Nyugen Kie^ entered the room, Sasha was stunned by her beauty and the very grace of her walk. At the same time, Sasha detected a young woman who had been abused and dehumanized in life and particularly in the KGB Swallow system. Sasha's instincts told him Nyugen Kie^ was the person for Operation Red. He questioned her briefly about her field assignments to date. Nyugen Kie^ answered the questions in a bewitching voice that would stimulate lust in any man. Sasha made the decision, Nyugen Kie^ was the right person for Operation Red. He thanked Nyugen Kie^ before dismissing her; he canceled the other two interviews.

A female sergeant escorted Petrov back to Colonel Sokolova's office; Colonel Sokolova did not offer Petrov a seat and brusquely stated, she understood his visit was finished. While KGB Colonels generally did not treat KGB captains with much respect, her conduct toward Captain Petrov was grossly beyond the norms of KGB professionalism. Captain Petrov was poised and respectful as he requested Nyugen Kie^ be assigned to him for a sensitive First Chief Directorate operation.

Petrov's mere request caused a bellicose outburst from Sokolova, she shouted,

"Who do you think you are coming into my facility and demanding anything, much less a personnel transfer."

He reached across her desk grabbing the phone and placed a call before she could physically restrain him from using the phone. Sokolova listened to his brief remarks, that,

"he had a problem at the Swallow facility",

Captain Petrov simply smiled as he handed the phone to Colonel Sokolova.

Sokolova did not know who was on the other end of the call, so she controlled her rage, answering in a professional tone:

"Colonel Sokolova here"

A blasting voice responded,

"General Mikailovich here, what the hell do you think you are doing impeding a First Chief Directorate operation – unless you are eager for a remote posting in Siberia or some other shithole – give Petrov whatever he wants and do it now – he is there under my orders on a priority First Chief Directorate operation."

Before Sokolova could respond, General Mikailovich hung up. Shocked and worried, Sokolova knew her professional survival was at stake. She looked at Captain Petrov with malice and hate but stated in a forced calm voice:

"Nyugen Kie^ is transferred as a subordinate to you, just to you personally, transfer effective immediately. Nyugen Kie^ may travel back with you now to KGB Headquarters"

KGB Headquarters filled the large Lubyanka building on Dzerzhinsky Square; a statue of "Iron Felix" Dzerzhinsky, constantly surveilled the Headquarters from his towering position in the center of the square. Iron Felix was the father of the KGB having organized the Cheka during the Bolshevik revolution. The Cheka established a level of fear and terror across Russia unknown since the Mongol invasion. The sinister nature of the Cheka never changed, despite many name changes over the decades, the latest incarnation being the KGB. Whether Cheka or KGB, the institution, by whatever name, was always an instrument of terror for the Soviet Union and a dangerous threat to Soviet adversaries worldwide.

Gritting her teeth, Colonel Sokolova asked in a calm voice which belied her fury and rage,

"Is there anything else I can do to assist you, Captain?"

Captain Petrov politely and hypocritically thanked her, commenting that he would like to depart for Moscow with Nyugen Kie^ immediately. Colonel Sokolova picked up the phone and issued the necessary orders in a loud demanding voice, knowing she would be humiliated behind her back as the staff circulated rumors about the young captain calling her out and how a senior KGB officer read her the riot-act on the phone, embarrassing Sokolova in front of a female sergeant and Petrov. No matter, she would take her fury out on the staff and Swallow students later.

Nyugen Kie^ walked into the waiting room 15 minutes later carrying a small suitcase and dressed in the same drab shapeless grey uniform, which passed for a dress at the school, the same ugly garb she wore during her interview with Petrov. Nyugen Kie^ had her 'game face' on to mask the anxiety she felt with the abrupt and unexpected changes imposed on her life. Who was this Captain Petrov? Where did he get such power and influence as a lowly captain? Would her life go from bad to worse?

Petrov already knew much about Nyugen; she was 25 years old, a veteran KGB intelligence operative with a chain of clandestine sexual compromise successes. Now, with Nyugen as the potential central player on his team, Petrov was poised to launch an operation that could provide the greatest challenge and potentially the greatest intelligence coup in KGB history.

Petrov would learn as time passed, Nyugen's life had been very cruel eventually bringing her to where she was now, a KGB prostitute. She was a child of Marxist-Leninist parents, not a little girl of a loving French father and caring Vietnamese mother. Her parents were more devoted to Karl Marx than they were to their daughter. Her parents were ardent, fanatical devotees of the 'Communist ideology', which became a substitute 'religion' for them. The parents both were well-educated in the French dominated colonial land of Indochina. As Vietnamese nationalists, they gravitated into the Marxist-Leninist belief-system during the 1930s. A Comintern talent-spotter marked them as good candidates for training as agents to promote the Soviet brand of Communism in Southeast Asia. The future parents of Nyugen traveled to Moscow at the end of the 1930s for training as agents. Their training period encompassed a time of extreme turbulence and danger in Russia. The "Great Terror" was still in full swing as the lethal Stalin purges took a daily toll of victims. War loomed from the west as Hitler prepared to invade and conquer Poland in the fall of 1939, using that strategic positioning as the precursor to Barbarossa, the June 1941 Nazi invasion of the USSR.

Her parents plunged into the spy training with an energy possible only in true zealots. The birth of Nyugen Kie^ was a temporary distraction from their pursuit of Communist sainthood. Nyugen grew up in a chaotic time, intensifying her deprivation of the parental emotional support, essential for the healthy emotional growth of a child. She received little love and no nurturing from her parents who held all their devotion and energies for the Communist Party. Nyugen sought solace in her studies and a personal fantasy that her future would hold some happiness.

By the age of 15 she had grown into a beautiful young woman despite the meager diet during the war years. She was tall, 5 feet 8 inches, for a Eurasian female and well-endowed with full figure. Kie^ had all the physical attributes of a beautiful young French-woman. She is stunning and drew the attention from all men and stirred their male libidos. The omnipresent KGB had monitored her parents and watched Nyugen develop physically and intellectually. The KGB noted Nyugen was exceptionally intelligent in addition to her beauty. With the Great Patriotic War concluded and Nazi Germany destroyed, the USSR now looked outward to spread Communism and Soviet influence worldwide.

Her parents were dispatched back to Indochina to set up a KGB spy network. Kie^ would not miss them. Except for sharing an apartment with her parents, Kie^ and the two communist zealots were virtual strangers. Nyugen Kie^ was abandoned to the fates and remained in Moscow unaware her destiny was already written by the KGB.

Early on, she had learned just how deceitful and cruel the KGB-world was. She met a person whom she believed was her caring mentor; she knew him as Captain Vladimir Rostov. Rostov was a superb agent handler and manipulated her with a diabolical methodology, giving her what she thought was his love. Of course, he was not immune to the seductive qualities of the sultry Asian temptress. Rostov and Nyugen Kie^ engaged in a steamy sex affair that could have been a best seller as an erotic romantic novel. Kie^ thought she had achieved her fantasy and she would do and did anything for the young KGB officer, Vladimir Rostov. She became "Rostov's thing". He betrayed her in a savage manner as he brutally coerced her into the KGB "Swallow" program, abandoning her in the same callous way her parents had. Once again, she was bereft of emotional security. The "Swallow" training was humiliating, degrading, and dehumanizing. The operational assignments corrupted her very soul. Even so, Nyugen Kie^ was a "natural" as a clandestine operative, adept at tradecraft, deception, and seduction as ingrained parts of her persona.

Walking to the waiting room, the female Sergeant whispered to Nyugen Kie^,

"another guard said she heard Sokolova talking to the Captain, something was said about him taking you to Lubyanka."

An icy chill ran down Kie^'s spine. Many taken to Lubyanka went directly to the basement and disappeared forever. Credible rumors about basement cells used for interrogation, torture, and execution were part of the currency of terror in the Soviet Union. Rumors about death in the Lubyanka base were wide-spread in Moscow, because they were true. Stories about drains in the floor needed to dispose of the copious amounts of blood the many executions generated and the bullet to the back of the skull for 'enemies of the state'.

Kie^ thought, what could I have done to become 'an enemy of the state'? Captain Petrov greeted her pleasantly which reinforced her trepidation. Smooth and dangerous, she concluded. To make her confusion complete, this KGB Captain had a driver and a car, how is that possible when only the top KGB Generals had official transport with a driver? Resigned, Nyugen Kie^ accepted her fate as a powerless pawn to be used at the whims of the KGB.

Kie^ had suffered so many indignities from the KGB, death in the Lubyanka basement might be a relief from all her pain. She did walk through Dzerzhinsky Square once and saw that virtually all pedestrian-comrades were turning their eyes away from the Lubyanka building as they walked by, as if just seeing the KGB building would cause their arrest. She had never driven a car and did not know the street patterns in Moscow, so she looked out the car window awaiting her fate. Much to her surprise, they stopped at an apartment building near the Baumanskaya Metro station, an apartment building guarded by two-armed Militia officers. She had no idea this was an exclusive residence for senior KGB officers.

Captain Petrov was greeted obsequiously by the guards. The driver took her luggage, such as it was, one small, dilapidated cardboard-suitcase. When she reached to take it, the driver shook his head, no. Petrov told her to follow him and proceeded to the elevator. The driver went to a back elevator with all her worldly goods in that little suitcase. Petrov and Kie^ rode the elevator in silence to the seventh floor. Petrov reached for a set of keys and opened the door of 'apartment 21'. As she entered apartment 21, she was overwhelmed by the elegance. The apartment was not the usual cramped two rooms. She could not tell how many rooms were in this wonderful 'apartment 21'. There was a knock on the door, the driver entered and set her suitcase down and asked Petrov if there was anything else. Petrov replied:

"Yes, we want to go to the GUM in 30 minutes"

GUM was the only legitimate department store in Moscow. It catered to the Soviet elite and foreigners and in any event was far too expensive for the average Russian. GUM was situated in a massive building on Red Square across from the Kremlin. Kie^ was sure she was dreaming.

Captain Petrov spoke pleasantly, telling her to follow him; they passed two rooms and stopped at a third. Petrov told her,

"This is your room; please unpack and take a bath".

The bath, well, now she knew why she was there, Swallows provide sexual gratification as ordered, for KGB spies and for KGB officers. She thought, make the best of this while it lasts. Kie^ undressed and took her bath. To her surprise, instead of engaging in sex, they went to GUM.

She had dressed in the best dress she had, but she felt and looked shabbily attired compared to the rest of the snobby-elitist GUM shoppers. Though she felt uncomfortable, she did enjoy looking at the luxury goods in the marvelous GUM department store. Petrov led her to an upscale women's shop, the condescending looks, directed at her quickly vanished when they saw the uniformed KGB captain with her. Captain Petrov spoke with authority to the sales-clerk. He directed the clerk to fully outfit the Kie^ with clothes, shoes, 'the works' and burn the dress she was wearing. The female sales-clerk obsequiously rushed to bring various outfits for Kie^ to try-on. When they were through shopping, the driver carried several large packages to the car and they departed GUM and returned to 'apartment 21'.

Kie^'s head was swimming as she tried to process what was happening. She had many simultaneously conflicting feelings. For the present, Kie^ decided to take a low-profile. Captain Petrov was plainly in-charge and he obviously was very well-connected in the KGB. She expected he would clarify her situation in due time. For now, she can just enjoy her good fortune while it lasts. Her idea to enjoy it 'while it lasts', was cut short as Petrov ordered her sit with him in the living room. He told the cook to bring them glasses of sweet-tea, and then began to ask Kie^ a series of probing questions.

Street-wise, Kie^ dutifully, but carefully, answered each question. She knew this was a test, perhaps a trap. Petrov would already have known all the answers to this series of questions. In addition, he was taking her measure as she interacted with him during this potentially dangerous situation for her. Petrov listened with the incisive senses of an experienced case officer who was used to hearing lies, evasions, and attempts at deception.

As the interrogation continued, anxiety returned for Kie^, had she made a mistake during a previous Swallow-operation; had she made an inappropriate comment to another Swallow - and that other Swallow was a KGB informant who reported her? She thought, the trip to the Lubyanka basement may still be in her near-future. Despite the Petrov smiles, Kie^ felt a rising level of fear, fear which she was sure Petrov would detect. After a second glass of hot sweet tea, served in a clear glass in a metal frame with a handle, Petrov thanked her for her cooperation and suggested she might want to retire to her room to rest. Kie^ thanked him and moved quickly to her room, a 'suggestion' from Petrov was an order, not a social pleasantry.Petrov analyzed his interaction with Kie^. He learned a great deal in the brief time with her. Kie^ was street-wise but in a way that was much more so than the typical 'Swallow'. She had a solid intellect that was yet to be tapped by the KGB. At the same time, Sasha observed, Kie^ was damaged goods. Her personal adversities and the emotional abuses had created havoc with her self-esteem, depriving her of a sense of personal worth. Kie^ was on the precipitous downhill path of self-destruction. A path so many Swallows found as a way of escape from the Hell which was a Swallow's life-prison. Kie^ was on the way to clinical depression and hopelessness, knowing she was working in a KGB that did not care about her. Nyugen Kie^ was just a KGB moving-part to advance the interests of the State. Just as the cruel and exploitive nature of the spy business used human vulnerabilities as opportunities for the case officer to exploit people. Petrov would exploit her as needed for the Operation Red mission.

Petrov evaluated how he could exploit Kie^'s vulnerabilities to advance KGB objectives. The good case officer became the rescuer, the provider of all that the agent needed to achieve stability, plus fulfill the essential satisfactions and needs in the agent's life. In the harsh world of 'smoke and mirrors', the case officer would 'complete the Mission' with a clinical, unemotional detachment. Despite his professionalism as an intelligence officer, Sasha felt conflicted. He felt an empathy for this young woman whose life had been so sordid and cruel. In the background, another feeling lurked. Sasha Petrov found the sexual allure of this young woman enticing and distracting. Her allure attracted all men that way. She has all the potential to be an outstanding operative, but she is emotionally wounded at this point in her life. He believed she could heal and become whole again —and she could play a decisive role in Operation Red.

In her room, Kie^ agonized about her near-term future. In her emotional state, Kie^ fell back on what she knew best. She would use her potent sexual wiles to seduce and manipulate young Captain Petrov. She had not missed any of the lascivious glances Petrov cast her way since they first met at the Swallow compound. Of course, she had encouraged his desire by certain movements as an implied promise of bliss. In her shaky emotional condition, she determined to act boldly and quickly. Going back to the 'apartment 21' living room, she found Petrov in a contemplative mood, sipping vodka. Using her most innocent voice, Kie^ asked the captain,

"Would you like to see me in the dresses, you bought for me at GUM?"

Sasha considered her question and concluded, there was more to this than Kie^ doing a fashion show. This action by Kie^ will tell him a great deal about her now and for the future.

Smiling, Sasha said:

"Yes, I would very much like to see you in the new dresses."

Kie^ thanked him using her most suggestive smile, honed at the 'Swallow school', a smile that implied dreamlike pleasures for a man. Returning to her room, Kie^ quickly undressed and brushed her long black hair, checking the mirror, Kie^ felt a renewed confidence, no man can resist her. She stepped to the door and, leaning out, asked Captain Petrov to come to her room. Petrov moved quickly down the hall to her room. When he arrived, he found a naked Kie^, appearing as the seductress in a lustful dream. Reacting instantly as virile young men had done since boys and girls lived together in caves, Sasha started to move toward Kie^ to take her to bed. By his second step, a survival instinct kicked in, he was an experienced intelligence operative, and he saw the move by Kie^ as a 'provocation', an attempt to compromise him. Instantly, back under control, Sasha composed himself by asking Kie^ to try on the red dress first. He stepped around her to sit on her bed as he watched her put on the red dress. Sasha smiled in personal amazement that he had resisted her charms. Even so, he mentally noted, I will taste her charms at my timing, which will be soon. Petrov complemented Kie^ on how nice she looked in the red dress, going farther to say,

"You make the dress look beautiful".

Kie^ was shaken by the self-control Captain Petrov had exercised as she stood naked before him, radiating sexual ecstasy to be had in the nearby bed. What had happened? Was there something wrong with this young man? She had never been rejected by a man before.

Sasha asked her to try on the black dress and continue the fashion show. Two dresses later, he instructed her to wear the red dress that evening when they went to dinner at the Europa restaurant.

Located in the historic Metropole Hotel, the Europa Restaurant was famous for its cuisine and notorious for the exorbitant prices. The guests to this exclusive restaurant were wealthy foreigners, senior Communist Party members, the elite of the privileged nomenklatura ruling class, and, of course, senior officers of the KGB.

Every head in the room turned as the KGB Captain in a splendid uniform and an exotic Asian beauty in a red dress walked into the restaurant. The men hid lustful smirks while the women did not hide their envy. Kie^ fell back onto her Swallow training as she elegantly followed Captain Petrov to their table. The golden mushroom soup was world-class, the expensive black caviar on squares of buttered bread thoroughly enjoyed, and they decided to choose a traditional Russian dish for the main course, picking the humble but tasty pelmeni. For dessert they had the classic Russian Napoleon Cake accompanied by cognac. Kie^ struggled to process this enigmatic Captain Petrov. Sasha thought, she will heal; and we will be rewarded as "Heroes of the Soviet Union", I will be recognized as the reason for Operation Red success.

For Nyugen Kie^, she had learned since childhood, survive this day, tomorrow is not now and never will be, if you do not survive this day. Deprived of love and approval, she would do anything to receive some love, some caring, and some acceptance.

The KGB had reentered her life in a very different way. Captain Petrov, a rising star in the KGB, charged with making Nyugen a useful asset for Operation Red. Kie^ quickly became obsessively devoted to the handsome KGB officer who might rescue her from the hell of being a 'Swallow'. This Captain Petrov was kind to her and seemed to give her a certain genuine affection. She did not yet understand that she was part of a grand plan and Petrov would be her operational handler in that plan. The fact was, she was just thrilled to be out from under the 'Swallow hell', that alone was enough for her.

As the KGB and US protagonists drank to perceived respective future successes, a certain irony resided in the workings of both their plans. As an epic clash of American and Russian warrior-intelligence cultures developed in the 'world of smoke and mirrors', neither the American generals nor the Russian generals imagined how their clandestine combat, would stretch around the world, nor that this combat would be shaped to a large extent by the actions of two young women.

Annie Hoffman, 26-year old NSA analyst, could have been out of Hollywood central casting as the beautiful innocent girl from the US Midwest. Nyugen Kie^, a hardened KGB operative at age 25, was an exotic Eurasian beauty who exuded sexuality just as the dangerous Sirens in Greek mythology lured sailors to their deaths on the rocks of lust. The two young women shared a physical attractiveness and brilliant intellects. Beyond the beauty and brains, they could not be more different. Annie Hoffman was a devout Christian and a super-patriot for her country. She lived her life with a commitment to her faith and her country. Nyugen Kie^ was streetwise, emotionally scarred, a hardened KGB operative. Nyugen Kie^ held no ideology sacred, except her ideology of personal survival.

Operation Red was an elegant plan conceived in the tradition of Russian maskirovka (deception). Petrov used the 1939 statement by Churchill, "a riddle, wrapped in a mystery, inside an enigma" as his template. Operation Red used deception of allies and enemies alike to disguise the ultimate objective for Operation Red to recruit a high-level spy in the US State Department. Petrov understood the path to the KGB objective would take many twists and he would have to be continually adapting to the realities which evolved:

The KGB would use an in-place low-level deep cover mole in the US State Department personnel office to spot a recruitment target for the high-level penetration of the State Department. Once that target was identified by the low-level mole, the decision on the method to approach and recruit the target would dictate how the remainder of Operation Red would unfold. The illegal had patiently waited and diligently worked for years to be assigned to a human resources personnel job where he had access to State Department personnel records.

The "illegal" would 'spot', that is identify, a candidate recruitment target. The target would have one or more personal vulnerabilities. Target vulnerabilities include: flawed morally, greedy, egotist, disaffected by his lack of State Department promotions, a heavy drinker, and, is married, a womanizer. The latter vulnerability made the target vulnerable to sexual compromise and blackmail. The KGB would be patient and wait until the target was assigned to the Embassy in Saigon. At that time, the KGB case officer could access the target while operating under the US counterintelligence 'radar'.

Having the target in Vietnam was ideal as the US counterintelligence had a very limited presence in Vietnam; the military counterintelligence resources were focused on security problems created by US forces, such as loose talk by GIs to bar girls, enemy attempts to recruit GIs, and specific attempts by North Vietnamese intelligence to place agents inside South Vietnam military. The CIA station in the US Embassy was understaffed by the many tasks and operations the station personnel had ongoing. The South Vietnamese counterintelligence organization was ineffective. It was an ideal situation for the KGB, a high probability of little or no surveillance of KGB recruitment contact of the US target.

Petrov conceived a deception plan to give layers of KGB misdirection, respectively, to the Americans, the North Vietnamese, and the South Vietnam security services. The first layer of deception was a proposal to North Vietnam for a joint KGB/North Vietnamese operation to penetrate of the South Vietnamese Army command and administrative system. The KGB would provide advanced technical equipment, including an encryption system, plus on-the-ground KGB advisors and technical trainers. North Vietnam would, in-turn, provide support by using in-place North Vietnam moles for the penetration of the ARVN. KGB/North Vietnamese would jointly-manage the communist spy operation in South Vietnam to assassinate US Army advisors. It was a win-win for the KGB. A key part of the deception scheme was the encryption system provided to the North Vietnamese by the KGB. That encryption system was obsolete and a surety to be compromised by the NSA – the obsolete encryption system was the bait for the KGB trap to misdirect the Americans.

The Americans would have to respond to the threats to US troops, specifically the targeting the US Army military advisors. The KGB would leave a bread-crumb trail of evidence to point the Americans in the direction the KGB chose. If the KGB ally, the NVA, suffered in the process, all the better because the Americans would think they were winning.

While the Americans are chasing the mole killing American advisors, the Operation Red case officer will make contact with the US target in the US Saigon Embassy as soon as the target is posted to Saigon. That recruitment contact will exploit 'the fog of war', the chaos, and fury of the Vietnam War.

The Americans had a more difficult problem. They did not understand the scale and nature of the security problems causing the combat deaths of American advisors. The Americans could not be proactive until they had initially 'connected-the-dots'. Thus, they were vulnerable as false trails led them in the directions the KGB wanted them to go.

Operation Peregrine was the US response to the US predicament – find the enemy, fix the enemy, neutralize the enemy. Peregrine used layers of cover to disguise how they planned to terminate 'the threat to US advisors'. The Peregrine plan was a step-by-step 'discovery effort' using powerful resources available from NSA and CIA to support the deployment of an experienced special operations clandestine team. Once on-the-ground, the Peregrine team would fill-in any gaps in the initial counterintelligence plan provided by the Pentagon and the team would execute the necessary actions.

CHAPTER 4   THE ILLEGAL

The clandestine world is based on misdirection, deceit, lies, and deception. There are only two rules: "do not get caught"; "complete the mission". Clandestine operations, conducted by the KGB, the US JCS Special Projects, CIA, DIA, and the military services apply the same "principles" to plan and execute their spy operations. Though the principles do not change, no two operations are the same because the 'human factor' dominates.

While following the same basic principles, the KGB and the US intelligence community often use different terms for the identical operational activities. For example, the terms 'legend' (KGB) and 'cover' (US) mean the same clandestine practice: develop a story, which is used to conceal and protect the true identity and activity of intelligence officers and spies. The legend/cover requires secrecy, deception, and effective tradecraft to successfully accomplish the mission and to protect sources, methods, and operations from compromise by counterintelligence services, enemy or friendly.

Birth of an Illegal

The KGB has employed the 'illegal operation' since the 1920s into the 1960s, deep-cover spies are embedded in enemy countries. These operations are run by Department S, the most secretive unit in the KGB. The KGB 'illegal' is carefully chosen to work in a target country and is given extensive training in order to be able to thoroughly integrate himself into the social fabric of a hostile society.

The "illegal" is the epitome of maskirovka (Russian deception). An illegal could be a radio operator, a case officer, logistics support person, a mole, or a 'sleeper'. The sleeper lives his legend while waiting for an assignment. At times, the sleeper may wait for years to get a specific mission. In the case of the Operation Red 'illegal', the circumstances were fortuitous. This illegal was sent to the United States years before Operation Red was conceived by the KGB.

Originally, the illegal was to obtain a job in the US government in a low-level civil service position and work his way up the civil service employee career progression ladder. In this case, once in place, the illegal was active but had only minor operational duties until the KGB reached out to give him a specific task for Operation Red.

In 1939, Department S had been watching Hans Fischer for over two years. Fischer was a Volga German. The Volga Germans are ethnic Germans who colonized a region along the Volga River in southeastern Russia and lived there since the 18th century.

Hans Fischer was recruited by the NKVD from the Volga German community in 1939. The 1939 date was important for Hans, because, when Nazi Germany invaded the Soviet Union, June 22, 1941, Stalin turned his vicious paranoia on the Volga Germans. The Volga Germans were marked as traitors and large numbers of Volga Germans were deported to Siberia and other locations in the Soviet Far East. Many Volga Germans were arrested as 'enemies of the state' and duly executed.

Hans Fischer was a fervent communist during the 1930s and was a candidate to join the Communist Party of the Soviet Union when the NKVD approached him. The NKVD agent who contacted Hans was typical of those times, a stocky menacing thug. These thugs instilled fear in every Soviet citizen. Taken by surprise, Hans was immediately fearful as every Soviet citizen was when the NKVD came around.

Fischer spoke German with a native fluency, spoke Russian fluently, and spoke English reasonably well, but with a strong German accent. The ideological and linguistic factors made Hans an excellent candidate to be a KGB penetration agent into the US government, a "mole" for the Soviet Union. The NKVD officer told Fischer that he was chosen to serve the Communist Party in a special way.

At the same time the NKVD contacted Hans, the NKVD reached out to Helga Schmidt, another Volga German. Helga's reaction to the NKVD contact was identical to Hans', she felt terror and vulnerability. Helga had a similar profile as a communist activist and strong supporter of the USSR and she had gift for languages.; The NKVD gave Helga the same 'pitch' as they had given Hans, she was chosen as one who could serve the Party in a special way.

They were transported to the illegals training facility about 50 miles southeast of Moscow, "the American Village". "The American Village" was a replica of a typical small midwestern American town sited far back in a birch forest enclosed within a high electrified-fence, barbed wire, and guard towers. A permanent instructor-cadre resided in the high-security training facility. The cadre all spoke fluent American-English, had lived in the United States for varying periods

The first time Hans and Helga met one another was at the NKVD briefing which set out their clandestine missions. To their dismay, they discovered they would deploy together to the US as a husband and wife team. Their mission was to find employment in the US government, initially as foreign language linguists; and work their way into jobs which would give them access to the sensitive information the NKVD wanted.

They would pose as Jews fleeing Nazi Germany. David and Dora Hochstadt, completed their ''American Village' training in nine months and were secreted out of the USSR to travel through the Balkans to Lisbon for their final travel leg to the US. Lisbon was a hotbed of intrigue with every significant intelligence service in the world plying the back-streets and bars in a myriad of nefarious activities and dangerous schemes.

David and Dora Hochstadt entered the US at Ellis Island and were granted a 'special refugee' status. Following the NKVD plan, once they were admitted to the US as refugees, they would change identities once more – now, coming forth with a legend as James and Nancy Smith, long-term US citizens with validating false documents, birth certificates, social security cards, driver licenses, all the 'normal' documentation every

James and Nancy Smith, traveled to Washington DC to find work in a city that existed for the US Government bureaucracy. The State Department was in desperate need of personnel who were fluent in foreign languages. James would become a Russian and German translator for the State Department. Nancy had the good fortune to obtain work in the State Department as a Russian and German linguist. James and Nancy, formally of 'The American Village" in the USSR, could commute together to the US State Department for their NKVD/KGB day jobs.

James and Nancy, the Illegals are Activated for a Specific New Mission

After another day at the State Department working for the KGB, after twenty-years of collecting relatively innocuous materials from State Department personnel files and transferring the data to their KGB handler using a combination of dead drops, the US Post Office, and personal meetings, James and Nancy Smith have a new mission.

The KGB intended to use the low-level State Department-mole, James, to spot a recruitment-target for a high-level penetration of the US State Department. Once that target was identified by James, the optimal method to approach and recruit the target would be clear and dictate the way the remainder of Operation Red would unfold. This spotting process was to be the payoff for the years James had patiently waited and diligently worked to be assigned a human resources job where he had access to State Department personnel records.

The KGB was paranoid about the internal and external security of the KGB spy operations. Department S severely restricted any information within the KGB about Department S 'illegals' and, in particular, the identities of persons trained as illegals. Even the powerful First Chief Directorate had to have authorization from the Chairman of the KGB, or his First Deputy Chairmen, to access Department S operational information.

Captain Alexandre Petrov was well prepared when he contacted the Chief of Department S to discuss his HUMINT target requirement. He presented a compelling case for Department S to provide clandestine support from an established illegal in the USA. Petrov had his authorization from the Chairman of the KGB, as required by the security protocol for Department S. Petrov had two additional sources of leverage: KGB Chairman Semichastny called KGB General Sychov, Chief of Department S, instructing him to give Captain Petrov all requested support for Operation Red. Captain Petrov's father, KGB General Oleg Petrov was the head of the Second Chief Directorate counter-intelligence and domestic security, as well as being a long-time friend of General Sychov. Petrov's father made a personal call to General Sychov to suggest energetic Department S support of Operation Red was a good career move in the KGB internal-political jungle.

James was an ideal State Department employee; efficient, hard-working, always on time, and willing to 'help-out' on other tasks. Promoted in HR several times, by 1950, James was in a position to review virtually all State Department employee records and employment applications. This was the HR appointment his Soviet masters intended decades before for him from the inception of this 'illegal' operation.

One of the new-generation KGB officers, 35-years old, casually dressed as a typical American, visited James and Nancy at their home on a weekend. After using the decades old bona fides and code-phrase to identify himself as their KGB contact, he gave James a new mission to 'spot' State Department personnel as targets for a specific recruitment. The candidate target had to meet criteria: the target must be in-line for posting to a sensitive job in the State Department, preferably the INR; the candidate must have certain vulnerabilities as typified in the acronym MICE (money, ideology, coercion, ego). The KGB officer gave James new instructions how to contact him once James identified suitable recruitment candidates. The KGB contact emphasized the need to find the candidates quickly, all the while, observing the need for absolute secrecy.

The KGB officer studied James and Nancy carefully, one of the problems with illegals was a tendency to "lose the faith" once they have lived in the target country for an extended period. The most successful illegals remained fervent disciples of communism. Many illegals posted to western countries, particularly the United States, succumbed to the allure of the materialistic benefits and hedonistic pleasures in the host countries which were unavailable in the Soviet Union, except to the senior Communist Party officials, KGB officers, and senior military officers.

If the temptations of the West corrupted an illegal, the individual became ambivalent and tried to avoid the risks inherent in doing their spy missions. The KGB officer thought, those unreliable 'illegals' should have been detected during the vetting and training in the Soviet Union and sent to the Gulag for reeducation. The KGB contact did not detect any of the corrupting negative traits in James and Nancy. Their 'commitment to Communism' was still evident as James and Nancy remained steadfast and eager to accomplish their mission for the CPSU and the Soviet Union.

Armed with his new KGB mission, a new code phrase, and a method to contact his KGB handler, James began to think, how do I do this mission without getting caught? James mulled over different methods to identify the candidate targets for recruitment as a Soviet spy. The 'criteria' provided by the KGB were useful but did not help with the mechanics of the search process. The number of potential candidate targets would be very large. It would not be possible to review all those records 'quickly' to find a singular candidate or multiple viable candidates. Furthermore, if James began reviewing records in large numbers, he would draw attention from his co-workers, and possibly even from State Department internal security. The MICE filter was useful but not sufficient.

An epiphany hit James, Human Resources was a relatively boring job and generally looked down-on by 'the elite' in the State Department. As a result, the rumor mill in the State Department Human Resources department was always in overdrive as a diversion from their daily boring jobs, a diversion giving the HR worker an opportunity to mock the 'State Department elites'. That HR rumor-mill would be one part of his method to find the candidate recruitment targets. He also had to find an excuse to review personnel files that might be outside his normal purview. On Monday, he would explore exploiting the rumor idea to defeat State Department security obstacles and dangers.

As usual, when the Human Resources department work began each Monday, the official work starts slowly as people chatted and exchanged gossip in their little cliques, what happened over the weekend, each gossip-monger trying to be more lurid in his revelations than the previous person's garish scandal mongering. James circulated around the office to hear several discussions, keeping a low-profile in the process. That Monday morning provided a goldmine of salacious information about many senior State Department employees: which employees were having sexual affairs, who had serious problems with bosses and colleagues, who was drinking too much, and the petty slurs by the smirking behind-the-back gossip mongers and back-stabbers.

James suppressed a smile after making the rounds of several groups. Three names were consistently mentioned among the many rumors; these three would be the first State Department employees he would investigate. One name in particular jumped out to the become the focus of his recruitment candidate list: Calthrop Winston Simmons. Simmons had just emerged from a personal trifecta-disaster, miraculously coming through unscathed. The rumor was, Calthrop was involved leaving-the-scene of an accident while driving drunk, and he had a mistress in the car at the time. The only reason Calthrop was not in jail and his TS/SCI clearance revoked was the forceful intervention by his very wealthy, supremely influential father-in-law who was on a first name basis with the President. His father-in-law was influential with everybody in DC who had significant political clout.

A motivated 'James the Illegal' went to his desk to clear any urgent matters and read the Calthrop Winston Simmons personnel file. After reviewing the Simmons personnel file, James found more devastating information. Information which would result in any other person being fired, his clearance pulled, and legally liable for the lying during his State Department hiring process. Calthrop had provided false information in his background investigation form about the possible use of illegal drugs. Calthrop's personnel record documented very poor performance in his State Department job as a branch chief in the Bureau of Intelligence and Research (INR). The INR was the State Department organization representing State in the US intelligence community for highly classified intelligence matters. Simmons had survived only because everyone from the Human Resources Department Head to the Secretary of State was afraid of what Calthrop's powerful father-in-law would do if any punitive disciplinary actions were instituted and would cause negative consequences to Calthrop's State Department career.

Regardless, the DWI incident, though swept under rug, allowed the State Department to take action against Calthrop. Simmons was given the choice, he could be placed on formal probation or he could volunteer for a two-year assignment in the US Embassy in Saigon. He quickly volunteered for the Saigon assignment and prepared for a move to Saigon in early 1964. James smiled as he considered his report for the KGB. Calthrop Simmons was the poster-boy for a MICE-based recruitment. Gathering further information from casual conversations with HR colleagues, James added rumor tidbits to expand the spotting report with information not documented in the State Department HR personnel file.

The target 'spotting report' was rich in detail for a future KGB case officer to recruit Calthrop as a spy. James hand-wrote the first draft of the spotting report:

"Calthrop Winslow Simmons was a child of privilege, spoiled, avaricious, and an egomaniac. An early observer might detect a potential for Winslow to be categorized as a dangerous narcissist or even a borderline sociopath. As Calthrop grew into chronological adulthood, he displayed a stilted maturation which did not match physical growth with emotional maturity. Calthrop's aspirations and expectations for life were unrealistic by any measure. He fantasized that he would be honored within the US IC as a leading intelligence analyst and sought after by all the young-women in the IC for his innate desirability. When

63

reality slammed against his delusional aspirations and the unrealistic expectations of his arrested emotional development, Simmons consistently exhibited unstable behaviors.

Even so, Simmons managed to achieve certain goals that most observers would envy. Calthrop married well, as they say. His wife, Xenia, is the daughter of Constantin Drakos, an unscrupulous and extremely wealthy man who was compulsively obsessed with gaining personal power of every type. Xenia is selfish, very spoiled, and totally self-centered. She was unattractive, her body thin to the point of anorexic, with a shrill fingernail-on-the chalk board voice. Her only qualities which would attract a suitor were her father's money and his ability to make her potential husband a guaranteed success in any Government job.

She and Calthrop could be a pair of flawed bookends for all their similarities in personality defects. Simmons jumped at the chance to have such a powerful father-in-law use his influential political weight for him in the Washington political jungle. His father-in-law could ensure Calthrop had employment advantages he did not deserve. Calthrop joined the State Department INR with dreams of fame and personal glory, but with no clue that these goals had to be earned rather than bequeathed.

Simmons was assigned to the State Department intelligence unit, INR, with a TS/SCI clearance. A TS/SCI clearance normally required several months of background investigation before the adjudication decision to grant or deny the clearance. Without fanfare, Calthrop was granted a TS/SCI clearance shortly after the application was submitted. All it took was a private call from his father-in-law to the Secretary of State to intervene in the background investigation process. Miraculously, Calthrop has his TS/SCI clearance in three weeks.

Simmons is not a brilliant man, but he possesses a reptilian-type of focused intelligence that is matched by a reptilian lack of emotion and empathy. He performed at a barely satisfactory level in his State Department intelligence career but was promoted rapidly, thanks to the shadow-influence of his father-in-law. With an early promotion to a relatively senior grade, GS-14, he should have been pleased and comfortable with his situation in life. Instead, Calthrop was resentful he was not a GS-15 and angry that some of his egregious behavior was recorded in his personal file. He grudgingly accepted the punitive posting to Vietnam in hopes he would find this new job as the key to his quest for personal glory. Calthrop called his foreign assignment, his 'stand-in-the-corner' Saigon disciplinary tour.

Simmons had a reputation as a heavy drinker and profligate womanizer. In Saigon, he is assigned as the Embassy intelligence liaison between the US Embassy, MACV, the CIA Saigon Station, and the Vietnamese military and intelligence services. Calthrop would have access to some of the most sensitive classified information in the war zone. He was the poster-child for recruitment by the KGB.

The richly documented spotting report from the HR illegal included a copy of Simmons' State Department personnel file. The HR file photo showed a man in his mid-30s with a face beginning to show the ravages of a dissolute life. He is still handsome with light brown hair parted on the left side and combed in the 1950s style. An aquiline nose complemented a strong chin and gave him a look of an aristocrat. five-feet nine inches tall at 180 pounds, Simmons relished his self-image of a ladies' man.

The spotting report would be read and reread by the few individuals cleared for Operation Red. The report contained page after page of salacious gossip and rumors of depraved behavior by Calthrop and his wife Xenia in their ceaseless affairs and revealing insights into their darkly scandalous married life, rumors which gave details of the sordid debauchery and depravity which comprised the sex life of Calthrop and Xenia, who preferred to be called Xin to rhyme with 'sin'.

James forwarded the spotting report to his handler using the standard dead drop procedure. James made the requisite signal, a chalk mark on a specified stone fence, to indicate the drop is loaded.

James' KGB handler broke into a broad smile as he read the report. This report is the stuff that creates a promotion for a KGB officer. The handler wrapped the report in a tamper-proof envelope and placed it in the Soviet Embassy diplomatic pouch for hand-delivery to the KGB First Chief Directorate, KGB General Aleksandr Sakharovsky.

The report arrived at KGB headquarters. It was exactly what Captain Petrov needed to go forward with Operation Red. The "illegal" successfully spotted a target who was an excellent candidate for recruitment, the target was deeply flawed, greedy, egotist, disaffected, angry at his lack of State Department promotions, a heavy drinker, and though married, a womanizer. The latter situation made the target vulnerable to sexual compromise and blackmail. Furthermore, the target had volunteered, under untoward circumstances, to go to the Embassy in Saigon for a minimum of two years, in an effort to boost his flagging career. When Sasha saw the spotting report, he called his boss, KGB General Aleksandr Sakharovsky. Captain Petrov was in General Sakharovsky's office ten minutes later – where they broke out the ice-cold vodka.

CHAPTER 5   LAUNCH OPERATION PEREGRINE

Major-General Wojcik stood at attention briefly before he announced – Peregrine is a Go! The eleven men responded in unison – Hoo-yah! – with loud clapping and cheering. Bull Wojcik smiled relishing the esprit de corps of these warriors. He let the enthusiastic response wind down before he began the briefing on the next actions to deploy the Operation Peregrine team to the war zone.

The General reviewed the three integrated steps to prepare for the Peregrine team deployment. First, a detailed review of the current intelligence and an initial plan how the Team and NSA would work together now and after the deployment. There was a similar procedure to be developed for CIA. Second, training to prepare the team to be totally ready physically and mentally for a difficult mission. A key objective in the training was to build unit integrity, cross-train, and deploy a team that watched each other's backs. Finally, there was a major logistics challenge. The need to maintain security meant the team would make minimal draws from military stocks, except for weapons. The other essential materials necessary to sustain an independent, self-sustaining operation in-country for the duration of the deployment had to be acquired from civilian sources. The team had to anticipate the unique needs for this clandestine mission and ship the unit materials in a way that does not draw undue attention to the team. The clandestine nature of the mission requires a secure low-visibility base for the launch from the US and a covert operating base in Vietnam. Once in-country, they would need to enlist a reliable trustworthy indigenous fighting force that will be loyal to the team as bodyguards and work off the books.

General Wojcik continued,

"This team has a powerful advantage. The President ordered a virtually unlimited supply of 'black money' be made available. Most of you know about the 'special', some would say dubious, acquisition skills of our legendary 'logistics procurer' and 'dog-robber', Master Sergeant Wilbur James."

Bull quickly quieted friendly military-tribal derisive remarks directed at Sergeant James. He looked at James and said in a commanding voice,

"Wilbur, you will keep the receipts for the records" – instantly generating more improper comments and laughter – as the General intended, building team cohesion:

"The formal training will begin on Monday. The team will send Captain Robert Williams, LT Gary Baumgartner, Captain Reginald Denning, Gunnery Sergeant Jacob Risner, Warrant Officer Carl Renner, and Master Sergeant George Washington Jones to NSA for three weeks training and planning. A CIA training session is scheduled after the NSA-stint. The CIA training includes the commissioned officers and Warrant Officer Renner case officer and counterintelligence training at 'The Farm', a classified CIA training facility located on the Camp Peary military reservation in Virginia. Those going to the Farm will be using cover names, false backgrounds, to avoid disclosing any personal information and absolutely nothing about the mission, including the mission operational location."

"The rest of the Team will prepare the logistics deployment plan. Master Sergeant James has overall responsibility for the logistics preparation. I will approve the logistics plan before any 'black money' is spent."

"Once the training at The Farm is completed, the full Team will deploy to Eglin Air Force Base in the Florida for training in all aspects of what we anticipate in Vietnam. We need to have the team "ready" for the field operations in Vietnam in six to nine months."

Monday morning, preparing to depart DC, the Peregrine NSA training-group tried to get in a Hertz rental car. There simply was not room to fit the six rather-large men into the four-door sedan. Captain Williams returned to the Hertz counter to explain, "we just do not fit into that car." The Hertz lady said they had this new van which should work - and the six were off in the van to NSA for coordination and training. Driving to Fort Meade in the Monday morning commute was start and stop in the rush hour traffic. Gunnery Sergeant Jacob Risner piped-up with "I would rather be in a fire-fight than this commute shit". Warrant Officer Carl Renner laughed about the 'tiny car'– what a piece of crap – trying to put 1400 hundred pounds of – how would you describe us – into a 600-pound capacity car. Master Sergeant George Washington Jones retorted – I think that actually goes as – 1400 pounds of shit into a 600-pound bag. Laughter all around, and then, back to the irritation of the DC traffic. Captain Williams was pleased by the banal banter as it was one of the steps for these individuals measuring one another and bonding. They all knew about one another, each team member was picked as an elite special operations operator, but once in the combat zone, reputations mean nothing – what you do is all that matters. Each man wanted to know if the man beside him has his back and each one wants to know - are these men as fully committed to The Mission as I am?

They saw the exit for NSA and begin to search for visitor parking, which they found immediately but finding a parking spot in visitor parking was not so immediate. Lieutenant Baumgartner observed,

"We have gone from start and stop, to driving in circles in a government parking lot – DC sucks".

When the visitor paperwork was completed and visitor badges in-hand, they asked for directions to the meeting room. The security guard told them summarily, in a pedantic voice, "no visitors are allowed in NSA unescorted." A call to Dr. Slade's office resulted in a security-minder arriving who herded them to the conference room. Looking around the conference room, they felt at home, it was just like a thousand other government conference rooms – decorated in 'drab and dreary'.

They took places at the conference table and waited in-silence, which did not last very long. Annie Hoffman entered the room, she was dressed in a white blouse, a plaid pleated skirt, white knee-high socks, the popular brown penny-loafers, and her shoulder length blond hair completed a vison of a dream-girl. She carried a pile of TS/SCI briefing slides. Annie immediately had their attention; an inappropriate, stage left, sotto voice comment by Gunnery Sergeant Jacob Risner broke the silence,

"Wow, we got Marylin Monroe for a teacher. Ain't she that one the President has in the White House to massage his back and whatever?"

Annie walked unperturbed to the front of the room. Turning to face the smiling team members, actually leering team members, she placed her briefing slides on the table announcing,

"I am Annie Hoffman. I have never been to Hollywood or the White House. I am from Indiana. I am an NSA analyst who will be working with all of you on Operation Peregrine. As a security protocol reminder, you are not to leave this room without a security officer accompanying you."

None of the team members ceased smiling but they all sat up straighter in their chairs.

Annie passed out an agenda and they began their training at the No-Such-Agency headquarters. As soon as Annie started her briefing the smiles were replaced with a professional attention for every word she spoke and every word on the slides. She covered the background of her investigation and how she approached the 'why' behind the soldier's dying words – "they knew we were coming"

"Something happened in March 1962 which was the enemy trigger-pull initiating a series of compromises of US and ARVN operational security. These compromises led directly to the deaths of American advisors. The patterns we identified are not circumstantial but show carefully planned and well executed enemy ambush operations based on deception and information from a mole inside the South Vietnamese government. There is a pattern of VC communications which correlates specifically with the ambushes. The singular note in all this is that every one of these ambushes beginning in 1962 to the present involved an ARVN unit with US Army advisors. Up to the Ap Bac ambush, the attacks targeted relatively small ARVN units and did not provide obvious indicators or warning that there was a wide-spread integrated action ongoing by the VC. All the evidence shows the ambushing of ARVN units with American advisors is centralized as a VC/NVA strategy to kill Americans."

The team members asked questions about the reliability of the data. Their main concern was the possibility that the assumed assassination threat was actually just circumstantial unrelated events.

Annie responded confidently,

"On the surface the intelligence could appear circumstantial, but there is a timeline continuity and coherence of a carefully planned and well executed strategy to ambush US Army advisors".

Dr Slade sat in the back of the room listening to Annie's briefing. When she was done, he introduced himself, saying, modestly, he would be in support of Annie for the project, the reality being, he was her new boss. Then he asked,

"Any further questions? Annie was the analyst who discovered the ongoing assassination threat to the US advisors".

There were no additional questions. Dr. Slade discussed the agenda for the next day, he told the team that he would be bringing in technical folks, you know, the people you guys probably call 'geeks', which generated brief laughter from this bunch of 'shooters'. The 'geeks' would go over what type signals they are looking for and the information resident in the collection results so far; signal power, frequencies, the strength and weakness of direction finding, encryption issues, and other technical parameters as they relate to Operation Peregrine.

Realizing the team would only be at NSA for a brief period, Baumgartner knew he needed to make a move now before one of the other banditos on the team beat him to it. Annie was smart, beautiful, and had an engaging personality. Baumgartner's brain shifted from the analytic conclusions, technical aspects of signals and communication intercepts and to – how do I impress Annie? Dipping into his glib opening-lines bag-of-tricks – Gary walked over to Annie who was packing the classified slides into her briefcase. As he gave her a come-hither smile, Baumgartner said,

"We are travelers in a strange land. Can you suggest a good place to eat this evening?"

Annie broke into a smile and brief laughter, responding,

"That is the worst, the most inept, pick-up line I have ever heard."

Gary appreciated her sense of humor and had to agree with her – "yes, it was bumbling".

Annie thought, here is one of those sailor 'girl in every port' guys. The type to steer clear of. She coolly commented,

"You boys look like the type who eat raw steaks and drink beer. There is a fine place for steaks and beer near your motel". The place is not much on ambiance or decorum but cooks serve the best food in this area. It is family owned and very popular locally."

She provided directions to the "All Good" restaurant.

Gary shook his head and remembered, the 'if at first you don't succeed' thing – he took a simple starboard-tack – he was a sailor –

"Would you join the team for dinner this evening?"

Annie looked at him, responding after a contemplative pause,

"I will meet you there at 1800"

Annie arrived exactly at 1800 hours. When she entered the All Good restaurant she saw three tables pulled together to accommodate 12 diners. The rest of the team had traveled to the restaurant from DC to meet Annie. The restaurant was busy, as it always was. Annie wondered, how did they get three tables on short notice? When she entered eleven large-muscular men stood to attention, all smiles and waited for her to approach the empty chair. Every eye in the restaurant was turned to watch LT Baumgartner politely pull her chair back and she was seated.

Intentionally, Baumgartner did not sit beside her but took his place across from her. As soon as Annie sat down the rest of the team took their seats and Annie was inundated with welcomes. The conversations were light-hearted and pleasant. She asked the team where each man was from. Going around the table, each man told her his hometown, rank, and service. Most were from small towns, farms, and ranches. Two were bona fide city boys. She was surprised to hear that Baumgartner was from a small town in Indiana not far from her family farm.

As the excellent food was devoured by the team, Annie continued to ask bland questions about the team members. She noticed they seemed to address each other by last names. Annie asked why the use of last names so frequently, the surfer, Sergeant Wilson answered,

"It is because our first names are so similar".

When Annie looked quizzically at Wilson, he clarified,

"All our first names are Sergeant, except for the officers".

Sergeant Podowski saw that as a moment to add,

"By the way the Marylyn Monroe comment was out of line this morning, you have to understand Sergeant Risner is a jerk". (which evoked laughter from all, including Risner.

Podowski could not let it alone adding,

"You are better looking than Marylyn," (causing Annie's face to redden).

All the team members were on their best behavior, even cleaning up their usual crude-language, although that took a great effort for some of the team. It was obvious that the team had developed an instant respect for Annie, starting with her earlier in the day pleasant put-down of the Risner 'Marylyn Monroe comment', impressed by her knowledge about the operation, and finally her downright ability to be comfortable with this gang of 'hard cases'. Some of the team were already in the protective-mode, seeing Annie as a younger-sister.

She thoroughly enjoyed the 'evening with the boys'. These men were not what she expected, based on the rumors that Special Operations snake-eaters were a rough bunch. In fact, they were intelligent, convivial, and friendly, even sophisticated, but still a rough bunch. Smiling, she bid them,

"Good night, see you all tomorrow for 'geek' time".

The team weighed on her mind as she sat in her living room, hoping they had a positive impression of her that matched the positive impression she had formed about them. There was one thing that did correlate with the rumors, as the team projected an amiable attitude toward Annie and a very professional approach to the work, there was an intangible aura about them that played similar to background music that is always there but does not dominate the ambiance of the moment. This 'intangible' had several dimensions: they had a constant sense of their surroundings, accompanied by a readiness to respond to danger, plus an unavoidable undertone that they were dangerous men, True Believers, who would remorselessly do anything necessary for the mission and for their Country. Annie thought as she processed this 'dangerous men aura'. She smiled about the only sailor on the team, Baumgartner from Indiana, despite her resolution to stay away from him, she had to be careful as he was a fellow Hoosier, she might like him.

The next morning found a van full of six disgruntled special operators, stranded in a traffic jam on route I-95 from Laurel, Maryland to Fort Meade. Were all the thousands of NSA employees using this same route at the same time? Captain Williams remarked,

"Last evening was a good meal and Annie 'is good people' ",

This evoked a 'HOOYAH' from all. Risner changed the subject to his interest in one of the waitresses in the "All Good" restaurant last night. Williams was relieved that the traffic was now moving so they did not have to listen how Risner's hormones were stirred last evening as he ogled the waitress. Same-o, same-o, so it seemed.

73

Again, the visitor lot offered no empty parking-slots until completing several circuits of the visitor lot. Who were all these people? Captain Williams decided to ask Dr. Slade if the team could have a parking spot assigned for the duration of the training, maybe they could use Major-General Wojcik's name.

The first bright spot of the day was Annie's arrival, no clever comments from the team this time, just a sincere good morning. Annie did give Lieutenant Baumgartner a lingering gaze which was not lost on the rest of the men, men who survive by having an acute sense of situation awareness. She thought afterwards, why did I look at him like that?

The NSA geeks arrived, all the players joined enthusiastically into the discussion topics for the day: collection planning to build a data base which would show eventually who and where the bad guys were. The NSA geeks were phenomenal in their technical knowledge and ability to put that communications signals collection information into a practical real-world perspective for an operational team of shooters. The day was intense as the team and the geeks collaborated to construct a working plan: signals, frequencies, modulations, signal strengths, signal direction-finding, encryption, patterns, direction finding collection techniques to identify patterns that would compromise the bad guys. By the end of the day, all the participants were ready for a break.

Beyond the technical discussions, three important matters came to the team's attention. First, among national priorities used to allocate NSA resources, Peregrine was in the top ten, this was a biggie. Second, NSA was going to dispatch two direction finding collection teams to Vietnam, their sole mission would be to support Peregrine from classified collection sites in the Saigon area. Third, the team would not communicate with the NSA in-country folks. All communication must be routed through Annie.

As the classified materials were being turned-in for safe storage, LT Baumgartner moved to speak to Annie, trying to do so unobserved – yeah right! The team watched them with smirks but no comments. Annie's attitude toward the dashing sailor was changing. Now she actually wanted him to ask her out. Annie thought back to her original resolution to steer clear of this muscular young sailor. At this moment she felt a stirring in her heart that had no parallel objective explanation in her mind. It was not the romance novel 'love at first sight', it was more a compulsive feeling that she wanted to get to know this sailor form Indiana in a very personal way. Mildly conflicted, she realized she might be falling for him.

As Gary walked toward her, she greeted him with a smile and asked coyly,

"What can I do for you Lieutenant?"

This possible double-entendre was not lost on Gary, but he avoided saying what just went through his mind as a response to her question, instead, he took the safe approach. Following the sailor's creed, 'a girl in every port', he wanted Annie to be his 'girl in the NSA port'. As he thought about Annie, he sensed she was a person of impeccable character and clearly had an exceptional intellect. These are lasting qualities that transcend physical attributes. Gary was falling for Annie and thinking, maybe this is not another 'girl in a port'. He smiled and asked,

"Have you ever visited the US Naval Academy in Annapolis?"

"No, I haven't."

"Would you like to have a native-guided tour of Annapolis and the Academy this weekend? And as an added attraction, there are some great seafood restaurants there?"

Smiling inwardly, her heart warmed, she responded,

"That is rather bold, LT Baumgartner. Are you asking me out on a date?"

"Yes, yes I am!"

"Lieutenant Baumgartner, my mother told me to never date sailors."

"Your mother is a very wise woman. I never date sailors myself."

"I need to think about going on a date with a sailor – (delay of about five seconds) – what time Saturday?"

"1100, does that work for you? We can have a light lunch at an interesting sandwich place out on West Street, do the Academy and Annapolis thing in the afternoon, and go to this great seafood place located on the Annapolis harbor. Sound like a plan?"

"Sounds good, let me give you my address."

"I already have it. I am a special operations guy! By the way, wear comfortable walking shoes with low heels. You will be my drag for the day."

A dark look passed briefly across her face as Annie responded in a restrained tone,

"I am not so sure about this "drag" thing."

"The drag thing is a 'good thing'. I will explain more Saturday. I have to catch-up with the team now."

Annie just shook her head, thinking, why do I like him?

The Friday meeting with the geeks was a seamless continuation of the previous day, but with more specifics on the operational planning. Annie and Gary both seemed to be more reticent in their interaction that Friday, under the false impression the rest of the team had not picked up on 'there is something afoot' with our Annie and the sailor guy. After a productive day, the geeks, the operators, and Annie packed-up for the weekend. Monday would be for further planning of the sensitive and complex operation involving Peregrine and NSA.

By now, the team was focusing on Baumgartner as their immediate collection "target." The team took notice that Annie and 'the sailor' just nodded at each other as the team departed the conference room, breaking the pattern of exchanging comments each previous evening at the close of the workday. A definite "tell" and bad tradecraft by the Navy guy. During the ride back to their motel, Captain Williams engaged in a deliberate provocation, inviting Gary to a 'serious team imbibing' event Saturday night. The team would walk to a bar near the motel, walk for protection against over-enthusiasm, resulting in excessive-intake of adult beverages. Baumgartner gave a lame non-excuse why he could not participant in that rowdy behavior,

"Can't make it tomorrow night. Already have a plan, thanks anyway"

His response was greeted by smirks and guffaws from the rest of the team. They had him.

Exactly at 1100, Gary knocked on Annie's apartment door, Annie immediately opened the door with a brusque,

"I just knew you would be on time, exactly on time".

She smiled and raised her foot, pointing at her low-heel soft leather shoe.

"Will that work when you - drag me?"

Baumgartner, sailor clever, knelt down to hold her ankle while he 'inspected her shoe'. She just shook her head, thinking, how often she shook her head when dealing with this US Navy Lieutenant. After a long pause for the 'shoe inspection', Baumgartner pronounced,

"The shoe is satisfactory for the outing today".

Annie grabbed her coat. as they walked to the car, she reminded him,

"You promised to tell me about this 'drag' thing."

"Well, the term 'drag' is a traditional terminology at the Academy for the Mids' weekend dates. As Midshipmen were not allowed to ride in cars, they had to in effect, "drag" their dates around the rough historic cobblestone sidewalks of Annapolis, that is, to support them lest they fall on the colonial type sidewalks."

Gary added, coyly.

"You know we sailors have many Academy traditions".

Annie ignored his last comment, suppressing a smile, instead, avoiding falling into the 'tradition trap', she added,

"That is a relief, your "drag" comment implied I bored you,"

The day together was like a romantic movie. The sandwich shop on West Street was quaint and the food great. She clearly understood why Gary recommended she wear comfortable walking shoes as she endured walking the historic cobbled sidewalks of Annapolis. First, to the US Naval Academy, walking through Gate #3, Baumgartner showed his officer ID and was given a smart salute by the Marine guard. They both enjoyed the tour; by the native-tour-guide, as Gary nostalgically remembered his days at the Academy and how he was enjoying his time with Annie. She appreciated the historic significance and beauty of the various military. Plus, she enjoyed the time, her time with 'her sailor'.

They walked to the Naval Academy Chapel where the term 'beautiful' absolutely fit. The solemn cathedral, the stained-glass windows, large wooden pews, the classical dome and magnificent limestone structure combined to echo a reverence for God and service to our Country. The obligatory stop at John Paul Jones crypt under the Chapel produced some humorous antidotes from Gary's Plebe Year. Most of the antidotes would not be included in Academy brochures. They walked along Chapel Walk and turned east to view the home of the Brigade of Midshipmen, Bancroft Hall, a massive multi-wing edifice housing 3600 Midshipmen.

Going through the huge time-aged metal doors, they entered the Bancroft Hall rotunda area and proceeded up the wide granite stairs to Memorial Hall – the silence in Memorial Hall set a mood for solemn reflection and introspection – the great naval battles remembered and the great personal sacrifices that produced those naval victories for the US Navy and recorded in murals and pictures on the walls of this hallowed room. Memorial Hall was a place to give respect and thanks to those who so faithfully served the nation.

After a brief view of the roof of the mammoth mess hall from the Memorial Hall balcony, a mess hall which served 3600 Midshipmen three meals a day at tables seating 12 Midshipmen per table. Annie and Gary continued with a walk around the perimeter of Bancroft Hall, another reason for comfortable shoes as the perimeter was indeed long. Gary pointed out his room where he lived during his First Class year (senior year) – fourth deck, the top 'deck' in Wing 3. There were six wings to house the six battalions of the Brigade. He showed her the seawall with the long running track paralleling the huge rocks forming the seawall. Gary explained,

"Midshipmen who broke Academy regulations had to get up before reveille to run punishment laps, quickly noting, with a very innocent smile, I never broke any" – before he could complete his prevarication - Annie playfully punched him in the arm to verify her disbelief in his incredulous claim of innocence.

Leaving Academy grounds through Gate #1, the two began their walking tour of historic Annapolis. The Annapolis harbor was three blocks from Gate #1. He showed her the restaurant for their evening meal and they proceeded from the harbor area up Duke of Gloucester Street to Church Circle where the Maryland Inn, a famous colonial-era inn was still operating on Church Circle as a hotel, impulsively, Baumgartner blurted out,

"Maybe we could stay there sometime"

Annie's face colored, as she thought, that would be great, but she tried a mild put-down to mask her true thought,

"That remark is what I would expect from a sailor".

They walked around Church Circle to State Circle turning onto Maryland Avenue, the street many Mids called 'robbers' row' for the small tourist shops and many casual-eating offerings. Seeing Annie was tired from their safari, Gary suggested they stop for a cup of coffee. Relieved at a chance to rest, good walking shoes notwithstanding, Annie told the former Midshipman native-guide to pick the place. Picking a favorite little sandwich shop from his back-in-the day Academy time, they contemplatively sipped their coffees. Gary broke the quiet by asking Annie if eating early would work for her, explaining that the restaurant would be crowded soon. Midshipman who wanted to impress their drags would inevitably choose this harbor-side eatery great food and a most pleasant ambiance.

"Why Lieutenant, are you trying to impress me?"

"Yes, yes I am!"

"Then, let's beat the rush, lead-on."

The Middleton Tavern lived up to billing, exquisite ambiance and great food. Gary recommended she try either the Chesapeake Bay Stuffed Rockfish or the Maryland Crab Cakes. Annie chose the crab cakes, so, Gary picked the Rockfish. Their choices complemented with a good bottle of chardonnay wine. They spoke briefly of the day but spent most of the time reminiscing and contrasting their experiences growing up in rural Indiana with what life in colonial Annapolis had to be like. The waiter brought their wine and they toasted 'to a good day in Annapolis.' Annie and Gary felt comfortable together in their light ranging conversation and sharing a taste of each other's food. Annie loved the crab cakes, but she really prized her tasty-bite of Gary's rockfish with Chesapeake Bay blue crab stuffing. It was her turn now to 'blurt out', she looked at Gary,

"I want the Rockfish next time".

Immediately realizing what she said, her cheeks took on a pink blush. Gary smiled as in, "right-on."

The drive back to Annie's place was relatively quiet as both savored the day and both wondered how they were going to deal with the classic first-date issue, what do we do now? Arriving at Annie's apartment, they looked knowingly at each other, both thinking the same thing, what they would like to do versus what was more appropriate for their first date, not wanting to possibly spoil the day with some over-the-top behavior. Each waited for the other to make a first move.

Annie saved the day:

"I would like you to come in for a drink, but I have early NSA Watch Officer duty tomorrow and I probably should get needed rest after being the drag-for-a-day today."

Gary replied, "ok, a drink sounds great, maybe next time."

They shared a goodnight kiss that lingered more than a 'casual' first-date kiss should last.

Once in her apartment, Annie leaned against the door, muttering to herself – Damn, I am falling in love with a sailor.

Gary had to discipline himself to pay attention to his driving. He kept rerunning his remembrance of 'their kiss'. This was not in-keeping with the original plan to have a friendly 'good time', this relationship could get serious and I'm on the way to war. Smiling, I think a plan to get serious with Annie is better than a plan for a one-time good time.

A week later, after dinner at a local Italian restaurant, they pulled into the parking area at Annie's apartment complex. She asked Gary if he wanted to come-in. Before he could answer, she said she wanted him to meet Porter, her roommate, adding, he is very nice. Gary said in an even voice, but with a firmly set jaw, he would like to come in. When she opened the apartment door, a male Siamese seal-point cat raced to meet her. As she picked the cat up and turned to Gary, she smiled broadly announcing, this is Porter. Gary just shook his head muttering something like, you got me.

The apartment complex catered to lower grade, lower paid civil servants. Many young NSA employees lived in the complex. Her apartment was as shipshape as his room was back at the academy, clean and neat. He thought, ready for inspection. Beyond that, the apartment was quite modest, a living room, small kitchen with attached dining area, a bedroom, and bathroom. The living room window looked out over the covered carports, one assigned to each tenant. The living room furniture was consistent with the unpretentious setting, a moderately priced couch and chair which were 'moderately' comfortable. When alone, Annie spent most of her time laying on the floor relaxing in a pile of large pillows in her living room. Annie had saved her money while at the Defense Language School for her two extravagances, an RCA Victrola radio-record player and a double bed which barely fit into the small bedroom. She and Porter listened to music laying on pillows in the living room and

80

reading books in bed. GS-7 Annie barely had enough money for rent, food, and gas until she was miraculously promoted to GS-11 and finally had a little bit of discretionary income.

Porter accepted Gary on cat-terms. Gary could pet him, and Porter would purr. But Porter was very possessive and protective of 'his Annie'. Porter had an uncanny skill to always position himself between Annie and Gary in virtually every situation. Porter's stealth and perseverance were admirable in his devotion to Annie.

The three weeks TDY flew-by as the team was finishing the NSA part of the Peregrine training. Annie and Gary spent most of each weekend together: touring the Washington monuments scene, visiting the Smithsonian, going to movies, watching TV, and playing cards. Annie rejected, out-of-hand, playing 'strip poker', muttering, "you sailors!"

The initial planning with NSA was complete, punctuated by a meeting with Dr. Slade and the combined NSA-Peregrine team (analysts, geeks, and the Peregrine shooters). Dr. Slade thanked the visitors adding,

"The top leadership in the NSA chain of command is involved in Peregrine. We will support Annie as she is the Project Manager running the project on a daily basis".

The team broke into a brief spontaneous applause and a couple shouts – way to go Annie! Slade smiled and nodded in respect to Annie and to the team. Dr. Slade told them the combined team would meet with the NSA Director, Lieutenant General Blake, tomorrow morning at 0900 in the Director's conference room. The combined team shook hands all way round and the military members prepared to depart that workday early. Annie and Baumgartner stepped aside to set a time to meet that evening.

The 0900 meeting was directly to the point, Lieutenant General Blake reiterated the President set Peregrine as one of the highest priorities for the Intelligence Community. NSA would be supporting Operation Peregrine with all needed resources. The NSA Director looked at the group, pausing to evaluate the faces of the special operations personnel, General Blake thought, "this is one tough bunch." General Blake gave each man a handshake and – "Good Hunting."

The previous weekend had been a momentous turning point in their relationship. Annie and Gary talked about what they would do the coming weekend, their last weekend at NSA for now. Annie looked at Gary with a smile he had not seen before, sort of a combination of a naughty school-girl and a temptress, the sailor was smitten by that smile, that special smile was followed by Annie innocently saying,

"What about that Maryland Inn thing in Annapolis?"

Trying to play a 'Mr. Cool', Gary responded in a businesslike tone,

"I will check on a reservation; they should not be too busy this time of year."

Annie smiled and punched her sailor in the arm before she kissed him. Gary gave a false yawn, betraying his nonchalance by running to the phone to make a Maryland Inn reservation, booking the classic King Room for Friday and Saturday nights. And, with a wicked smile, Gary said,

"I think we will just have to depart early Friday to beat the traffic".

The weekend in Annapolis was an idyllic romantic interlude for Annie and her sailor. Friday night they dined on excellent food in the Maryland Inn Treaty of Paris Restaurant, followed by a few drinks in the Maryland Inn Drummers Lot Pub, a bottle of a superb Merlot followed by relaxed sipping of Hennessy XO Cognac and toasts to the future. The conversation drifted back to Indiana and how dramatically different the lifestyle and local culture of Hoosier-land was from the Washington scene. The cognac was mellow, and by now, so were Annie and Gary, very mellow indeed. During the past weeks they had not ventured into sexual intimacy; they each had privately and independently decided to make a respectful journey to explore a mutual emotional intimacy first - and then, see where their continued journey would lead them.

They looked at each other, rather dreamy-eyed. Gary, carefully choosing his words, that, "it was probably time to go to the room". instead of 'it was time to go to bed'.

Whether it was the warmth of the cognac or just a feeling of comfort in each other's presence, or both, they laughed in unspoken acknowledgement how lame the evasive 'go to the room' line was. Gary grabbed the unfinished bottle of crazy-expensive cognac and left a good tip for their waiter. Annie took her sailor's arm and they decided to do it the colonial way, use the stairs instead of that modern elevator-thing. As they ascended in a quiet mutual rectitude, each repressed a smile on reaching the room on the third floor and they entered the well-appointed historic room. Gary set the bottle of cognac on the table. They kissed passionately and spontaneously began robustly laughing together, from there-on, it became like a slap-stick movie scene as they raced to see who could undress first and win a sprint to the bedroom. They determined to make some history of their own in that historic room.

The next morning, they woke with sweet and tender memories of their new intimacy last night. Annie looked at Gary and asked,

"How do I tell my mother that I woke up naked and there was a naked sailor beside me?"

He pondered this thoughtful interrogatory, while his sailor's eyes did the sailor-ogling thing of the beautiful naked woman beside him. After giving due thought to the gravitas of her question, Gary gave his profoundly insightful answer,

"Don't tell her".

An answer which caused both of them to burst into hysterical laughter. As solemnity slowly returned, they agreed it was time for them to take a shower before satisfying their voracious hungers.

Both were ravenous. Annie remarked,

"It must be the sea air,"

Gary started to give a different answer, but Annie shushed him to avoid titillating the people with children at a nearby table. Gary ordered the steak hollandaise with two sunny side-up eggs, whole-wheat toast dry, breakfast potatoes, orange juice and black coffee. Annie was feeling adventuresome, so she ordered 'Sea and Eggs': Poached Eggs on Chesapeake crab cakes, English muffin, hollandaise sauce, and breakfast potatoes with black coffee. Noting Gary's raised eyebrows, Annie said in her best Wizard of Oz voice,

"Look sailor, we are not in Indiana anymore".

Lingering over breakfast, they planned their day. First, they would return to the Naval Academy as they had only toured the eastern half of the campus during the last visit. Gary promised her some USNA western-half campus stories with a probability that some of the stories might be true. For lunch, they would cross the Chesapeake Bay, transiting over the Bay Bridge to enjoy lunch at one of the several good restaurants near the eastern end of the bridge. That evening, they would return to Middleton Tavern, for a return encounter.

Their second visit to Middleton Tavern was pleasant as the first enjoying the food, each other's company and anticipating the return to the Maryland Inn. They walked back up the hill, this time, following Main Street to the Maryland Inn. The conversation as they walked was one of those unremarkable exchanges that occur when neither party is ready to discuss – the serious stuff - where they go next for the future as a couple. During a brief sojourn in the hotel pub for wine, they did recognize the reality that Gary would leave on Monday for 'The Farm'. Back in the room the spontaneous exuberance of the Friday night sex play was replaced by tender shared-caring embrace, each thinking how to deal with the future. That caring extended into a gentle intimacy which added yet another dimension to their relationship.

The next morning was mechanical as they ate breakfast and then packed to depart Annapolis. The near future weighed on both as they traveled up Maryland Highway 2 in a mutual contemplative silence toward the Fort Meade area. Annie asked Gary if he would like to stop at her apartment to listen to music while sharing some wine before he went to his motel to pack for The Farm. Gary nodded his head while commenting on their mutual tastes in music, how they shared a wide eclectic interest in a range of music. That range was 'wide', including classical, the big band sound, and now, the new era of rock and roll.

Once in the apartment, Annie asked what music genre he preferred today. Gary responded,

"The classics seem right for this afternoon".

Annie retrieved a 33-rpm album titled "The Best of the Classics"; the play list began with their favorite, Rachmaninoff's Concerto in C-minor. They sat together on the couch sipping wine and listening to the vibrant strains of the concerto. The mutual reflection set a solemn tone matched by the musical genius of Rachmaninoff in this work. Finally, Gary looked at Annie and said,

"I like sipping wine with you".

Annie rolled her eyes as she expected one of Gary's intentional 'lame' lines would follow, but all that followed was unexpected:

"I like sharing wine with you because – I love you Annie"

As the concerto played on, the room held a poignant emotional pause. Annie had not expected this from Gary. She knew he had affection for her and great respect, but love! A lump rose in her throat as the import of this simple statement of his feelings impacted her. A tear ran down her face, which concerned Gary. Have I offended her? He held her chin with his left hand as he gently brushed the tear away with his right hand.

"I'm sorry, I did not mean to cause you any pain or discomfort".

"You silly sailor, I wanted so much to hear you say that. I love you, Gary, I love you very much."

As the concerto chords reached a crescendo, wine glasses were set aside as Annie and Gary kissed, savoring a prolonged embrace. Now, they had 'freedom' to talk about their future. She would remain behind at NSA while he went to training at The Farm and deployment to the Vietnam war zone. How do they envision their love within the concerns and stresses of this dangerous real-world, it was something they would work out together.

CHAPTER 6   LOGISTICS

When the Peregrine officers deployed to The Farm for case officer and counterintelligence training, the Peregrine NCO cadre deployed to Field #3 on the Eglin Air Force Base in the Florida panhandle. Eglin was the largest air base in the world, covering, 732 square miles with many different military units and several operational sites remote from the main base. The secretive Special Air Warfare Center (SAWC) had its headquarters at Hurlburt Field, Field #9 frequently used Field #3 for classified mission training. The SAWC 1st Air Commando Wing, had covertly deployed to South Vietnam in 1961 and would support Peregrine operations in Vietnam. Field #3 was an ideal location to "hide" the Peregrine team in the US. Master Sergeant Wilber James would lead the NCO team at Field #3 as they prepared all logistics matters for the team deployment to Vietnam.

The first item on the logistics prep list was to set up a cover organization to conceal the identity of the end-user, the Peregrine team. The cover organization would purchase, requisition, and otherwise acquire, a wide range of equipment and supplies from commercial sources. This layer of security was needed to ensure no leaks occurred due to curiosity from vendors regarding the unusual and diverse acquisition list. The cover organization had to have its own firewalls to hide the true purpose of its role in Operation Peregrine. The cover organization would be a legally registered company, paid taxes, had an operating headquarters location, and function in all external ways as a typical legitimate business.

The Peregrine cover organization was the "International Export and Import Company Ltd", incorporated in Panama. CIA personnel, expert in setting-up and managing cover organizations, would run the cover organization for Peregrine. SAWC was briefed that Team Peregrine would operate from Field #3 for an unspecified period. The JCS ordered SAWC to render any support requested by Peregrine. Beyond that, SAWC did not have a 'need to know' regarding the Peregrine mission.

Air Police from SAWC were dispatched to Field #3 to provide general security at the Peregrine base.

As soon as the team stored their gear, Master Sergeant James convened the NCOs to assign responsibilities and set forth individual assignments. The NCOs would provide inputs on what they would require for their respective functional needs while in Vietnam. One of the daunting issues was to ensure that Peregrine arrived in-country with all they needed for a self-sustaining secure operation. Except for requisitioning weapons, ammunition, and certain military communications gear, International Export and Import Company Ltd would order the rest from civilian commercial sources and contract for air-shipping to Saigon. Even so, the experienced CIA personnel running International Export and Import Company Ltd raised their eyebrows when they read parts of the initial requirements list:

One 1963 Wurlitzer juke box model 2700

One box of top-ten hit records for each year as follows: 1935-1948, big band 78 rpm; 1948-1955, 33 rpm big band and country; 1949-1963, country and 'rock and roll' hits, 45 rpm.

Four air shipping containers loaded respectively: one-container, top-line vodka, one-container, top-line bourbon whiskey, one-container, top-line cognac; one container top-line single-malt Scotch whiskey. (liquor often was a better trade/bribe commodity than money to extract help from the US military in Nam. On the South Vietnamese side, simply bribing in US dollars – it is always about the money)

Two pallets of Dortmunder German beer (the team members really like Dortmunder)

One pool table with 16 pool cues and two sets of pool balls

One boxing heavy bag and two boxing speed bags

45 individual 8000 BTU window air conditioners and four 5-Ton A/C units (the team would use 25 of the 8,000 BTU units to cool living quarters, offices, and conference rooms.

The remainder of the 8,000 BTU would be high-value barter items to 'acquire things' in-country from US military contacts. One 5-Ton unit would provide cooling for the ammunition and weapons bunker in the compound, the remaining units would be stocked as high-value barter items).

The rest of the 'initial list' was routine administrative materials and food items, relatively boring by comparison. International Export and Import Company Ltd would charter 707 freighter aircraft for the trips to Vietnam and back. CIA air crews would fly the chartered aircraft.

Master Sergeant James arranged for the transfer of five million dollars in cash (three million in one-hundred dollar bills; two million in used twenty dollar bills) from the Peregrine 'black money' account to the CIA Saigon Chief of Station. He would hold the money for the Team to use for bribes, agent payments, purchase of local real estate, and the other contingencies common to clandestine operations. Sergeant James requested the CIA Station search for a large walled villa, for base of operations and quarters for team personnel, plus space for secure storage of equipment, parking vehicles, and housing for an indigenous security force which will serve as bodyguards, compound security guards, and certain combat duties as required by the Peregrine team.

CIA Saigon responded in two days, a facility which fit all Peregrine needs was about to go on the market, with a fire-sale urgency. A French company had attempted to enter the tin market through exploration for tin deposits in Vietnam. Not surprisingly, the company had gone bankrupt given the chaos and disruptions due to the ongoing war. The company left three executives in-country to handle the sale of company assets, including the Saigon area property. CIA used a Vietnamese cutout to bribe the three executives to keep the property off the market for at least three weeks.

Master Sergeant James notified CIA Saigon that he and a representative of International Export and Import Company Ltd would arrive in Saigon within the next 3-5 days. International Export and Import Company Ltd would be the entity to purchase the property, if the property fits the Peregrine in-country needs. Sergeant James reached out to an old Special Forces friend, Master Sergeant Hank Svensen, currently stationed in Saigon with MACV-SOG. The Military Assistance Command Studies and Observations Group was the cover name for a covert-action unit running highly classified SOG operations into Cambodia, Laos, North Vietnam, plus special in-country missions. James said he would be in-country in a few days and wanted to talk to his old buddy when he arrived, Sergeant Svensen's reply message was, "you pay for the beer".

Master Sergeant Hank Svensen and Master Sergeant James were old friends going back to their days during the Korean War as young airborne-rangers in the Eighth Army Ranger Company. The Eighth Army Ranger Company would forge part of the special operations concepts which led to creation of the US Army Special Forces. After Korea, Svensen and James were reunited in the late 1950s serving in the 10th Special Forces Group, Bad Tölz, Germany. This long-term personal and professional relationship would resume in Saigon in five days doing 'deals' over some beers while planning how to kick enemy-ass.

Three days later, representatives of the International Export and Import Company, 'civilian' Wilber James and 'civilian' John Smith (one of the CIA International Export and Import Company Ltd cover organization 'employees') checked into the Hotel Caravelle. Having coordinated with CIA Station by classified cable, the two International Export and Import Company "reps" hit the ground running. John Smith made calls to the Vietnamese cutout to arrange a meeting the next day with the bankrupt company executives, to inspect the property. James called Svensen to set a meet in two days at their old watering hole, a bar off Le Loi Street.

As soon as James saw the property, he thought, problem solved. The tin company executives said the company was asking $450,000 for the property, an overprice of about $200,000. James counteroffered with $225,000 but with a service fee of $75,000, paid in cash, $25,000 to each of the three executives. One further condition was, the sale had to close in the next four days. Greed flashed in the executives' eyes as they requested time for a brief caucus. The executives knew the bankrupt tin company was desperate for money and would accept the International Export and Import Company $225,000 offer.

More important to the three Frenchmen, they had a singular opportunity to quietly walk away with $25,000 each as a service fee (read bribe). The brief caucus was a blatant 'tell' that the bribe offers were working. The tin company executives agreed to accept the offer (and service fees). All parties shook hands as James indicated, 'John Smith' would handle the rest of the deal, including the service fee cash payments.

After the corrupt Frenchmen and the well-paid Vietnamese cutout departed, James and Smith took photographs of the property and decided what immediate changes were needed. Smith executed a circuitous countersurveillance route to the US Embassy to meet with CIA station personnel. Smith needed to draw $300,000 in cash from the Peregrine

90

black money to close the deal 'now'. CIA Saigon sent a limited-distribution TS/SCI cable back to the Peregrine project office at Langley giving a status report on the purchase. 'Civilian' James returned to the hotel to prepare for the discussion tomorrow with his SOG Special Forces buddy.

The "Texas Bar" had not changed since the two friends' last tour; it was the standard "buy me Saigon tea" (a greatly watered-down cheap whiskey rip-off) for the Vietnamese bar girls. After getting the 'Saigon tea', the girls would 'persuade' the young GI to buy a ridiculously overpriced drink for himself. As former customers, during a past tour of duty, the smoky interior of the bar was déjà vu. Reinforcing the sense of déjà vu, one bar girl whooped when she saw them:

"Hey GI, you numbha ten, where you been?"

Vaguely remembering the bar girl with the thick red lipstick, the guys laughed as 'Li', or whatever her name was now, continued her phony tirade:

"You buy me an my friend big Saigon Tea, buy now, have old table waiting, buy me tea, then you numbha one GIs"

Rationalizing this was part of their cover, the two sergeants ponied-up a large wad of piasters to pay the exorbitant bar bill. They sat with the bar girls for about 15-minutes engaging a non-stimulating repetitive conversation of 'you buy me more Saigon tea, I be you good friend' and a Americans' banal reply, 'we are not done with our drinks yet'. It was the standard script for 'intellectual conversations' with To Do street bar girls in the 'rip-off the GI' bars. Thanking the girls for the lovely evening, the sergeants left to go upscale at the Caravelle hotel bar. Svensen was very surprised when James said they would have a drink at the Caravelle. Svensen commented,

"What the hell, did you win some high-stakes poker game? Do you know the prices of drinks at the Caravelle? Those are exorbitant prices that they charge that 'weenie' crowd who frequents that place?"

"I know the prices because I am staying there."

"This is real bullshit. Are you still in the Army?"

"Hank, I need some stuff and I am 'sort of' still in the Army".

The SOG warrior instantly understood that some type highly

91

classified mission was involved. As they drank the Caravel expensive cognac, with Svensen gasping at the price put on James' hotel bill, James went directly to what he needed:

"Hank, I need to hire some mercenaries, about 20-40 fighters, good fighters, reliable and loyal, and need them soon, but right now would be better."

"How long would you need them?"

"Not sure, maybe a year."

"Nungs are the best. The going rate per Nung fighter is around $47 per month and in some cases small allowances for families. You can't get more loyal tough fighters than the Nungs. The Yards are great, but much less sophisticated and Yards do not do well in a sustained fire-fight."

"Look, I will pay each fighter $100 per month, plus a family allowance, and provide a secure living space, depending on how many Nung fighters we get."

"Now I understand how you can afford the Caravelle. You have 'a boo-coo' bunch of black money. I may have just the ticket for you. There is a Nung clan that is in limbo and was just relocated in a temporary set-up, north of Saigon. Damned tough bunch of bastards and top notch loyal. I know the clan chief. You want to meet them tomorrow?"

"You betcha Tonto, I will need a personal weapon for the trip, as we 'civilians' do not carry."

"Pick you up at 0900 and will bring some hardware for you. Might be smart to have a few dollars with you to seal a deal if you like what you see."

Hank arrived promptly at 0900 to pick-up his friend waiting at the hotel entrance. They stopped at a SOG safe-house to get weapons for James, outfitting him with an M-16, a 45 caliber, semi-automatic, 1911 model sidearm, four frag grenades and several clips of ammo for both weapons – and a helmet. The route took them north of Saigon to a rather bleak group of tents surrounded by a few strands of barbed wire. James observed several armed Nungs around the poor-excuse for a camp. All the armed men were young. The career of a Nung mercenary was not conducive to reaching a ripe old age. The road-dust had not settled when the Nung clan chief emerged through the camp entrance to greet them.

Ban Chen, head of the Nung 'Li clan', was an impressive man about 45-years old. He had facial scars from old wounds and a wiry "don't mess with me" demeanor. Ban Chen and his men had worked with US Special Forces on several occasions conducting patrols deep in VC territory. Ban and several of his men spoke passable English. There was a great mutual respect between the Special Forces men and the Nung fighters.

The clan had operated with ARVN units and the Nungs had no respect for the Vietnamese soldiers. They witnessed the ARVN avoiding combat with the VC and the ARVN was always quick to run when things got hot. The ARVN had abandoned the Nungs more than once in fire fights, leaving the Nungs to fight their way out.

Ban Chen greeted Hank with a warm embrace and extended his hand to James. The three went to Ban's tent where he offered tea and small rice cakes. Hank opened the discussion, telling Chen that James needed some 'best-fighters', leaving the rest for a direct exchange between Ban Chen and James. Chen explained the bleak camp that was 'home' for the Li Clan, for the moment. The Li Clan had previously been holding an isolated outpost as an intelligence collector for the ARVN. The outpost was attacked by a large VC force, the ARVN failed to support the Nungs and the clan fought a desperate battle for survival. The 'Li clan' made a fighting retreat while inflicting a lot of casualties on the VC attacking force. Their reward from the ARVN was this unpleasant, unsecure, miserable camp.

James listened intently, sipping the tea occasionally. When Chen was finished, James asked questions about the number of fighters in the clan, their combat experience, and how many women and children were part of the clan. After Chen answered in detail, James was comfortable the 'Li Clan' was an excellent fit for the team mission. James proposed the 'Li Clan' 'join' his group located in a Saigon compound. When James described the terms of pay and opportunity for the families to be in safe quarters, the normally stoic Ban Chen broke into a broad smile, grasped James' hand with two hands and shook it vigorously, Chen asked, "when do we start?"

"Hank, is that Motor Pool Sergeant buddy of yours still in-country?"

"He is, but he rotates in about a month"

"Can you pull a couple of cases of good booze out of the SOG stash to set up four deuce-and-a-half's with drivers for the next two days to

93

move these folks to the new compound? I will restock your booze 2-for-1 in our first shipment 'from CONUS'. Probably two weeks from now."

"No sweat, let's get back to Saigon and get the ball rolling."

James, turned to Chen and told him,

"We start today. Begin packing. Trucks will be here tomorrow."

Chen thanked James and gave a formal bow. He turned, shouting orders in Chinese, the camp burst into activity.

Master Sergeant Wilber James met that evening with 'John Smith'. Smith laughed, relating how the French executives had signed the papers that day, greed is a wonderful motivator. After spreading a few modest bribes around, the purchase papers were recorded with the Vietnamese bureaucracy. The International Export and Import Company of Panama now owns a large commercial property in Vietnam. James briefed him on the Nungs being inbound tomorrow and the following day, about 120 total including women and children with their possessions. Smith and James decided to give the second warehouse to the Nungs as living quarters and sort the rest out later.

James asked Smith if he could stay on for about five days until James gets a small Peregrine cadre in-country. Smith answered,

"Done for the stay-behind and I will meet the Nungs tomorrow at the compound and get them settled-in."

James told Smith he gave Ban Chen, the clan chief, $1000 to bridge any Nung personal moving costs from that current shithole-camp to get to the "Adjunct Inspector General Team #4" compound - and to ensure the Nungs can buy food.

Civilian, Mr. James, used the tried and true, money talks and bribery walks, to get a first-class seat on a commercial flight out of the Saigon Tan Son Nhut airport the next day.

Master Sergeant Wilber James needed a day back at Eglin Field #3 to overcome the jetlag beating he took from the approximately 25,000 miles in-the-air, transiting many time zones, over the six-day trip to and from Vietnam. Back in the saddle, Wilber found just what he expected, all the logistics preparations were proceeding with a clockwork professionalism, the first shipment would be ready to go in three days.

The Peregrine team needed to deploy an advance team to support departure of the "Adjunct Inspector General Team #4" in two more days. James selected Master Sergeant Jones and Sergeant First Class Podowski for the advance team, the two Peregrine sergeants deployed 48 hours later.

CHAPTER 7   THE FARM AND APARTMENT 21

The Farm – Camp Peary, Virginia USA

An unmarked CIA staff car picked-up Captain Williams, Lieutenant Baumgartner, and Captain Denning at their motel near Fort Meade. Warrant Officer Renner's assignment was changed from travel to The Farm to remain at CIA Headquarters for specialized analysis training.

All three had been though the training rigors necessary to qualify as Special Forces operators and were comfortable they would easily complete the training at "The Farm". These three, along with their Peregrine comrades were the modern gladiators; tough, fearless, and committed to the Mission – woe to any and all who might stand in the way of them doing their Mission.

"The Farm" is a CIA classified training facility located on the grounds of Camp Peary, Virginia. Secretive, but not so secret. The existence of the CIA training facility was a 'rumor' widely spread in the surrounding communities. The Farm facility was part of a World War II Seabee base. The Farm, off Interstate 64, was closed to the public since 1951. Camp Peary is physically guarded and secured with fences, razor wire, sensors, roving patrols, and stationary guard towers. The CIA knew KGB agents had Camp Peary under constant surveillance, trainee personal cars were not allowed to avoid license plate copying and photography of occupants. The only way trainees could access the base was on a CIA bus, with heavily tinted windows concealing the occupants, or a CIA aircraft using the 5000 foot long airstrip deep inside the Camp Perry grounds.

The Peregrine officers would be trained as case officers to spot, recruit and control HUMINT agents, i.e., spies. In addition, they would receive training in counterintelligence (CI) and counterespionage (CE). Normally, each course would be approximately a year in length. However, the urgency of the Peregrine mission dictated that the officers would attend accelerated versions of the courses, four months in the HUMINT course and two months in the CI/CE course. When the officers arrived at CIA Headquarters main gate using a limited access road off the George Washington Parkway, two security officers greeted them and took them directly to the airstrip on CIA Headquarters grounds. The Peregrine boarded the Pilatus Porter aircraft for the flight to "The Farm".

They settled into comfortable private rooms to begin the case officer training the next morning. The harsh conditions and challenging physical aspects of all their previous training seemed to be absent from the case officer course. That previous 'shooter' training was set by the rule, train as you fight, a realism that resulted in high dropout rates, injuries, and even deaths. Now, the training was 'defeat the enemy with your intellect and deft adaptation to changing conditions'. The officers would learn that both courses at The Farm would be more stressful mentally than they anticipated. The case officer training was totally consistent with the 'train as you fight' maxim, the CIA maxim was 'train as you spy'; both approaches stressed realism as the they would face at the hands of the enemy. In-country, Peregrine operations would need clandestine human sources for information which is not available through other collection channels. The case officer course was designed to develop the skills needed to recruit and control human intelligence sources, spies.

The classroom work was put into practice in realistic field exercise with CIA personnel playing the roles of the recruitment targets. Realistic challenges, including recalcitrant human targets and active CI opposition, forced the candidate case officers to employ sophisticated tradecraft including countersurveillance techniques, surveillance methods, use of dead drops, secret writing, locks and picks for surreptitious entry to rooms and buildings, flaps and seals (covert opening of mail and packages), clandestine communication, clandestine signaling, brush passes, basic operational skills essential to protect the lives of the case officer and the spies.

The people-to-people interactions requiring the abilities 'to read' and manipulate people were an intense challenge for the case officer trainees. The recruitment process is a well-structured procedure: spotting the target, assessing the target, developing the target, delivering the "recruitment pitch", and handling the recruited spy who performs his directed missions. However, as in every endeavor, the devil resides in the details. The devil here is the wild card of 'individual human behavior'. Each potential spy presented a set of demands different from all other recruitment targets. The case officer had to design a unique approach for each target. Thus, while the process is well defined, the implementation in the field was nuanced and specialized to recruit and handle each spy as a unique individual.

The recruitment process begins with the' intelligence requirement'. What information is required to Satisfy the requirement? Spotting is the next step, identify a 'person' as the target for recruitment. The spotting process must find the one person, out of possibly thousands, who can and will provide the information needed to answer the questions addressed in the intelligence requirements. That human target must have "access" to the needed information. Next, the target must have personal vulnerabilities that can be exploited for recruitment. Typical vulnerabilities would be greed, past or current behaviors that could be a basis for blackmail or coercion, personality flaws such as extreme egotism, asocial behaviors, or leveraging the target's ideology beliefs.

Once a potential target is identified, a meeting with the case officer is set to assess the target. The meeting circumstances are always problematic. Why and how would the case officer contact the target? The reason to meet has to be natural and not raise any suspicions by the target. Once the initial contact was made, why would the target agree to the necessary second meeting with the case officer? The case officer's objective in these early meetings is to objectively evaluate the target. Does he or she actually have access to the information sought for the mission? What personal vulnerabilities does the target have?

If the target has access and shows a potential for recruitment, the case officer will 'develop' the target. The case officer, all the while maintaining his cover. The case officer works to build a rapport and personal trust with the target. (the trust is one-way, the target trusts the case officer; but the case officer never trusts the target or the recruited spy) The case officer wants the target to see the case officer as 'the one person' who can fulfill the target's personal needs, whatever these needs be: money, friendship, security, emotional fulfillment. The case officer offers the target comfort and satisfaction. Once the case officer has prepared and primed the target, the target is ready for "the pitch".

"The Pitch" is the moment of truth – the target is being asked to betray his country, take extreme risks, and allow another person to control part of his life as the spy responds to the case officer direction. The case officer typically will break cover during "The Pitch" and reveal he is an intelligence officer, thus, making the target "witting" (aware that this is an intelligence operation). Making the target witting is important for the case officer to solidify control over the target and maintain future security in the operation. After the successful pitch, the case officer begins "handling" the recruited agent (the spy). If the pitch goes awry, the case officer must 'get out of Dodge' as fast as possible using a preplanned escape and evasion plan to evade enemy security forces.

The Peregrine officers found their experience at "The Farm" over the next four months case officers training intense and well adapted to the real world of espionage, "train as you spy". They appreciated the operational differences between HUMINT and special operations. Case officers worked alone with no backup. Special operations were typically conducted by a team that succeeded by stealth, situational awareness, and team firepower. Case officers succeeded by guile, subterfuge, and their wits, or as the case officer fraternity says, 'good dancing shoes'. The case officers were always threatened by enemy and even faced problems from 'friendly' security forces. Everywhere the case officer operated, he broke the laws of that respective country, were a threat to that target country's security, and subverted the country's citizens to become traitors.

The highlight of the case officer training were the realistic field training exercises. The exercises were conducted in urban environments and rural areas. An instructor from The Farm would role-play the 'target' during a recruitment process and the 'Pitch'. The target would confront the 'case officer' with a variety of problems such as: he is late or misses the meeting; a nervous target who is reluctant to accept the ''Pitch'' to become a spy; a target who demands more money; a target who threatens to expose the case officer to security forces, along with inadvertent problems occurring by the ubiquitous Murphy's Law, such as a chance encounter with local police while involved in a suspicious activity. A daunting challenge during these training exercises was the active opposition of FBI counterintelligence surveillance teams participating in the exercise. After duly defeating the FBI teams, overcoming other problems, and persuading the 'target' to accept his dangerous role of becoming a spy for a foreign power, the Peregrine officers graduated, certified to perform as case officers in the field.

The two-month CI/CE course began immediately after the case officer school. The CI/CE training dealt with developing competencies and skills to find and negate enemy intelligence operations, catch enemy spies and enemy case officers. Essentially, how does a Peregrine 'CI officer' learn to catch a spy? In effect, the CI trainee learns how he can undo everything he just learned in the case officer training course. The foundation concept in the CI/CE course was, the evidence is always there, find it, that information would compromise the enemy operation.

The knowledge and experience from the combined training courses at The Farm would serve the Peregrine team well once they began operating in Vietnam to find, fix, and eliminate the threats to US advisors embedded in Vietnamese military units.

Though both courses were demanding, the weekends were free for study or other pursuits. Baumgartner determined he wanted to study Annie as his 'weekend other pursuit'. CIA operated a bus departing for Washington late each Friday afternoon and returning to The Farm late Sunday evening. The bus parked in a guarded secure garage in DC. There were four exits from the garage with two exits being at the end of tunnels allowing all the riders to avoid surveillance. Annie would meet Gary at one of the exits, as previously agreed. Annie was driving the sailor's ocean-blue metallic paint 1962 Corvette, which was anything but a covert vehicle. Annie blushed every time an NSA co-worker asked about the car, a car which was definitely 'not Annie'.

Annie and Gary would stay in the Washington area on the Friday nights, enjoying the fine restaurants serving the politicians of DC, along with lesser mortals. On Saturday morning they would drive to picturesque Ocean City, Maryland, to relax in a rented cottage . Ocean City was a local-tourist secret, carefully protected by the visitors from Baltimore and eastern Maryland, to keep the beach relatively uncrowded. The beach was wide with soft-brown sand that extended from the Ocean City boardwalk to the Atlantic Ocean surf. The social atmosphere was family-friendly and pleasant for all locals and visitors. Several good restaurants graced the town, completing what was an almost perfect setting where strangers greeted one another with a smile. In that setting, the locals noted that their rented-cottage neighbors, Annie and Gary, spent a lot of time in their cottage, Gary explained, with a smile, when asked, "we are trying to avoid getting sunburned" – his light-hearted explanation always resulted in raised eyebrows and smiles from the local folks.

On a rainy weekend that September, Annie and Gary went into NSA instead of the beach. There had just been a major development. Annie learned that a KGB cipher clerk defected in London. CIA and NSA were informed by MI-6 of the defection and the respective intelligence services kept the defector information limited to a few individuals in each service. The US and UK had, a "special relationship" for intelligence matters. CIA, NSA, MI-6, and GCHQ shared selected information in a way no other services on the planet shared classified data. The code-clerk defector would be debriefed at GCHQ, the British equivalent of NSA. GCHQ would give NSA access to the defector in about ten days.

NSA submitted a list of priority questions they wanted to ask the defector. To the surprise of GCHQ, one of the NSA questions was about an obsolete KGB cypher system that had not been used in years. When GCHQ informally inquired why NSA would ask about an obsolete cipher, NSA politely ignored the British inquiry. NSA did not want to share the reason that this obsolete KGB cypher was the encryption method being used in Vietnam for communications by the 'mole' betraying US advisors. If NSA could crack the obsolete code, Peregrine would take a mighty leap forward to identify the 'mole'.

NSA sent a four-man team plus an NSA Russian language translator, to GCHQ in late October to debrief the KGB code-clerk defector face-to-face. NSA prioritized the topics for the first debriefing session; the obsolete KGB cypher code was number 4 on the priority list.

When asked the question about the old KGB encryption system, the defector, very tired from the continuing intense interrogations, burst into a loud tirade. The NSA translator laughed as he explained, the defector had just delivered a very Russian vulgar response, which in a polite summary was – 'why are you asking me about this old shit?' After a brief moment for the defector to regain a semblance of control, the defector minimally expanded on the 'old KGB encryption system'.

Basically, the defector gave a truncated reply, 'the old encryption method you asked about had been discarded years ago for an improved encryption technique; what is the next topic?' The NSA analysts were clearly upset to receive no actionable information on this NSA priority issue.

Two days later, while the defector was providing high-value information on the priority 5 issue, the defector surprisingly digressed, as he said he did remember a couple things about the old cipher system. Excited, the NSA analysts listened carefully as the defector recited from memory:

"The old KGB encryption method had been declared obsolete several years ago and sent to the archive. The obsolete cipher process was used only for a brief period in selected minor KGB operations in Europe. It had two major problems: first, it was difficult to use due to a cumbersome input process to take open text into the encrypted form. However, the most serious problem was, when an error was made in the cumbersome input process, the encrypted result had a fatal glitch. The glitch resulted in an unintended pattern in the transmitted message causing a major security problem if those messages were intercepted by the enemy".

ending his input stating, that was all he knew on that subject.

The NSA team could not suppress smiles, though smiling was usually bad form during an interrogation. They now may have the path to decrypt the Peregrine related messages. These 'old cypher' messages were still being transmitted daily in Vietnam. As typical to the world of 'smoke and mirrors', valuable new information raised new questions. Why would an old, a flawed encryption method suddenly be in daily use by the NVA mole in Vietnam? The NSA team sent an urgent eyes-only message to Annie at NSA headquarters.

Happy about the information from the defector, no one stopped to think, at that point, the timing was certainly a very fortuitous 'coincidental' event for NSA and Peregrine. An immutable rule- in the intelligence business is, 'there are no coincidences.' In addition, no one picked up on the fact that the code clerk defector was considerably older than all known KGB code clerks. Furthermore, the defector had a certain polished and suave mannerism uncommon in low level code-clerks.

Gary and Annie's relationship matured during that summer. They could not communicate during the week for reasons of CIA and NSA security. Thus, each weekend was even more important for them. They became totally comfortable with each other as they shared hopes and dreams. Hopes and dreams that began to coalesce as mutual desires for them as a couple. Yet, the coming Vietnam deployment for a dangerous mission was always a dark cloud overshadowing the future.

During one rather personal talk, Annie asked Gary if the team would deploy before Christmas. It was now early November 1963 and pressure was mounting to get the Peregrine team deployed to Vietnam. Gary was not sure, given the possible impact from the ongoing defector debriefing. Annie asked, if Gary was still in the CONUS, would he go with her to Indiana to spend Christmas with her family?

Apartment 21 – Moscow, USSR

Sasha sat at the kitchen table in his luxurious KGB apartment enjoying coffee along with a buttered hard-crust roll. He was thinking about the day's training for Nyugen Kie^, his mind digressing, he analyzed how his impressions of Nyugen had evolved. He now had a more nuanced perspective of her, seeing her as very intelligent, street-smart, clever, and appeared to be coming out of the incipient depression she had been slipping into at the Swallow training facility. Thinking in English, I have discovered 'a diamond in the raw'. He laughed out-loud at the double meaning of 'in the raw' and, caught his error in the English phrase. It should be, 'diamond in the rough'. Laughing one more time, I like my 'in the raw' version better. Returning to a serious mode, he began to modify parts of the training plan for the day, a knock on the apartment door interrupted him, he asked the cook/housekeeper to answer the door.

When the cook opened the door, she saw Captain Petrov's driver and a KGB courier with a locked briefcase chained to his wrist. The driver said the courier has an urgent message for Captain Petrov. The cook invited them in and told them to wait while she announced the visitors. Petrov told her, bring the visitors to the kitchen; the cook shook her head ruefully, this young man is entirely too casual, she repeated, the courier is from Lubyanka. The uniformed courier entered the kitchen and snapped to attention and saluted, then, he realized the man at the table was lounging in a cashmere bathrobe. Looking beyond the kitchen, the courier surveyed part of a magnificent apartment. The courier had delivered messages to many senior KGB officers. None, except the top KGB generals, had apartments to match this one.

Looking at the young richly garbed man at the table, the courier asked to see Captain Petrov. Petrov countered with an order, give me the message. The courier fell back on security protocol as he stated he had to see Captain Petrov and verify Captain Petrov's identity. Sasha stood up and went to his bedroom where he retrieved two identity documents. One document was a small red hard-cover two-page, hinged booklet. This document was for public use showing his authority as a KGB officer. The second identity document was color coded with his photo and was used only in KGB facilities for access sensitive operations. Now verified that the man in the bathrobe was Captain Petrov, the courier unlocked the briefcase, passing the message to Petrov.

At that same moment, a casually dressed beautiful young Eurasian woman entered the kitchen but immediately turned back when she saw the courier, confounding the courier even more. Petrov signed for the message and quickly scanned the text. He returned the message to the courier with the signed receipt. Petrov congratulated the courier for following KGB security protocol in the delivery. He turned to his driver and ordered the car brought around for an immediate trip to Lubyanka. The courier saluted and departed, totally confused.

Arriving at the KGB Headquarters, Captain Petrov called General Sakharovsky reporting he was in Lubyanka and requested permission to visit the KGB registry to read an eyes-only message before reporting to the General. General. Sakharovsky responded,

"Report to my office immediately, I have a copy of the message in front of me".

Hurrying to the 7th floor, Sasha thought about the General, a living-legend in the KGB for his spy networks operating against the Nazi fascists during the Great Patriotic War, known in the West as World War II. General Sakharovsky's aide, a KGB Colonel, showed Captain Petrov into the General's office. The General greeted Sasha warmly and asked the Colonel to close the door and see he was not disturbed.

Sakharovsky handed Petrov a lengthy, 'eyes-only' cable for General Sakharovsky, from the Rezident, the head of the KGB effort in Washington DC. As Petrov read the cable, nodding positively at several points, General Sakharovsky opened the small refrigerator in his office, removed a bottle of ice-cold vodka, filling two Russian-size shot glasses to the brim. As soon as Petrov finished reading, the General proposed a toast to Operation Red. Downing the vodka shots, they discussed the Rezident's cable forwarding the spotting report from the Illegal in the US State Department. The report provided information which was exactly what was needed, to prepare a recruitment plan and move forward with Operation Red.

The smiles eased a bit as they deliberated on the spotting details which were "virtually perfect". When was anything 'perfect' in the world of 'smoke and mirrors? Could this be a dangle? Had the Illegal been turned and now was a double agent? What if the information was a US provocation?

Eventually accepting the information in the cable as likely accurate, Sakharovsky and Petrov began the planning the next phase of Operation Red. The next phase had three interlocking steps. KGB Moscow would conduct an internal security investigation on the Illegal in the State Department human resources office to ensure he was not a double agent.

Petrov would accelerate the training of the 'Swallow' for Operation Red. Finally, Petrov would set actions in motion for deployment of a KGB team to Vietnam to support Operation Red.

Sasha was deep in thought as the driver navigated the light Moscow traffic back to Apartment 21. He visualized the separate parts of Operation Red now converging toward the coup de maître and smiled, he was the genius actually orchestrating all parts of the operation, while the General gets the credit with the KGB Chairman.

Sasha thought about the accelerated training for Nyugen Kie^, flashing back in his mind to two weeks earlier, when he invited her to move into his bedroom, and, how pleased she seemed to be. Sasha and Kie^'s relationship had evolved from senior-officer and subordinate to one of 'mentor and lover'.

Arriving back in apartment 21, Petrov instructed the cook to make a cold lunch; put the food in the refrigerator and go home for the rest of the day. Sasha told the driver he could go home for the rest of the day. The cook and the driver were happy with the time off, but each privately speculated, what is going on: the cook who had a maternal concern for the young Captain and the driver who smirked about what the afternoon Apartment 21 'training' would be.

Once Sasha and Kie^ were alone, Sasha assumed the official role of KGB Captain Petrov, her mentor. He gave Kie^ a security warning about the extremely sensitive material he was going to share with her. He told her she would play a critical role in Operation Red. She listened carefully for any potential danger to herself in the Petrov, 'critical role', comment. Sasha set out the Operation Red mission objective: recruit a high-level mole in the US government.

Kie^ thought, well just another 'Swallow' job, her face displayed disappointment, which Sasha immediately detected as he read her facial "tell" and her body language. he said,

"This is not just a 'Swallow' assignment".

Kie^ was shocked that he seemed to read her mind, as he explained what he had learned during their interactions over the past weeks and what his conclusions meant,

"I see a great opportunity for you in the KGB, as a KGB officer, your 'Swallow' days are over."

Kie^ suppressed tears that were forming in her eyes; she could not reply as she tried to process what Captain Petrov just said. She just nodded her head and waited, was there a negative 'other shoe' waiting to drop?

Stressing the secrecy and sensitivity of Operation Red, Petrov began the operational briefing. Kie^ would be trained as a KGB operative, a case officer. On successful completion of that training, Kie^ would be promoted to KGB Junior Lieutenant and assigned to special duty under Captain Petrov for a secret compartmented task. (Sasha smiled as he thought – the swallow becomes a lioness). For Operation Red, Nyugen Kie^ would use a legend which included many truthful factual data points, as the best legends always include genuine backstop-information if possible.

Her legend would be, she was a refugee separated from her biracial parents during the chaotic ending of French colonial rule in Southeast Asia. The incipient civil war escalated into actual combat between the Northern communists and the Southern non-communists. Her legend had modified her true relationship with her ardent communist parents, to parents who were to wealthy capitalists, a French father and Vietnamese mother. In her legend, her parents were greedy and very wealthy, making excessive profits from the French Indochina War. Living in Hanoi, her father was prescient that there would be a retribution against him if the communists came to power. Her father set up a substantial trust fund in Paris for Nyugen Kie^. Her Vietnamese name Nyugen Kie^ was used in Hanoi, her true birth-name was Brigette Murrain, her father's last name and a French first-name. Kie^ would work under her Vietnamese name in Operation Red.

The legend continuity has her father sending her to a boarding school in Paris as the communist forces seized power and proclaimed the northern territory as the "Democratic Republic of Vietnam" . Her parents joined the refugee exodus to the south to escape the communist reprisals against the rich, there was an arrest warrant out for her father.

Per her legend, Nyugen Kie^ never heard from her parents again. Nyugen Kie^, now a young woman, had decided to return to South Vietnam to search for her refugee parents. She had ample funds using money from her trust fun. She would travel to South Vietnam with false papers identifying her as a French citizen. Once in Saigon she would rent an apartment to begin her search for her parents. During this process, the KGB would construct additional 'truths' for her legend and enable her to contact her recruitment target.

Petrov knew that legends without backstopped details were essentially a death warrant for agents. But backstopping alone was insufficient. Nyugen Kie^ would have "to become the boarding-school girl in her mind", not just recite something about a boarding-school girl. Details, were intrinsic to survival under cover. She had to know how to use the Paris metro, where are the movies, where does a young woman go for a drink, what are the current topics of discussion in Paris, be aware of the Algeria troubles. She had to be fully conversant with the information that make the spy's legend credible. Kie^, the spy, must internalize her legend persona, to "become the boarding school girl" not just memorize the material. Kie^ needed to internalize her legend to the point where, 'in her own mind', she believes she is that 'Paris school girl'. An accomplished spy does not see the legend as a "role" in a movie or play; the accomplished spy transforms herself into 'the person in the legend'.

Petrov went through the First Chief Directorate to have orders issued to the KGB security office to obtain Nyugen Kie^ official KGB identity documents, the Red Book and the internal security badge. A rigorous training regime was set to drill Nyugen Kie^, every day, on her legend with companion-training on how the case officers assesses and recruits a target to become a spy. She would train in the French language to rehearse and refine her legend. In a later part of the training, she would use English, as the target only spoke English. Kie^ learned English as part of her training as a swallow. Her deployment to Saigon was scheduled for early 1964.

The next action was to draft a priority message to the Paris KGB Rezident. Requesting the Rezident to have a KGB operative purchase a complete wardrobe for a young woman. All clothes must be of French manufacture and carry French labels; sizes and colors were provided in an attachment – dresses, skirts, blouses, slacks, various shoes, raincoat, undergarments, stockings, cosmetics, soaps, shampoo, and all other items a wealthy French woman in her mid-20s would use. The full complement of purchased items should be sent by diplomatic pouch to Moscow, Attention: Captain Petrov, First Chief Directorate. Shipment no later than ten days from the date of the message. Kie^ would wear her French wardrobe daily for the duration of the training to give the garments a normal-wear appearance. Thus, when she arrived in Saigon her clothes would have a normal-wear appearance and not draw attention as a wardrobe of new clothes, plus, her shoes would be comfortably broken-in.

Kie^ was shocked and surprised, the training was not what she expected, she thought the legend training would be academic in nature. The training was not 'academic' but was realistic, just as being in the field facing the enemy is not an academic exercise. The training was brutal, almost as bad as the 'Sparrow' training. The KGB instructors focused on mission success and field operative survival in a hostile environment; there was no concern about the trainee sensibilities. The rationale was, if a trainee cannot handle the harsh-training regimen in Moscow, the trainee would certainly fail given the realities and dangers of the field.

She began using a training-legend developed specifically for the Moscow portion of the case officer training. The first sessions were low-key as she and the instructor went over the legend and then went over the legend again and again. The tenor of the interaction constantly changed. A new instructor posed a series of role-play exercises beginning with the 'casual encounter'. The casual encounter role-plays were a series of scenarios every operative would likely encounter in the field. Innocent questions about life in Paris, where did you buy those shoes, what did she think about a recent event in Paris, what were all Parisians talking about, what did she study in the private school, and so on. Innocent questions that could create deadly suspicions if the answers were incorrect or poorly presented.

The nature of the questions became more complex and aggressive with each instructor.

'I have a friend that goes to your school, do you know her', how did you get to Paris from Vietnam as a child, how did you get a French passport, how long have you had your apartment in Paris, I heard you speaking Russian on the phone, why would you do that, and other probing interrogatories that must have immediate definitive credible answers.

At that point, it was clear there were terminal weaknesses in her original legend. They decided to drop the boarding school and make schooling by a private tutor among the changes to the original legend.

Each day, Kie^ had to read three French newspapers and the English language newspaper, the International Herald Tribune.

During rehearsals of the revised legend, the whole tenor of the training changed again. She was subjected to a series of hostile interrogations with simulated enemy security forces. The KGB internal-security department officers conducted this part of the training – the KGB internal security thugs were famous for their brutality.

The new case officer training-format began with Kie^ entering a hostile country and dealing with customs and immigration officials, questions about her documents, how did she get her visa, why was she there, did she have any contraband or prohibited items, did she know anyone in that country.

After that 'easy' phase, Kie^ experienced a highly realistic arrest and interrogation by KGB officers acting in the roles of enemy security forces. Although the KGB trainers did not apply the usual KGB savage physical punishments, which are routine for third-world interrogations, the trainers did have a retinue of techniques to create extreme psychological and mental stresses. Kie^ resorted to the way she survived 'Swallow' training and her field experiences as a 'Swallow'. She used an emotional and psychological defense of generating a mental state, "I am another person in this experience", that created-person became her surrogate in the horrific experiences a 'Swallow' endured. While this psychological device only mitigated the immediate agonies, it gave her a survival mechanism to deal with the stresses of the KGB interrogations about her legend. One thing was clear, she needed practical on-the-ground, day-to-day experiences in Paris before deploying to Saigon.

The legend and case officer phases of her training provided experience how to "live her legend" under stress. While the legend training was harsh, even brutal at times, it was designed to give her resilience against invasive physical and psychological methods used by enemy security forces trying to break her story. She gained an appreciation of the enemy techniques and evolved personal defenses to cope with enemy subterfuges. She came to understand that her 'legend' was her shield, she even extended that thought to the KGB motto and the KGB badge, "the Sword and Shield of the Party".

The process was harsh, the case officer trainers took a path to build her confidence and develop a new sophistication in her skills to recruit and control a spy. The training was realistic and focused the 'art of guile', living by one's wits, and being able to sense the target's weaknesses and vulnerabilities which the case officer exploits to the maximum during the recruitment process.

The CIA and KGB are congruent in their commitments to protect the identities of their spies, starting from the time the spy was identified as a potential target. The potential target's true name is immediately filed in a secure eyes-only, need-to-know repository. The potential target is assigned a number as a "spotted individual", that number could not be directly linked to the potential target. each day The case officer is the only one, outside of the Repository, who knew the target's true name.

During her case officer training, Nyugen had to refine her skills to cope with the vagaries and uncertainties of dealing directly with a target as a unique individual. She had to exert control over that individual and manipulate him. This was not just 'Sparrow' sex-work to compromise a target. This time, she was in-control of her life and, as a case officer, the driving force in the espionage operation, not just a one-time-use sex-tool in an operation.

Her case officer training instructors had no knowledge of her mission or the target. Petrov provided the instructors with a generic target profile to give the training more focus; but that profile would fit thousands of targets. The profile was an American male, heavy drinker, womanizer, married, highly egotistical, greedy, and self-centered; characteristics that tracked well with the MICE vulnerabilities for recruitment: money, ideology, coercion, ego. As her case officer training progressed, Kie^ was enjoying every moment, she was excited to get up each morning, kiss Sasha and travel to the training site. Her trainers recorded her performance in their training journal comments –' The officer is a natural, great instincts' – 'the trainee has performed in a superior manner in each part of her training" – "this officer is capable to handle high-level spy operations".

On the way back to apartment 21 after a training-day which had gone particularly well, Kie^ thought about Sasha. Sasha has redeemed me and regenerated my spirit, he has healed my soul. There was an intensity in her thoughts that only a person who has been pulled back from the abyss of despair could know and feel. She smiled, she was 'empowered', she would show Sasha some 'real gratitude' tonight after the cook departs.

The KGB case officer training was based on interactive role-play; the trainee case officer would work through the basic steps essential to recruit a target. An experienced KGB case officer would play the role of the target and actively engage the trainee in a realistic set of problems. Problems that typically emerged in many forms during a recruitment. The trainee had to deal with each challenge in real-time, there were no 'time-outs' – it was - "Fix the problem or fail", and do it in "real-time", right now – just like it happens in the field in the real-world.

Kie^ went through three different role-play cycles on the streets of Moscow with various KGB officers acting as her targets. Each cycle introduced new security issues and the KGB role-play targets presented major challenges for her. This involved complicated human interactions in which Nyugen must sense and immediately design a response that exactly fit the problem. She may have to calm the target; motivate the target; reassure the target; threaten the target, in the jargon of spy handling, "work the target".

Kie^ designed and wrote three narrative recruitment 'pitches', how she would persuade each of the role-play targets to agree to be a spy. The three 'pitches' were presented to the KGB lead Training Officer for review and approval. Her narratives addressed known or perceived needs and vulnerabilities that she had discerned from interactions with the target in the assessment and development phases and described how she will manipulate the target to 'buy' "The Pitch". During the field exercises, she was under surveillance by 'internal-security hoods' from the KGB Seventh Directorate.

As Kie^'s training progressed, all the instructors were impressed how she dealt with each operational problem. She exhibited quick thinking and a native ability to improvise and adapt as each emerged. While impressed, the instructor in charge of her training suppressed his anger at her continued successes. Major Yuri Grushchkov wanted her to fail. Grushchkov did not accept that women should be officers in the KGB, especially in operational roles as case officers. He knew Kie^'s training was sanctioned by a high authority, so he had to be careful in his attempt to sabotage her receiving a certificate as "operationally qualified".

Grushchkov was responsible to review each of her training exercises conducted on the streets of Moscow. He used these reviews to insert formidable complications and impediments in each exercise. In one exercise, he had a dead drop located in a dead-end alley, a siting that was virtually impossible for Kie^ to service without detection from the KGB surveilling her during the exercise. Grushchkov also set a brush pass between Kie^ and her target to be accomplished in an open area of a park where she could be observed from several directions.

Kie^ could read men. Grushchkov was an open book to her. His facial and physical tells complemented his rude comments to her face during the training sessions showed his deep seated antipathy toward her. She was friendly with one instructor who let her read the draft training plans before they were sent to Grushchkov. When she was given the final scenarios for her field exercises, she could see the pitfalls Grushchkov had inserted in each exercise. Kie^ analyzed each if of his traps determined to find a way to defeat his attempts to destroy her future in the KGB.

The dead-end alley offered no secure approach to load the dead drop and was actually a violation of tradecraft procedures in the choice of location. She identified an alternate dead drop in a hollow log in a nearby park where she could not be seen. She would place the compromising documents in the new dead drop before proceeding to the trap Grushchkov had set. Walking into the dead-end alley she stopped appearing to be confused, she made a slight movement which the surveillants could construe as loading the dead drop. The surveillants photographed her actions and were prepared to report to Grushchkov that she had failed this part of the exercise. However, when the surveillants checked the alley dead drop, it was empty. She had out-maneuvered them. The alternate dead drop was good tradecraft, Kie^ won this round.

The open area brush pass trap presented a different threat as Kie^ still had to pass compromising material to her target. The brush pass is executed as the operative momentarily has a physical contact in a public place with the agent. During the contact lasting less than two-seconds, a note or a very small packet would be exchanged, a highly risky action for both the operative and the agent. Again, Grushchkov demonstrated bad tradecraft in forcing a brush pass that did not allow for use of a crowd to mask any contact. Kie^ knew the brush pass would be photographed and the agent in the exercise would be arrested as he exited the park and searched' for the compromising materials. Kie^ entered the park carrying a folder, as she approached the agent she stumbled and grabbed him to avoid falling but dropped the folder in the process. The agent helped her gather up the papers scattered from the folder. The whole scene appeared as a clumsy attempt to conduct a brush pass with compromising information being transferred during the inept process. Smirking surveillants photographed the obvious security breech and waited to take the 'agent' into custody at the park exit with the compromising materials on him. However, the agent was clean, he had no compromising materials of any type on his person. Kie^ had circumvented the trap by whispering a warning as they gathered the paper from the folder, instructing the agent where he would find the material in a dead drop near the park. Kie^ thwarted Grushchkov once again.

Major Yuri Grushchkov was one of the surviving KGB brutish thug relics from the Stalinist era. Low intellect, driven by primal urges and personal biases, these thug types thrived in the dystopian culture of the KGB. He was furious that this woman had outwitted him so far in his efforts to damage her KGB career. As he read the official inputs from her instructors who documented her superior performance throughout the case officer training, Grushchkov realized he had few options left to make a negative impact in Kie^'s training report. Calling a meeting of her instructors, Grushchkov complemented them on the reports they submitted. He announced that Kie^ had one more exercise to complete as directed by higher authority. They would give her the "wooden box" interrogation test.

Captain Alexi Perishenko voiced his concern, tentatively,

"Comrade Major, the KGB Vice Chairman issued an order that the "wooden box" interrogation method was absolutely prohibited for use in KGB training, and could be used only in hostile interrogations".

Smirking to hide his worry about violating this high-level order, Grushchkov decided to bluff his subordinates,

"I will ignore your impertinence Captain Perishenko. Higher authority has authorized this additional exercise as a special circumstance. I will personally conduct the training exercise, scheduled for tomorrow morning".

Perishenko despised and feared Grushchkov. He knew if something went wrong during the "wooden box" session Grushchkov would try to shift the blame onto the instructors. The "wooden box" method had been prohibited for good reason. During the last two attempts to use the "wooden box" method in training, one trainee died of a heart attack and a second trainee had a mental breakdown and is still institutionalized in an insane asylum. Taking one of the instructors aside, he whispered,

"We have to cover our asses when this Grushchkov idea goes bad. I am going to prepare a secret memo that we protested the decision to use the "wooden box" technique in training. If there is no problem, I will destroy the memo. If there is a problem, I will have the memo in our files as protection. Will you sign the memo with me?"

"Yes, I will sign it and am sure Voladia will as well".

As directed the previous day, Kie^ reported to take part in a final training exercise. This was an unexpected addition to the training syllabus which was officially completed three days ago. Adding to her consternation, she was greeted by Major Grushchkov and three thuggish sergeants, none of her regular training officers were present. When she saw the mocking smile on Grushchkov's face, all her survival instincts kicked-in. He informed her they were going to a site outside the Moscow Ring Road for the exercise and directed her to a closed van. Grushchkov and one of the sergeants sat in the back of the van with Kie^.

"You have done exceptionally well during your training Lieutenant Nguyen. I suppose part of the reason is your experience as a swallow. Is Captain Petrov pleased with the results of your case officer training?"

Kie^ maintained an impassive expression as she saw the trap developing. Her orders from the First Chief Directorate were explicit, provide no information that connects her with Captain Petrov or any specific First Chief Directorate operation.

"I do not know any Captain Petrov comrade major".

"Please Lieutenant, I have been briefed on your mission. I am ordering you to provide information to help focus this last part of your training".

"Comrade major, all I was told is to report for training and I would receive additional orders after the training is complete. I cannot tell you what I do not know about a future mission or comment regarding a Captain Petrov I do not know".

Grushchkov's face turned dark red in anger, but he could not suppress a smile, "the wooded box" will make her tell the tale. The van passed the Moscow Ring Road and turned off on a dirt road into a birch forest, once out of sight of the main road, the van was stopped at a chain-link gate by three heavily armed KGB border guards. Flashing his pass, the van entered the compound pulling off onto a rough side road to a clearing in the forest. Grushchkov ordered Kie^ to get out of the van. Kie^ stepped out of the van to see a hole dug in the ground, a hole that looked like a recently dug grave. There was a coffin-like wooden box beside the grave with a lid leaning against the open box. Grushchkov and the three thugs, surrounded her,

"Now lieutenant, I am ordering you to answer my questions about Captain Petrov and your mission".

"Comrade major, I told you, I cannot tell you what I do not know about a future mission or comment regarding a Captain Petrov I do not know".

"Get in the box lieutenant".

When Kie^ did not move, two of the thugs grabbed her arms and threw her face down in the box as the third thug placed the lid on what now was her coffin.

Kie^ felt the vibration and heard the hammering as the lid was nailed shut. She struggled physically to turn onto her back and tried to control her emotions as she felt a rising panic at the thought of being buried alive. Trying to turn over in the tight confines of her tomb, she scraped her face and tore her hands on the rough interior of the box. The darkness was total and almost tangible; her exertions and resultant heavy breathing turned the air into a fetid failing source of oxygen. She tried to use her mental abilities to maintain her sanity as she pushed against the lid and silently called out to Sasha, you saved me once, please save me again. She bit her lips to avoid crying out.

Grushchkov was disconcerted when he could hear scratching sounds but no cries for help from Kie^. He leaned down to shout,

"Just agree to talk to me and you will be released immediately".

Kie^ heard his false promise for salvation. In the midst of this terror, she had resigned herself to whatever fate held for her. She thought of Sasha, quietly whispering the words,

"Sasha, I will always love you".

She felt her coffin move as if lifted, then it was suddenly dropped crashing into what she assumed was the bottom of her grave. The impact temporarily knocked her senseless, but the onslaught of panic sharply returned her wits.

"Lieutenant, I am losing my patience, this is your last chance, will you just talk to me?"

When Kie^ did not reply, a less smug Grushchkov nodded, and the thugs began to shovel dirt on top of the coffin.

When the first shovel of dirt hit the top of the "wooden box", Kie^ knew she was being buried alive. She called on every mental and emotional strength she had to hold onto her sanity.

Grushchkov's face was covered in sweat as he realized this scheme was failing which could have dire consequences for him. He ordered the thugs,

"Get the box out of the hole! Do it now!"

When the thugs pried the lid off, they found Kie^ unconscious, face and hands covered with blood. They roughly lifted her out placing her on the ground. Grushchkov was now in a state of panic. He did not care if she died, he was concerned about shifting the blame for the debacle he had created.

The fresh air brought Kie^ back to a conscious state. She summoned a reserve of physical strength to stand before she walked unsteadily to board the van. Her silence was a wrenching threat to Grushchkov. He ordered the thugs to leave everything and drive back to Lubyanka.

Grushchkov obsequiously offered Kie^ a handkerchief to wipe the blood and dirt from her hands and face. A false smile and plaintiff voice replaced the haughtiness he projected before everything went wrong for the sweating major.

"Lieutenant, I am happy to report you have passed this test with the highest grades ever recorded. Our training report will be you are fully ready for a field assignment. Congratulations".

Kie^ gave Grushchkov a look which left him rightfully fearful for his future,

"Thank you major, I have learned much during the training, particularly the final test you personally administered".

When Kie^ entered apartment 21, Sasha rushed to her side after seeing her bandaged hands, swollen lip, and the scratches on her face. After hearing the story what Grushchkov had done to her, a cold fury encompassed Petrov. He suppressed his impulse to beat Grushchkov to death. Instead, he called a friend in KGB personnel and then called General Sakharovsky's aide to request a meeting with the General in the morning.

That night, Sasha cradled Kie^ in his arms as she slept. She sought solace in his caring to help purge her mind and soul from the ordeal she had just endured.

Two days later Major Yuri Grushchkov was on a plane to the Congo to be one of the KGB advisors to Patrice Lumumba. The Congo had descended into a third world hellhole of savage violence, lawlessness, and danger at every turn. Betting odds were against Grushchkov returning from the Congo to claim his pension.

The new senior training officer reported to Captain Petrov, Junior Lieutenant Nyugen had passed her courses with high grades and demonstrated exceptional instincts for field operations. In the view of these experienced instructors, Kie^ was a "natural" and ready for deployment to the field.

CHAPTER 8   DEPLOY TO THE WAR ZONE

The 'smoke and mirrors' game evolved to worldwide scale as the secret-war protagonists engaging in the Operation Red versus Peregrine conflict moved from Washington and Moscow to include Vietnam. The killing fields in Vietnam became up-close-and-personal as the tip of the spear for the melee between the two enemies. So far, the KGB deception plan had consistently swept the chess board, winning every encounter. As the conflict moved to the deadly ground of Vietnam, the rules of the game remained the same: lies, deception, misdirection, chicanery, seduce, beguile, illusion, cheat, conceal, and kill. Two antagonists constantly seeking new techniques and methods to outwit and destroy the enemy.

The KGB had been running the deception phase of Operation Red in Vietnam since 1962, coordinated by a senior KGB officer sent to Hanoi as liaison with the North Vietnamese intelligence services. A KGB communications team was operating a radio-transmitter communications hub from a secret Russian-North Vietnamese base in the A Shau valley.

The five-man KGB A Shau radio team consisted of three radio operators, a Spetsnaz commando for security, and a KGB Warrant Officer team leader. The three radio operators would rotate back to Moscow during 1963 in a sequenced replacement process. The Warrant Officer and Spetsnaz commando would rotate home in 1964. Consistent with the long-range Operation Red objective, the replacements represent a significant change for the next phase of the KGB plan. KGB Captain Alexandr Petrov would be located in Saigon and assume command of the Vietnam Operation Red team. KGB Warrant Officer Andre Vladimirovich Klimov would serve as the Deputy Commander located in the A Shau camp. He was Spetsnaz specializing in 'wet work' (an assassin).

KGB Junior Lieutenant Nyugen Kie^, will operate as the case officer in Saigon to deliver the coup de maître, recruit the Operation Red target. Kie^ would work under Petrov as her operations officer in Saigon though that was not officially stated before her departure for Saigon.

Given the impact of the information from the KGB code clerk defector, Major-General Wojcik decided to put deployment of the full Peregrine team temporarily on-hold. The team would continue to complete the logistics acquisitions, shipping the equipment in-country to the Peregrine compound, and use the two-man advance-team in Saigon to direct activities there. The three officers at The Farm would return to NSA after completing their training.

Major-General "Bull" Wojcik scheduled immediate personal travel to Vietnam to meet with the MACV Commander, the CIA Station Chief, and the SOG commander. Bull controlled SOG from DC which was a closely-guarded secret. He would brief selected senior officers on Operation Peregrine and emphasize to each of these senior US officers,

"Peregrine was authorized by the President MACV, CIA, and SOG will render any and all support requested by the in-country Peregrine team". Awareness of the Peregrine program was extremely restricted no information about Peregrine would be given to any person not read-into the program. Major-General "Bull" Wojcik is the only person who could approve a person being read-into this TS/SCI compartmented program.

As NSA analysts reported they were on the verge of a breakthrough decrypting the old KGB cipher, a national crisis struck, President John F. Kennedy was assassinated on 22 November 1963. The assassin, Lea Harvey Oswald had a murky background which spawned a wave of conspiracy theories, including, Oswald was a KGB agent. A nationwide trauma of grief and sorrow swept across the United States, regardless, the American system of government functioned effectively during the crisis with a virtually seamless transfer of Presidential power to Vice President Lyndon Johnson. Despite national mourning, all the usual national security threats to the US continued. Soldiers died in Vietnam; the existential Soviet nuclear threat persisted; the US intelligence community continued to collect and analyze the information extracted by various nefarious methods from the many enemies of the US. All the while, at the national level, political power relationships were realigning in Washington DC. In the CI/CE world, the Peregrine Presidential Authority established by President Kennedy remained as a top national priority. NSA, CIA, and the Peregrine team intensified their work even as they mourned the loss of President John F. Kennedy.

Two weeks after President Kennedy's assassination, the NSA analysts announced they had 'cracked the KGB old cipher code' and were beginning to decrypt and analyze archived messages from Vietnam which used the obsolete KGB cipher method. One of the top priorities in the analysis process was to understand why anyone would use the problematic old KGB cypher system. While the Soviets often gave Third World clients old equipment, this system did not pass the smell test for many on the Peregrine team. Regardless, the decryption breakthrough was the strategic turning point the Peregrine team needed to construct an aggressive plan for the in-country operation to identify and neutralize the North Vietnamese mole.

The team celebrated the NSA success and waited for the deployment order. On his return from Vietnam, General Wojcik set the date for the team deployment to Vietnam as 2 January 1964. The team members began to make immediate contacts with families and friends to settle arrangements for their 1963 Christmas holidays. Annie contacted her family on their farm near Geneva, Indiana. She told her parents she would be home for Christmas and would like to bring a friend with her, asking respectfully as always, if bringing a visitor was alright with her parents. Her mother responded, of course her friend was welcome. Naturally, her mother asked who the friend was? Annie told them he was a US Navy Lieutenant, and he was from Indiana. Both her parents looked at each other smiling, Annie's mother saying,

"Your Navy friend is quite welcome for Christmas. By the way, how long have you known him?"

Annie replied,

"I have known Gary for a few months in a work-related situation. Gary's parents are deceased and the family home in Syracuse, Indiana had been sold."

Annie's father winked at his wife, Rachel, who responded with a smile.

General Wojcik told Captain Williams the two team members on the advance team in Vietnam could have ten days leave to return to the CONUS for Christmas if their current duties would allow. With a smile, Captain Williams said,

"I expect their 'current 'duties' will allow Master Sergeant Jones and Sergeant First Class Podowski to return for the Christmas holiday".

Sergeants Jones and Podowski would redeploy with the full team on 2 January 1964. It went unspoken that this could be the last Christmas with their families for some team members as the uncertainties of a war zone deployment always were in the minds of military families. The personnel at Field #3 and the International Export and Import Company accelerated the logistics preparation to have all equipment and supplies in-country by 2 January 1964.

Indiana Christmas 1963

The brief Christmas leave for Annie and Gary was scheduled to begin on 17 December. But the NSA analysts had some important new information to share. Duty takes the priority, Annie and Gary spent the first day of their leave in an NSA SCIF. They would drive the ocean-blue metallic paint job, 1962 Corvette to Indiana on 18 December. Gary mused that the Corvette was not the ideal car if there was a lot of snow for an 'Indiana White Christmas'; he mused further, "what the hell, I am a special ops guy, I can handle it."

Leaving early the next morning, the weather was friendly as was the Pennsylvania State Trooper who stopped a blue Corvette, which had been traveling at a semi-racing-speed. Gary had been going more than a little bit over the Pennsylvania Turnpike speed limit. Seeing the flashing red light in his rear window, he took his foot off the gas and immediately the 340 horsepower V-8 engine roar diminished as he pulled onto the Turnpike berm.

He looked in the driver side-view mirror to see a squared-away State Trooper approaching the now-still Corvette, a six foot tall, broad shoulders no-nonsense law enforcement officer in sharply pressed shirt and trousers with razor-edge creases was looking back at him through the mirror. Gary punched the power window-button and proceeded to open his billfold to present his license. The Trooper noticed a military ID card under the driver license as Gary removed the license. The Trooper studied the driver's license, asking a question which the Trooper already knew the answer:

"Are you military?"

"Yes sir, US Navy."

"Where are you going in such a hurry?"

"We are on the way to Indiana for Christmas."

"Been to Nam?"

"Yes sir, and I am going back to Nam next month."

"You know you were driving well over the legal speed limit."

"Yes sir."

The Trooper returned Gary's license and held out his right-hand. With a grim but friendly smile, the Trooper looked Gary in the eye,

"1st Marine Division, Korea, Chosin Reservoir (the Chosin Reservoir battle was one of the bloodiest actions during the Korean War and one of the most heroic fights recorded in the annals of the US Marine Corps). Have a Merry Christmas and keep that speed down – stay safe in Nam."

"Thank you, officer, (shaking the Trooper's hand), 'roger' on the speed and you have a Merry Christmas too."

The drive from Fort Meade to the Hoffman farm took about eight hours and it was December dusk as they pulled into the farmhouse lane. The Hoffman home was similar to most Indiana farmhouses in that area, a two-story wood frame family-farm home. Annie's mother, Rachel, had been repeatedly glancing out the front window all day, even though she knew they would not arrive much before evening. Finally, she saw a little blue car coming up the lane. She muttered to herself,

"Good Lord, what kind of car is that?"

Annie's family represented all that was good in rural Indiana. Hard working, self-sufficient farm families who loved their country, went to church on Sunday, and never complained about working 365 days each year.

Gary parked and got out to retrieve the luggage. Rachel saw a tall ruggedly handsome young man get out of the sporty blue car. As Rachel moved to open the front door, Annie sprang from the car and ran toward the house. Mother and daughter met on the front porch, tears of joy flowing from their eyes as they hugged. Gary approached the porch carrying two suitcases. Rachel reluctantly disengaged from hugging Annie, offering her hand to the clean-cut husky young man. Gary set one suitcase on the ground and shook Annie's mother's hand, roughened by years of helping with the farm work. Rachel contemplated the sailor with a bit of skepticism. Annie saw her father coming up to the house after finishing the evening chores in the barn. Annie shouted, "Hi Dad", as she raced to meet him. Annie's Dad, Fred, hugged her warmly and they walked arm-in-arm back to the house. Fred looked Gary up and down, initially approving of the muscular young man before him and they shook hands with equally powerful grips.

Annie's mother was the local beauty who married her high school sweetheart after graduation from the small local school. At 5 feet eight inches tall, 160 pounds, long blond hair, now streaked with gray, Rachel had a pleasant smile to complement her imposing figure. Farm life demanded much from the Indiana farm wife working as hard as her husband to fulfill the daily duties of farm life. Cooking, washing clothes, and cleaning were the 'light work.' The 'other work' cultivating and taking care of a large garden, the flock of chickens, canning and preserving food, plus lending a hand for some chores took a toll on farm wives. Their skin was coarsened by the sun and weather, hands were calloused, and many farm wives appeared aged beyond their years. But virtually all these women cherished their freedom on the farms and sense of achievement feeding the family plus taking pride providing food for many additional American families. Rachel's passion was reading books. Geneva was too small to host a library. Every two weeks she would travel to the library in Marion, Indiana to return a stack of borrowed books and pick-up an eclectic assortment of books (classics, histories, and contemporary novels) to fill the evenings the next two weeks, reading before bedtime.

Fred, six feet tall, 180 pounds, brown hair, could be the typical farmer found anywhere in Indiana. Square shoulders, a farmer's tan (face, neck and forearms), lean with solid muscles, large rough hands from the daily work tending livestock, ploughing, repairing farm equipment, lifting heavy bags of seeds, moving feed bags for livestock, dealing with fertilizer bags, plus challenges from the vicissitudes of the weather, all demanding a commitment of 365 days every year. Fred's idea of a vacation was going to church on Sunday and going to a movie once a month with Rachel if the chores were caught-up.

Entering the house, Rachel told Gary he would have the room on the right, at the top of the stairs. For an instant, a cold-wind seemed to pass through the entry way, not from the December weather, but from a chill of sad memories as the Hoffman family all thought this was the first time anyone had used Annie's brother's room since he was killed on Iwo Jima. Unaware of the family's emotional memories relating to the room, Gary took his suitcase up to Robert's old room. Calling down, Gary asked where to put the other suitcase. Rachel called back, as the moment of tension passed, put it in the room up the hall on the right. Asking if they were hungry, Rachel said dinner was about ready, and what a dinner it was, large servings of roast beef, mashed potatoes, gravy, lima beans, home-baked bread, a big piece of cherry pie with milk and coffee, a quintessential Indiana farm family dinner.

Gary and Fred retired to the living room while Annie and Rachel cleared the table and washed the dishes. Fred was not a naturally talkative man and Gary hated small talk. They sat in silence for a few minutes, Gary respectfully waiting for Annie's father to take the lead in whatever conversation there might be. Breaking the silent interlude, Fred asked,

"What do you do in the Navy?

"I am a SEAL."

"What the hell is a SEAL?"

"Well, SEAL stands for sea, air and land, SEALS are a type of Navy special forces."

"I have heard of the Army special forces, are you like them?"

"No sir, we are not like them. We are much tougher, better fighters and certainly more handsome."

Fred roared with laughter, this young man reminded him of his US Marine Corps son.

"Damn, lets have a beer! Sailors do drink beer, don't they?"

With that, Fred and Gary began a pleasant evening. Gary appreciated being back in the Indiana culture. Annie and Rachel joined them after doing the dishes and the female presence did tone the discussion down a bit, but it remained lively. Annie's parents were curious about her job in Washington. Annie used the NSA cover story that she worked in a State Department administrative office, a boring job that stimulated few follow-up questions. So, Annie's parents turned their attention to their visitor, Annie's mother began with:

"Who are you, Gary, and what do you do in the Navy?"

Annie's father interjected,

"He is some kind of those special forces guys."

Rachel gave Fred a disapproving look and asked Gary,

"Exactly what is a Navy 'special forces guy'?"

Gary was thinking, I wish I had used the State Department cover story too. But the upcoming deployment to Vietnam would have made that 'admin cover story' an unbelievable stretch. Gary glanced at Annie, who just smiled back, wondering how her Academy wonder-boy would get out of this. Gary mentally donned his case officer dancing shoes and took to using a tried-and-true ruse, the 'in the beginning' modus operandi path, hopefully bore the listener to tears well before reaching any heavy-duty sensitive material.

"I was born here in Indiana, Syracuse, near Lake Wawasee."

Rachel may live on a farm, but she saw a con-job when it was emerging. Annie received her superlative intellectual genes from both parents, but her mother knew which parent's genes dominated that arena. Annie settled back to watch and enjoy the, what next, how does Corvette TS/SCI boy handle this? Rachel was on the case, without saying bluntly, 'stop the bullshit and give me a straight answer', going to the point, again,

"Annie told us you were from Indiana. What I asked was, what do you do in the Navy as one of those special forces' guys as Fred so elegantly explained?", giving Fred another dirty look.

Gary understood, Rachel had broken the code and would demand to know more. He suspected Annie had indicated to her mother that Gary was more than just transportation for her return home Christmas 1963. Gary accepted the fact; her parents deserved honest answers within the limits of security.

"Navy SEALs conduct a variety of classified missions for the US military and are not always under Navy command. A Navy SEAL receives unique training in many military skills including parachuting. Because of security considerations, I cannot be specific about the classified missions, but I will say, I am proud and blessed to be a SEAL and serve with the very best men in the US military, my comrades-in-arms are the best military men in the world."

Fred nodded in satisfaction and a bit of pride. I like this guy. Rachel looked at Gary solemnly, this boy is so like my Robert, as she tried not to begin crying. Rachel lightened the conversation, making a wry look at the empty beer bottles.

"You two need to go to bed after drinking all that beer. Fred is a farmer and has to get up early."

To the Hoffman family's surprise, Gary was up before Fred, dressed in heavy duty jeans, paratrooper boots, and ready for work. Rachel was a little embarrassed their guest might feel he had to earn his keep during a Christmas visit. Fred shook his head and told Gary to get a good breakfast as there was a lot to do today. After Fred and Gary finished breakfast and went out to work, Annie asked her mother, "do you like him?" Rachel nodded her head, yes. Her mother was afraid to talk because she was about to cry, then she said, "he is so like Robert", as tears ran down her face. The days flew by as Christmas approached. Fred and Gary worked during the day and drank beer and talked in the evening; Mother and daughter enjoyed each other's company talking and preparing food, before joining the men in the evening for banter and making fun of the men drinking beer.

The plan for Christmas Eve was to attend the local Baptist church Christmas Eve service. Before supper, Gary asked Annie to walk down to the barn with him as he wanted a moment of privacy with her. The air was cold and refreshing as they strolled to the barn. Once at the barn, they stood in the twilight leaning on the rail of a cattle pen. Gary told Annie, again, that he loved her; and he had a personal Christmas gift. He opened a small blue-velvet gift box which encased a gold chain with an attached gold medallion, the gold medallion was his US Naval Academy 1961 class crest. Annie took the gift in her hands and pressed the medallion to her lips, then she kissed him, her eyes glistening. She spoke in an emotional-husky voice:

"I have something for you, but it is up at the house."

Gary helped Annie snap the chain around her neck and they walked back to the house in silence, holding mittened-enclosed hands. As soon as they entered the door, Annie raced up the stairs to return with a slightly larger gift box than the blue-velvet box, handing her gift to Gary. He opened the box there in the hall. The box held a beautiful stainless-steel Bulova Accutron Astronaut watch, a watch which Gary knew Annie could not afford. He kissed her. They hurried to supper, which Rachel was putting on the table. Annie was aware that her mother was staring at the gold necklace and the USNA crest medallion. Her dad was oblivious as he bantered with his new friend as they were telling each other Indiana stories. Gary was glad to be back home in Indiana for Christmas.

The church service was appropriate for the season, reminding the 120 worshippers that the season was about Christ's birth and how 'God the Father' loved his precious Son and had sent Jesus Christ to redeem mankind. On the drive home, Annie thought about how the pastor was the one, who unknowingly, set this 1963 Christmas visit in motion some six years earlier when he helped her get a scholarship to Indiana University.

Christmas day was a time for all to relax after finishing the obligatory chores taking care of farm animals. In a family gift exchange, Gary gave Annie a luxurious white cashmere sweater. Annie gave Gary a compact folding pocket-tool with many blades and gadgets. Gary gave Annie's parents a book about the Naval Academy including pictures of the US Naval Academy grounds and buildings. As they all turned a few pages, Annie said the pictures were as beautiful as the Academy actually is. Fred and Rachel both turned their heads with raised eyebrows before continuing to leaf through the book.

The 1963 Christmas on the Hoffman farm near Geneva, Indiana was a wonderful time, though poignant due to Gary's upcoming deployment to Vietnam. Annie was pleased her Dad and Gary hit it off from the get-go; laughing how Gary helped her Dad with the farm chores during the day and they drank cups of hot chocolate and beer during the evenings, actually mostly beer. Now, on the day after Christmas, they put the suitcases into the Corvette for an early departure. Gary had to pack his gear to catch his flight tomorrow to Eglin Air Force Base, the first leg of the Vietnam deployment.

The ride back to Maryland gave them time to talk about the visit, the latest NSA breakthrough by the analysts, and their future together. They dispensed rather quickly with the visit and NSA discussions to go to, what about us now?

Annie was wearing her Christmas sweater and the gold chain with the Naval Academy medallion. Gary told her,

"You look great in that sweater and the crest."

"They both mean a great deal to me (spoken with a catch in her voice), thank you"

"You mean a great deal to me Annie. The sweater and crest were gifts from my heart. I want to see you wearing them for a long time into the future. I want a long future for us. "

(a long pause as both thought about what to say next)

"I will worry about you in Vietnam. I will pray for you. And wait for you."

They rode in a measured silence for over an hour, each deeply absorbed in thoughts about the future and their future. When they finally spoke, the topics were the mundane of packing and the trip tomorrow to Andrews Air Force Base for his flight to Eglin. They decided it would be most efficient for Gary to take a cab to Andrews for the early morning flight. He had too much gear to fit into the Corvette and Annie needed to be at NSA early. Before arriving at Annie's apartment, they stopped for Chinese food. Once at the apartment, they continued to discuss perfunctory topics such as Gary placing Annie on his auto insurance since he would leave his Corvette for Annie to drive while he was deployed. Packed and ready for an early launch the next day, Annie and Gary retired to her bedroom; the evening before the deployment was marked with a tender intimacy between them.

Waiting for the taxi holding hands, they were both thinking, and looking to the future when they could hold hands once more. The taxi honked his horn; the driver helped Gary load his gear. Gary kissed Annie and departed for the war, as untold millions of warriors had departed homes since the ancient wars between tribes of enemy cave dwellers and all the other wars which continued from that time to this time, this continuation was the "Vietnam War".

Each team member had a memorable Christmas with family and friends. The team rendezvoused at Eglin Field #3 on 27 December 1963 to complete final preparations for the 2 January 1964 deployment. Logistic lists were checked and rechecked. Follow-on actions tasked to the logistics cover agency, the International Export and Import Company. Phone calls made by the team to family members and a lot of beer was consumed on the evenings of 27-30 December, there would be no New Year's Eve party for the team.

CHAPTER 9   WHEELS UP EGLIN AFB
DESTINATION VIETNAM

The 11-man team boarded a bus to travel from Field #3 to Eglin Main Base. As the team loaded their weapons and personal gear onto the bus, the bus driver stood amazed at the weaponry the team members carried. He could only speculate what other killing gear was concealed as he read the labels on the crates being loaded onto a truck for transport to Eglin Main: shotguns, AK-47s, a variety of handguns including the reliable 1911 model Colt .45, silenced High Standard HDM .22 semi-automatics, other hand guns (Glocks, Sig Sauer, Berretta and foreign models the driver did not recognize), a variety of grenades, sniper rifles, Stoner 63 machine guns, Thompson submachine guns, various foreign weapons, and some unmarked crates. They loaded crates of ammunition to match all the weapons. The driver remarked to one of the team,

"Looks like we will be safe if attacked on the way to Eglin Main."

A look from an imposing hulk in jungle fatigues, Sergeant First Class Podowski, made the driver decide to get on the bus and wait for the order to depart. The International Export and Import Company 707 charter-aircraft. was configured for cargo and 30 passengers. The CIA crew, with two extra pilots, welcomed the team on-board, a rough-looking bunch of grim men heavily weighed-down with weapons and personal gear. All other logistics loading was completed early, refueling was done.

Captain Williams shouted,

"Why wait, go for launch now – we need to kill some bad guys".

The team responded with a hearty HOOYAH!

Liftoff was rescheduled for 2100 hours, 1 January 1964, two refueling stops on the way, Alaska and Okinawa, touchdown some 23 hours later at Tan Son Nhut airport, Saigon, Vietnam.

The CIA crew revved the engines and requested takeoff clearance, but the control tower told the 707 to hold.

A few minutes later, Major-General Wojcik, in jungle fatigues with no name tag, looking every bit as mean as his 11-man bunch of rowdies on the plane, drove up in a van. The General boarded the aircraft, greeting each team member personally, shaking hands, laughing, slapping NCOs and officers on their backs. At the same time, the General's Aide, an Army captain, and two master sergeants were unloading the van. Two large cardboard boxes full of KFC meals, a crate of Big Mac's and Quarter-pounders, four cases of cold beer, and a case of fresh fruit. The team gave the Major-General a hearty HOOYAH and high-fives all way round. As soon as the General departed the aircraft, the tower gave clearance for an immediate take-off. The food was passed around to the flight crew and the team; all the food was consumed well before the 707 reached cruising altitude.

The team settled in for the first leg of the flight. Four members of the team sat on the deck playing poker, three members were reading, and one immediately went to sleep. The three officers went to the rear of the passenger seating area to discuss the initial actions necessary when they were boots-on-the-ground in the war zone. The officers discussed the status of the team and individual team members. The officers agreed, their team was ready – lean and mean. The officers knew in this complicated and sensitive operation, the team would be doing a lot of improvising. The plan was a start and a guide, but on-the-ground situation awareness will set the type and tone for team responses to the threats they will face.

During the flight to the first refueling stop, master scrounger Wilber James thought it would be a shame to waste the exceptional priority assigned to the flight plan. Though a civilian flight, General Wojcik had ensured the flight carried a priority accommodation for refueling at the two military bases. James walked to the cockpit to radio a message to Base Ops at Elmendorf Air Force Base, Alaska. Citing the aircraft priority, James used an officious-voice to order 25 VIP box-lunches and two cases of cold beer, preferably German beer. Have the lunches ready at the refueling position at touchdown. Our flight plan priority states, no base personnel other than the refueling team and the persons from the Officers' Club mess delivering the food are to have access to the refuel site. Repeating the priority, James closed the radio link with a brusque – "OUT", and broke the connection. Noting the flight priority and the nature of the 'request', many eyebrows were raised as the Base Ops Duty Officer called the Officers Club.

Captain Williams, seeing James exit the cockpit, wondered what 'Sergeant you-need-it-I'll-get-it' was doing in the cockpit. Captain Williams did not ask a question, he just raised his eyebrows; Master Sergeant Wilber James nodded his head,

"Just getting some food delivered while we refuel".

After touchdown at Elmendorf, the CIA pilots trailed the Base Ops "Follow Me" truck to a secluded parking spot on the ramp. Two fuel trucks, a fire truck, mobile stairs, and a van were parked waiting for them. Immediately on engine shutdown, the stairs moved into place and the fuel trucks took positions to begin the fueling. When the white-vest waiters entered the aircraft with cartons of VIP box lunches and the German beer, they were shocked to see men in unmarked jungle fatigues, some cleaning weapons, two sharpening Fairbairn-Sykes commando daggers, and the rest of this intimidating bunch ignoring them. The CIA crews switched-out and the rested crew moved into the cockpit. The Eglin to Alaska crew would eat and then sleep during the next leg of the flight plan. The engines were started as soon as the fuel trucks were clear. An immediate takeoff clearance had them airborne on the way to Okinawa for the second refueling.

Watching the aircraft depart, the two white-vested waiters smiled as they thought, wow, their story would add real grist for the base rumor mill, as they described how they had just delivered food to a bunch of Vikings in jungle fatigues. On-board the 707, after devouring excellent VIP box-lunch meals with German beer, the team settled in for sleep, experienced soldiers know when to grab shuteye.

The flight to Kadena Air Base on Okinawa was unremarkable. The refuel stop was an instant replay of the Elmendorf experience as James made his authoritarian call to Kadena base ops giving his meal delivery order. Fuel and top-of-line line food, and cold German beer were provided efficiently for the team and air crews. Another air crew rotation and back in the air – next stop Tan Son Nhut International Airport, Vietnam.

As the 707 moved to assigned Tan Son Nhut International Airport ramp parking and the passenger door is opened – it was 'deja vu all over again' for these veterans of one or more previous tours in Vietnam.

The open aircraft-door allowed a rush of the pungent smells of the Orient, a cocktail of odors overcomes the olfactory senses for a few moments. The familiar hot humid oppressive air told them the jungle was waiting and the painful urban noise-level was yet another reminder – we are back in Nam.

The team had their personal gear and weapons packed and was ready to deplane. To his irritation, Master Sergeant Wilber James did not see the trucks and unloading work-party that had been ordered to meet the flight. He saw an overweight supply sergeant, smoking with several other GIs. Master Sergeant Wilber James, wearing unmarked jungle fatigues, ordered the supply sergeant to get off his ass and get the 707 unloaded; The overweight-supply sergeant, giving James the 'who do you think you are' look, responded,

"I'll get to you when I am ready."

James removed a card from his pocket and thrust the card into the fat supply sergeant's hand with the command:

"Call that number shithead and do it now."

The supply sergeant walked slowly to a nearby shed with an outside phone. James watched the supply sergeant shift his weight from foot to foot and say 'Yes sir' into the phone several times. The supply sergeant made a second call before he walked back to James with an obsequious smile. Handing the card back to James, the now groveling supply sergeant told James,

"The trucks are on the way with a forklift, please let me know if I can help in any way, sir."

With a jeep in the lead, four deuce-and-a-half trucks, a 40-foot flatbed arrived. Each vehicle was driven by a Nung, accompanied by a heavily armed Nung riding shotgun. James knew the Nungs from his previous visit. The Nungs smiled when they saw James and hands were shaken all around. James introduced each team member to each of the Nungs as the team members took the measure of the Nungs as the Nungs took their measures of the team members – both sides thinking the same thing about each other – they look like some mean bastards.

The Nungs and Americans mounted-up for the convoy to the 'compound'. Captain Williams rode in the Jeep and the rest of the team dispersed to the trucks. Nungs and Americans readied weapons as they pulled out of Tan Son Nhut airport. One reassuring observation verified they were in the right country. As before, Saigon traffic was a nightmare with the only relief coming after the nightly curfew. Cyclos, the three-wheeled bicycle taxis, were everywhere weaving precariously through the military and civilian traffic. The Cyclo 'taxi' driver sits on a raised seat behind the passenger, peddling, smoking cigarettes and striving to avoid an accident. The passenger sits on a street-level bench-seat in the front of the three-wheel contraption, serving as a potential bumper in case of accident with the added benefit that the passenger's head was at the same level as the diesel-smoke belching exhausts of the deuce-and-a-half Army trucks on the streets of Saigon. Completing the thrills of Saigon traffic were a mix of bicycles, motor scooters, buses, gas powered-taxis, all in the midst of undisciplined pedestrians with a toxic cloud of exhaust fumes accentuated by blaring horns and no traffic rules – or traffic rules which everyone ignores. GIs believed they were safer in a fire fight than riding in a Saigon Cyclo.

As the Peregrine convey passed through the compound gate the team's first impressions are positive, this facility will serve us well to complete the Mission. The compound was surrounded by a ten-foot, four-inch thick concrete wall capped by barbed-wire, the compound walls measured 1200 feet long and 500 feet wide. Two 20,000 square feet warehouses are situated to the rear along the north boundary wall. A soccer-size sports field was across from the warehouses. Two 19,000 square feet three-story buildings stood at the opposite end of the north wall. One building had been constructed as living quarters for the employees of the Tin Indochina Limitée company and the second three-story building was for office and two conference rooms. The Peregrine advance team had constructed a reinforced-concrete ammunition and weapons storage bunker between the warehouses and three-story buildings. Overall, the compound is ideal for the Peregrine team operations. A sign over the gate indicates the facility housed the "Adjunct Inspector General Team #4".

The history of the compound was symbolic of the changes sweeping the world in the aftermath of WWII. Historic empires were crumbling under the forces of nationalism and self-determination. France suffered a national humiliation during WWII and was determined to reassert French control over the former French colonies in Africa and Southeast Asia after WWII. Speculators and investors in France jumped on the start-up company Tin Indochina Limitée business prospectus which promised massive near-term profits from mining tin in Vietnam. Hundreds of millions of Francs flowed into the Tin Indochina Limitée coffers. In

1953, Tin Indochina Limitée built the lavish compound in Saigon as the flagship site for their tin mining operation. The hopes of the company and investors were dashed from the outset as the Vietnamese no longer wanted foreign rule of Vietnam or foreigners, particularly the French, in their country. Despite paying huge bribes to the Viet Minh for permission to prospect in safety for tin, the political and security chaos from 1954 onward doomed the company to bankruptcy in 1962. No one wanted to purchase the large vacated compound and the Tin Indochina Limitée affair became a scandal in France. That scandal gave the International Export and Import Company Ltd an opportunity to purchase the compound on-the-cheap and make three bribe-susceptible Tin Indochina Limitée executives rich in the process.

The trucks are greeted by two huge German Shepherd dogs and four fierce-looking Nung guards. The dogs had earned the admiration of the Nungs that morning when they saved a three-year old Nung girl who was threatened by an aggressive King Cobra. The dogs barked and feinted at the Cobra with one dog always staying in position between the child and the hooded snake. A Nung fighter joined the fray to dispatch the King Cobra with a machete. The big snake went into a tasty stew with some pieces reserved for grilling – jungle hors d'oeuvres – and some snake meat for the dogs' evening meal – it was a very big snake.

The Team decided the compound was great, very defensible, comfortable living quarters, and plenty of storage space. One warehouse was in use as the Nung Li Clan families living-quarters and the other available for team equipment storage and vehicle parking. After stowing personal gear in their living quarters, the team convened in the dining/bar area, to drink beer and listen to the Wurlitzer juke box which was playing the smooth rock-and-roll song, Sea of Love by Phil Phillips – a unique welcome as the team goes to war.

The next day, jet lag aside, the Team is up early, turning out for a serious work-out and a run using the sports field area. The Nungs had seen this crazy behavior by Americans before. So, the Nungs not on duty just went back to sleep. After PT, showers, and a hearty breakfast prepared by the Nung cook, the Team convened for the 'get-the-show-on-the-road' staff meeting. The first agenda item was a review of the security protocols, including the organizational cover, what was the public to see and know about the" DoD Adjunct Inspector General Team #4"?

Captain Williams reviewed the team cover story.

"The cover story for the DoD Adjunct Inspector General Team #4 is: we are a JCS team here to conduct a classified administrative investigation and report back to the JCS Chairman". "I will contact the CIA Station Chief to establish a working arrangement with the CIA station.. Master Sergeant Jones will contact the SOG for initial coordination".

"All NCOs will use their true names because, they, without exception, will meet special operations personnel they knew from a previous tour in Vietnam. The DoD Adjunct Inspector General Team #4 cover for the NCOs assignments is: all the NCOs were assigned by JCS to provide security and support the DoD Adjunct Inspector General Team #4. The NCO personal-version of the cover story for their friends, was, the NCOs are being screwed over for past sins, some sins in the not so distant past, and given the assignment to babysit some REMF wienies as punishment."

Continuing,

"Team members are not to use their 'get-out-of-jail free ' cards (Presidential Authority Card) without my approval or LT Baumgartner's, unless it is an 'in extremis' emergency, such as, a situation which would compromise the security and cover of the Peregrine Mission. Every team member will be armed when outside the compound".

"James, Podowski, and von Eisenberg will complete getting the compound squared-away. Use Nungs as needed. Have the compound ready-to-go in three days. During free-time, all NCOs are to reach out to friends in-country and establish informal networks for information and potential sources for 'special supply' needs – meaning, permanently borrow, as in steal, bribe those who you need to, and 'those other things' the boss needs. Captain Williams does not want to know how we 'do special-logistics' in Nam".

"Jones will begin training the Nungs and evaluate if they are combat ready. Identify ten Nungs as bodyguards and train them to execute certain actions requiring tradecraft such as surveillance and countersurveillance".

"Renner and Risner will set-up a secure intel room – the Team version of a SCIF. After that, they will update all the intel and brief the team. Target complete, three days".

"After I coordinate with the Station Chief, Wilson will contact CIA comm center personnel to set up communications procedures between the

Team and the Saigon station. All clandestine operational messages will go through CIA. Wilson will set-up a comm cover-site in the compound to send deceptive open-text administrative message traffic back to the Pentagon".

"PT 0600, breakfast 0730, staff meeting 0800 – questions?"

The next morning staff meeting went as Captain Williams expected. Each of the consummate professionals on the Peregrine team had been very diligent the previous day in the pursuit of their assigned objectives. During the morning briefing in the secure intelligence room, each team member documented progress on their objectives.

Williams had contacted the CIA Station Chief to setup the working arrangement with the CIA Station. The contact point for Peregrine was the Deputy Chief of Station, Orval Berringer, an Ivy League holdover from the OSS days. Orval, preparing to retire after this tour, looked on the assignment as a low priority until the Station Chief advised Orval of the Presidential Authority for the Peregrine Operation. Orval immediately assigned the Peregrine liaison responsibility to one of the Station case officers, Jake Reynolds, Jake was in his early thirties and rock solid as a highly motivated effective clandestine operator.

James contacted the SOG establishing old-ties with old buddies for information sharing and coordinating 'things'. Anticipating the comings and goings of future recruited-agents, Peregrine spies, Renner and Risner reported the team needed to acquire a safe house to protect the Peregrine home-base compound from unwanted attention, They needed updated information from NSA, specifically, the requirement was to give the Saigon location for the 'suspect mole' radio transmitter site as well as the radio receiving and transmitting location in the A Shau valley. CIA, DIA, and NSA should provide the organizational charts for the ARVN General Staff and ARVN intelligence.

Jones reported he was reorganizing the Nung fighters with Ban Chen, head of the Nung 'Li clan' giving the direct orders to the fighters. The intent was to build Nung morale by maintaining Nung leadership and; at the same time, the Peregrine team would build rapport with the individual Nung fighters.

Wilson stated the Peregrine cover communication facility was 'ready to go' He would begin transmitting the 'cover messages' starting today to provide credibility and backstopping for the Adjunct Team #4 cover. The

GRU and KGB are listening from clandestine sites in Saigon and offshore ships to collect communications intelligence. He had a plan to drive the GRU analysts nuts. He would send a message later in the day talking about firing up the Wurlitzer. The GRU guys would bust their asses to "decode" the meaning of Wurlitzer, Operation Wurlitzer? The GRU was already stretched thin trying to track the fast-changing US order of battle as US advisors and troops poured into South Vietnam.

Von Eisenberg noted he set up a medical room in 'the office' building. He was coordinating with Jones to train selected Nungs in combat medical techniques".

"Doc" von Eisenberg set a stack of eleven paper cups on the conference table with two one-gallon jugs of potable water on the table. Before "Doc" could take the next action, the Vietnam vets were groaning, throwing in a few 'oh shit' remarks and other crude epitaphs. Giving his best 'bedside medical smile', "Doc" produced a small box with eleven large, orange chloroquine anti-malaria pills. One per man each week, no waivers,

"some of you wimps may get the 24-hour diarrhea or might want to try to sleep for 15 hours after taking these not-so-little orange beauties, if you need help, see me and I can help.

James, Podowski, and von Eisenberg reported on the compound readiness: Additional needs for compound security are in a draft plan for officers' approval today. They will reach out to friends in-country and establish informal networks for information and 'special supply' needs – read permanently borrow, i.e., steal; who do you bribe plus some other things the Boss really does not want to know - stuff.

CHAPTER 10 WHEELS UP PARIS
DESTINATION VIETNAM

This dacha, vacation cottage deep in the birch tree woods, contained no hidden-bugs to eaves-drop, no phones, no prying ears or surveilling eyes – it was just the two of them enjoying Sasha's father's KGB General Officer perk, a private dacha.

The citizens of the communist state, the Union of Soviet Socialist Republics, lived in fear every day of their lives. This was a country where a national hero was a 13- year old boy, Pavlik Morozov, who betrayed his father for crimes against the State. That crime was forging minor administrative-documents that helped impoverished citizens and had no impact on the functioning of the State. Regardless, Pavlik's father would be executed as a result of his son's denunciation. It was a common practice for comrade-citizens to betray and denounce other comrade-citizens over matters large and small. The denunciations were usually without merit, just reprehensible personal attacks by petty, malicious individuals who used the system for their personal advantage.

In denunciation cases, the Second Chief Directorate could take actions ranging from opening a file, arrest, shipment to the Gulag in Siberia, or execution. In this draconian environment of fear, no one was safe from denunciation; no one, including KGB Captain Alexandr Petrov, a rising KGB star and well-connected officer. Everyone knew about the omnipresent perpetual official 'watching' and the unofficial surveillance of a citizen by another citizen. comrade-citizens would betray friends and family, while the Second Chief Directorate listened and watched every Soviet citizen.

Sasha's cook, a babushka-type person (grandma-type) liked the young captain, but that did not stop her from filing weekly reports on Captain Petrov and Kie^. What did they talk about; were there any security beaches; how often did Captain Petrov and Kie^ have sex and what kind of sex-play did they have? The cook held no malice toward Petrov or Nyugen but simply did the bidding of the Second Chief Directorate out of her fear of punishment for not reporting an 'incident'. Captain Petrov's driver reported weekly on the young KGB captain for the same reasons as the cook, to protect himself in the event Captain Petrov fell afoul of the 'the system' and the driver had not reported him first.

Sasha expected and accepted the conduct of the cook and driver as one more part of the paranoia endemic in the USSR. Thus, he took measures to exhibit only positive behaviors for the cook and driver to report to the KGB. He is careful to find secure methods to privately communicate with Kie^ on sensitive matters. A telling and savagely cynical 'saying' within the KGB was – "no one had friends in the KGB". Of course, the saying was not totally true, there were friendships that ranged from casual acquaintances to those who trusted a friend with his or her life. Even so, another KGB maxim was – "everyone is guilty of something. We just have to find out what that is".

Romances, as loving relationships, within the KGB ranks were frowned-on, this facilitated and exacerbated the pettiness and jealousies naturally existing between various individuals. At the same time, the KGB implicitly allowed casual sexual affairs as unremarkable. Sasha could not think of a KGB colonel or general, including his father, who did not have one or more female KGB officers on his staff – his 'personal private' staff. Another cynical KGB phrase was – 'females in the KGB all know the path for career success is through the bedroom'.

As part of the KGB apparatus of fear, KGB Captain Petrov and KGB Junior Lieutenant Nyugen understood the dangers and knew very well how to play the 'game'. Sasha and Kie^ intentionally gave the cook and driver occasional salacious tidbits for their reports. Petrov knew 'Apartment 21' was bugged, despite the proforma periodic electronic sweeps to detect 'bugs'. The 'bugs" were in place and the electronic sweeps were 'for show'. Their recorded bedroom sex-play would corroborate the cook and driver reports. Sasha and Kie^ would go 'for a walk' as needed to have their privacy in Moscow.

Her case officer training completed, Captain Petrov and newly promoted Junior Lieutenant Nyugen planned the next two steps of Operation Red. She would travel to Paris for three weeks to immerse herself in the sounds, smells, gossip, and cultural mores of living in Paris. At the end of her Paris experience in French lifestyles to support her legend, Kie^ would board an Air France-Air Vietnam code-share flight from Paris Orly airport to Saigon Tan Son Nhut International

142

Airport. She would occupy a first-class seat as part of her legend, as a 'trust-fund' girl.

Petrov and his team would deploy to Vietnam while Kie^ was in Paris to be in-place when she arrived in South Vietnam. Petrov's team would travel to Hanoi from major airports in Europe using false papers. Once in North Vietnam, part of the team would traverse the Ho Chi Minh trail to the secret camp in the South Vietnam A Shau valley. Petrov would travel under cover to Saigon. The Saigon Operation Red radio operator would arrive by ship to the Saigon harbor.

As Sasha and Kie^ faced imminent separation in the early stage of the Operation Red deployment, Sasha decided that he and Kie^ needed some personal private time together. They would spend a few days in his KGB General father's. dacha. The time at the dacha was idyllic for Kie^. She had developed a passionate love for Sasha, who was her mentor and had showed a protective caring for her she had not experienced before in her life- and, Sasha was now her lover. Kie^ was determined to tell Sasha how she felt. She was not sure if he reciprocated 'love' beyond the sexual intimacies they had. Kie^ wanted his love but she would be content, in any case, to just be part of his life. She gave Sasha a longing gaze, thinking she would do anything for her KGB captain.

During a contemplative walk in the silent birch forest, Kie^ turned to Sasha and said emotionally,

"I love you Sasha."

Sasha's response was to take Kie^ in his arms and kiss her with a passion that matched hers. The two had crossed some mythical line in the KGB world of relationships. They knew the difficulties they would face as lovers rather than 'casual players in a strictly sexual affair'. In Kie^'s mind, they were, soulmates, a term that Sasha would be unlikely to use though he understood the term contextually. Sasha had not intended to fall in love with Kie^ but here they were in each other's arms.

Even though their personal relationship had changed, a truism remained constant for both of them, Do the Operation Red Mission". At the same time, Kie^ wanted to see no dramatic change in their existing overall relationship. Kie^ wanted to remain as boss-subordinate on the professional side, lover-lover on the personal side, somehow fusing these two sides as one. However, there was still a shadow of doubt that her Operations officer in Saigon would be Sasha. There could be another

KGB officer appointed for the Saigon portion of the mission. Kie^ would not know for sure who her Saigon operations officer was until she was contacted by him in Saigon.

The "swallow to lioness' transformation was complete. She was self-confident in her new role as a case officer. KGB Junior Lieutenant Nyugen recognized the great personal debt she owed Captain Petrov. The 'omnipresent risks' of the field operation and the potential KGB retaliatory threat for their romance made their bond even closer as "Sasha and Kie^". They were only safe when alone in a secure environment like the remote dacha. Her intimacies and affection for Sasha were real; he had rescued her from the 'Swallow degradation' and given her status and a sense of self-worth, he loved her.

The KGB First Chief Directorate planners were consummate masters when constructing legends for KGB operatives in foreign countries. Part of the meticulous preparation was obtaining genuine documents, whenever possible, to construct a authentic trail of documentation as the solid backstop for the agent's legend. Pierre Legrand was a Paris attorney who tried to ingratiate himself with the Soviet Union Embassy in Paris, portraying himself as a communist sympathizer . Legrand in reality was merely a clever crooked lawyer who was equally happy to take payments from capitalists or communists, preferably in cash, moreover, cash preferably in US dollars.

When Legrand was approached by an 'unidentified man' to document and back-date a foreign trust, plus create a bank account for an individual named, Nyugen Kie^, Legrand's response was, "how much will you pay for this work?" The unidentified man told Legrand he would be paid $5000 dollars to create a trust fund of $200,000 US dollars, the funds ostensibly from Nyugen Kie^'s father. A separate bank account would be funded by an additional $50,000 US dollars. The trust would name Nyugen Kie^ as the beneficiary of a revocable inter vivos trust. Legrand was delighted with the payment as offered and quickly set up a back-dated trust, duly filed by a transfer of $200,000 deposited with the Banque de l'Indochine Paris office plus $50,000 in a draw-on-request account.

The $5000 cash payment was agreed to be made to Legrand at an isolated-site in the heavily wooded Bois de Boulogne Park west of Paris. The lawyer left his apartment on the payment day, arriving at the appointed site in the Bois de Boulogne forest. After getting out of his taxi and a short walk to the agreed secluded meeting site, he saw two heavy-set men smiling and waiting for him. Legrand recognized one of the men as the person who paid him the down-payment for the trust document legal work. Smiling, Legrand walked forward and reached out to shake hands, the nearest man took his hand, returning Legrand's smile, and then violently head-butted Legrand. The second man pulled a syringe he had behind his back and thrust the needle into Legrand's neck. The yellow liquid in the syringe was a lethal invention from the Moscow KGB labs, the liquid would render the victim into a paralyzed state instantly, killing the victim in less than 10-seconds. The two 'wet work' goons quickly undressed the Legrand corpse, piling his clothes and shoes neatly on the ground. They begin the gruesome process to render the corpse impossible to identify: they cut off his hands, no fingerprints; pulled his teeth out with a pair of heavy pliers leaving no dental record; and smashed his face with a rock until his face was unrecognizable. The 'wet work' goons threw the body into a shallow grave they had dug earlier and spread a chemical on the grave to stop animals from digging up the body. Satisfied that all was in order, they loaded the clothes, his personal jewelry, severed hands, and Legrand's passport into their car and casually returned to the Soviet Embassy to engage in many rounds of drinking ice-cold vodka. Just another day for 'wet work' veterans of the Lubyanka basement. Legrand was never seen again as the KGB tied up loose-ends for this part of the Nyugen Kie^ legend.

There was a flourishing black-market in Paris for French passports and other identity documents, including blank genuine documents, if the buyer had enough money. KGB technical services already had a stash of blank genuine French passports and did not need to resort to the black market. Kie^ had two sets of false documents: one set for travel to Paris from Moscow as a South Vietnamese national and one set of documents for her time in Paris and travel from Paris to Saigon as a French citizen. She would continue to use the 'French citizen' cover documentation in South Vietnam. She traveled to Paris three weeks in advance of her travel to Saigon, using a false Republic of Vietnam passport to avoid an arrival stamp in her false French passport. She used the three-weeks to gain essential background knowledge as she participated in a broad range of Parisian experiences to bolster her Paris knowledge in support of her legend.

Sasha admitted, he was smitten with Kie^, she was intelligent, beautiful, and it was obvious to him, she was in love with him. To his surprise and dismay, he wanted to protect her versus what his normal KGB case officer behavior should be, 'how do I exploit her to the KGB advantage'. This mental contradiction was a dilemma, his duty to the KGB demanded that he "use Nyugen" in any way the KGB operation required. Their new relationship of love could present a future problem. Sasha's KGB duty could result in a formula which did not work well in the cruel world of 'smoke and mirrors' when it clashed with his love for Kie^. Regardless, Sasha was committed to make his intimate 'secret' personal relationship with Kie^ work as they did The Operation Red mission together. A KGB officer met Kie^ at the airport to exchange her South Vietnamese documents for her 'French citizen' documents and drove her to an apartment the KGB rented for her.

Her visit to Paris was a dizzying time for her. The French culture and dramatic intensity of life in Paris stood in such contrast with the drab Moscow environment. The shops and stores offered a range of goods that dazzled her as she now thought of 'the great GUM' as a rather average shopping venue by comparison. Moreover, she found the experiences revealing that other ways of life existed, other people laughed, and seem to have freedoms she had not imagined.

She did the standard tourist circuit visiting the Eiffel Tower, Musée du Louvre, Cathédrale Notre-Dame de Paris, Avenue des Champs-Élysées, Musée d'Orsay, the river ride down the Seine River looking at the left and right bank sights, absorbing the magnificent architectures and observing how Parisians went about their daily lives. The art works by Renoir, van Gogh, Manet, along with the many works by genius-artists made the comparison with the political art of the Soviet Union showing the communist political art to appear clumsy and childish. She dined in many of the elite expensive restaurants in Paris. Her favorite upscale dining was at the L'Escargot Montorgueil, classic French cuisine, with onion soup, steak tartare, and the delicious buttery and garlicky snails.

Her legend as a vibrant young woman in Paris would not be complete without an immersion in the Parisian café culture of Saint-Germain-des-Prés as the most Parisian quarter of all Paris. "The Left Bank" offered nightclubs, bars, restaurants serving local delicacies, and shopping as she did not dream existed.

After the three-weeks bolstering her legend in Parisian living and French mores, Kie^ boarded the Air France flight to Saigon. Her checked French baggage was filled with haute couture clothing from the top fashion houses in Paris and other accoutrements which a wealthy young French woman 'needed' for international travel. She located her first-class seat and ordered a dry wine aperitif. The flight was not crowded as the Vietnam War had driven the tourist traffic virtually to zero and the French were not popular as the Vietnamese remembered the Indochina War and colonial times. She departed Paris with knowledge and experiences that gave substance and credibility to her legend. However, there was something personal bedsides backstopping her legend, she found herself pondering what she had seen as life in the West.

CHAPTER 11   WHEELS UP MOSCOW
DESTINATION VIETNAM

Planning and training are imperatives for any successful intelligence operation. However, in the field, the situation on the ground frames the operational environment and forces the shooters to adapt to the realities they face. The plan and training set a baseline to adapt to new situations. The KGB illegal operating as a mole in the US State Department Human Resources Department informed his handler that the recruitment target, Caltrop Winston Simmons, was preparing to depart for the US Embassy in Saigon assigned as, Intelligence Coordinator. A job with no real power, but a position that gave Simmons access to the greatest secrets of the Vietnam War, a potential goldmine of information for the KGB. But gaining intelligence about the Vietnam War was an interim first step, the long-range objective was to recruit Simmons and insert him as a KGB mole in the State Department INR.

General Sakharovsky trusted no one with the totality of the deceptions in his plan. Sakharovsky always intended Captain Petrov would be in Saigon as the Operation Red operations officer for case officer Nyugen Kie^. For reasons buried in the KGB security obsession, Junior Lieutenant Nyugen was not told before her arrival in Saigon who her controller would be in Saigon. In the true KGB paranoiac secrecy, Petrov was left in the dark as well by General Sakharovsky. Captain Petrov was told after Junior Lieutenant Nyugen left for Paris to prepare for an immediate deployment to Saigon. Petrov knew there were other candidates in Moscow, including one of her case officer training instructors. Prior to the deployment order, Petrov was worried the romantic relationship between him and Kie^ had been compromised by an informer. He was greatly relieved when General Sakharovsky told him he would be the Operation Red commander in Vietnam.

Petrov's radio operator, Technical Sergeant Ivan Perlinkov would set up a clandestine radio transmitter in Saigon. Perlinkov was one of the 'new generation' of KGB operatives slated for duty in foreign assignments. Ivan Perlinkov was unremarkable in appearance at five-feet eight inches tall and 180 pounds. An 'average' face, appearing in his 30s, created a physical image of the classic 'gray man' drawing no attention. At first impression, no one would suspect Perlinkov was trained in hand-to-hand combat and could play the role of traditional lethal KGB thug, as needed. The radio operator had well developed language skills as Perlinkov spoke English and French in addition to his native Russian. He would use English in Vietnam as he wanted to avoid the antipathy against the French. Perlinkov had experience as a cypher clerk for two years in the KGB London Rezidentura giving him experience operating in a foreign culture. Perlinkov would operate in Saigon under cover as a business representative for a British company importing handicraft novelties from Vietnam. Perlinkov's legend name in Vietnam was Peter Martin, a common English name.

The Operation Red A Shau radio site team used a Russian military aircraft for the long journey from Moscow to Hanoi. This travel was a natural cover as the USSR operated a virtually constant stream of military aircraft delivering military equipment to North Vietnam. The A Shau team would unload in Hanoi, reload the A Shau equipment and men into trucks for the next stage of the trip from Hanoi to the start of the Ho Chi Minh trail near the juncture of the North Vietnam, South Vietnam, and Laos borders.

The Ho Chi Minh trail was a continuous work in-progress as the trail was upgraded in sections to support truck traffic, in addition to the army of porters carrying supplies as individual loads through the jungle. Along with the improvements to stretches of the 'trail' were underwater bridges, slightly below the water surface to disguise crossing sites from air reconnaissance, effectively masking the daily movement of troops and war supplies to the south. Most of the porters used bicycles, which they would load with equipment and walk the loaded bicycles down the trail as what was a high-density north-south traffic pattern for equipment and NVA troops going south, and empty bicycles and porters returning north to reload and repeat the trip When the truck portion of the trail ended, the team and equipment would complete the trip to the A Shau valley by foot. The radio equipment would be distributed among the large number of porters who walked the trail.. The Operation Red A Shau team would gear-up and walk the rest of the way to the A Shau camp located on a mountain ridge

Captain Petrov traveled a less rigorous route as he backstopped his legend for Saigon. Petrov departed Moscow for Paris traveling as a

Soviet diplomatic courier which allowed Petrov to freely pass French customs and passport control using his diplomatic passport in the name of Ivan Ivanovich Serov. Petrov/Serov had the 'diplomatic pouch', a brief-case in this instance, chained to his wrist. As Petrov boarded the Aeroflot flight in Moscow, the 'wet work' goons were in the process of murdering Pierre Legrand in the Bois de Boulogne. At the same time, KGB B&E (breaking and entry) boys from the technical services section in the Paris Rezidentura had picked the lock on Legrand's apartment. The B&E boys searched the apartment for any records of the trust fund Legrand had prepared. The KGB thugs loaded an array of Legrand' clothes into one of Legrand's suitcases, a wardrobe suitable for a long trip outside France. Putting the apartment back into the original order, they left no traces they had been there. They mailed a letter from Legrand to the landlady, telling her Legrand was sorry he missed her before he departed to Asia on an ex-tended business trip. 'Legrand' told her he wanted to keep his apartment and a courier would bring rent payments the next day for one year – pay-ment in cash.

The immigration and customs procedures are suspended for a diplo-matic courier. Diplomatic courier Petrov/Serov traveled directly to the Soviet Embassy where he paid his regards and a greeting from his KGB General father to the Paris Rezident. The Rezident, a powerful man in the KGB, greeted Petrov more warmly than the Rezident actually felt, "who was this upstart Captain", it was irritating to receive a personal cable from General Aleksandr Sakharovsky. The cable was brief to the point of brusque, "give Captain Petrov every courtesy and any support he requests".

Petrov knew that many of the 'KGB long-knives' awaited him if Operation Red is not a resounding success. Petrov would drop the diplo-matic courier ruse after the visit to Embassy and use the Legrand identity to travel from Paris to Bangkok to leave a false trail of Legrand leaving Paris for his extended business trip. The tech services had his Legrand French passport ready with the appropriate Thai entry visa and modified the ID photo after removing the Legrand photo and replacing it with Petrov's photo. KGB field officers were expected to speak at least two languages; Petrov spoke three: Russian. French, and English, all fluently.

Petrov was informed that the Legrand question was permanently re-solved. He understood, Legrand was dead. With a smile, the tech services officer told Petrov he had a surprise, placing Legrand's suitcase on the table filled with Legrand's clothes and personal effects. Smiling, the technician commented, Captain Petrov could use the actual garments as part of his legend. Petrov suppressed the need to call the tech an idiot. Instead, he calmly observed that Legrand was overweight and shorter than Petrov – the idea to use these clothes was bad tradecraft – actually just stupid.

Petrov had the foresight to ship a suitcase with French clothes for himself in a separate diplomatic pouch. He asked the tech if a reservation had been made on the Air France flight to Bangkok tomorrow. A chastised tech opened a file and produced the first-class ticket for a Monsieur Pierre Legrand, Paris to Bangkok. Petrov/Legrand spent the night in the embassy; the next morning Petrov/Legrand gathered his suitcase with his French clothing, his Legrand passport, wearing Legrand's watch, and pocketed his first-class ticket, before traveling to Paris-Orly Airport by cab, which he hailed at a nearby railway station to avoid the cab driver associating him with the Soviet Embassy.

Arrival in Bangkok was uneventful, He took a cab to the historic Oriental Hotel on the banks of the Chao Phraya River. He had two objectives for the three-day stop-over in Bangkok. First, he wanted to eliminate any jet lag factor before arriving in Saigon. Second, he would assume another false identity for his legend in Saigon and Bangkok. He is an American businessman, Woodrow Carter from New York. A KGB support agent delivered a suitcase to Petrov/LeGrand/Carter's room. The suitcase filled with American clothes and toiletries. The suitcase had a clever concealment device designed and installed by the KGB Technical Services department in Moscow. The false bottom was filled with $10,000 US dollars and false documents to backstop his Saigon legend as 'Woodrow Carter', an American businessman.

The Bangkok support agent handed Petrov/Carter his American passport, a somewhat-worn US Passport that contained the various entry and exit stamps expected for an international business traveler, plus a one-year business visa to enter South Vietnam. The support agent took the false French documents and the suitcase with French clothing with him when he returned to the Soviet Embassy Rezidentura.

During the next three days, Petrov/Carter did the Bangkok tourist thing, eating Thai delicacies, sightseeing, viewing many statues of Buddha, and continuing to build his legend with experiences to support his legend. Petrov was surprised to see the Air Viet Nam aircraft was a venerable Douglas C-54, a four-engine propellor aircraft. The flight to Saigon Tan Son Nhut International Airport took two hours. The passport control and customs processes went smoothly. Petrov/Carter had a five-day reservation at the venerable Majestic Hotel, a Saigon luxury hotel since the 1920s. The taxi ride from Tan Son Nhut presented the kaleidoscope of the humanity and smells of 1964 Saigon, a pungent welcome for Sasha. He would use the next five days to study the streets, people, and develop a sense of Saigon.

The Saigon radio operator had arrived three-weeks before. His legend identified him Peter Martin, listed as ship electrician, on the Corrola, a Panamanian registered small freighter. In fact, the Corrola was a false flag ship as it belonged to the KGB and was used as a COMINT collection platform off the Vietnam coast. While in the Saigon port, the radio operator left the ship, ostensibly on shore leave, and never came back. He carried a table-model AM radio stashed among the kit in his sea bag. If anyone opened the back of the AM receiver, the truth would be obvious, the AM radio was a sophisticated compact transmitter-receiver built by the KGB Moscow Technical Services Department. The sending key was hidden in a concealment device in the operator's luggage and the materials to construct a directional antenna would be purchased locally in Saigon. The radio operator, per his legend as a business representative of a British company importing novelty goods, purchased a small walled villa, now the Operation Red safe house in the Cholon district of Saigon. The safe house was unremarkable located on a relatively quiet street. The previous occupants were French who departed as the South Vietnamese attitudes toward the French vacillated between unfriendly to hostile. Peter Martin also leased an apartment near the race track and would use that top floor apartment as his radio transmission site and backup safe house.

Petrov moved into the Cholon safe house five days after his arrival. After confirming his arrival to Moscow he sat at the typewriter to prepare a coded message to Kie^. They would meet day after tomorrow.

CHAPTER 12   LIVING THE LEGEND IN SAIGON

Kie^ called the Caravelle desk-clerk to have her breakfast tray removed and bring a fresh serving of café au lait. In less than ten minutes, the tray was gone, and a steaming carafe of Café au lait awaited her. She needed the caffeine as support for her intense mental planning session. She would commit nothing to writing for security. The next several days will be dedicated to establishing a credible foundation for her legend in Saigon. This foundation includes noticeable public actions seeking information from official sources about her parents. These legend backstopping efforts would satisfy the curious who asked, why was she in Vietnam. A separate track is to establish a social presence within the 'correct social networks', the elite and the Saigon 'movers and shakers'.

She needed to brush up on her Vietnamese. She learned Vietnamese as a child, so she had a native pronunciation, however, her vocabulary was stilted as she seldom used Vietnamese since then. She spoke fluent French with no accent, and fluent Russian, which she would use only in the confines of the safe-houses. English was needed for contact with the target, Mr. Calthrop Winslow Simmons. Kie^ spoke English fluently with a slight accent. She learned English as part of her training as a 'Swallow'. She specialized in seducing KGB recruitment targets who only spoke English. For psychological theater in her meetings with Calthrop, She would affect an Asian-accent when speaking English.

She decided to approach the hotel concierge for 'advice' about the search for her parents. The concierge, Wie Li, 35 years old, was average height at 5-feet five-inches tall and presented a mildly theatrical appearance in his red and blue hotel livery. The always smiling Wie Li was smooth as he interacted with the hotel guests leveraging his experience, knowledge, and connections to encourage generous gratuities from the guests. The concierge's pleasant manner plus his speaking fluent Vietnamese, French, and English made him a natural for interactions with the guests. Kie^ decided the exchange with the concierge would accomplish two objectives: the concierge would be flattered that she asked for advice; as a result, he would tell everyone on the hotel staff how the valued guest had confidence in him. In turn, the story of the valued French-Asian guest seeking to find her parents would become a widespread credible rumor. The concierge appreciated how the rumor would bolster his stock with the hotel manager, plus, likely earning a significant gratuity from the beautiful French-Asian woman. The concierge quickly began to spread the information to the hotel staff about the honored guest approaching him for help finding her parents.

The challenge to join the 'correct elite' of Saigon wartime society loomed large and daunting. She had discussed this problem in detail with Sasha during the planning in Moscow. How does an outsider penetrate the snobbery of an established local elite? How does this sexy woman do so in a manner that does not appear to be a 'come-on', at least not a blatant 'come-on', to the men in the 'elite group'. The solution was obvious, in Saigon, you join the exclusive Le Cercle Sportif Saigonnais Club.

Finishing her second cup of café au lait, she dressed for her next subterfuge. Taking the elevator to the ground floor, she approached the concierge displaying her seductive pleasant smile. The concierge immediately gave her his full attention, asking in French –

"How may I help you mademoiselle?"

She briefly explained, 'in strictest confidence', doing so helplessly, that she was in Saigon trying to find her parents. However, she was not sure which government agencies she should contact. Could the concierge tell her where to start, with the police or who? Assuming the proper expression of grief for her plight (even as dreams of dollars or piasters in gratuities dominated his thoughts), he said would make some contacts and report back to her.

Smiling her innocent 'sweet Kie^ smile', she thanked him,

"Please take any needed time to make your contacts". She added, "Please reserve a car and driver for me; I will need the car for about four days."

Kie^ slipped the concierge a modest tip in piasters, equivalent to a US dollar, and both parties were satisfied with the transaction.

She decided to walk around District 1 for the rest of the day to familiarize herself with the streets, sights, sounds, and listen to people speaking Vietnamese. District 1 is at the heart of the city, typical of an urban center: embassies, businesses, shopping centers and restaurants. The district houses many famous buildings such as the City Opera House, the Notre-Dame Cathedral, the Reunification Palace, plus banks and financial institutions. The Ben Thanh market was a popular shopping location for the locals. She decided to have lunch at the Continental Hotel as part of the orientation. Returning to the Caravelle after four hours of 'getting 'the lay of the land' in District 1, she was tired but pleased with the progress on her KGB assignment in Saigon. Calling room service, she ordered Chateaubriand, a bottle of burgundy wine, and crème brûlée for dessert, the Vietnamese food could wait for another day. She listened to a Vietnamese radio station for an hour for the news and practice listening to the local pronunciations. Finally, to bed, tomorrow will be another busy 'legend' day.

After breakfast the following morning, Kie^ decided to avoid the elevator and walked down the stairs to the ground floor where an enthusiastic concierge rushed to meet her. He told her the car and driver were waiting and would be at her convenience whenever she needed transportation. The concierge gave her a sheet of paper in French, the paper included a list of agencies which could be of assistance as she searched for her parents. Some agencies had specific contact persons for refugee inquiries. Other government offices were just names of agencies with addresses. The concierge said he would have more information by that afternoon regarding additional refugee agencies.

Very pleased, she gave the concierge a generous gratuity of three dollars, a large sum of money for the average Vietnamese who earned less than $20 US dollars per month. She asked the concierge to have the driver ready in 30 minutes. Kie^ was at the hotel entrance on schedule 30 minutes later, the concierge introduced the driver, who would drive the hotel four-door black Citroen, for the honored Caravelle guest, Mademoiselle Nyugen.

The driver quickly moved to open the car-door for access to the back seat, greeting her in French. She thanked him in Vietnamese and requested they speak Vietnamese today. Ordering the driver to take her on a tour of the city, she requested the driver identify points of interest during the ride. She studied the street patterns and allies as they toured the city. This knowledge would be critical when she planned her surveillance detection routes (SDR). The tour of the city was very thorough allowing her to note the location of the Cholon safe-house as they passed by the walled villa address. Returning to the hotel, she told the driver to be ready at 0900 hours tomorrow. She gave the driver a modest gratuity in piasters as she exited the Citroen. Another evening meal in her room, listen to Vietnamese on the radio, and to bed. Kie^ is very disciplined, but she thought of this discipline being more to Sasha than the KGB.

While Nyugen Kie^ would rather continue the orientation around the city and study the Vietnamese culture, she understood that people would expect her 'natural' priority would be the search for her missing parents. She and Petrov had discussed and considered the 'search' in detail. Kie^ had to appear as an 'anguished daughter' searching for her parents, parents missing in the chaos and confusion of war. Of course, the unacceptable consequence of the search would be to actually 'find her parents'. To ensure against that unacceptable consequence, Kie^ and Petrov concocted a cover story that ensured 'the parents' could not be found. It was very simple to take part of the true story of Nyugen Kie^ being separated from her parents, modify a couple aspects so her legend still worked as credible. For the 'search', Petrov and Nyugen changed the names of 'her parents' to people who were dead. They changed the former family residence from Hanoi to Haiphong. Finally, dealing with the back story on why Nyugen had a different name from her parents, her legend was that her father had been accused by the communist secret police as being a spy for France and her father was under a death sentence if they caught him. Her name had been changed to protect her as they shipped her to Paris with a trust fund.

The driver was waiting, Kie^ gave him the three destinations for the day: police headquarters, tax records, and property records. She had a contact suggested by the concierge at each agency. She repeated her cover story about her parents at each agency and her inquiry was officially recorded. Dutiful promises to help were made at each agency, with no agency having any intent to follow-up. The next day of visits were to immigration, the Saigon INTERPOL office, the Red Cross, the French Embassy, and the US Embassy (the latter two to get her request on each Embassy's records, giving her a future discussion point with her recruitment target). Satisfied that she had an adequate back-story for the 'missing parents' search, Kie^ turned to the thorny issue of an outsider becoming an insider with the Saigon elite.

The legend plan was to use the elitist Le Cercle Sportif Club to expeditiously gain access to the smug and powerful in Saigon society. The most exclusive club in Saigon is the Le Cercle Sportif Club, the club was developed around the turn of the century as a primarily outdoor sports facility with riding, sailing on the river, soccer, running-sports, plus certain indoor sports like fencing. Regardless of the sport, The Saigon Le Cercle Sportif Club was, always only for the rich and powerful. That aloof elite membership status became even more exclusive in 1933 when a large outdoor pool was installed – the elite had to compete with other elite for membership.

The list of members included all the 'powers-that-be' in Saigon: the very rich, the top politicians, senior Generals, wealthy, influential business men, and of course, the leading figures from the foreign power of the day – first the Colonial French, the Japanese during WWII, back to the French, and now the Americans. The US Ambassador, Henry Cabot Lodge Jr, belonged to the Le Cercle Sportif club, along with all the senior members of the Embassy staff.

The concierge had evolved into a paid informant for Kie^ as he brought tidbits of information to her every day, in hope to receive a payment from her for each of his revelations. She used her payments like weapons to motivate the concierge to seek out rumors that would help prepare her for future discussions with her target and the Saigon elite.

She casually asked the concierge questions about the Le Cercle Sportif Club. The eager-to-please concierge had no detailed knowledge of the Le Cercle Sportif Club, except one comment that was a great find for Kie^. He offered her the intelligence that the Caravelle Hotel manager and the two assistant-managers were members of the exclusive Le Cercle Sportif Club. She slipped him a wad of 150 piasters (the black market exchange rate being about 150 piasters to the dollar). At that time the South Vietnamese GDP per capita was a meager $118 per year, so a one dollar tip was a relatively large sum. The Honored Guest and the concierge both considered their information exchanges and monetary rewards as more than satisfactory. She returned to her room to think how to use the hotel manager club membership information.

The Caravelle hierarchy was a manager and two assistant-managers, all French, the rest of the hotel administrative and service staff were Vietnamese. Kie^ needed to move quickly on the membership problem as she had to be well ensconced in the Le Cercle Sportif Club before her target arrived in Saigon. She decided on a direct approach to the manager, taking care that he would not see this as a quid pro quo event – sex for membership sponsorship. But Kie^ thought, it really doesn't matter – whatever for the mission and Sasha.

Selecting a low-cut French dress, she proceeded to 'innocently' approach the hotel desk clerk, asking in French, if the manager was available. The clerk immediately called the manager telling him that Mademoiselle Nyugen would like to speak with him.

The Manager's office was on floor 1, as in the European system to designate floors, the office was on the floor above the check-in desk which was the ground-floor, numbered floor zero. In less than a minute, a slightly out of breath overweight Caravelle Hotel Manger opened a hidden door behind the check-in desk, the manager and the desk clerk both showed expressions of concern, did the esteemed guest have a problem with hotel service or staff? Heightening their anxiety, Mademoiselle Nyugen asked to speak privately with the manager. The manager responded,

"Of course, may I show you to my office",

He followed her through the hidden door walking behind her up one flight of stairs to his well-appointed comfortable office. The 53-year old manager was self-impressed with his position as manager and his position in the upper-crust of Saigon society. Overweight, a pencil-thin mustache above his full lips and flabby neck, the manager was typical of an officious French expatriate in the old French colonial empire. As he lustfully examined his guest, he offered her coffee which Mademoiselle Nyugen politely declined and went directly to her point:

"Monsieur Manager, please, I have a request. I would ask you to sponsor me for membership in Le Cercle Sportif Club."

"Mademoiselle Nyugen, membership in the Le Cercle Sportif Club is a most complicated matter." (stalling, as he searched his mind how to handle her request).

"Monsieur Manager, I do understand the prestigious aspect of Le Cercle Sportif Club membership. I understand that only the most important members are allowed to sponsor candidates for membership (leaning forward slightly in her chair to give him a better view of her ample cleavage). You know I am well able to pay the membership fee and the club dues (inferring paying any needed bribes). I am asking you as a Frenchman, rather than any of my American friends at the US Embassy. I see the Le Cercle Sportif Club as an important symbol of France in Asia."

160

The manger did a quick mental calculation – what is the risk for me in being her sponsor. Sponsors who recommend bad candidates, candidates who do not pay their dues or do not comply with Club behavior standards, are often are ostracized by other club members. At the same time, he knew very well that the club made accommodations for beautiful young women as 'decorative figures' around the pool, many of these young women are given 'permanent guest-member' status. There was no downside for him to be her sponsor and there may be some form of 'appreciation' from her in the future.

With a leering smile,

"Mademoiselle Nyugen, I would be most honored to be your membership sponsor I will start the process today."

"Thank you, Monsieur Manager, I am in your debt."

"Please call me François".

"That is gracious of you to be so helpful and kind François. I look forward to talking with you again".

The manager walked Kie^ back down to the check-in desk area and bid her a 'very good day'. The manager literally ran back up the stairs to his office and placed a call to his friend on the Club membership committee. The Manager began a graphic description, as only a Frenchman can describe a beautiful woman, and expressed the need for his friend to show 'good faith' in quickly approving her application with his sponsorship. His friend told him to invite Mademoiselle Nyugen for the required membership interview at her convenience.

In the elevator, Kie^ smirked, the cleavage does it every time for the weak ones. The smirk broadened into a smile, I already have my Le Cercle Sportif Club pool uniform, a skimpy black bikini. Later that morning, François called her to ask when it would be convenient for her to complete the obligatory candidate-member interview. She told him to advise his club-membership contact,

"Tomorrow at 1000 hours would be fine".

(another piece of the Operation Red plan fitting into place).

Wearing a different French dress, short and low-cut, she mesmerized the membership committee approving authority (who was thinking of François' graphic, lurid description of Nyugen Kie^ was on-target). The membership approving authority's behavior was virtually the same as the Caravel Manager's, eyes taking-in lustful images of the sexual Eurasian beauty. The membership committee chairman, Jacques Fabron, was a French expatriate who was out of touch with the reality, the old French colonial empire in Southeast Asia was defunct. Exalting in his power to give or withhold the coveted social status of Club membership, the 57-year old balding, pinched faced, lusting man behind the desk fantasized how he could use his power to seduce this sex goddess before him.

To further the impact of her visit, she asked if she could pay the membership fee now, in cash. Before the stunned committee chairman could reply, she pealed three one-hundred dollar bills off a roll she had in her purse. Paperwork signed, fee paid, the Club now had a new member. The committee chairman said he would have her membership credentials delivered to the Caravelle that afternoon.

In his rather high-pitched voice, Jacques Fabron asked,

"Is there anything else at all, I may do for you Mademoiselle? May I give you a tour of the Club?"

Kie^ gave him a smile that fueled his lust as she graciously declined his offer of a tour or 'anything else'.

Pleased, she relaxed on the ride back to the hotel. When she entered the hotel, the concierge advised her there was a message at the desk for her. The desk clerk gave her an envelope with a logo of a Saigon book dealer. It was the expected coded message for contact with her case officer. Great joy filled her heart and mind, along with a bit of trepidation – she sincerely was hoping and needing that Sasha would here in Saigon her Operations Officer for the mission and her Lover for her emotional stability.

CHAPTER 13   RESET - BACK TO BASICS

While the rest of the team were reading, drinking beer, telling war stories, cleaning weapons, or listening to the music on the juke box, the officers held a private meeting.

Baumgartner expressed the frustration the team felt,

"The team is pissed with the lack of progress. Dammit, Bobby, we are just spinning our wheels - this is shit – we need to stop waiting for NSA and CIA to give us info, the problem is, right now we are not being who we are. We are acting like a bunch of NSA analysts – bless 'em, they are great, and we need them – but dammit, we are shooters – we need to be. who we are, and we will get this mission done – Mission Complete!"

"Agree Gary, so what do we do?"

"First, we need to relook at the problem. We are missing something big time. We can't connect the dots because we haven't even identified all the essential dots. NSA, CIA, and General Wojcik are in support roles and will help, but this thing is on us. We need to look at the problem as shooters – the analysts can fill-in gaps as we go – but we are here now, no one ever has all the dots. Damnit, remember that picture of the vultures sitting on a wire, – the one vulture says to the other vultures – patience hell, let's go kill something."

Captain Williams turned to Captain Reginald Denning,

"Reggie, what do you think?"

"You know me guys, I have survived this kind of work for a long, long time. I did so by killing the other guy before he killed me. I have not said anything until now, but Gary is on target. We have not been who we are since we left DC. We were who 'we needed to be in DC', getting ready for the mission. Now we are 'among them', but still acting like we are in DC. We need targets to kill! If new dots get us there, fine. If we do not get new dots, we will find another way. This is as fine a bunch of shooters as I have ever served with – hell, they do not want to be sitting around listening to a juke box when there are bad guys out there to kill."

163

"Gary, for the team meeting tomorrow, you have it – get us on track – by the way we are going to stop calling this a 'staff' meeting, not one of the bastards on this team, is a 'staff guy', we are shooters – patience hell, let's go kill something."

"Got it Boss!"

The disgruntled team gathered for the morning meeting in a distinct atmosphere of, 'we sure do a lot of talking and then do not do much else except spin wheels'. Captain Williams set the tone as he gruffly stated

"It is time to get off our asses and kill some bad guys" –

The rest of the team nodded their heads but there was no rah-rah yet, they already had had plenty of words.

"Lieutenant Baumgartner is going to brief you on getting back to what we do"

The atmosphere changed in the room to one of anticipation.

"I am as frustrated as the rest of you. We have been waiting for someone to connect the dots for us. Hell, none of the CONUS team and certainly not us, have identified exactly, what are all the dots, much less how to connect the dots. We did good in DC preparing for this mission, but we are not in DC anymore, Toto – we are 'among um'! We are shooters, not analysts!"

That did bring a response for the team with vocal endorsements: damn straight! Hell yes! right-on! interspersed with the crude remarks, unacceptable in civilian polite society.

"Our job is simple: we find bad guys; we fix bad guys as targets; we kill the sons-of-bitches."

This 'back to who we are' comment further fired up the team and the rah-rah was back – it was, game-on, give me a target!

"So, here is what we are going to do. We now know that NSA cannot give us precise locations yet for the Saigon and A Shau radio transmitters. We are going to restate our intelligence requirements to NSA for better data, but we are not going to wait. The reality is, there are technical and security challenges that limit what NSA can provide.

For example, we know there is a transmitter here in Saigon and that transmitter sends a very narrow-beam signal in the direction of the

A Shau valley. The azimuth of the directional signal tends to be in the same orientation as the north-south geography of the A Shau valley. Even if NSA had accurate data on the Saigon signal power, they could not definitively determine the receiving site location in the A Shau. The security situation in the A Shau area is, you all know, A Shau is "shit-city" – one of the hottest regions you can find in 'Indian Country'. It is so hot that NSA cannot locate new collection sites in that region. We are going to go into the A Shau on the ground to sort this out".

A team HOOYAH eloquently stated this team was ready to go.

"Sergeants Jones and Risner are going to generate a plan how to get into the A Shau, get the information, and get out with our asses intact. They will have that plan ready no later than three days from this morning. The plan should contain an up close and personal Peregrine team recon. Add a small clandestine indigenous pre-patrol recon as needed."

"Sergeant Clayton and Warrant Officer Renner will integrate the Vietnamese organization charts we received from DIA, CIA, and NSA. There are choke points in the organization information-channels. The bad guys access the information channels to identify target locations for the ambushes. Once we identify the choke points, we can use timelines of the ambushes and Vietnamese personnel assignments to ID some bad guys to kill."

"Captain Williams and Captain Denning are going to identify HUMINT targets to recruit. We need insider information from the South Vietnamese military and the South Vietnamese government organizations which process the info the bad guys use to plan the ambush of the US advisors. We'll coordinate with CIA, but I don't expect much in the way of help from them."

"Sergeants Risner, Podowski, and Wilson, get your asses over to SOG and shake that tree. How would anyone on the VC side get information about SOG operations?"

"We have a whiff of serious problems for the CIA and SOG operations inside Nam and cross-border operations, apparently massive compromises have been occurring for some time. Captain Williams is going to see if CIA is going to play nice and share any information on that problem."

165

"The key here is, identify how the enemy moles get the detailed ARVN planning data info - the information the bad guys use to plan the ambushes of US advisors - who can tap into the 'choke points' – once we know that – it is lock and load – send some bad guys to Hell."

"Sergeant James, we need two more Jeeps"

"On it boss, you will have them before noon

"And Risner, that SOG thing on the bar girl informant network, that is very low priority".

Hoots and jeers followed, directed at Risner.

"Roger on that boss" - with distinctly less enthusiasm than James gave for his 'get Jeeps' response.

"If you get any crap from people while sorting out your tasks, you are authorized to use your – 'Presidential Authorization Priority – Don't Give Me Any Shit' card – just do so with great discretion and prudence. Any questions? OK, get moving, we are burning daylight"

Sergeant Jones commandeered the team Jeep with a Nung driver/ bodyguard. The rest of the team would have to wait on James to liberate two more Jeeps. Master Sergeant Jones had a close friend in SOG, Master Sergeant Clayton Matthews, a 'good ol boy' from Alabama, who would help with the A Shau 'sneak and peek' plan. Master Sergeant Matthews knew heavy-shit was coming down when he saw the massive frame of his friend, moving quickly, this was not a social call. Shaking hands as old buddies, Jones went directly to the point,

"My team needs to take a walk around the A Shau. How do we do it?"

Matthews shook his head ruefully, looked Jones in the eye and said seriously:

"You do that walk very carefully. That is Indian Country on steroids, boo-coo bad shit. Where do you want to go?"

"Right now, we have a north-south azimuth that essentially runs up the valley. We need to locate a specific radio transmitter on that azimuth. NSA tells us it is probably on the east-side of the eastern mountain range framing the valley."

"Jones, you better have your GI insurance paid-up for this trek."

"Do we have any assets in there which could do a first recon look to narrow down likely sites along that azimuth? The transmitter has to be in the high-ground which suggests some locations along the east side mountain ridge. We have the 1st Air Commando guys from Bien Hoa doing air recon, but we need boots-on-the-ground to have confidence before sending in a heavy-team."

"Do you know Billy Johnson?"

"Sure, if you meant 'Wild-Man', knew him at Bragg".

"Well, Billy's as crazy as ever. Wild-Man just got some REMF LTC's ass kicked by our General, but that is a story for a beer – you're buying the beer. Billy is in with some Yards not far from the A Shau valley, most of the Yards are farther south down in the Central Highlands. I think Billy would know how to do that recon and then maybe how you can live through a walk in the A Shau woods. Contact with Billy is not easy as he is in a hot area and keeps his Yards as low-profile as possible, but these Yards, I mean 'his' Yards, they love Billy and are fiercely loyal to him. Billy does good, hell better than good, Wild man and the Yards do outstanding work. You up for a planning trip upcountry?"

"Locked and loaded and ready to go. What do I need to do to set it up with Billy, to get some Yards to take a first peek?"

"Give me a day to contact Billy. Want some company for the trip?"

"You betcha for company, like the old days. I'll be doing you a favor to get your fat-ass out of a desk chair and you can see what real-soldiers do. It will be good to see ol' Billy again, always good for a laugh and no one I know gets into more bad-shit than Wild-Man."

Sergeant Jones and his Nung driver returned to the compound to find most of the team gone. James had done his 'hook or crook' thing and the team now owned two more new Jeeps. Late that afternoon, Jones received a call from Master Sergeant Matthews:

"I have progress on that that matter we discussed this morning. When would you like to get together?"

"How about tonight? We have a good cook and plenty of cold beer. 1800 work for you?"

"Sounds good, do you have maps?"

"Got plenty of maps and want to hear the Billy-REMF LTC story."

James made good on his reputation. Immediately after the morning brief, James called his motor pool buddy and told the Sergeant that he needed to "borrow" two Jeeps. The motor pool Sergeant had done a lot of business with James and asked James when he needed the Jeeps. James said he was on his way. James scarfed up two Nung drivers and they took the team truck, also 'borrowed' from that motor pool, loaded up a case of whiskey, two VC flags, and a carton of frozen steaks as the 'rental fees' for the two Jeeps.

Captain Williams continued the update session:

"I got some good shit from an Agency guy yesterday. I managed to shake that Deputy Station Chief bureaucrat-bastard who has been our contact. The Big-Man was 'too busy' to talk to me, so I was able to link-up with one of the Agency case officers, you know, Bill, Al, Joe, or whatever his real name is – but, this guy is the real deal, could be part of this team – good man – anyway, he said we should go to lunch, giving a wink as he announced that I was buying. We took the long-way walk to the restaurant using the great 'Saigon outdoors as our SCIF' for security. He started with the movie-line shit, "This conversation never happened". When I rolled my eyes, he just smirked and shrugged his shoulders".

Here is what he told me,

"The NVA is kicking CIA's ass six-ways from Sunday. The Agency is losing every team they send-out on cross-border ops, for you boys in the cheap seats, I said 'every team'. Apparently, the Agency is covering this up because it would create a political firestorm all the way to the President on the heels of the Bay of Pigs debacle."

I asked him a stupid question to see if he would give me the answer from 'the company memo' or 'tell the truth' for a change. I cleverly asked,

"How is the NVA doing this?"

His answer was precious:"

"Hell, if we knew, we would not be having this conversation. The Agency 'suits' in DC are panicked. We have brought in CI teams from the CONUS, put everyone at the Station on the 'how are they doing this to us' question. We have no real clue except the obvious there is a mole or moles inside 'somewhere', or there is communications security breakdown, but the comm security problem is so unlikely, the guy who said it was actually booed when he injected the comment, that guy is a real turkey. -Most of us are putting their money on a 'mole' somewhere in the system We just don't know where in the system!"

"We can work with this CIA guy. I knew this guy was real when he gave a painfully honest answer to my question".

So, I asked a broader question:

"Just how bad is the infiltration of North Vietnamese agents? Whoa Nellie, when you thought it was bad news up to now. I heard the answer I absolutely did not want to hear, he said, as if he read my mind".

"What I told you before was the good part. We do not have confidence in an explicit number for the number of North Vietnam agents who have infiltrated the South Vietnamese government and the ARVN, we can't count that high to quantify the actual numbers of bad guys on the inside. Furthermore, given that 'the large number' of moles and NVA agents infiltrated into the systemic whole of South Vietnam, every echelon of society and government. One can only conclude, we are going to lose this goddamned war. The number of moles and spies is in the many of thousands, agents sent from the North, agents recruited in the South, sympathizers, sleepers, moles; the number of agents is a security-threat horror movie."

The CIA guy continued his candid comments:

"What I heard about your group, yeah, there are internal rumors inside the Station SCIF and other US spooks, talking about you. I think you guys are working on just one-dimension of this mess. Maybe we could work together as US intel guys, contrary to the bureaucratic 'suits' who do intel 10% of the time and DC politics the other 90%."

"By then we had reached the restaurant, The Dead Fish, eat if you can afford it – where in the hell do they get these names for restaurants. I was buying, so he naturally ordered Birds Nest Soup, some fish dish, BBQ ribs and two kinds of rice, this boy was a hearty eater – I ordered the same thing and thanked God for lots of black money. Of course, we had 33-Beer – Ba Muoi Ba beer, the only beer in the world which has the marketing slogan – 'and you can't taste the formaldehyde'."

"Gentlemen, our problem is an order-of-magnitude more difficult than we believed previously. The folks in DC have no clue."

The cook had outdone herself that evening. Just as Master Sergeant Matthews arrived at the compound, she was preparing to serve Banh xèo and fried shrimp. Bánh xèo is a Vietnamese savory fried pancake made of rice flour, water, turmeric powder, plus a stuffing of pork, shrimp, diced green onion, mung beans, and bean sprouts. Tonight, the filling was all the above, heavy on the diced green onions and bean sprouts. Many bottles of ice-cold Ba Muoi Ba, '33 beer' were on the table. Matthews commented,

"So this is how you super-spooks live – high on the hog! And one shit-hot compound, any job openings?"

During dinner, Matthews proceeded to tell the REMF story, while swilling a lot of the team's beer in the process.

"This REMF LTC was in MACV personnel and for some reason he came across Billy's file. This REMF asshole sees that Billy was well into his second consecutive tour and was a Yard live-in advisor for both tours. Billy had taken no R&Rs nor the usual 'extend your tour' home-leave over those two years. So, this REMF personnel weenie decides that Billy has 'gone native'. So, this REMF jerk cuts PCS orders sending Billy back to the CONUS. When the orders hit SOG, Brigadier-General Martell called the MACV LTC and told him to get his ass over to SOG and do so now, be in my office within 20 minutes."

Jones and Mathews both knew General Martell well, having served under LTC Martell in Korea. Brigadier-General "Jack-the-Knife" Martell, 45-years old, six feet tall and 185 pounds was the quintessential 'lean and mean' warrior. The 'Jack-the-Knife' name stuck after Captain Martell led an OSS Detachment 101 guerrilla army of Kachin tribesmen operating behind Japanese lines in World War II Burma. Martell and his Kachins terrorized the Japanese nightly delivering silent death to Japanese soldiers of every rank. Captain Martell earned his moniker, 'Jack-the-Knife', during these stealthy lethal raids on the Japanese.

Brigadier-General Martell was intensely loyal to his SOG Special Forces troopers, defending the troopers from outsiders of any ilk. If a trooper required discipling, the General would administer such corrective actions fairly and expeditiously. Jack-the-Knife disliked bureaucrats and absolutely did not suffer fools.

"The MACV LTC arrived 10 minutes late, smug as only an REMF turd can be. General Martell ripped the REMF bastard a new one, and the REMF-loser departed SOG scared shitless. General Martell threatened to send the REMF bastard on a SOG patrol into the A Shau, he told REMF LTC - patrol orders were being cut even as they spoke. Unless the PCS orders for Billy were rescinded within one hour, the MACV REMF needed to gear-up for Indian Country. Thirty minutes later, a very contrite REMF LTC MACV personnel-weenie confirmed the PCS orders for Master Sergeant Billy Johnson were cancelled."

Sergeants Jones and Matthews retired to the secure room on the second floor, each carrying two bottles of 33 beer. Matthews explained the situation,

"Wild-Man was in for the job. Billy lived in a Montagnard Rhade village southeast of the A Shau. The Rhade are one of the many Montagnard tribes. Most of the Yard tribes lived in the Central Highlands making this Rhade tribe an exception. Their location in the vicinity of the A Shau is under VC observation some of the time. The security situation for this tribe and Billy is always tenuous and dangerous".

Sergeants Jones and Matthews laid the maps on the table to orient themselves on approaches to visit the Rhade camp and the relative position of the Rhade camp to the Saigon signal-azimuth passing through the A Shau. The discussion shifted to the plan how Jones would visit Billy to coordinate a Yard recon patrol to support a later Peregrine 'walk-in-the-woods'. The 'visitors' to Billy's camp would have to approach the camp at night. Jones asked Matthews:

"When can we go?"

Matthews answered,

"I arranged for Air America for a parachute drop two days from now. We walk from the DZ to the Rhade camp. Billy and a security-team of Yards will meet us at the DZ."

One of the Peregrine Nungs had parachute training and would go along with the rest of the gang for the 'Wild-Man visit'. 'The rest' of the gang for this first visit to the Rhade camp would be LT Baumgartner, Master Sergeants Jones and Matthews.

The special ops folks are meticulous planners and want as much time to plan and rehearse as possible. They understood that at times you had to be ready to go on a 'do it now' basis when the mission required. SOG allowed the Peregrine team to use a SOG firing-range near Saigon and all the Peregrine team spent time on the range with various weapons.

This was a simple coordination mission with no hostile VC contact expected and the hope "Murphy" was off duty from his perfidious and pernicious law. Each 'visit team member' could be packed and ready in less than 30 minutes. Even so, there were crucial planning details to be completed. Jones and Matthews decided to leave from Bien Hoa Air Base, about 25 klicks northeast of Saigon since there would be better security from the constant prying eyes watching a Tan Son Nhut departure.

Air America, operated by CIA, was flexible, Matthews would finalize coordination for the C-47. There were communications frequencies, call signs, code words, rally points, initial action plans, and more to prepare. Jones wanted to coordinate A-1E Skyraider air support if the team was not blessed by a Murphy's Law exemption and got in trouble. They would need extraction helicopters for the return to base after the 'visit' but would use SOG helicopters for the extraction rather than Air America.

This planning and coordination visit with Billy and his Yards would be an excellent training mission for the future insertion of a Peregrine patrol into the A Shau - a lot to do, but war is a 24/7 business – and this was not the first rodeo for any of this team. Billy and his Yards would soon be tasked to conduct a recon mission into the jaws of Hell, the A Shau.

CHAPTER 14   BACK AT THE RANCH

Annie was frustrated. She could not contact 'her sailor' directly due to security protocols and they could not use some private personal code in official messages. She was not even sure what name Gary was using. As a result, she felt her daily prayers for 'her sailor' were so very important. On the professional side, she was concerned about the glacial speed in advancing the NSA contribution to the Peregrine project. All that was happening at this point was that the project was not moving forward as desired and as needed to support the team in Vietnam. NSA was collecting more information every day, which confirmed the previous information, but in the aggregate, the additional information gave little new in the way of insights or actionable targets.

Annie thought, 'when you hit a dead-end, turnaround and find a different way', she stopped and smiled, oh no, I am becoming one of the bureaucratic 'phrase monger' types. Putting that thought aside, she began to look for a 'different way'. What are the precise determinations from the geek technical analyses of the Saigon and A Shau messages? Are there technical fingerprints we missed? Why the strange choice of an obsolete KGB encryption system? What might CIA be holding back? A parochial behavior the Agency tended toward at times. Annie flashed back to the advice she had been given by 'Charles the Lech'.

"The evidence is always there; you just have to find it".

So, start at the beginning, back to the original NSA signal analyses.

She called the 'geek analysts' to set up a meeting to review the Peregrine signal tech-data results. The young tech-analyst, Jim Maxfield, who had worked with Annie since the beginning of Peregrine, was always glad to see her. Like many tech geeks, he had a bit of arrogance about his tech-skills, but he was pleasant to deal with on a personal basis.

NSA geeks were little different than geeks found in every advanced research lab or scientific institute. The geeks thrived, indeed lived for, technical challenges that flummox and stymie other less intellectually-gifted individuals. The NSA geeks represented some of the most brilliant in all of 'geekdom'. Geeks are often criticized for a lack of social graces and interpersonal skills, plus a rather non-conformance dress code. The critics misunderstand because geekdom is a different culture that abides with a separate dialect, strong friendships based on technical prowess, and an earned sense of technical arrogance. Simply put, geeks are tribal and have their own culture. It should be noted that most people were intimidated by the geeks' intellects.

James 'Jim' Maxfield, 27 years old, 5-feet 7-inches tall and thin, is the primary geek-contact for Annie. Jim wore his hair in a close crew-cut, dressed in flannel shirts and blue jeans, selected black leather motorcycle boots as footwear, though he did not ride motorcycles. He graduated from MIT at the age of 19 with dual degrees in mathematics and physics. Jim and the rest of the NSA geeks all loved Annie and would shyly turn their heads to hide smiles when she entered the room.

The tech analyst patiently reviewed what he had gleaned for the 'signal take' so far; consistencies in frequencies, message formats, the mystery of the obsolete encryption use by the 'bad guy' Saigon radio base, and a powerful KGB encryption system was used for signals sent out by the A Shau base to Moscow.

The initial results of decrypting some of the Saigon transmissions were promising. The information provided by the KGB code clerk defection allowed NSA to exploit a decryption of the archived messages using the 'old KGB encryption process'. Though a powerful additional tool for the tech-analysts, that decrypted information had taken analysts a lengthy time to produce a coherent set of message details. The tech-analyst announced, 'that is it' after they reviewed a large number of intercepted messages, mildly dejected, they agreed they were making no additional real progress. The current intercepts just add to what we know with no further insights. The continued decryption of messages with the old KGB cypher will certainly add more and likely lead to a breakthrough but it will take time. Annie knew the tech-analyst was outstanding in his work. She respected him and the tech-team and would not challenge his technical work. But she had an intelligence officer's intuition that the geeks and other analysts had not fully appreciated what was there in front of them.

Annie asked the tech geek if she could look at the actual messages as original encrypted text, the raw COMINT intercepts. The analysts pulled up a sequence of messages which appeared as a garble of the encryption within a repeating message format. Annie asked about a blurp, a short discontinuity, in the format. The analyst told her that was 'just static'.

She asked Jim if he had seen other instances of 'static'. The analyst shrugged and told her static was not that rare. Annie intuitively knew there was something there, now to determine what the 'something' was. As they scrolled through the Saigon radio transmitter messages, the 'evidence' hit them. There seemed to be a distinct pattern in the appearance of the 'static' when compared with static in message sent form Saigon to the A Shau site and time-related messages sent from the A Shau base. Annie tasked Jim to check their total 'take' of Saigon and A Shau messages for the appearance of 'static'; then provide that data to Annie so she could examine a possible correlation of a static-pattern related to ambush events on the ground in Vietnam.

Two days later, Annie returned, asking hypothetically, if this was not 'just static', what else might it be? This was the type question any tech geek loved, challenging and off-the-curve. Annie did not disclose she found a correlation between the 'static' events and ambush events in Vietnam.

Jim gave Annie a brief tutorial on disguising data using codes versus encryption. With a smile, he told her, the guys down in Research have been playing with an idea to hide information within a message, very cutting edge stuff. The technical term they are using is "Steganography", a technique that can hide code in plain sight, such as a blip in a message format or a pixel within the array forming an image. Annie and Jim smiled as they saw the answer. They Tech Geek literally jumped out of his chair to take the Saigon messages with 'static' anomalies down to the Research Geeks.

The next morning, Jim, tired but excited, called Annie,

"You have to come down here right now!"

Unshaven, red-rimmed eyes, but thoroughly pleased and excited, Jim told Annie that he and the Research Geeks had worked all night. They made a breakthrough around 0300 and spent the rest of the night/ morning verifying their discovery. The Russians lagged far behind the US in computer technology and many other advanced technology areas. Regardless, the Russians had been the first to put a man in space to give perspective on how the Russians approached technical challenges from a different angle.

Given the Russian relative weaknesses in advanced computer technologies, the Russians fell back on their historic strength for solutions, 'Russian mathematicians'. The 'static' in the enemy messages was a clever technique in which a message 'internal to the overall message' is highly compressed into a very short time frame, the result looked like a brief garble, or 'static' when the transmitted message with static is sent. The knowledgeable person receiving the message with embedded 'static' could extract the 'static' and decompress the 'static' to reveal the sender's 'internal message'.

The 'static' technique is relatively low-tech and very Russian and the Russian Steganography application was effective. A eureka moment, analysis of the Peregrine Saigon radio traffic was a NSA breakthrough in their analysis process for the "COMINT take" of all intercepts of Russian communications containing "static". For the Peregrine operation, the NSA discovery provided a new expanded perspective of the problem they faced. It was time for another urgent meeting with her boss, Dr. David Slade.

Dr. Slade cleared his meetings calendar to hear what Annie said was 'urgent'. After Dr. Slade heard what the Geeks in 'Research and Analysis' learned about the Soviet technique to hide data in-the-open in messages, he shook his head, thinking what else have we been missing? At the same time, he broke into a broad smile, this technical breakthrough for analyzing Soviet messages was due to the persevering efforts of a person he had started to think of as his protégé, Annie Hoffman. Dr. Slade recognized that the new insight into the Saigon radio-base comms meant an expansion of the NSA Peregrine mission. He needed to talk to the NSA Director and Bull – and needed to do so ASAP.

As Dr. Slade arranged a meeting with Lieutenant-General Blake and Major-General Wojcik, US Navy Lieutenant Gary Baumgartner was simultaneously drafting a message for Major-General Wojcik to be sent though the CIA comm system for security. His message marked 'Immediate' precedence, - a high priority used only for critical information. LT Baumgartner asked in cryptic terms if Major-General 'Bull' Wojcik would be visiting Saigon soon. If such a Saigon visit was not in the immediate future, Captain Williams, and Lieutenant Baumgartner should make a brief visit to the Pentagon. Please advise soonest. The game has changed and not for the better!

Major-General 'Bull' Wojcik responded to the message from LT Baumgartner with terse answer.

"We will meet in Hawaii in three days; advise of your travel plan, the NSA Project Manager will accompany me."

Baumgartner had a broad grin on his face reading the message from the General, Annie would be at the meeting in Hawaii. After confirming travel arrangements, LT Baumgartner sent an initial response to Major-General Wojcik;

"US Army Warrant Officer Carl Renner would accompany Baumgartner to the Hawaii meeting."

Within a few hours, an embarrassed US Navy Lieutenant amended his initial message to the General:

"Peregrine Saigon has a situation. Baumgartner and some friends need to take 'a little walk in the woods' and do it within the next two days. Could the General hold the meeting in Hawaii in ten days from now?"

Major-General Wojcik replied,

"See you in ten days"

"A Walk in the A Shau Valley Woods"

The A Shau Valley is a strategic and tactical nightmare for the South Vietnamese and US militaries. The valley runs roughly north and south, is about 25 miles long and frames part of the Vietnamese-Laos border. The valley is narrow with much of the bottom land covered with tall dense elephant grass. The bottom land is flanked by steep mountain ridges covered in densely forested jungle, ranging from single-canopy to triple canopy forests. While the topography is problematic in a tactical sense, the strategic problem is the root of the nightmare. The A Shau valley is integrated into the Ho Chi Minh Trail, which is the NVA and VC lifeline for supplies and replacement personnel from North Vietnam to the combat areas in South Vietnam. Thus, loss of the A Shau valley would be a severe threat to North Vietnam ambitions to conquer the South. The NVA understood this quintessential strategic threat to their objective of conquest and responded by sending some 20,000 NVA troops to be bivouacked in the A Shau valley area. Their mission is to dominate the A Shau area and secure the northern portion of the Ho Chi Minh Trail.

Putting the 'big-picture strategic issues' and 'little-picture tactical issues' aside – for the American GI grunt 'humping it' through the jungle on the ground, the A Shau was just another Vietnamese hellhole: strategic and tactical merged meaninglessly into just more misery to be endured by the GIs – trying to avoid being bitten by the deadly neurotoxin-venom cobras, kraits, or some unknown viper; trying not to be stung by masses of insects; suffering the large biting ants; the science-fiction appearance of giant-centipedes which had a bite that delivered incapacitating pain; not getting caught in the sharp hooks of the 'wait-a-minute' vines; the droning of flying-stinging insects; oppressive heat and humidity; cleverly disguised holes that had sharpened punji stakes, deadly wooden spears placed in the bottom of the hole, highly infectious points dipped in feces, waiting to impale a GI's foot; trip-wires hooked to explosives that would put you in a body bag; but the most deadly threat in the A Shau valley is the thousands of combat-hardened NVA troops who bivouacked and patrolled the Au Shau region.

The North Vietnamese made three serious communications security mistakes: first, they always used the same frequencies in the transmissions from Saigon; second and most important, but mysterious to NSA, they used an obsolete KGB encryption method (which was finally broken based on 'new' information after the defection of KGB code clerk). As Annie discovered, there was a distinct pattern tying the Saigon signals with the ambush events. While the continued NSA collection and analysis will provide increasingly accurate location information on the Saigon transmitter, the exact location of the A Shau comm hub will remain elusive. NSA signal collection and analysis for Operation Peregrine indicated that somewhere along a consistent azimuth, Saigon bad guys sent messages to an A Shau radio receiving site which then directed message traffic for the NVA to 'kill American Advisors' in ambush operations. While interesting, the information is operationally of limited value unless the exact location of the radio site was known. NSA could not pinpoint the A Shau radio location, NSA could only narrow the search to the azimuth with the high-probability the site would be on the east side of the mountains forming the A Shau valley. Without 'boots on the ground confirmation, the NVA A Shau radio site location was just an educated guess, the Peregrine team had to take a look – an up-close-and-personal look.

Annie and a couple other NSA analysts pondered the highly fortuitous timing of the KGB code clerk defection. Further muddying the analytic waters, when given a polygraph exam, the code clerk polygraph test produced an inconclusive result, neither an outright indication of deception nor validating truthful responses. Using the polygraph in a cross-culture environment was always problematic but the result added to a growing list of concerns. Was this one of those 'too good' 'smoke and mirrors' occurrences? If this timely 'intelligence gift' was just 'too good', it was 'too good' for a reason – what was that reason?

The venerable Air America C-47 cargo plane departed Ben Hoa Air Base one-hour after dusk to arrive at the drop zone in full darkness. Master Sergeant Billy Johnson had led a Montagnard reception team to the DZ area the evening before. Wild Man Johnson was a legend in the Special Forces community: 6-feet 4-inches tall at 210 pounds, Billy was lean and mean, taciturn, more comfortable living with indigenous tribes than in 'civilized' society. He was the epitome of the Special Forces trooper who was sent to organize locals to fight and gather intelligence for the US. Billy 'Wild Man' Johnson was truly fearless, but his fearlessness was tempered by detailed planning to mitigate the risks and the fact he cared deeply for 'his people'.

Sergeant Johnson brought 20 Montagnard fighters with him to the DZ. The Yards would ensure the DZ was secure for the drop, the VC often placed watchers at likely DZs and LZs. The VC watchers would fire warning shots if any enemy force dared to insert a team into the VC territory. The shots would be the signal for VC attack forces to close on the DZ or LZ to destroy the enemy insertion force.

If a VC watcher is present, the Yards would silently kill the watcher. If the DZ was clear of VC watchers, Johnson's team would place flashlight markers down the center of the DZ. If the pilot did not see the markers, the C-47 would abort the mission and divert back to Ben Hoa Air Base. In addition to the four-man Peregrine team, the C-47 carried three air-drop containers with supplies for the Yards and their families. The 20-man Yard contingent would porter the supplies from the DZ back to the village. The 250-pound containers were loaded with food, medicine, practical goods such as cooking pots, knives, and some candy treats for the village kids. Johnson had been recently resupplied with weapons and ammunition before this drop.

As the C-47 approached the DZ the aircrew could see the string of lights marking the DZ. Diving to an altitude of 800 feet, the aircraft lined-up for the drop. The Jumpmaster gave the signal – 'two-minutes before 'green light''. The drop sequence would be: two aircrew loadmasters would push the three containers out the door as fast as possible after 'Green Light'.

The Peregrine four-man stick of jumpers, LT Baumgartner, Master Sergeant Jones, Han Li (Peregrine Nung) and Master Sergeant Matthews (SOG) would immediately follow, having completed the jump prep sequence – 'get ready, standup, hook-up, equipment check, sound off, shuffle-to-the-door, stand in the door' ready to exit the aircraft after the third cargo container was pushed out the door.

"GREEN LIGHT- GO! – EXIT THE AIRCRAFT,"

Peregrine troopers jumped into the darkness and the majestic solitude during a brief descent to the ground.

Before all four of the Peregrine team had landed, 15 of the Yards were unpacking the cargo containers as the rest of the Yards stood security. The DZ was cleared of all evidence of a parachute insertion. Personal and cargo chutes were removed along with the cargo and cargo containers – the women in the Yard village prized the parachute cloth for many uses. As soon as the container loads were distributed as individual packs, the 25-men faded into the jungle and went to ground. They would silently wait until they were sure that no VC detected the drop and no VC were in pursuit. After moving into defensive positions, the team listened intensely for any sounds that did not belong in the normal cacophony of nighttime jungle noise.

After one-hour, Sergeant Johnson sent Yard scouts ahead of the main body and the procession traveled the trail safely to arrive at the Montagnard village the next evening. The tribe rejoiced at the return of the Rhade fighters and all had childlike glee as they examined the food and other gifts the Americans brought for the tribe.

The Montagnards are believed to have settled in the central highlands well before the arrival of the Vietnamese who made their residences in the lowlands and coasts of what would become known as Vietnam. The relationship between the Montagnard and the Vietnamese was generally hostile, starting from the initial contacts between the two peoples. The dark-skin Montagnard were discriminated against from the first contacts with the Vietnamese because of their darker skin-tone and their different culture. The fact was, the North Vietnamese and the South Vietnamese both hated all the Montagnard peoples and the Montagnards returned the hatred in-kind.

After the French were defeated and left Indochina, a Vietnamese civil war began between opposing factions in the North and South. US

180

Special Forces troops and US Army advisors to the ARVN. Special Forces troopers first made contact with the Montagnard in the late-1950s, and that contact expanded as the Special Forces began a program in the early 1960s to establish US outposts in remote areas of South Vietnam to combat the growing VC presence outside the urban population centers. The Special Forces found the Montagnards a compatible freedom-loving culture. These first contacts were a precursor to a close and lasting bond between the Yards and US Army Special Forces.

After arrival of the team and distribution of the presents, there was a celebration, lots of food and rice wine – and then more rice wine. The next morning, the Peregrine team, Wild-Man Johnson, and four Rhade fighters sat down to discuss the objectives for the upcoming Yard recon patrol into the A Shau. LT Baumgartner explained the problems of finding an enemy radio center located in the A Shau valley. Baumgartner laid out the map covered by a plastic overlay with a grease pencil line from Saigon through the A Shau valley. The radio camp was located somewhere in the A Shau along this azimuth line. Given the radio signal and antenna characteristic, the radio comm center would be located somewhere on the higher levels of the mountain crest on the east side of the A Shau valley.

The Yards indicated they knew this area intimately but, like most indigenous peoples, they did not read paper maps as westerners. Wild-Man pointed to the known local landmarks, swamps and clearings as marks on the map, which Yards used to register as the mental maps for the ground and jungle they knew very well. The Yards went into an animated side-discussion in the Montagnard language, which Johnson understood and spoke fluently. As the Yards discussed the situation, Wild-Man translated the conclusions the Yard fighters reached. First, they knew the area well, though they had not been in this particular area since the large numbers of NVA troops moved into the A Shau valley area. Second, the approaches to the A Shau from this area were what the NVA and Americans would call "impenetrable jungle". The NVA would think it was an unlikely approach to the expected location of the radio center. Third, and the Yards laughed during these comments by Wild-Man. He translated for the visitors,

"They are laughing at you for calling it "impenetrable jungle".

The Yards could do a 'look-see' recon patrol to determine if there was an NVA camp and radio site at the azimuth-crossing on the east crest of the mountain range. The Peregrine team shook hands with the laughing Yards, congratulating them in recognition of the Yards' superior jungle knowledge and tradecraft.

Billy and two Yards would covertly search the ridge line along the east side of the A Shau mountain in the next few days. The Peregrine team began preparations to return to the DZ for a SOG helicopter extraction. The Yard patrol objective was to find the antenna array that was necessary for the radio site to receive and transmit signals. The Peregrine visitors produced a set of photographs which showed the types of radio antennas likely to be in an array on the crest. As the Peregrine visitors geared-up for their hike back to the DZ for extraction, the villagers expressed thanks for the gifts, all the time smiling, laughing, patting the Peregrine team on their backs, and shaking their hands.

Five days later, Billy and the two Yard fighters, Duan Ho and Chu Zhu, returned from their covert patrol. The Peregrine compound radio crackled with a cryptic message from 'Wild-Man': "Gold Ring. What now?"

The Peregrine team finalized the planning for an in-depth recon by a combined Peregrine and Montagnard patrol. This patrol would be high-risk, deep in Indian Country. The A Shau valley, dominated by a large NVA presence, was one of the most hostile environments in Vietnam. The planning would be meticulous. The choices of the insertion LZ and the extraction LZ were discussed and discussed again. No matter how often they examined the locations for an emergency exfiltration LZ, the choices were bad or much worse. In the end only one emergency extraction LZ was viable, and this site was six miles from the recon target.

The A Shau recon team set the respective radio Call Signs as:

Blue 1: LT Baumgartner

Blue 2: US Army Captain Reginald Denning

Blue 3: US Army Warrant Officer Carl Renner

Shadow 1: A-1E two-ship air support flight leader

First Responder 1: Flight leader of the SOG extraction two-helicopter element

The indigenous members of the patrol were the Peregrine Nung, Han Li, and the two Montagnards, Duan Ho and Chu Zhu, who made the initial covert patrol. The indigenous members would not have radio call-signs.

In this recon operation the extraction could be from a 'hot LZ'. The team decided the SOG would provide the best solution for the extraction challenge and the rather routine insertion. A decision of critical importance remained, who would provide air support if needed. The team decided to request air support from the 1st Air Commando Group at Bien Hoa, specifically, the team would request two A-1E aircraft, each with maximum munitions loads designed to support this recon mission (snake and nap (high-drag bombs and napalm canisters), 2.5 inch rockets, and 20 mm cannons with high-explosive ammunition).

Specialized intelligence collection equipment for the mission included a 35 mm camera with high-speed film and two battery-powered stay-behind listening devices. Team observations and notes would complete the intelligence-gathering plan.

Captain Denning called his Nung driver for travel to Bien Hoa to close the 'detail loop' regarding the 1st Air Commando Group air support. The rest of the details for communications and other needs for the mission were nailed down in two days. The recon team drew extra ammo, grenades, and tear-gas crystals, the latter in case the NVA used dogs to track the team. The ingress route, egress route, and the emergency escape route were plotted on the maps the officers would carry. Communications frequencies and code words were put on small cards encased in plastic to avoid moisture damage. Officers would carry these classified cards which often were the difference between a team living or dying.

Planning completed with the mission launch date set. The team would meet the Yard guides at an LZ near the Rhade village with an on-ground time of 45 seconds for the helicopter pick-up of the two Yard guides, then fly to the A Shau insertion LZ. Plan A was to move through the "impenetrable jungle' to the eastern mountain ridge, patrol north along the ridge line to the location where the Yard patrol saw the antenna array. After photographing the array, checking for a supporting camp with the radio transmitter, and emplacing listening devices, the Peregrine patrol would covertly go back into the 'impenetrable jungle' for a secure trek back to the insertion LZ, which now would become the extraction LZ. Plan B was, if detected by the NVA, the patrol would run like hell north along the ridgeline trail to the emergency extraction LZ. Plan B did not sound good, spoken or on paper. The secondary extraction site was six miles (ten kilometers) east along the ridge-line trail. However, that LZ was the closest LZ which gave the two extraction-helicopters room to land.

SOG launched two UH-1 Slicks on time from Bien Hoa Air Base taking a flight direction which would indicate a destination in the opposite direction from the first insertion LZ. VC agents outside the base constantly monitored the air traffic in and out of the base. Once out of sight and hearing, the Slicks turned onto new flight vectors to the interim LZ to pick-up the Yards, pick-up was completed in 21-seconds and the Slicks flew to the insertion LZ. During insertion, part of the security process would be to make three false insertions to confuse any enemy in the area. To mask the actual insertion, the door gunners were ordered not to employ the standard suppression fire to prepare the LZ. The door gunners were only to fire in response to hostile fire. Insertion was done at dusk without a hostile reception and the team moved quickly off the LZ into the surrounding jungle where they set up a defensive position to listen for indications the insertion had been detected.

After an hour, determining no enemy were in the immediate area, the team moved deeper into the jungle for the rest of the night. Once in-place, a defensive position was established with three of the team staying awake to be spelled two hours later, repeating the process until full daylight. At daylight, the team ate a cold breakfast and sanitized the site to leave no signs the patrol had been there.

The Yard guides led the patrol into the 'impenetrable jungle' area for the approach to the A Shau valley target, following the same path as the Yard 'look see' recon patrol had done a few days before. Though experienced in jungle warfare, the Americans found the 'impenetrable jungle' to be, well, 'impenetrable jungle'. No trails, lush foliage, the jungle was triple canopy in that area, plenty of insects. The Yard jungle-craft seemed miraculous to the Americans. The Yards found animal trails that were not obvious to western eyes, even after the Yards pointed at the obscure trails. The jungle animal trails tended to skirt the worst of the 'wait-a-minute' vines and avoid the trees and bushes that had poisonous sap. The Americans and the Nung followed exactly in the steps of the Yard guide. The second Yard brought up the rear to erase any sign they might left which could betray the patrol's passage. The guide and the rear guard would change positions every 30 minutes to ensure the lead-guide would be fresh and alert. At the end of the day, the Yards, who both spoke some English, pointed at what passed for a clearing in this tangled jungle foliage. The Yard guide told the team to use hammocks to stay off the ground because of poisonous snakes and biting insects. The security roster for the night was set, all ate a cold meal, and settled in for the night with the raucous nighttime jungle-noises playing in the background.

The next day was the same, walking in the Yard guide footprints and staying alert. That night was a repeat of the previous night. As much as possible, they team used hand signals for communication to maintain silence. That evening, over their cold meal, Duan Ho, the senior Yard guide, told LT Baumgartner, they would leave about 0400 tomorrow to reach the place where the Yards had seen the antennas. The jungle would thin as they approached the crest of the ridge. Four members of the patrol would take a defensive position near the antennas while Blue 1 and Blue 3 took a closer look. All hands reviewed Plan A and Plan B, along with silent prayers they would not need Plan B: Plan A was to have a look-around, take some pictures, plant the listening devices, and sneak off back into the jungle to the exfiltration LZ; Plan B was, if discovered, they would blast away weapons on full-automatic and run like hell to the exfiltration LZ. Just in case they had to go to Plan B, they would stack rucksacks at the ridge defensive position, to be abandoned if they had to run for their lives. In the event of a Plan B, the team would only carry weapons, ammo, first aid packs, and water in a race-for-life to the extraction LZ, about six miles from the target.

Moving more slowly as the jungle thinned and the first glimmer of sunrise showed in the east, they arrived at the spot that Duan Ho had suggested for the defensive position. Blue 1 nodded his head observing this was the optimal location, even though they had a long crawl to reach the antennas. The rucksacks were stacked, the patrol members moved into field-of-fire positions to cover the approach by Blue 1 and Blue 3. Faces streaked in green and black camouflage paint, Blue 1 and Blue 3 began a low crawl to the antenna array. Reaching the antenna array without incident as first light was illuminating the hillcrest, Blue 3 took several pictures of the antenna array using the fast 400 ASA film for the early morning low-light conditions. Though barely audible, Blue 1 and Blue 3 both tensed each time the camera film was advanced with a slight click.

Finding antenna cables leading downhill, Blue 1 hand-signaled they would follow the cables. The low crawl was more difficult now as the cable path was across an area of loose rocks, after following the cables for about 50 meters, the terrain dipped sharply.

At this distance, Blue 1 could not see the cables over the edge of the change of sharp incline. As Blue 1 and Blue 3 crawled further over the loose rocks to the edge, they could see a hooch that appeared to be the cable termination point and the likely communications center. Taking a couple minutes to mark his map and make notes, Blue 1 hand-signaled they would check-out the hooch/comm shack. Blue 3 rolled his eyes and looked for a path to quietly crawl down the sharp incline.

Blue 1 and Blue 3 reached the back side of the hooch without incident; both of them were soaked with sweat and experiencing a tsunami flow of adrenalin. Blue 1 gave a hand-signal for Blue 3 to emplace both recording devices along the back of the hooch.

While Blue 3 removed the devices from their carrying pack and concealed the voice-activated recorders against the back wall of the hooch, Blue 1 peeked around the corner of the hooch. Blue 1 could see part of a camp, 30 meters distance further down the slope, but what really got his interest was a Caucasian walking up the trail from the camp toward the comm hooch. Great intel, but really bad timing and bad positioning for Blue 1 and Blue 3. Blue 1 gave the danger signal to Blue 3 and pulled back from the hooch corner. Blue 3 had just completed hiding and activating the battery-powered listening devices. The listening devices could be interrogated by a passing-aircraft and would respond with a silent radio burst of conversations surreptitiously recorded from the hooch.

Blue 1 decided to wait until the 'Caucasian' went inside the hooch, intending, once the occupants settled down in the hooch Blue 1 and Blue 3 would begin what they hoped would be a clandestine retreat up the rocky slope. Both checked their weapons were on full automatic fire, safety off. They leaned against the hooch back wall to listen when the 'Caucasian' entered the comm center. Blue 1 thought he had observed a rare American GI defector until Blue 1 and Blue 3 heard two voices – speaking Russian. Blue 1 raised his eyebrows and signaled to start the crawl back up the steep incline.

Just as Blue 1 and Blue 3 reached the top edge of the steep incline, they heard a shout in Vietnamese – a challenge to stop. Looking back they saw an NVA soldier, he had been walking toward the latrine without his weapon. All three of them, Blue 1, Blue 3, and a frightened NVA, soldier in his underwear, begin to run in opposite directions as fast as they could. The NVA soldier shouted warnings. Blue 1 and Blue 3 sprinted to the defensive position, repeatedly shouting the password to avoid being shot by their comrades. Now the team faced the long-distance run to the emergency extraction LZ, six miles down the ridge-line trail.

Blue 1, Blue 3, and the rest of the patrol in the ridge defensive position heard the initial AK-47 shots – they all knew what that meant. The shots were a warning to all NVA in the area to take up arms and pursue. To make things worse for the patrol, the numerous NVA bivouacked in the A Shau were dispersed in small camps to avoid detection by American reconnaissance aircraft. The dispersion of the small camps increased the threat to the patrol – instead of the boo-coo NVA coming from a single direction, behind them, boo coo enemy would be coming at the patrol from several directions at the same time. Confirming the bleak conclusion that they were in deep shit, the patrol heard answering NVA shots all around, as NVA pursuers grabbed their weapons and joined the hunt to kill or capture six men.

Blue 1 quickly assessed the patrol chances of survival as 'slim and none'. The patrol escape route was effectively surrounded by several NVA camps loaded with troops eager to kill them. The patrol had to avoid being pinned down by a sustained fire fight which would slow them down as they ran for their lives in the heat and humidity - six miles to the Plan B extraction LZ. Two things were necessary for patrol survival: first, run like hell to stay ahead of the pursuing NVA; second, have the A-1E air support bring down hell on the pursuing NVA. Blue-1 estimated that the patrol could reach the LZ in about 55 minutes on a sustained full-out run.

Blue 1 yelled for Duan Ho to take the lead and get them to the extraction LZ 'didi mau' – use the trail and avoid the jungle cover, as speed was their best weapon to survive. The rucksacks were booby trapped before being abandoned. Blue 1 grabbed two claymore mines to take with him. The whole team did the 'didi mau', slang Vietnamese for "go quickly", racing along the mountain crest trail. Blue 1 ordered Blue 2 and Blue 3 to bring up the rear while Blue 1 followed Dong Ho with the rest of the team in between lead and the rear guard.

As the patrol literally ran for their lives; Blue 1 yelled into his handset radio as he gasped for breath. He was calling for the two A-1E aircraft, flying an orbit out of sight and hearing to do their air support thing to take-out the closing NVA horde – and do it now!

"Shadow 1 this is Blue 1; Shadow 1 this is Blue 1: we are in deep shit – bad guys after us – we are running north along the mountain crest trail toward the emergency extraction LZ. Do you copy?"

"Blue 1 this Shadow 1: copy, we are five minutes out. Need to see smoke to identify you."

"Shadow 1 this is Blue 1: will pop white smoke when you are in-close – do not want to advertise our current position on the trail. This will be a very hot LZ extraction."

"Blue 1 this is Shadow 1: the extraction Slicks are about 35 minutes out from the LZ."

"Blue 1 this Shadow 1: Will advise extraction Slicks, 'hot LZ!'. Shadow 1 and Shadow 2 are carrying the weapon loads per the plan. Save your breath for now – the cavalry is on the way."

The initial sprint had turned into a fast-paced run with no enemy fire directed at the patrol, yet, but the NVA signal shots were firing all around them, increasingly closer to the trail. Enemy contact was certain in the next few moments.

Blue 2 heard AK-47 shots not far behind them – these signal shots sounded like NVA running on the same mountain crest trail. Blue 2 heard dogs barking, he stopped briefly to scatter some tear-gas crystals across the trail – once the dogs sniffed the crystals, the dogs would be useless for days.

Blue 2 resumed the race-for-life understanding the NVA knew the patrol was on a narrow path running to the north – the NVA officers were shouting encouragement to the pursuing troops – faster, we will kill the enemies now. By now, both the fleeing patrol and the pursing NVA had settled into a steady fast run to sustain the long-distance game. The patrol knew, to have a chance to escape, the patrol had to slow the NVA pursuing from behind. The next immediate and greatest threats would be from NVA troops rallying from the small camps, trying to cutoff the patrol.

Baumgartner stopped to tell Blue 2 and Blue 3 to keep going. He would follow as soon as he set out a claymore mine. Quickly attaching a trip wire to a bush, Blue 1 armed the claymore and rejoined the patrol for the race to the Plan B LZ. The NVA troops running down the crest trail were totally fixated on the chase and did not detect the trip wire. 700 steel balls blasting from the claymore shredded half of that NVA platoon. The Peregrine patrol could hear the claymore blast and the immediate screams of the NVA dying and wounded. That would delay the pursuit from the west only momentarily, these NVA troops were combat veterans, hardened in many battles. Their renewed chase would be even more motivated by the deaths of their comrades.

Knowing the first claymore blast and the resultant NVA casualties would inflame the survivors to greater exertions to kill the patrol, Blue 1 set the second claymore about one hundred yards further down the trail. The crazed NVA survivors raced with reckless abandon until an NVA soldier hit the second trip wire triggering another devasting blast and further casualties. A surviving NVA officer intervened to order the chase forward but to exercise caution for more tripwires. This would buy the patrol a few more seconds in their race to survive. All now depended on the arrival of the A-1E cavalry.

Blue 1 raced back into his position behind Dung Ho. Blue 2 and Blue 3 resumed their roles as rear guard. The sense of danger that combat veterans develop electrified Blue 2, he sensed and then saw an NVA trooper emerging from the jungle on the left flank – and then two more – all three were aiming their AK-47s at Blue 3. Before the enemy could open fire, Blue 2 delivered a torrent of fire, taking down two of the NVA – as the third enemy tried to shift fire at Blue 2, Blue 2 killed him.

Simultaneously, two more NVA troops had emerged from the jungle, this time on the right flank. Blue 2 and Blue 3 whirled to engage the new threats. One of the NVA troopers opened fire with his AK-47 on full-automatic – his aim was bad. The bullets were close but no hits and Blue 2 took out the erratic-aim shooter with a three-round burst. The second NVA shooter took better aim at Blue 3 and fired a three round burst. One shot hit Blue 3 in the elbow spinning Warrant Officer Renner around and down. Blue 2 killed the NVA gunman before he could unleash a second burst.

As Blue 2 and Blue 3 fought a desperate firefight, with Blue 3 now down, the rest of the patrol reversed direction and raced back to help the outnumbered rear-guard. As the patrol 'meager reinforcements' arrived and began to lay down cover fire, Blue 1 assessed the situation and issued orders:

Blue 1 yelling to Han Li, "Blue 3 is hit, put a tourniquet on his upper arm".

The two Rhade fighters took up covering-fire positions on either side of the trail.

Blue 1 saw Blue 2 fall as he was hit by at least two rounds of AK-47 fire, two more NVA soldiers had emerged from the jungle to assault the patrol rear guard. The Yards took out both of the NVA before these enemy could unleash more rounds on the patrol.

Blue 1 ran to Blue 2's side, US Army Captain Reginald Denning was dying; Captain Denning was trying to speak, even as a bloody froth formed at the corners of his mouth. LT Gary Baumgartner leaned down to hear Blue 2 utter his last words, which Denning spoke in German, "Ich bleibe hier, auf Wiedersehen, meine Kameraden" – "I am staying here, goodbye my comrades". Captain Reginald Denning summoned the last of his strength to salute Gary Baumgartner. Baumgartner saluted back and held Denning's hand as the light-of-life left his friend's eyes, tears formed in Gary's eyes knowing his brother-warrior had fallen.

The team members could hear more NVA troops running through the jungle seeking to cutoff them off and kill every man in the patrol. Blue 1 ordered the Rhade fighters to take point and run down the trail to the LZ. Han Li took the Blue 3's unwounded arm and helped him stand to resume the race-for-life to the extraction LZ. Blue 3, supported by Han Li, was able to run at a fast jog. Blood continued to seep from his shattered elbow despite the tourniquet. His partially severed arm, hung loosely from the elbow down, attached only by a few strands of skin

Blue 1 pulled out his radio; speaking into the radio as he ran down the trail:

"Shadow 1 this is Blue 1: we have two men down – lots of bad guys in hot pursuit"

"Blue 1 this is Shadow 1: We are thirty seconds out – what do you need?

"Shadow 1, give us 'snake and nape' on both sides of the trail, I am marking the initial aim point now with Wille Pete – (white phosphorus grenade generating a dense cloud of white smoke along with deadly particles of burning phosphorous) – hit the bastards in a southward pass – we are running north"

"Blue 1 this is Shadow 1: I see you on the trial – GET SMALL!"

Just before the two A-1E aircraft passed over the patrol, engines roaring, Blue 1 yelled to the patrol – "GET SMALL!" The patrol members hit the ground anticipating the air strike on the pursuing NVA would be 'danger close'. Paralleling the trail on either side, Shadow 1 and Shadow 2 began the air strike, starting at the white phosphorus smoke marker. The first weapons on target were two 250-pound Mk 81 bombs 'the snake' hitting the NVA running along the sides of the trail, then the 'nape', 500-lb. M-47 napalm canisters followed. The bomb blasts generated a concussion wave that swept over the patrol as they hugged the ground. Blue 1 looked up as the concussion wave passed and saw a wonderous act of courage and devotion – Han Li used his body to cover the wounded Warrant Officer Renner to protect him from further injury.

The patrol heard the fearsome woosh of the napalm igniting and smelled the fiery death spreading over the pursuing NVA who received a 2,000 degree payback for the life of Blue 2. The patrol was up and running again.

Blue 1 estimated the patrol was about one-half mile from the LZ. Every patrol member felt as if his lungs were on fire. Parched throats ached with each raspy breath, the collective patrol was sure that their legs had turned into stone and became sources of pain as they forced themselves forward agonizing step by step, driven to survive despite personal pain and being slowed by Blue 3. At that moment, Blue 3 and Han Li stumbled and fell, landing on Blue 3's wounded arm. Blue 3 did not cry out or attempt to get up.

Blue 1 ran to his fallen comrade and gently turned Blue 3 on his back. Carl Renner was going into shock. His pupils were enlarged, breathing rapid but shallow, skin tone ashen. In addition, Carl was severely dehydrated. Carl was in critical condition requiring professional medical aid. If the patrol did not move now and fast, they all would all die on a remote mountain trail in the A Shau Valley, Vietnam. Blue 1 slung his Thompson submachine gun over his chest and told Han Li to help get Carl on his feet. Once they had a semi-conscious Carl standing, Blue 1 bent down, as Han Li assisted, to place Carl Renner across Blue 1's shoulders for a fireman's carry.

Blue 1 contacted Shadow 1 as he ran behind the rest of the patrol with Carl across his shoulders:

"Shadow 1 this is Blue 1: we are in a world of hurt. We need you to rain 'all hell' on both sides of the trail. Start at the LZ, fly south - give them 20 mm and everything else you have. I am popping willie pete to mark our position. Estimate we are about a quarter-mile from the LZ."

191

"Blue 1 this is Shadow 1: We see the white smoke, are making the run now to kill some bad guys in your neighborhood. GET SMALL"

Blue 1 yelled – "GET SMALL – Help is incoming".

The patrol survivors hit the ground, temporarily deafened by a rising decibel level as the two A-1E aircraft, 2800 horsepower engines at full power, roared by, four 20 mm canons delivering high explosive death to NVA on either side of the trail, snake and nape followed the cannon fire along with 2.5 inch rockets, this torrent of weapons was followed by cries of the NVA dying and wounded.

"Shadow 1 this is Blue 1: you did good buddy, thanks – we are about one minute out from the LZ – what is status of the exfil choppers?"

"Blue 1 this is Shadow 1: lots of the bad guys will not show up for NVA evening chow – Exfil choppers are on station waiting for a hot exfil"

"Shadow 1, this is Blue 1: – prep the LZ with rockets and 20 mike-mike"

"Shadow 1 to Blue 1: Roger on the LZ prep - call if you want more of our services there – we are off to make the LZ safe for our side".

"Shadow 1 this is Blue 1: we will pop yellow smoke at the LZ – repeat, Yellow Smoke – tell the chopper door-gunners not to fire into the yellow smoke."

The two A-1E aircraft delivered a devastating curtain of rockets and 20 mm cannon fire to clear a border around the LZ as protection from any enemy who might lay in wait.

Blue 1 ordered Han Li to pop yellow smoke as they entered the LZ. The four members of the patrol still on their feet were staggering, their vision beginning to blur from exhaustion and dehydration. Blue 3 was in critical condition as he was bumped along, carried by Blue 1.

Shadow 1 and Shadow 2 moved into a standby orbit southwest of the LZ. The A-1E pilots saw yellow smoke on the west side of the LZ and gave fist-pumps in each cockpit.

"First Responder 1 this is Blue 1: we have popped yellow smoke - west side of the LZ, do not fire into the yellow smoke. Standing by for exfil – have one WIA".

"Blue 1, this is First Responder 1: you call we haul – will be on the LZ in ten-seconds; door gunners will not fire on Yellow Smoke"

The two SOG slicks flared and touched down, door gunners hosing-down the LZ borders with M-60 machine gun fire, excluding the area of yellow smoke. The patrol still on their feet ran out from the yellow smoke cloud to board a rescue chopper and depart a very hot LZ. The on-board medic and one of the door gunners pulled each member of the patrol into the chopper, each patrol member was 'running on empty' and was having trouble climbing onto the helicopter deck. As soon as the patrol was on-board, both choppers lifted-off using full power, prayers, and ferocious M-60 machine gun fire by the door gunners to shield the helicopters from enemy ground fire.

The on-board medic gave Blue 3 morphine and applied a new tourniquet. The door gunners gave the A Shau valley landscape one final sustained burst of fire and turned to look at the exhausted, sweat-soaked, filthy-clothed passengers laying on their helicopter deck. The patrol survivors had their eyes closed. After a brief moment, the door gunners produced four canteens of water and gave the canteens to the patrol members, along with reassuring pats on the patrol members' shoulders.

The extraction flight route was to Danang Air Base as the closest American medical care facility, a small but sophisticated hospital associated with the low-profile 1962 deployment of US Special Operations aircraft units to Danang. The medic started a saline drip and began giving Blue 3 plasma, Warrant Officer Carl Renner, had lost a lot of blood on the run down the trail. He would lose his left arm below the elbow, if he lived.

An ambulance was waiting on the ramp to move Warrant Officer Renner for emergency surgery. The exhausted patrol went directly to the Air America ramp area to catch a C-47 back to Bien Hoa. The flight back to Saigon was mix of emotions for Gary Baumgartner: he was thankful he survived the walk in Indian Country; was thankful that all but one of the patrol had survived; and satisfied they had completed the mission collecting significant intelligence information. Nonetheless, Gary was emotionally distraught that he did not bring Captain Denning's body back to the Peregrine team. Gary thought of the final handshake with Denning – and, though dying, Denning was calm and resolute – the true warrior. Baumgartner knew he had made the correct decision. Had they tried to

193

carry Denning's body the final miles, there would have been six bodies on the trail rather than one. Seeking closure, Gary nodded his head, thinking quietly to himself, *Reginald Denning was my friend and my comrade.*

The A Shau Valley 'walk in the woods' debrief

The Peregrine team gathered in the compound conference room, but the usual banter and irreverence was not there. Each team member was contemplative and solemn.

US Navy Lieutenant Gary Baumgartner spoke in restrained voice:

"Before I start the brief, I want to give tribute to our friend and teammate, Erik von Hausfeldt. We knew our quiet warrior friend as US Army Captain Reginald Denning, a veteran of US Army Special Forces and the French Foreign Legion. The Legion knew him as Foreign Legion recruit, Reginald Denning. Captain Williams and I learned his true name as we are doing the usual 'disposition of personal effects' drill."

"Most of us had heard the rumors, we did not think that Reginald Denning was his true name. Today, when we opened Reggie's footlocker to inventory his possessions, we found a series of surprises."

"A small blue velvet box was hidden under the his civilian clothes. Opening the box, we found a "Knights Cross with Oak Leaves and Swords" presented to Waffen SS Captain Erik von Hausfeldt for leadership and courage in combat, leading German forces to rescue a Wehrmacht company trapped behind Russian lines and about to be overrun by the Russian forces. The "Knights Cross with Oak Leaves and Swords" is comparable to our Congressional Medal of Honor. There was a certificate with the Knight's Cross giving more details of the rescue action by Erik. Captain Williams and I already knew Erik was a damn fine soldier, an outstanding soldier, while this was amazing, there was more."

"Continuing to sort through Erik's effects, we found a red velvet box similar in size to the blue velvet box. When we opened the red box, the contents were almost beyond belief, given the German military decoration we had just seen. The red velvet box contained "The Legion of Honour" which is the highest French order of merit for military bravery. The award was made to French Foreign Legion Captain Reginald Denning for utmost bravery, leading his French Foreign Legion Paratroop company operating behind enemy lines in Indochina."

194

"We are privileged to have known a remarkable man, probably the only guy in the world to be awarded such prestigious decorations from two different countries, Erik fought in hellacious battles in three different armies on three continents and fought these engagements under different names, always with great courage and honor"

"Erik, your Peregrine comrades toast you – in whatever Valhalla you are in now – we salute you - our friend and brother"

Standing at attention, the team gave a roaring HOOYAH and saluted before they emptied their glasses."

As to the rest of the story,

"The A Shau Operation debrief has three parts":

"Part 1: I hope to hell we never have to go back there."

"Part 2: Billy Johnson's Yards were amazing. Their jungle knowledge and jungle tradecraft are without peer. The Yards are brave and loyal. They stood tough in the fire-fights we had along that damned mountain trial. Our guy, Han Li, is one of the most loyal and bravest fighters you will find anywhere. We need to give Han Li's family a reward for his courage on the A Shau op.

"The intel take was significant. The pictures of the antenna array will help the NSA nerds refine their technical conclusions. Carl planted the listening devices which could produce some industrial-strength intelligence information. SOG is going to do a flyby tomorrow to take a shot at interrogating the devices. And we determined there are Russians on site, apparently in-charge of the radio communications site."

Murmurs circulated the room after the 'Russians' comment.

"Part 3: Warrant Officer Carl Renner is stuck in an Army hospital in Danang, Carl will lose his left arm from the elbow down. Carl is chomping at the bit to rejoin the team and we need him back here. The bastards at the Danang hospital are going to medevac Carl to an Army hospital in Japan. Who is up for a rescue mission to spirit Carl out of the Danang hospital? We will bring him home to the compound where Doc can take care of him and we will put Carl back to work helping with intel analysis."

The team jumped out of their chairs as one, shouting hoo-yah – every man then yelled,

"I'm in! When do we go?"

"Everybody get another beer. We don't have much time - Carl is likely to be on a Medivac airplane soon."

Boys Will Be Boys

The 'rescue Carl' planning was done in just three beers. It was going to cost the team several cases of liquor but that was no problem. Of course, there was the minor issue of a possible court martial. The plan was to run a covert operation to break Carl out of the hospital for a clandestine transit back to the Peregrine compound, all the while keeping Carl under wraps while they figure out how to explain all this to Major-General Wojcik. – The consensus was, resort to the ever-useful concept - 'it is better to ask forgiveness than ask permission'. The team was ready to launch on the rescue/kidnap mission.

The kidnap-team traveled to Danang in a borrowed SOG aircraft. A SOG contact in Danang met the team and supplied them with a pilfered ambulance and surgical scrubs. Armed with forged orders, dressed in scrubs, the 'medical' team would penetrate the hospital, place Carl on a stretcher, telling anyone who asked that Carl was going for a special consultation and would be back in about 2 days for transfer to the Army hospital in Japan. The kidnap team would put Carl in the ambulance along with the rest of the Peregrine pirates, and race to the air base to get on an Air America plane, using Air America would avoid any US military procedures at the Danang air base.

The kidnap operation in Danang went exactly as planned – hell, the Peregrine guys did this sort of thing for a living.

The ambulance pulled up to the ER entrance and three individuals jumped out. One individual was dressed in sharply pressed Army fatigues with the rank of major on one collar and the Medical Corps insignia on the other collar. The name tag on his fatigues was Doctor Jeremy Ellison the kidnap operation cover name for Master Sergeant Karl 'Doc' von Eisenberg. The other two individuals exiting the ambulance, carrying a stretcher and a small knapsack, were large rough looking men in hospital scrubs. Sergeants Jones and Podowski were intimidating to the point of discouraging any questions from hospital staff bystanders.

Doctor Jeremy Ellison carried a folder with all the proper orders and releases. As Doctor Ellison walked into the 'patients ward', he saw an attractive young nurse. Her name tag identified her as First Lieutenant Worthy. Doctor Ellison, with a broad smile, immediately engaged Nurse Worthy congratulating her on the fine facility here in Danang. Before Nurse Worthy could do more than thank the 'doctor', Ellison told her he was there to transport patient Renner to a facility in Saigon to evaluate a prosthetics procedure for use in a combat zone. After asking Nurse Worthy her first name, he told nurse Elizabeth Worthy they were on a short fuse due to an aircraft waiting to depart for Saigon. Doctor Ellison presented Elizabeth with the required orders and releases from the folder. She was overwhelmed by speed of this interaction and unsure what she should do.

Seeing her anxiety, Doctor Ellison took her arm and guided her aside as the burly attendants in ill-fitting scrubs began to place Carl Renner on the stretcher. Carl suppressed a knowing grin, immediately realizing what was happening. Doctor Ellison gently held Nurse 'Elizabeth's arm in what was more of an embrace than a restraint. The doctor leaned over to whisper, "I expect to be back in Danang soon, could we have dinner then?" The now totally flustered Nurse Worthy smiled responding in a whisper, "I would like that". Doctor Ellison wrote her phone number on the back of the now empty folder, leaving Elizabeth with a handful of papers. Shifting to an authoritative voice, Doctor Ellison asked one of the stretcher bearers, for the small knapsack. The knapsack clinked as the stretcher-bearer handed it to the doctor.

As the handsome doctor turned back to Elizabeth, the ambulance driver entered the ward to gather up Carl's personal gear and carry the now unhooked IV stand to the ambulance, joining the stretcher bearers procession. Doctor Ellison handed the knapsack to Nurse Worthy who started to take it with one-hand. The knapsack was heavy and unwieldy, Elizabeth used both hands to hold the knapsack and not drop the official papers. Physically immobilized for the moment and mentally distracted, Elizabeth gave Doctor Ellison a 'promising smile'. The good doctor smiled back, very suggestively, telling her he hoped to see her soon. He turned and followed his colleagues to the ambulance.

Nurse Worthy walked over to an empty bed and set the heavy knapsack on the bed with gentle clink. Opening the mystery bag, Elizabeth discovered three bottles inside: a bottle of VSOP Remy Martin cognac, a bottle of, Stolichnaya Vodka, the highly prized vodka rarely found in the West, and a bottle of single malt Glenfiddich Scotch whiskey. Smiling a 'sort of innocent' smile, Elizabeth fantasized about a future meeting with the handsome Doctor Ellison – totally unaware she had become an accomplice to "the abduction of Carl".

After reconnecting the IV, Master Sergeant "Doc" von Eisenberg examined Carl on the flight back to Saigon pronouncing him ready for duty. The "boys" were all back in the compound before dark. Cases of liquor delivered: one case to the SOG guy in Danang, one case to the Air America crew, and three cases to co-conspirators at SOG headquarters.

As to immediate medical treatment, Doc prescribed,

"Give Carl a beer and send him to bed".

Captain Williams congratulated the kidnap team and said,

"Now we wait to see if the shit hits the fan".

The team had one more card to play to bring closure to the 'Kidnap Carl' caper. A forged medical-movement order was prepared and sent to the Danang Hospital. The order authorized the transfer of US Army Warrant Officer Carl Renner, immediately, to Special Medical Facility #4 in Saigon. Confirmation of arrival attached.

Williams and Baumgartner smiled - Thank you, Clausewitz for the 'fog of war' – plus the predictable bureaucrat's response: order received, order filed, case closed. No one ever inquired officially about 'where is' US Army Warrant Officer Carl Renner.

Well, there was this one comment later by Major-General Bull Wojcik.

CHAPTER 15   THE CHOLON SAFE HOUSE

One fear tormented Kie^ while she was in Paris and continued to haunt her in Saigon. There was ambiguity as who would be her operations officer in Saigon. Originally, it seemed certain it would be Sasha, but she overheard comments before she left Moscow for Paris suggesting that Sasha would have other duties. The thought that she might not see Sasha in Saigon weighed heavily on her.

The initial excitement to meet her operations officer at the Cholon safe house quickly dissipated, followed by an overwhelming anxiety. What if someone had discovered the forbidden romance between two KGB officers? What if Sasha had fallen afoul of a back-stabbing KGB enemy? What if Sasha is assigned to 'other duties'? Kie^ had suffered so much in her life, was her happiness with Sasha to be taken from her as well?

Regardless of her apprehension, Kie^'s personal discipline motivated her to prepare for the meeting with whomever the case officer may be. She reviewed her progress in Saigon. She had solidified her legend with contacts at the Cercle Sportif, attended high-society parties, and backstopped the reason she was in Saigon as searching for her parents. She had developed two informants, her driver and the hotel concierge, who provide her a constant flow of rumors about the political situations as seen from the viewpoints of the people on the street. The one thing missing was knowing the identity of her Saigon controller. She dreamed and wanted that mystery operations officer question to be resolved – she needed Sasha to be her controller and operations officer – she just needed Sasha.

Using solid tradecraft, she had established surveillance detection routes (SDR) to detect and lose any surveillance when she approached the safe house. The SDR routes were set up to expose a foot surveillance, vehicle surveillance, or combination thereof. She developed two separate routes for the safe house. Though there was little reason she would be under surveillance at this point, SDR routes were professional tradecraft and provided security for the future.

She had a restless night before the scheduled safe house contact. Her last few weeks involved a 'build-your-legend' mode with swimming at the Cercle Sportif, having the men at the pool lust as she walked by in her black bikini or the orange bikini, having scrumptious lunches at the Cercle Sportif, taking tennis lessons at the Cercle Sportif, in the evenings she would dine in an upscale restaurant or go to a society party - and now, she was swimming laps to avoid gaining weight.

Kie^ was very discriminating in accepting invitations to posh parties and dinners with the Saigon elite. She wanted to establish an image of a knowledgeable individual who could converse on many subjects at a dinner party or in any serious discussion. Kie^ reinforced the part of her legend as a wealthy sophisticated young woman by eschewing any behaviors that could make her appear like a coquette. She assiduously avoided any actions that would label her as a 'party girl'. While her natural beauty and erotic sexuality were potent assets, these traits often caused an inconvenience as she was constantly approached by men and a few women with proposals which were subtly suggestive to blatantly rude, and, on occasion, pornographic propositions. None of this fazed Kie^, given her training and field work as a KGB 'Swallow'. She had a knack to reject or defer those men or women seeking sex and do so in a way which was not demeaning or insulting to the petitioners. In the same way, She developed a pleasant style to accept or decline invitations to various events of declared-importance by the rich and powerful in Saigon. As a result of her exclusiveness to accept but a few of the many invitations, she was sought after as a 'social prize' to attend the elitist soirees.

While cultivating the image of a convivial but serious person, Kie^ stayed true to the Cercle Sportif pool culture where attractive female members and the eye-candy' guest members displayed alluring figures in their skimpy bikinis, along with knowing smiles. When not at the pool, she often wore the plunging necklines which diverted all males to her cleavage. Adept for each situation, she chose more demure French dresses to fit the occasion as part of her image of a sophisticated, wealthy women. Of course, she used the allure of her breasts and cleavage as strategic weapons when the 'physical asset' displays suited needs of her mission.

Intelligence operations tend to be successful in direct proportion to the planning and preparation going into the respective operations. Nyugen worked diligently to create her 'knowledgeable and sophisticated' persona. Each morning the concierge delivered local and international newspapers to her room. She would scan the International Herald Tribune, the most recent edition of the New York Times, Le Parisien, Le Monde, The Times from England, and she avidly read the weekly news magazines Time and Newsweek for information of interest. Her most valuable source for what was on the minds of the Saigon elite came from the concierge and his informal network who gathered the gossip of importance in Saigon. The concierge passed the juicy tidbits of gossip to her every day and received a generous gratuity each day for his 'local intelligence' work. Such gossip was the coin of the realm for elite Saigon insiders.

She mentally rehearsed scenarios for future interactions with her recruitment target. She read books in English which, unlike Moscow, she could freely purchase in the local bookstores and from street vendors. By KGB standards, many of these 'American' books would be considered subversive. She rationalized that she was doing research on America to support Operation Red.

As the evening wore-on, the intense focus on preparing for the meeting tomorrow was replaced by an introspective examination of her life. She did not think out-loud for fear of potential listening devices in her hotel room, but she wished she could voice her fears and worries about the future. Kie^ needed a catharsis to calm her emotions. As her mind raced, she thought about her persona and identity. Who was she? She was not French; she was not Vietnamese, and she certainly was not Russian. Was she just some freakish creature of the KGB? What would happen to her when her usefulness to the KGB waned? The only thing she cared about was Sasha. He was the only person she had known in her life who seemed to truly care for her, and she loved him in return with all her heart.

At a US Embassy party, one of the wives talked to her about a range of American books. After the party, Kie^ bought two of the US books from street vendors which the Embassy wife had discussed: a volume of Longfellow's poetry and a book about the US Revolution. The Longfellow poetry themes and alliteration were comforting to her. The book on the US Revolution stood in great contrast to the indoctrination she had received about the Bolshevik 1917 Revolution. She thought about the soulless aspect of Soviet communism: no God, only the deified Lenin, the feared Stalin, and the absolute sovereignty of the Soviet Communist

Party. The book on the American Revolution could pose a danger to her if the KGB knew she read that book, so, she reaffirmed the rationalization that she was doing research on America to support Operation Red. Rationalization aside, two glasses of cognac diverted her from a latent depression.

Awaking the next morning, she ate a hearty breakfast to fortify herself for what would be a stressful and arduous day. Kie^ set out a disciplined timeline to arrive at the safe house at exactly 1500 hours. The rules of tradecraft were plus or minus two minutes from the set time for a clandestine meeting. Outside that time window, abort the meeting and go to the scheduled fallback meeting location and time. Her SDR would allow two hours for the approach to the safe house, plus time for a light lunch as part of the SDR. She called the concierge to request her car and driver be at the hotel by 1230 hours.

At 1230, the concierge opened the car door for Kie^. As the driver obsequiously greeted her, she presented the image of a person relaxed and in no rush. Just before getting into the car, she casually scanned the area looking for any cars parked with the motor running. She checked the color of any cars which had someone sitting in a parked vehicle. Only then would she tell the driver to take her to the market in Cholon. She knew the driver would take Nguyen Hue street, turn left onto Le Loi, travel through the traffic circle at the Saigon Central Market and proceed to Cholon. As the driver left the hotel entrance and turned onto Nguyen Hue street, Kie^ made an obvious gesture to take out her cosmetic mirror and check her make-up. She was actually checking the traffic behind them without turning her head; did any cars immediately pull out of parking spots near the hotel? What color cars were behind them?

Just before the driver reached the large traffic circle at the Saigon Central Market, Kie^ told him she had forgotten something, "go around the circle and back to the hotel". The tradecraft going around the traffic circle allowed Kie^ to track the cars behind them. Did any vehicle entering from Le Loi street go around the circle to take Le Loi street back in the opposite direction they just traveled following her? As the driver turned back onto Le Loi she determined no vehicle was following her car. At the hotel, Kie^ made a show of going into the hotel and returning a few minutes later. She repeated the previous travel from the hotel to the traffic circle, this time turning right out of the traffic circle into the Cholon district.

She previously located a restaurant that had a back entrance onto a small alley, she directed the driver to turn into the alley. Jumping out of the car as soon as it stopped, she told the driver she would take a cab from there and no longer needed him. Quickly entering the restaurant through the back door, Kie^ selected a small table with a view of both entrances, she could check anyone who entered after her. Her stomach was tight from stress over the pending meeting at the safehouse. Who would be there, waiting for her?

Though not hungry, she ordered food to appear like the other customers in the restaurant. She ordered a bowl of egg-drop soup, a plate of fried rice and a pot of tea. After 40 minutes, she paid the bill and departed out the front door. She began her meandering walk to check for surveillance, and, if necessary, lose any foot surveillance. She first walked away from the safehouse taking a circuitous route back toward her destination. Checking her watch, she noted, it was time to knock on the safehouse door – with great trepidation she knocked and waited.

She heard footsteps coming toward the door, locks being released, and the door opened – Sasha is standing in the open doorway! Her eyes filled with tears as she ran inside to hug him tightly and kiss him. Sasha responded passionately kissing Kie^ as he pushed the door closed with his foot, they held each other in a joyous reunion.

Without a word, she followed him to a bedroom, both shedding clothes as they literally jogged, leaving a trail of clothing and shoes from the door to the bed. The passion in their making love was resonated by mutual sounds of pleasure, and the cries of two orgasms. They lay back on the bed emotionally and physically spent. As they recovered, more kisses and exchanges of mutual vows of 'I love you' – as each of the KGB lovers uttered the depths of their feelings for each other.

Kie^ felt a brief fear race through her mind and body – is this a dream? Temporarily exhausted, they fell into a dreamy sleep in each other's arms. When they woke, they were ravenous. Going to the safe house kitchen, Kie^ found a well stocked pantry with food ready to be warmed. Kie^ and Sasha worked together to warm portions of fried rice, bar-b-que pork, spring rolls, plus a side of squid salad with hot peppers, onion, nức mắm fish sauce, and tomatoes with basil.

As they ate, Kie^ tried to express her joy at seeing Sasha in Saigon and knowing he would be her operations officer, adding with a suggestive smile, they would have to meet secretly in the safe house – meet 'frequently' in the safe house. Feigning anger, Kie^ confronted Sasha, why he had not told her he would be her operations officer in Saigon. He calmly but firmly told her that his silence was part of the security protocol, leaving out the part that he was not told until a brief time before his departure. After the meal and cleaning up the kitchen, Sasha filled two large glasses of a very good red wine he brought from France and they got down to another type of 'business', the business of spying.

She briefed him in detail on the various actions she had been taking to support her legend in Vietnam. In particular, she talked about each consequential individual she had contacted since she arrived in Saigon. Sasha asked several questions about the Cercle Sportif crowd, the Embassy people she had met, and how the various individuals had coalesced into the inevitable cliques which form in expatriate communities or in an elite local societies. All these 'elites' thrived on the rumors, petty jealousies, and snide backbiting. How do these factors create expected and unexpected security problems for the operation? He was interested in her daily routines and what patterns she might have established. All in all, a professional prelude to the additional planning which would follow.

Sasha told her how the low-level mole in the US State Department had identified Kie^'s target, Calthrop Winslow Simmons and verified Simmons received his travel orders for assignment to the US Embassy in Saigon. He would arrive in Saigon seven-days hence. Sasha produced the spotting report, written on 'flash burn' paper, documenting what they knew about the target to date:

The report described a narcissist who would have no personality at all if it were not for the plethora of personal flaws in his character.

MOST SECRET - Spotting Report Calthrop Winslow Simmons

Calthrop Winslow Simmons is a textbook candidate for a study of psychosis. Outwardly Calthrop is somewhat handsome and a glib but superficial talker. He could even be charming when he set his mind to it. Behind his physical and social façade, Calthrop was seething with rage and anger. Despite his many apparent social advantages, he felt the world had not treated him fairly, particularly in his State Department career. Calthrop's aspirations and expectations for his life were unrealistic and when these thwarted aspirations and expectations were slammed against his arrested emotional development, he evolved into a twisted Hyde-like character. Calthrop is not a brilliant man but possessed a reptilian type of focused intelligence that was matched by a reptilian lack of emotion and empathy.

He is married to Xenia Drakos, the daughter of a secretive wealthy tycoon who is possibly the most powerful man behind-the-scenes in the US. Calthrop exploited his father-in-law's influence to overcome the obstacles his prior malign behavior had placed in his planned way to fame and respect. He was appointed to a coveted position in the State Department INR, thanks to his father-in-law. All the externals indicated Calthrop should be envied by all those who knew him.

Calthrop's warped personal reality was something quite different. In his mind, he had been denied the adulation he thought due to him, despite his lack of personal achievement.

His wife Xenia was a pinched-face spoiled brat, a shrew of a woman whose very voice grated on him. To say the woman was selfish and self-centered was an understatement. In Calthrop/s view, her primary redeeming qualities were her father's money and power to help Calthrop. Calthrop did like, Xenia's psychosis of degeneracy, which was an appealing trait for him. Her excursions into a world of sexual fantasy which she put into action were legendary. Calthrop and Xenia also shared the non-virtues that seem prevalent in children of the privileged: a sense of entitlement without effort, arrogance without achievement, and condescension in place of compassion. In these non-virtue areas, the Simmons were a good match.

When Calthrop received his orders for a two-year assignment to the Saigon Embassy, neither Calthrop nor Xen gave a first thought, much less a second thought, that Xenia might accompany him. The marriage was real, though some may say surreal. A loveless union of two pathological degenerates in a twisted co-dependence. As the departure date neared, Calthrop was planning new debaucheries in Saigon and Xen reveled in the many names of young men and a few women in her 'sex Rolodex'. Her pathology of sex role playing, attempting to supersede the excesses of Kama Sutra and make it a passé, a book for sex peasants, and denying there were any bounds which defined her life. Xen thought the only thing she would miss with Calthrop were the sex role playing games, she smirked, thinking about playing the dominatrix in her garter belt, long stockings and stiletto heels as she brought 'bad boy Calthrop' to heel. The smirk changed to a wicked smile as she thought, many of the young men in the Rolodex were 'bad boys', willing bad boys. Xen would little miss what's-his-name in Saigon.

Calthrop's background was not what one would call Middle America. A child of wealthy parents who circulated in the elite society of the East Coast, he saw his world crumble around as his father frittered away the family fortune in bad investment after bad investment, which his father made in an alcoholic haze. His mother was the source of gossip and ridicule as she screwed every male she could find, as long as she was sober enough to pull their trousers down. One of the taunting gossip items was, how could Calthrop be "as right as he appears", coming from this boozy parental-union. Other 'behind-the-back smirks' speculated, there may have been some residual genetic problem or brain damage to the lad.

Calthrop's father-in-law, Constantin Drakos, was an enigma. Virtually unknown to the American public, the President would interrupt a cabinet meeting to take a call from Drakos. Every Representative and Senator in Congress sought to curry the favor of this powerful shadowy man. Drakos did not particularly care for Calthrop. As animals in a pack sense a member which is 'not quite right', Drakos sensed there was something not quite right about his son-in-law. At the same time, Drakos enjoyed the privilege of power and was personally entertained to manipulate events surrounding Calthrop Simmons. Constantin Drakos had Calthrop placed in a senior position in the State Department INR, although Calthrop was in no way qualified. Calthrop saw the position as his path to respect and his ticket to fame. Calthrop could not conceive or accept that he was absolutely unqualified to fulfill the duties commensurate with the security aspects of his sensitive position as intelligence analyst.

Thanks to the influence of his father-in-law, Calthrop was made a senior grade GS-15 within the INR and granted a TS/SCI security clearance. Calthrop should have been pleased and accepted a degree of comfort from his status and situation in life. However, his serious character flaws of drunkenness, womanizing, and lying, along with a DWI hit-and-run accident damaged his pursuit of adulation from State Department senior bureaucrats. To atone for his horrific behavior, he had to accept a posting to Vietnam as penance. Calthrop held hopes of finding a key to his quest for glory and resuscitate his failing career by working in the Saigon Embassy.

Once in Vietnam, he would assume his job as the State Department liaison with the CIA station, MACV intelligence, and Vietnamese military intelligence, a position that included little power and certainly no glory. But in this position, Calthrop did have access to some of the most sensitive and secretive materials related to the war and intelligence operations in Southeast Asia.

Calthrop was frustrated and his anger intensified. He lacked a moral compass to give him any aspect of objectivity regarding his behavior. He drank to excess and was a profligate patron of prostitutes in the US. It was in these relationships with prostitutes that Calthrop revealed some of his deep seated mental psychosis, a mental malady which Calthrop carried as part of his immoral baggage. His abusive treatment of the working-girls became a compulsion. He hoped he would have ample opportunities in Vietnam to continue his deviant and abusive behavior.

Calthrop was the epitome of a coward and hoped the proximity of the US military would protect him from the real risks always afoot in Saigon.

Kie^ read the spotting report three times to indelibly inscribe the detailed set of information in her mind. After she concluded studying the document, Sasha burned the flash paper document in an ashtray, one sheet at a time.

Sasha and Kie^ understood Calthrop was a dangerous man because the likelihood he was sociopath. Kie^ had experience dealing with abusive men during her time as a 'Swallow'. Most times while conducting swallow operations, she had backup KGB goons observing as she compromised the men. These thugs would intervene if the target became physically abusive to the swallow.

In Saigon, she would be on her own in the initial meetings with the target. Sasha and Kie^ agreed that they should wait until after the first meeting between Kie^ and the target to discuss how she would 'work' the target and exploit his vulnerabilities. They needed to understand how Calthrop might relate to her at the outset. The important thing now to use the venue established for the initial meeting; a venue that should not raise any suspicions by the target nor any 'red flags' for Embassy security.

Sasha explained how the KGB had set-up a cover organization in France to sponsor a 'business opportunities seminar in Saigon'. The seminar would be an elitist invitation-only event hosted in the Saigon Continental Hotel. The event would include a cocktail hour, a lavish complementary dinner, entertainment, and a brief presentation after dinner which essentially would be 'a list of individuals and companies in Europe' attendees could contact regarding doing business in Saigon. The KGB intent was to make the event a social-status prize, for which an 'invitation' to be sought after by the elite of Saigon.

Kie^ would be able to meet Calthrop in public, in a natural environment where people interact with friends .and strangers. The objective was to entice the target into a second meeting with her; an objective that should be rather straightforward based on Calthrop's womanizing proclivities and 'case officer' Kie^ showing Calthrop some of her cleavage along with a bit of suggestive conversation.

As in all sound planning, they designed a back-up plan. If for some reason, Kie^ did not make contact at the 'business event', it was a virtual certainty the target would join the Cercle Sportif as all senior Embassy officials did. she would contact the target at the Cercle Sportif pool, noting she missed meeting him at the Continental dinner but was pleased to see him here at the pool.

Sasha gave Kie^ detailed background information on the US and South Vietnamese counterintelligence (CI) and counterespionage (CE) capabilities. CE operations are designed to detect and neutralize enemy spies. CI operations are designed to protect against the enemy obtaining intelligence on the friendly forces and government. An effective system of CE and CI requires significant resources of personnel, money and equipment. South Vietnam lacked the needed CE and CI resources. The CE and CI challenges for the US and South Vietnam security organizations were daunting given the North Vietnam commitment to flood South Vietnam with spies and moles, plus exploiting the large number of North Vietnamese sympathizers already living in-country.

The massive penetration of the South Vietnamese military and government, plus the systemic corruption in South Vietnamese governmental structure, resulted in a relatively ineffectual CE/CI capability against the North Vietnamese and, most important for Operation Red, virtually no capabilities dedicated against foreign intelligence services like the KGB and China. Though the US had the resources potentially available for a comprehensive CE/CI program in

South Vietnam, the US focus was on North Vietnam and gave a low priority for KGB operations in South Vietnam.

Sasha emphasized that the relatively low CE threat to Operation Red did not relieve Kie^ or him from continuous vigilance, proper security measures, and professional tradecraft. He emphasized, part of this vigilance was for Kie^ to be aware of communist agents in South Vietnam who might inadvertently cross-wires with Operation Red. The VC were a possible threat to assassinate Calthrop as a senior official in the US embassy and she could become collateral damage. Sasha admonished her that she could not be lax at any time in situation awareness. For security, she would not write the standard HUMINT "contact reports" but would deliver the 'contact reports' verbally to her operations officer, meeting with him after each contact with the target.

Sasha retrieved the red wine and they proceeded to finish the bottle – before deciding they needed to "rest" more in bed. After a vigorous 'rest', Kie^ and Sasha were hungry again. Kie^ examined the well-stocked pantry and refrigerator. She told Sasha she would prepare the evening meal to polish-up her cooking skills. Laughing, Sasha sat down to watch her demonstrate her culinary skills.

The refrigerator provided a variety of options. Kie^ decided to reheat the rest of the pork from lunch adding sliced green onions and sliced carrots, steamed rice, a chicken broth soup with noodles and onions, pickled cabbage, jasmine tea, and guava for dessert. It was clear that Kie^ had not cooked much in her life – but the results that evening were tasty - and Sasha was happy.

After the meal, Sasha broke out a bottle of white wine. They discussed if Kie^ spending the night would create any security or legend issues. Sasha contemplated the security question for about seven seconds and announced officially, 'there was no security concern'. Two bottles of white-wine later - they were back in bed

CHAPTER 16   BEAT THE WAR DRUMS AND START THE WAR DANCE

Working directly for the JCS Chairman had written perks plus unwritten perks, and, as the Chairman's Deputy for Special Projects, there were advantageous black-money contingency options. The 1254th Air Transport Wing based at Andrews Air Force Base operates 'Air Force 1' for the President. 'Air Force 1' is on alert 24/365 for a 15-minute takeoff. The 1254th Air Transport Wing also provides high-comfort air transport for luminary government VIPs. Those not-so-important non-luminary government personages are provided 'much less-luminary' aircraft types to clearly emphasize the 'pecking order' in DC.

While Major-General Wojcik could use the JCS Chairman's prerogative to use an 1254th Air Transport Wing 'luminary' aircraft for the flight to Hawaii, the request would draw too much attention and become a security problem. So, Major-General Wojcik opted instead to use one of the "International Export and Import Company Ltd" cargo/passenger configured Boeing 707 chartered aircraft and keep a low profile to fool the Washington crowd. The flight time from Washington DC to Hawaii was approximately ten hours. Major-General Wojcik's aide arranged for all involved in the Hawaii meeting to stay in the Visiting Senior Officers quarters at Fort DeRussy on the beach in Honolulu. LT Baumgartner and Gunnery Sergeant Jacob Risner USMC arrived from Vietnam three hours after the General's aircraft touchdown. Gunnery Sergeant Risner replaced the wounded Warrant Officer Renner for this planning meeting.

Major-General Wojcik, Annie Hoffman, and Captain Ben Albert, the General's aide, were on the Hickam Air Base ramp to greet LT Baumgartner and Gunnery Sergeant Risner as they deplaned. LT Baumgartner and Gunnery Sergeant Risner delivered sharp salutes which General Wojcik returned just as crisply. Baumgartner turned to Annie and said formally,

"Good afternoon Miss Hoffman"

General Wojcik immediately retorted,

"Spare us please, you know Miss Hoffman well enough to call her Annie"

The General gave Annie a nod, actually a signal, and Annie raced to hug and kiss 'her sailor'. Gary thoroughly enjoying the kiss and her embrace, felt self-conscious as his memories from his Academy days – specifically, the regulation of 'no public show of affection' which allowed for 'no public show of affection'. The General, with a grin, said it is time to go to our quarters, we will reconvene in the SCIF in one hour. Baumgartner fully understood the General's grin when he discovered that the rough-tough OSS warrior had ordered his aide book adjoining rooms, actually connecting rooms, for Annie and 'her sailor'.

After quick showers, LT Baumgartner and Gunnery Sergeant Risner USMC reported to the SCIF. Annie and General Wojcik were seated at the conference table. The General stood up and took LT Baumgartner aside:

"Gary, I was very sorry to hear about Captain Denning up on that hellhole-ridge. Denning was an outstanding soldier and a good man."

"Thank you General, he was indeed an outstanding soldier and a good man. But there is a complication in the story. Reginald Denning's real name is Erik von Hausfeldt. He was a German Waffen SS officer during WWII. We found this out as we did the next-of-kin process. It is a wild-story and Captain Williams will need your guidance for the disposition of final affairs."

"I am always up for wild-stories - wild-stories are about all I get from your team – We will talk about Captain von Hausfeldt later."

With everyone again seated at the table, General Wojcik announced that, as the only 'pretty one' at the table, Annie would kick-off the discussion with an update from NSA, before she could begin, Bull added,

"By the way, Miss Hoffman is now a GS-14".

With a special smile for Baumgartner and a pleasant smile for the rest, Annie began her briefing on NSA progress and current issues.

She covered three issues in this initial briefing. Foremost was the discovery that the previously presumed "static" in the Saigon messages. The breakthrough recognized the occurrences of 'electronic interference' were not static, the apparent static was actually steganography, a secretive technique using highly compressed messages deceptively inserted in the host-messages to look like static. The 'static' in the host-messages use a different KGB encryption system, a more sophisticated cypher process. NSA is in the process of searching old intercepts to see when this steganography technique was first used. General Blake has assigned more technical analysts to the Peregrine program to investigate the 'static' in the Saigon messages. Second, there is still a mystery why certain signals used an obsolete, flawed KGB encryption system. The opinion at NSA was that the obsolete, flawed encryption system was a clumsy attempt to misdirect the US – but misdirect to what? Then there was the "coincidence" in the timing of the KGB code clerk defection. NSA was reexamining the Saigon traffic 'take' since 1962 and a pattern seems to be emerging, more work needs to be done. Third, a new KGB encryption system and new message format have been intercepted from Saigon. This appears to be a new radio site and the location of this transmitter is not yet precisely determined We do know it is a different location than the site being used to coordinate attacks on US advisors. In addition, there are confirmations of radio signal activity from South Vietnamese provinces that relate to the targeting of US advisors. Annie stopped at that point, noting the other presenters today likely will have inputs which further impact NSA thinking and analyses.

Major-General Wojcik turned to LT Baumgartner to give the Peregrine update from the Saigon perspective.

"Lieutenant, you have the floor. By the way, did you and your team actually kidnap Warrant Officer Renner?"

(Annie's eyes widened in surprise and dismay – What? Kidnap!)

"Sir, I'm not sure kidnap is the right word".

"Stop right now – when you are in a hole, stop digging".

"Aye-aye sir – stop digging."

"Fine, you and I will talk more about the nefarious hospital escapade after this meeting."

Annie looked at Gary and raised her eyebrows; Gary pretended to ignore her.

"Yes sir. General, I have quite a bit of information which is new to the mix, some as recent as just before we departed Saigon for this meeting. There is some good news and some bad news. Gunnery Sergeant Risner will present the 'good news'."

"General, Miss Hoffman, the good news relates to taking down the bad guys who are targeting US advisors. We have actions in work which will isolate and identify the top bad guy, the 'mole' who is acting as a 'principal agent' for multiple, enemy spy networks. We recruited an ARVN officer in the Joint General Staff personnel office. This agent is a greedy combat-dodger who is providing the names and backgrounds on several ARVN officers who have been assigned to positions which give access to the data needed to set-up the ambushes, including the Ap Bac, January 1963 massacre."

"We have solid inputs from CIA and DIA on how information flows in and through the ARVN Joint General Staff. We constructed a matrix to cross match the radio transmissions with all these data. Warrant Officer Renner is working this problem as we speak. The good news is tempered by other sensitive information which LT Baumgartner and Captain Williams have acquired. LT Baumgartner will tie all this together, adding in our first 'take' from the listening devices the A Shau recon patrol implanted in the back-wall of the A Shau radio hooch."

Annie's eyes widened when she heard that Gary had been in the notoriously dangerous A Shau valley.

Risner continued,

"The day before yesterday, a SOG light-aircraft, with the electronic-gear needed to interrogate the listening devices, overflew the NVA camp we recently 'visited'. Both devices responded to the interrogation and provided duplicate information. We installed two in case one failed. The listening devices recorded several conversations in Russian between KGB radio operators. First, the camp commander, who appears to be a Russian named Warrant Officer Andre Vladimirovich Klimov, concluded the intrusion by the US patrol was a coincidental event rather than a targeted recon. Captain Denning's body was identified by an NVA patrol as US, but there were no documents on the body which compromised anything beyond the US involvement in a recon patrol, a typical 'Indian Country' recon patrol by SOG in NVA areas of Vietnam."

"Klimov decided they did not need to move the camp. Part of the decision was driven by the camp being the ideal location for the antennas. So, we can expect more 'take' from the listening devices. There were discussions between the Russian radio operators about a new signal from Saigon and the need to keep that signal compartmented with retransmissions of that signal only to KGB headquarters in Moscow using the high level encryption. The Russians had a laugh about how gullible the North Vietnamese were to not detect the hidden parts of Operation Red. While this is not highly specific, the recordings benefit us using the Russian chit-chat to help connect the dots. We do not know what Operation Red is."

Gary picked up at that point to deliver the 'bad news':

"The bad news is information the team has obtained from SOG and CIA. All this information has an indirect correlation with why Peregrine was originally sent to Nam to sort out the threat to our advisors and 'end that threat'. This background information is politically damning and could cause problems up to the highest levels in DC – possibly big problems. First, I want to look at Project Safeguard"

"Stop Lieutenant! Stop now! You are not cleared for Project Safeguard information. Project Safeguard is a tightly compartmented Top Secret program"

"General, you hired me to do the Peregrine mission. I am doing the Peregrine mission. All the information I am going to give you is directly tied to the Peregrine mission and is essential to saving American lives. These data are material to US national security. Since I already know this 'information' – the cat is out of the bag – what I am asking is – what do you want me to do with what the team and I have learned?"

General Wojcik paused for an extended period studying LT Baumgartner's face – and thinking – he is as brash as I was in the OSS at his age - putting that aside, - let's do the right thing and deal with the classification need-to-know as we go forward.

"Lieutenant Baumgartner, you are right. I hired you and the team to do a mission – the Peregrine mission –and you and your bunch of bandits are taking no prisoners in the process. Here is what we are going to do – everyone in the room, listen closely. You are going to hear Project Safeguard information for which, you are not cleared. Everything that is said in this room today will stay in this room – got it? I will give more guidance after we see just how devious and clever this Peregrine bunch really is. Proceed Lieutenant."

Nodding his head, Gary continued,

"Aye-aye sir. Project Safeguard is a SOG operation to insert agents, teams and singletons, into the denied area, in this case that would be North Vietnam as the prime target, but also Laos and Cambodia. Project Safeguard has been betrayed from the inside since Safeguard attempted the first over-border insertion. There has not been a single success to date – every team and every agent has been killed, captured, doubled, or is in prison.

"The number of lost agents is staggering; 250 men, lost and counting! There are compromised SOG teams operating radios under North Vietnamese 'control' feeding us false information However, the North Vietnamese have not been all together that clever. For example, we know Team Romeo is compromised. They are supposed to be north of the DMZ in the Vinh area, sending the radio transmissions from a location near Vinh. But the current Romeo radio transmissions are verified as actually coming from the Hanoi area – that is, the Romeo signals are emanating from a site 120 miles north of the location where the team claims to be near Vinh. I could go on with more details, but I think you get the picture of an operational disaster and enemy agent penetration of one of the most secret US organizations in Vietnam, SOG."

"The over-the border operations by CIA have been just as dismal. The data we have on the CIA cross-border fiasco are not as specific except for the "total failure" part. It appears the Agency has lost about the same number of agents during a similar period, some 200-300 agents. As if this is not bad enough, this mess is further complicated, so far, CIA and SOG swept all of these problems under the rug. They are afraid of "being off the Washington political script" and seeing careers end because of DC politics backlash in Saigon."

"Is that all Lieutenant?"

"No sir, that was the basic background information. Here are the team conclusions: there are three major enemy networks in operation which converge in Saigon; one network operates to kill American advisors embedded with the ARVN. A second network operates against the Agency unit running 'cross-border' ops and the third network works

216

against SOG cross-border ops. We believe all three networks converge to a single 'principal agent'; we called him "the Spider". He is the heart of the North Vietnamese spy web. The Spider controls the Saigon radio communications and makes operational decisions for all three networks. The information Annie provided about the 'static' reinforces the idea a principal agent, the "Spider". We take out the "Spider" and you give all three networks 'a big hurt' – but the networks will likely resurface, in time, with a new Spider or Spiders. We have an idea of where the "Spider" is organizationally sited in the ARVN command, but not who he is – at least not yet. We expect to have him in our sights soon"

With an intense look, "Bull" Woznick asked,

"Where do you think he might be?"

"We believe he is near the top of the ARVN Joint General Staff in a department called Deconfliction Division. We are actively pursuing an op to smoke him out."

"General, I want to add, we understand this is a political problem 'way above the combined pay grades' of the Peregrine team - the political ramifications are profound. South Vietnam appears to have North Vietnamese agents at virtually every South Vietnamese government institution, from top to bottom. Having said that, I am confident we will do the mission assigned to the Peregrine team: take out the bastards targeting and killing American advisors.

As to the greater political problem, as a grunt-level strategic observation, if we don't find a way to deal with the North Vietnamese agents and moles operating from 'the inside', it will be impossible to win this war. It is a war of intelligence – the US military can kick the shit out of the NVA on any given day on battlefield – hell, six guys up on a ridge in the A Shau plus a couple of Air Commando A-1Es sent about 300, likely more, of the bastards to Hell in less than two hours."

Needing to consider the new information from the team, the General closed the session for the day, including a couple light comments directed at Gary and Annie,

"Thank you for your inputs today, brings back unpleasant memories when Hitler was running amuck in the first two years of WWII. We were disorganized and uncertain what to do. Lieutenant, I want you to meet me tomorrow, here in the SCIF at 0800. All others convene at 0930 for your return-to-base orders and assignments. Everyone, have a good meal tonight and get to bed early".

The General did not wink at Baumgartner and Annie – but he might as well have – Annie left the room with a deep red blush and a sly smile – she was followed closely by Gary.

Gunnery Sergeant Risner, sideling up to Lieutenant Baumgartner, asked if it was alright for him to go to Honolulu to see an 'old friend'. Baumgartner gave Risner a knowing grin,

"See you in the morning Gunny".

Gary and Annie walked slowly back to the 'adjoining rooms', each lost in her and his individual thoughts. Arriving at the rooms, Annie gave an innocent smile as she affected the Gone With the Wind southern accent of Scarlett O'Hara, asking,

"Is this how you Yankees spend government money, you rent two rooms – but use one room and waste one room?"

Assuming the mellow baritone of Rhett Butler, Gary replied,

"Darling, with the connecting door open, this is a two bedroom suite. More important, you focused on the wrong issue. You should not be looking at the money thing as in what is the 'bang for the buck' in this room deal. You should be thinking, how do I get a 'bang from the buck' in this room."

Annie was forming a wide grin when she saw Gary rip off his shirt and throw it across the room, Surprised, she dropped the Scarlett accent and loudly said,

"What are you doing!"

As Gary reached for his belt, he replied with a mirthful smile,

"I am winning our contest as who can get undressed the fastest."

In a quandary, she thought, what contest, oh no, he has a head start, an exasperated Annie yelled,

"Gary you are cheating!"

Continuing the Rhett melodious baritone, a smiling, Gary responded,

"Yes, yes I am cheating, and I am winning."

With a broad smile Annie went into frantic disrobing. She was throwing her clothes around the room – her blouse caught on the corner of the desk chair, her bra landed on top of the bedside lamp, one shoe fell into a waste basket, and the rest of her garments were strewn around the bedroom. Slightly out of breath after the fury and flurry of a manic strip show, she turned to face Gary. A quirky thought passed through her mind as a smile begin to spread across her face – now lets see, in the Indiana parlance, would I be 'buck naked' or 'naked as a jaybird'?

The smile was quickly stifled when she saw Gary standing there fully clothed, except for the shirt he had thrown across the room.

Gary gave her his most innocent smile and calmly announced,

"You win."

Without a word, lips tightly pursed, Annie, 'naked as a jaybird', walked over to Gary and gave him a 'teachable moment' playful punch to his shoulder, as any strong Indiana farm girl likely would do. Summoning an authoritative voice, she said,

"Get in the bed Lieutenant."

They managed the rest of the time that afternoon to make up for the time lost due to demands of the mission. They arrived punctually for their dinner reservation that evening at the DeRussy Officers Club dining room. Gary devoured a large porterhouse steak, medium rare, grilled asparagus, and a salad with French dressing. Annie enjoyed a filet mignon, medium rare, a baked potato with sour cream, and a salad with French dressing. They shared a bottle of wine; and finished with crème brûlée for Gary and tiramisu for Annie.

One part of their conversation was somber when Annie asked about Reginald Denning. She remarked what a gentleman Reggie was around her, reminding her of the classic Old-World aristocratic gentlemen she had seen in the movies. Gary agreed Reggie was sophisticated and classy, and added he was a great soldier. Gary told her about the Reggie/Erik revelation, medals, and all. They decided to have a toast to a friend and comrade. Gary ordered the best cognac the Officers Club had for that poignant tribute.

Back in the room after their pleasant dinner, Gary mentioned the General's admonition, 'get in bed early'. As he turned to hear Annie's reaction, she was already in bed beckoning him to join her.

219

At 0730 the next morning, LT Baumgartner was drinking coffee, waiting for General Wojcik. He was expecting a major ass-chewing about the 'kidnapping' before they get down to the current challenges they have on their hands. General Wojcik arrived at 0740, LT Baumgartner stood. The General shook his hand before pouring a cup of coffee.

"Tell me about Erik von Hausfeldt."

Gary related what he and Williams found going through Erik's footlocker, adding what they read in von Hausfeldt last will and testimony. Erik wanted his medals to go to his brother, Goerzt von Hausfeldt and the funds he had in a Swiss bank account to go to two German WW II military veterans' charities.

Baumgartner and Williams had speculated that Erik had been transferred to the Western front fighting Americans when Germany surrendered. They concluded Erik found a dead American solider about his size and switched uniforms with the American, Reginald Denning. Taking Denning's ID plus his dog tags, Erik left the body of 'dead German soldier' who was of no interest to the Americans. Erik moved on to France where he joined the French Foreign Legion, as did many former Waffen SS soldiers. After some time, Erik, now Denning, an American, asked the Legion to send his false identity information to the US Army in occupied Germany to verify a MIA status for Reginald Denning. Furthermore, the back-story gave Erik a solid cover story to later join the US Army after fulfilling his time in the Legion.

The General said he would assign the Erik 'last will and testament' problem to his aide.

"Now Lieutenant Pirate, tell me about Warrant Officer Renner, how is he doing?"

"He is doing fine and is at the compound, deep into the ongoing analysis work. Doc checks on him medically two to three times a day. Carl Renner is a tough bastard."

"Did you cover your tracks from the Danang hospital outing?"

"All indications are the Danang hospital has closed their record on a US Army Warrant Officer Carl Renner being transferred to a unit in Saigon. No AWOL charge was filed and, if I might say, we got in and out of Danang clean."

"Well done Gary – this incident and conversation never happened regarding your criminal breaches of Army regulations, kidnapping, and falsifying official records. Give my regards to Warrant Officer Renner. And if you ever repeat what I am going to say, I think you can fill in that blank on the 'consequence form'. Gary, you remind me of a very brash OSS officer when he was about your age; Could have been my twin, looked a lot like me – except I was younger and more handsome in a crude sort of way".

"Tell me about your plan for the "Spider"."

"The plan is simple in concept – but tough to execute. As a bunch of shooters, we used two maxims. First, the basic 'find the target, fix the target, kill the target'. Second, why does Occam's Razor, always look at the simplest obvious answer first? Because the simplest answer is the best place to start and often is the answer. An essential assumption was, there is zero probability the North Vietnam Ministry of Public Security could 'guess' the exact times and exact locations of virtually all of the SOG and CIA insertion missions plus the time and place information needed to ambush the American advisors. The geography of the campaign assassinating American advisors in South Vietnam and the SOG and CIA compromises cover all of South Vietnam, and large parts of Laos, Cambodia, and North Vietnam. The North Vietnamese successes involve many different VC and NVA units. This is a very complex and sophisticated threat

"There has to be a central location that links all the diverse operational planning and execution actions. So, modify the 'follow the money' rule to a 'follow the information' rule. The information central location has two nodes: one resides in the A Shau valley at the camp we recently 'visited'. We understand that the A Shau base is not the head of this snake. The A Shau node is just a radio message clearing site; they forward messages to Hanoi and Moscow and send action directives back to NVA forces in South Vietnam. The central location has to be in Saigon due to decision timing constraints".

"The NVA has exhibited poor tradecraft by using the same frequencies and message formats over and over; the radio sites are fixed and have not moved around. The KGB is playing games with us and also playing games with Hanoi – the obsolete KGB encryption system is a calculated attempt at misdirection. We concluded that the old KGB encryption system was intended to be compromised to mislead the US and screw over their North Vietnamese ally. We are not sure, as yet, just why about the latter. As to misdirecting us, a similar question exists. What are the other Russian objectives in this operation? The 'convenient' defection of the KGB code clerk reinforces our conclusion the KGB is running parallel and simultaneous deception operations against North Vietnam and the US".

"The radio site in Saigon is their key vulnerability; find the Saigon radio location and we have a direct path to the 'Spider'. We need a major increase in NSA resources to DF-and-fix the radio transmitter location in Saigon. Once we have the Saigon location, we will place the site under 24-hour surveillance. It has to be serviced by couriers and 'the Spider' himself likely visits the radio site frequently. Following the couriers will give us links to other moles in the South Vietnamese government. We are continuing our correlation of message traffic by the NVA mole with information provided by the agent we recruited in the ARVN Joint General Staff personnel department. The movement suspects we have identified so far in the General Staff and the message traffic timing will narrow the search for the mole. Our exceptionally greedy ARVN-agent thinks he is supporting a US study on personnel assignment practices."

"We will use our Nungs for the surveillance. We have set up our network of unwitting double agents which will give us a channel to plant deceptive information to "find the target" – after that, we will kill the Spider."

"That 'sounds like a plan' Lieutenant. I like it plus the increased security aspect cutting out dependence on CIA only using our folks and the Nungs. You'll get the extra NSA support to precisely locate the Saigon radio. Do you need any other additional resources?"

"For now, we are good, the team is confident we have the right people working the problem in Saigon. Depending on the scope of the NVA networks which we ID, we may need to bring in more shooters when simultaneously scarf up the bad guys and take them out."

"As an aside from the team, we thank you General for your support – I am aware that you already knew what I related about the overall situation in Nam. From our perspective, the team subscribes to what we call "the 10% rule" which assumes the North Vietnamese Ministry of Defense Intelligence Department has achieved a level of 10% penetration in every important South Vietnamese institution, using agents sent from the North, recruited agents in the south, and sympathizers for the Northern cause. This aggregate collection of enemy spies is so widespread and proliferated - moles, intelligence collectors, and agents of influence are essentially everywhere – we do not see how this war can be won without a draconian house-cleaning to root out these North Vietnamese spies."

"Good work by you and the team – give them a HOOYAH from me. In the next meeting this morning, I want you to repeat the plan you described to me. We will return to our respective bases tomorrow. That timing should give you some 'beach and sun' time today with GS-14 Hoffman."

"And yes Lieutenant, I knew all you told me about the mess we face in this war. I will want to have more discussions with you later on these problems. Now, let's get to the next meeting, wrap it up, and get you and Annie down to the beach this afternoon."

The 0930 meeting was proforma to a large extent. Gary briefed the group on the plan, General Wojcik summarized the results from the two days in Hawaii assigning tasks to the participants. He "directed" everyone to enjoy the rest of the day and to be ready to RTB (return to base) the next morning.

Annie and Gary made their plan for the rest of the day: lunch at the Officers Club; some time at Waikiki beach, taking care Annie did not get sunburned, make a reservation to dine at the La Ronde restaurant, known for excellent seafood and famous as one of the three revolving restaurants in the world.

They decided to walk to the beach from the Visiting Senior Officers Quarters. It was another Hawaiian sunny day, light breeze, and temperature around 80-degrees. Carrying towels, Annie wore a dark-green one-piece swimsuit and Gary wore his khaki swim-trunks from SEAL training. The Pacific Ocean waves rolled onto the beach in low breakers. Finding an area away from other bathers, Annie and Gary placed their towels side-by-side. Gary rubbed suntan lotion on Annie's back before they ran to swim in the Pacific. Laughing and splashing each other like teenagers, the war was far away. Gary asked Annie if they should do the obligatory SEAL five-mile swim before going back to the Offices Club. In the same spirit, Annie punched Gary in the shoulder, implying she had other ideas for the exercise for the rest of the afternoon.

Back on the towels in dreamy solitude, neither was sure what to say. They wanted to protect and savor the idyllic moment they were sharing. The stresses of the war would return soon enough. Gary finally rolled on his side and asked Annie about her parents and if he had passed the test last Christmas. Annie talked about her parents' health and activities on the farm before she gave an ambiguous, possible double-meaning, comment,

"Yes, Gary, you passed the test at Christmas".

After a pretend-drama pause, she related how her Dad had been impressed with the sailor from Indiana: drinking beer; doing chores; and how they had a good time together. Then, as she smiled in a very tender way, tears welling in her eyes, she shared a confidence her mother had shared with her. She told Gary, in an emotion-filled voice, her mother had confided in Annie how Gary was so like her son Robert. That moment froze in time for them – neither knowing what to say – they just smiled intimately at each other and held hands.

Gary broke the moment, noting that Annie's shoulders were getting pink, and they should return to their quarters before she was seriously sunburned, reminding her, they had an early reservation at the La Ronde restaurant.

The La Ronde restaurant was the talk of Honolulu; The rotating restaurant on top of the Ala Moana Building was a pleasant novelty. The dining was excellent - they chose identical meals from the menu, shrimp cocktails, grilled mahi-mahi, steamed rice and a bottle of white wine. The conversation remained light talking about Hawaii and experiences in Indiana at Christmas, plus some suggestive comments that they needed to remember the admonition by the General – "get in bed early".

Back at the visiting officers' quarters bedroom, they both were thankful for the time they shared in Hawaii. They avoided talk of the morrow, when Gary went back to war and Annie went back to worrying and praying for him, as she worked diligently at NSA to support the Peregrine team. The evening was a tender intimacy that only a very few couples experience in a lifetime.

Two aircraft departed the next morning, one west to Saigon and one east to Washington DC.

During the return flight, Major-General Wojcik prepared a memo for NSA Director Blake, requesting expedited support for an enhanced direction finding operation in Saigon. Annie would hand-carry the memo to Dr. Slade and General Blake.

General Blake approved the request on receipt. NSA used the Peregrine cover organization "International Export and Import Company Ltd" to buy two used Renault panel trucks and two used Citroen panel trucks. NSA technicians reconfigured the truck interior-cargo areas with state-of-the-art DF gear to perform the enhanced direction finding mission. Logos were painted on the trucks, chosen so they would draw no attention or interest in the Saigon traffic. The undercover direction finding trucks with DF crews were delivered to Saigon two weeks later.

LT Baumgartner used the flight time to prepare a team action list Captain Williams approval.:

Sergeants Jones and Clayton will select four Nung 'snatch teams' and initiate training to conduct 'snatch a prisoner' operations in an urban environment. Sergeant Podowski will identify the type weapons and devices optimal for 'snatch' operations.

Sergeant Jones, Gunnery Sergeant Risner, and Warrant Officer Renner will select and train 20 Nung fighters in surveillance and tradecraft techniques.

Warrant Officer Renner will continue to analyze the enemy communication flows, timing, and information choke-points.

Gunnery Sergeant Risner and Warrant Officer Renner will develop additional target profiles for recruiting any needed additional Peregrine agent networks.

Master Sergeant James will 'do his thing' to ensure the team has every piece of equipment the team needs in this next phase of Peregrine action.

The Peregrine team was getting ready to lock-and-load.

CHAPTER 17 SAIGON HOOK-UP

The KGB front-company, Business International Ltd., began organizing a lavish event in Saigon as the cover to place Kie^ in contact with Calthrop Simmons. The KGB First Main Directorate released black-money funds for necessary bribes, pay retainers for entertainment, caterers, advertising, and other needed services. The advance spending for the many upfront bills for this ultra-extravagant event was a form of advertising that 'this is the social event of the year' for an urban warzone self-styled elite. General Sakharovsky convened the few KGB Headquarters staff cleared for the highly-classified compartmented Operation Red. The subject was the budget going forward. One staff officer obsequiously spoke up:

"Comrade General, this budget is excessive and inconsistent with the scale of Operation Red. Whoever proposed such a level of expenditures should be censored by the Party as irresponsible."

"Comrade Colonel, I personally proposed the current funding number on the table – to which I want to add a contingency fund beyond that original budget number. Now, a show of hands in support of release of the operational funds at the proposed level plus the additional budget augmentation."

The Colonel nearly dislocated his shoulder throwing his arm in the air. Sakharovsky gave the Colonel a look that was somewhere between a glare and a smirking smile – a combination suggesting early retirement for the officer who did not know when to keep his mouth shut. The other officers in the room understood that Chairman Semichastny and General Sakharovsky had expectations that Operation Red would embellish their professional records for future promotion within the CPSU. The funds were released the same morning, and, that same morning, 'the mouthy suck-up' Colonel resigned to end his KGB career.

Business International Ltd, ostensibly based in Paris, authorized their agents in Saigon to make all preparations for the 'business' conference. The basic plan was to throw a lavish invitation-only party in the Continental Hotel, a party limited to 200-invited guests. This would be the high-society signature-event of the year for the elite of Saigon – a 'must attend' event. These smug elite seemed insulated from the daily ugliness of the war, while, at the same time, most of that same elite were financially profiting from the war.

The first move by Business International Ltd was to acquire, for a modest bribe, the Cercle Sportif membership list (literally the' Who's Who' source for the insiders of Saigon). The next action drew the attention of the Saigon movers and shakers as Business International reserved the ballroom at the Continental; ordered the best catering in Saigon to augment the hotel kitchen; hired the ensemble from the Saigon Symphony Orchestra for entertainment; and, coordinated with city officials for security at this prestigious event. The coordination with the city officials would ensure that advance rumors would proliferate, causing an immediate competition for the 200 invitations. The strategy for invitations was to carefully select a cross-section of the Saigon elite: business, political, military, and foreign dignitaries. Among the latter, the top US Embassy officials were targeted for invitations, one of whom would be newly arrived Calthrop Winston Simmons, under cover as an Economic Attaché for his real INR job as an intelligence liaison officer.

The event agenda is an open-bar cocktail hour, a sit-down dinner with assigned seating, dining choices from a special 'Business in Saigon' menu, complemented by entertainment from the Saigon Symphony Orchestra ensemble. The business of the evening would be brief and consist of a glitzy multi-page brochure of companies in Europe interested in doing business in Saigon. The seating arrangement 'coincidently' would find Nyugen Kie^ sitting next to Calthrop Simmons, US Embassy. An additional decoration for the cocktail-hour would be the presence of some forty Cercle Sportif "guest members", who usually adorned the Cercle Sportif pool area during the week. These lovely young women "guest members" would fade away at the end of the cocktail hour when the dinner seating was announced. The competition for an invitation was intense with bribes offered, threats delivered, and fervent pleadings from "the important people" in Saigon for one of the prized invitations.

Kie^ studied the French clothes lining her closet. What would she wear for the 'business event?' – the need for professionally distinguishing while subtly risqué, erotic, or just your basic alluring – knowing all the women there would envy and hate her regardless of what she wore. The men would be 'stimulated' in accord to the dress choice in any event.

228

Understanding the type 'bait' needed at this first contact with the target, Nyugen chose the more modest 'basic alluring', as it would work as an implied promise for the future but not give a slutty impression and be more appropriate to avoid drawing undue attention from the self-centered crowd at this 'elite' business event. Nyugen made the short walk diagonally across the street from her hotel to the Hotel Continental to join the cocktail hour in progress. She mingled, talking to many of her acquaintances from the Cercle Sportif pool scene.

The cocktail hour was unremarkable in the sense it followed the usual script of the rich and powerful in any city around the world: rumors of who was having an affair; condemning corruption as bad but the money from it was good; wonderment that so-and-so received an invitation to this exalted event. The various discussions during the cocktail hour gave new meaning to the phrase, 'the trivial'. Simultaneous conversations, where at any given time, 100 people were trying to impress the other 100, vying to show how witty they were and how very important they were having been selected as one of the elite consummate-insiders invited to this exclusive event.

As Kie^ worked her way around the room, she looked for Calthrop, having studied his State Department personnel file photo from the KGB spotting report. She saw the target talking to a very attractive Vietnamese woman, obviously one of the "guest members" providing eye-candy for the cocktail hour. This "guest member" looked extremely bored as she smiled at Calthrop, weary as she endured Calthrop's extolling himself in effusive self-congratulatory language. A waiter in full-livery sounded a gong, indicating it was time for dinner. The young woman Calthrop had cornered, quickly disengaged, looking relieved as if she had received a pardon from a serious crime. She and the other "guest members" gracefully left the room in a choreographed exit.

Waiters, with seating charts, assisted the invited guests to their dinner places. Kie^ delayed, to be sure Calthrop was seated. Escorted by a waiter, she approached the table catching Calthrop eyeing her as she walked with the style of royalty. Calthrop jumped-up, with a predatory smile, to pull her chair back. Kie^ smiled back – thinking, 'game on', and she thanked him for his gentlemanly courtesy.

Calthrop introduced himself and offered his business card indicating he was an Economic Attaché in the US Embassy. Kie^ introduced herself as a new member of Cercle Sportif, invited to this event as a professional courtesy for her recent membership. She noted with an inner smile, Calthrop had been rather rudely examining her body since the time she approached the table. (game-points for the KGB). Calthrop droned on about his importance at the Embassy, his importance in the Washington DC scene, and, in general, how he was a man to hold in awe.

Kie^ gave intense attention, feigning interest in his self-laudatory performance, laughing at appropriate times, engaging his eyes at appropriate times, and even touching the back of his hand when Calthrop thought he had made a most humorous comment. In the back of his mind, Calthrop was very pleased how his pick-up lines were impressing this 'hot' Vietnamese woman. As he prepared to deliver his 'get her into bed tonight' coup de maître, as only a "chick-magnet" genius like Calthrop could, Kie^ preempted him with a sad smile, saying she had to meet friends after the dinner. She softened the blow to his ego by suggesting lunch at the Cercle Sportif pool three days hence. He enthusiastically accepted. The hook was set.

Calthrop went back to his Embassy responsibilities excited about the meeting with the beautiful woman, whom he had learned was Eurasian, not Vietnamese. Confident he had impressed her, he eagerly anticipated the pool-side lunch in three-days. For all his many flaws, Calthrop was a capable bureaucrat, that is, expert at covering his ass and shifting blame to others. He was a glib talker and could be charming at times. He was dangerous because he was more intelligent than most people gave him credit.

Calthrop was conflicted after his meeting with Nyugen Kie^ at the Continental Hotel 'business event'. Classified security access protocols in the early 1960s were strict, and TS/SCI clearances broke new ground for 'compartmented Top Secret security protocols'. New technologies such as satellite photography, satellite communications intercepts, and selected extremely sensitive projects were closely guarded, to the point that an individual with a TS/SCI clearance was required to report any and all contacts with foreign nationals. While the contact at the Continental could be dismissed as incidental, his plan to pursue Nyugen Kie^ sexually would not pass the security "incidental" contact test. He smugly decided that he was clever enough to evade the security rules and would not report the dinner contact nor future contacts with Nyugen Kie^.

Kie^ sat in her hotel room carefully reviewing the first meeting with the target. The meeting was a success as measured by HUMINT security and tradecraft standards. The 'first meeting' was natural and would raise no suspicions on the part of the target or any onlookers. She had gained a substantial amount of information from the target to begin the assessment phase of the recruitment and address the question, is he a suitable candidate for recruitment. She had set-up the essential follow-on meeting to maintain continuity with the target under totally natural and non-threatening circumstances.

As she reviewed the information she gathered that evening, she compared these data to the detailed spotting report. Both sets of information tracked well, except, in Kie^'s view, the spotting report underestimated the native intelligence of the target. She would not underestimate Calthrop's intellect. At the same time, he seemed extremely devious and likely prone to excesses in his behavior.

Kie^ applied her conclusions to the preparatory work required in the "assessment phase" in a HUMINT recruitment. Did the target have "access" to the information the KGB wanted? Yes, this target has excellent access to the sensitive information the KGB sought. The rest of the 'assessment process' was more subjective and risky. Was the target psychologically stable enough to function under the stresses of a clandestine operation? What were the target's personal characteristic which made him susceptible to recruitment as a KGB agent to spy on his country? Is the target likely to accept ongoing control by the case officer after recruitment? These questions would be the priority thrust as the assessment goes forward. The profound challenge was to evaluate how the erratic behaving Calthrop would actually function as a KGB spy, a question which had the final answer known only in the future. He was a man who had access to the US secrets, including the 'crown jewels' – US National Intelligence Estimates (NIEs). Kie^ had three days to construct the next step in the assessment process, the Cercle Sportif pool lunch.

Kie^ had prepared carefully, as she had learned to do during her case officer training. Sasha stressed the importance to prepare a 'ghost script' before launching each meeting with a target. This script gives her a constant sense of direction to reach her objectives for the meeting. Understanding the talk during the meeting would not follow the 'ghost script' verbatim, the script was a guide for the case officer to use, a 'path', to maintain the direction and content the case officer wanted to take the conversation. After completing and reviewing the ghost script, she carefully folded the compromising work-paper in a lengthwise accordion fold. Placing the folded note upright in an ashtray, she watched it burn in a controlled and thorough burn, she threw the meager ashes in the toilet, and checked-off that security-block as complete.

Calthrop had a simple objective, 'to get Kie^ into bed'. He gave little thought to detailed planning as he would rely on his 'natural gifts and skills' as a seducer of women. He smirked confidently as he went forward to greet Nyugen.

Kie^ sat by the pool in her eye-catching black bikini, sipping a French 75 cocktail, a drink made from gin, champagne, lemon, and sugar. At 1230, she noticed Calthrop standing in the pool entrance looking for her and at the same time, ogling the "guest members" in their skimpy bikinis. As Calthrop finally noticed her, Kie^ was standing, donning a white translucent knee-high pool cover-up smock. She waved to Calthrop and indicated to the waiter that he should move her drink to her table reserved by the pool. Dressed in grey slacks and a light blue polo shirt, Calthrop was nattily attired for poolside, but not for a senior US Embassy official during work hours. Kie^ offered her hand which Calthrop grasped with both of his hands and held her hand – too long. Suggesting they take their reserved table, she gently removed her hand from his grasp and led him to a pool-side table, already set for lunch.

A waiter was waiting, ready to take a drink-order from Calthrop. Calthrop asked Kie^ what she was drinking and ordered the same. With their drinks in-hand, he proposed a toast to their friendship, touching glasses. Kie^ asked if she might call him, Calthrop? Seeing this as an opportunity to make a 'move', he said:

"My friends call me Calthrop, but my close-intimate friends call me "Win", from Winston, my middle-name – would you please call me "Win"."

Kie^ smiled – even as she thought, how lame, you insufferable egotistical bastard.

"Thank you "Win", I so look forward to being a close-friend with you".

At this, "Win" raised his glass in a silent toast.

The assessment phase of the recruitment process requires the case officer to gain pertinent personal information from the target, doing so in a manner so the target is comfortable, not threatened, and does not become suspicious. The reciprocity technique, a form of elicitation, is employed by many case officers to psychologically manage the early assessment conversations. In the reciprocity technique, the case officer will use her legend to give 'personal information' to the target. The natural reaction by the target is to reciprocate by sharing similar personal information.

Kie^ began eliciting information:

"Win, I am so glad we met at the business initiative dinner. I told you then that my parents are missing. There is more to that story. My father was gracious to put a trust fund in-place for me in Paris. Since then, sadly, I learned people pretend to be your friends to try to get your money. I was lonely in Paris and am even more lonely here in Saigon."

Win thought, this is just too good to be true, a lonely rich beautiful woman implying she wants me to relieve her loneliness:

"Kie^, I understand your life has been very difficult up to now. I know that our close friendship here in Saigon will change all that for the better".

She gave Win her most innocent and expressive smile of gratitude, touching the back of his hand, all the while loathing him as a narcissist ass.

The assessment design is to subliminally establish benign forms of "control" over the target. Kie^ had begun this by establishing the meeting site, the time for the meeting, and preordering the meal, all actions individually seeming inconsequential, but were cleverly connected parts of a Pavlovian conditioning process. Kie^ had ordered the entrée dishes they would share as subtle bonding in this early stage of their relationship. The dishes were traditional Vietnamese and considered as festive dining selections: Vietnamese fresh asparagus and crab soup, Vietnamese cabbage salad with chicken, marinated grilled squid, Vietnamese grilled chicken, almond jelly with lychees, jackfruit and strawberries, plus, green tea to drink.

As they dined on the exquisite food from the Cercle Sportif kitchen, Kie^ asked:

"Win, how long will you be in South Vietnam?"

Win replied, adding coyly:

"At least one year, maybe more, I could stay longer depending on what happens in the near future. What is your situation here? As I remember from our first meeting, you arrived recently from Paris? Where do you live?"

"As I told you, I came to Saigon from Paris to search for my parents who went missing during the chaos and disorder in the late-50s. I currently have a room at the Caravelle Hotel, but I intend to have a more private accommodation in the future. What about your family and wife in the United States?"

"I am divorced and have no children, so I am here at the Embassy, lonely like you. I am quite free and looking forward to making new friends, close friends like you. My work as the Economic Attaché for the US Embassy is important, but it allows me ample time for a social life."

"Your work at the Embassy sounds exciting. Perhaps we could have a dinner together some time so you could tell me more about America. I always have wanted to go to America."

Kie^ used the rest of the conversation to glean personal tidbits about "Win" as she patiently listened to him drone on about himself. This was exactly the type conversation a case officer wants for an assessment meeting, a target that 'helps' by voluntarily delivering the assessment information – which always was a mix of true and false information,in Calthrop's case, inflated tales of his importance.

After another round of French 75 cocktails, "Win" said he had to be at a meeting in the embassy. He asked her to dinner at the Rex Hotel rooftop restaurant in three days for an American style meal. Kie^ thanked him profusely, accepting his invitation. She told him how much she had enjoyed the lunch with him and wanted to see him again. The Rex Hotel at 141 Nguyễn Huệ, had been taken over by the US military for senior officers' quarters, but the roof-top restaurant was open to all US officers and US Embassy senior staff.

Three-days later, Captain Williams and LT Baumgartner sat drinking beer in the team 'bar and fun' room – the juke box was blasting out songs like, "Come a Little Bit Closer" by Jay and Americans – as several of the team NCOs joked and drank beer. Williams and Baumgartner decided they needed steaks to go with more beer, it was time to hit the Rex Hotel roof-top restaurant. They corralled two Nungs as bodyguards/drivers and got in a Jeep for a robust meal of US steaks and American-fried potatoes with onions, plus some Rex roof-top entertainment. There was a Vietnamese rock and roll band there every night – some bands were good, some not so much, but all were loud.

Captain Bobby Williams and LT Gary Baumgartner were thoroughly enjoying the Vietnamese band and the cute-girl lead-singer, as the combo belted out their version of the Bobby Lewis hit, "Tossin 'n Turning". The band was young and reasonably talented – plus they had a sexy young woman on lead vocal – further enhancing the entertainment that evening. A very drunk Army LTC staggered up to the stage to engage the young woman, in conversation, or something – before the situation got totally out of hand, he was restrained by some less-drunk senior officers, to the hoots and jeers of the other diners. Great T-bone steaks, laughs, and beer – it does not get much better in the Vietnam war zone.

The band played on, used to such disruptions by drunk American officers. The background chatter, restored to a raucous level, mocking the drunk LTC plus the usual rough- language and jokes that were the standard social environment for the Rex roof-top restaurant. Then a semi-hush fell over the rowdy bunch of diners as an exotic, astonishingly sexy Eurasian woman in a green and black low-cut dress walked into the restaurant with some guy. Every eye in the room, excepting the band who played-on, focused on the singular-beauty looking for a table.

The team had decided LT Baumgartner would not assume his cover identity as a civilian but would remain openly as a Navy guy. Among the team, only Captain Williams would go the 'cover' route as a civilian to provide him more freedom of action for selected contacts. Captain Williams, under cover as civilian Jason Carter, let his hair grow to a respectable civilian length. As a civilian eccentricity, he carried a 35 mm Pentax SLR camera with him constantly. That 35 mm camera was sitting on the table that evening. As all the officers watched the Eurasian beauty, Gary told Bobby to get a picture of the 'mystery couple'. Carter moved the camera on the table to point at the target couple and took three surreptitious shots while the camera remained on the table. The 'some guy' proceeded the Eurasian woman to an empty table as the semi-hush transitioned to murmurs ranging from a gentlemanly appreciation of the Eurasian woman to some downright lewd comments. After the 'mystery couple' sat down, Carter adjusted the camera to unobtrusively take

235

three more images of the pair. Williams/Carter would take the pictures to CIA Station Saigon later, on just a hunch. The hunch would produce a surprising identification of the 'mystery couple' male-partner in the pictures.

Even as their male hormones are raging in the background, Special Operations guys exceptional primal-instincts kicked-in, - instincts which seem to be the province of case officers and Special Ops guys. This ability to sense danger or intuitively know something is 'out-of-place', animal-like senses which had preserved warrior's lives since the precarious days when cave-dwellers needed to survive the predators of the day. That essential 'sense to survive' continued today in the savage combat ongoing in the Vietnam jungles and rice paddies, and the urban crucible of Saigon. Baumgartner's 'case officer intuition' peaked – that is one uncommonly beautiful woman – but – she is dangerous. I can't be specific – but I know she is bad news. And who is this clown with her? The 'hunch' was spawned.

Telling Bobby to keep his beer cold and steak warm, Baumgartner left the table to run down the five-flights of stairs to locate the Jeep and waiting Nungs. The two Nungs sat in the Jeep smoking cigarettes, with gym bags on their laps, each gym bag contained a Swedish-K machine-gun, a 9mm Berretta handgun, and extra ammo magazines. Baumgartner told the Nungs about the woman in a green and black dress and some guy with her, expected to be departing the Rex, in an hour or so. One Nung was to follow the woman and the second Nung to follow the man to see where they go. They gave a casual salute replying, "OK Boss", Baumgartner gave each Nung a wad of piasters to take cabs back to the compound, knowing full-well these tough-wiry fighters would jog or steal a bicycle to return to the compound and keep the money for their families.

Back at the table, Bobby asked Gary what he did. As exchanges between warriors go, the response was succinct,

"I am having the woman and guy followed – something is wrong here".

Otherwise, the Eurasian beauty remained the erotic-focus for all the rooftop diners, the usual conversational din was reduced to a wave of background lascivious whispers complemented with leering gazes.

Kie^ carefully managed the conversation with Win, giving him the impression that he was in-charge and that she was slowly 'coming under his spell'. Kie^ was cunning as she threw him chunks of sexual innuendo 'bait', which Win gobbled-up - things like – she was lonely here in Saigon and found him interesting and a pleasant friend.

During the conversation, Calthrop continued to unwittingly reveal personal information about himself as he started to brag how important his job was to the Embassy and the US military in Vietnam. As Kie^ and Calthrop departed the Rex, the two Nungs became invisible as they stealthily shadowed their respective targets. Chen followed Nyugen Kie^ to the nearby Caravelle Hotel, where he found a place he could watch the front door surreptitiously. In the typical Nung dedication, he settled in for the night, returning to the compound the next morning to report. Wang followed Calthrop back to the Embassy. He wisely decided to return to the compound as having a gym bag full of weapons would be a problem if detained by the roving guards outside the US Embassy walls. Pilfering a bicycle, he arrived at the compound gate with a wad of piasters in his pocket, adding another set of stolen wheels to the compound stolen bicycle collection.

238

CHAPTER 18   SPIDER AND HIS WEB

A half-empty bottle of Jack Daniels whiskey sat on the table. A drunk Spider, well on the way to a being a very drunk Spider, looked at the glass of whiskey in his hand, laughing as he mumbled, trying to pronounce 'whiskey' in English.

"misky, whissy,"

Spider had purchased the American whiskey on the Saigon black market. He often drank western alcoholic beverages to excess – but seldom got as falling-down drunk as he was now. He was celebrating a trifecta victory over the Americans, killing more American advisors to the ARVN. Continuing to talk to himself in slurred Vietnamese, he mumbled,

"Uncle Ho would be proud of me, so proud. I am a hero for Uncle Ho and the people of the Democratic Republic of Vietnam. I am a 'great man' of the revolution."

This self-praise was part of his smug and confident demeanor, in his mind, he was the greatest spy the North had infiltrated into the South. He was the "principal agent" for many networks spying on the puppet-lackeys of the Americans. After the DRV victory over South Vietnam, the Spider would be lauded with awards, medals, and adulation by his communist countrymen.

The reason for the self-laudatory drinking spree were documented in three messages which he directed his radio operator transmit earlier in the evening. Each of the networks he controlled had provided crucial information which compromised American and Vietnamese operations – and the compromises would lead to killing Americans and their ARVN puppet-lackeys – lackey-traitors to the Vietnamese people.

Tomorrow night he would celebrate with his favorite of the two mistresses he kept in the radio communications building. His wife in Hanoi was not sure he was alive or dead, though she received his monthly pay at the end of each month. Finishing the drink in his hand, the Spider stumbled off to bed where he passed-out

239

When the Spider woke the next morning, the American whiskey had a modicum of revenge for the US. The Spider had a debilitating, head-splitting, incapacitating, hangover. The building was wired with an intercom to give 24-hour instant connections, if needed for time-critical messages. For this 'emergency', Spider called the radio room and told the radio operator to get both his mistresses to his room immediately. About five minutes later, Spider heard the door to his apartment open and the light footsteps of his two diminutive mistresses. When they saw the empty whiskey bottle, they knew what the problem was. They looked at each other and grinned.

The favorite mistress ordered the cohort mistress to go the kitchen and boil water for green tea. Both, suppressing giggles, went about the immediate task of dealing with his hangover. The Spider was not a pleasant man in the best of circumstances, and they hoped he would not take this hangover problem out on them. The Spider whispered they should call his office and tell them he was sick. Cold compresses, copious amounts of green tea, and fawning attention facilitated a recovery by mid-day, at least to the point the Spider was more or less ambulatory. By evening, some food and lots more green tea had worked to revive him back to his usual unpleasant self. After he checked for urgent messages, he dismissed both girls. Going back to what he remembered as his last lucid thoughts yesterday, he relaxed; he was a hero of the Democratic Republic of Vietnam – he had achieved great victories for his future rewards and legacy.

The back story on the two mistresses was rather typical for the great exodus of refugees from the North. People arrived in the South destitute and desperate. The lucky ones had relatives or friends in the South who would provide varying degrees of support. Those who had no supporting network shared the travails common to fugitive refuge-families throughout history. Whether previously of fabulous wealth and influence, or humble Catholics fleeing religious persecution, all these refugees, now bereft of money, were the same. They were shuttled into inhospitable refugee camps where every day was a fight for food and desperate struggles to satisfy basic human needs.

Before their arrival in the south, two of these many refugee girls, Hwa and Nu, were spoiled children raised in luxury by wealthy families in Hanoi. When the Communists exerted their draconian control in the North, both wealthy families became targets of the Public Security

240

Directorate for arrest, punishment in reeducation prisons, or execution. The two families, who were acquainted with each other as members of the Hanoi pre-war social-elite, fled for their lives to the South, leaving behind their money and perks. They arrived in the South as impoverished refugees with no prospects to resume their privileged lives, each day was a contentious hellish fight to survive.

The two spoiled teenage girls fumed with anger at their loss of privilege and status. They had become no different than all the poor people they previously despised and cruelly mocked in Hanoi. Their anger and frustrations morphed into blaming their parents for their plight, blame which soon became hatred for their parents. Hwa and Nu wallowed in self-pity mixed with the sheer hopelessness of facing a bleak future, a combination of depressing thoughts which dominated every waking moment for each girl.

Spider trolled refuge groups from the North looking for vulnerable young women who would do anything to escape the wretched despair of their refugee lives. He spotted Hwa in line to receive food dispensed by the South Vietnamese government. She was beautiful and projected a look of humiliation and anger with her body language. She was about to undergo the degrading loss of face begging for food. Beyond that, she was standing in line with people she looked down-on, people who were far beneath her status as, in her mind, she was still one of the elite. Her emotions silently peaked with a vitriolic fury, why had this happened to her! Adding to her raging frustration, she was wearing an expensive ao dai, now showing signs of wear from the many washings to combat the filth of the refugee center. Hwa lived in denial of the reality she was a refugee. She was determined to believe she was not like all the rest in that line.

Spider used an approach that had worked before – he would ask the targeted-girl for information. Sergeant Pham Binh, 5-feet five inches tall, 135 pounds, though 43 years old his face and skin appear wizened as one would expect in a Vietnamese man 15 years older. His physical appearance was the result of years enduring the harsh climate of the Vietnamese jungles serving as an NVA officer with the Viet Minh. Pham's slight physique and grizzled specter belied a vigorous highly-intelligent man who was a combat hardened veteran of guerrilla warfare. Moreover, Pham had a personal characteristic that served him well as an intelligence operative for the North Vietnamese Ministry of Defense Intelligence Department. Sergeant Pham/Colonel Wang was an exceptionally ruthless man.

Smiling obsequiously, Spider approached the young girl and asked her if she could direct him to a noodle restaurant located in that neighborhood. Though the man was smiling and not aggressive, she was repulsed by the old man in a lowly ARVN sergeant uniform.

Hwa, 15-years old, responded rudely and brusquely:

"I do not live here and do not know about any such restaurant. I am just helping a friend by standing in line for her."

Spider continue to smile and bowed slightly, while apologizing for intruding on her privacy. He asked in a humble voice,

"Could I make amends for my rude behavior? Would you allow me to buy you dinner if we can find the restaurant I believe is nearby?"

Hwa was very hungry and she wanted to rebel against 'everything' in her current situation - all the pain that the nightmarish refugee conditions imposed on her - what better way than to go to dinner with a stranger – a lowly sergeant. Her parents would be very angry. Hwa forced a smile and said,

"I would forgive you Sergeant if you would make amends by taking me to a meal"

In contrast to her evasive remark that she was standing in line for a friend, Hwa stepped out of line and followed Spider to the next intersection. He feigned surprise as they discovered the restaurant, just as he knew it would be there. The Spider had shuttled many young refugee girls through what was not a 'noodle eatery', but nicely appointed expensive restaurant. This restaurant was a well-known enterprise for excellent, but pricy, food. A seductive setting which the Spider had used before in his 'how to lure young women' ploy. The ARVN sergeant knew when to talk and when to be listen. He knew how to play their emotions and the desperate needs of his prey. The Spider was 'smooth'.

When the girl read the menu, she almost burst into tears as she recognized various food delights which she and her family routinely enjoyed during their halcyon days in Hanoi, delicious gourmet delicacies now seemingly forever lost to them. She looked at the Sergeant across the table who was carefully reading the menu. Hwa did not sense that the Spider was, in fact, was high in the food-chain of predators who preyed on young refugee-women.

Hwa ordered more entree dishes than she could possibly eat, which the Spider duly noted. She was starving, that is good. The waiter patiently transcribed her order of Pho, a savory noodle soup, banh xeo, a type of pancake filled with a combination of seafood and vegetables, vermicelli noodles, chicken, pork or beef slices, shrimp, sliced onions, beansprouts, and mushrooms; Ca kho to, a catfish fillet that's braised and served in a clay pot. Suddenly, Hwa realized she was making a fool of herself and truncated her ordering by asking for green tea.

Spider knew instantly how to play her embarrassment. He turned to the waiter and ordered the same dishes. Their leisurely meal was marked by a non-threating conversation, including a digression about the difficult conditions persisting throughout South Vietnam because of the war. The latter discourse irritated Hwa, as it sounded just like her father trying to excuse the family's current plight. Regardless of the conversation, Hwa was sated with food for the first time in weeks – good food that important people eat regularly, important people like her – this was how she used to eat. After the meal they stood outside the restaurant, Hwa wondered if this strange man would now demand sex from her. Instead, the Spider thanked her for a pleasant evening and asked if she would do him the honor of dining together again. A relieved Hwa said,

"I would be happy to dine with you again"

Spider asked Hwa how he might contact her, knowing this would pose a serious problem for her. Hwa was in a quandary. She would 'lose face' if he knew she lived in a refugee camp. Spider had set her up, but he intervened before her 'loss of face' destroyed his patient stalking. He politely asked,

"Can we meet one week from now, the same time at this restaurant?"

Comforted by the satisfying meal and thrilled at her escaping having to sexually service her host, she was ecstatic she did not 'lose face' by telling the truth that she lived in the wretched refugee camp. Hwa answered with an enthusiastic:

"Yes! I will meet you here, next week."

As she started to turn to leave, a most peculiar interaction occurred. The Spider reached into his pocket, commenting,

"I know your friend will be angry that you did not stand in line for her. Please take this to help her as you can."

Pham handed her six US 10-dollar bills – a wonderous amount of money for anyone in that despicable refugee camp. Without hesitation and too quickly, Hwa took the money promising again to meet him in a week.

The Spider watched her walk away, she seemed to erotically sway her hips under her expensive but well-worn ao dai, he nodded in a smug contentment – he could easily manipulate her.

During this rather surreal incident, Hwa did not immediately process the fact that the lowly ARVN sergeant just paid an exorbitant bill for their meal. Later replaying the evening in her mind, she did comprehend just how much money he had spent for the meal and the $60 in cash he gave her. She smirked, I do not know or care where this fool got his money. What I do know is, I can manipulate him to get more money from him. On the way back to the camp Hwa used one of the US $10 bills to buy a large amount of food for her family – as she walked into the camp she contrived her lie to explain the money to her parents, that is, account for ten dollars she would give her parents and for the money she spent on the food. She would secretly keep the rest of the money for herself.

Hwa decided to tell her parents a rather unbelievable tale that a drunk American had asked for directions. After she gave him the directions, the American gave her two US ten dollar bills and walked away. Her parents were suspicious of the preposterous story how she acquired $20 suspecting she had prostituted herself as so many refugee girls did.. Regardless, her parents accepted the ten dollars from Hwa and rationalized accepting her explanation for the money as part their own mental denial of their current plight.

Hwa reveled in the money she had been given by the strange ugly man in the lowly sergeant's uniform. She counted it and recounted it. She looked in her small hand-mirror, one of the few personal things she could bring with her from Hanoi. She thought, now I can have nice things again. We have this fool, who Nu and I can play and manipulate, and he has money. We are too smart and too beautiful for him to resist. In her arrogance and disdain for all the people she deemed inferior and below

244

her social status, Hwa temporarily forgot she no longer had the social status as an elite. Now she could more easily be in denial that she was just another hungry refugee in a soiled elegant dress. Reality hit her, as she looked away from the mirror and was shocked back to the truth of her current situation by her bleak surroundings, Hwa began to cry.

Galvanized into action, Hwa moved from her fantasy to formulate a plan that would take her out of the refugee hellhole and back to a modicum of luxury. She contrived how she and Nu would use the next meeting with the little-sergeant to gain an emotional control over the little-man and use their sexual wiles to get his money. They would use their native mental superiority and good looks to psychologically dominate Sergeant Pham Binh. Sergeant Pham Binh was a joke to Hwa, a pathetic needy man who they would soon subjugate to their wills and relieve him of a lot of his money.

Tomorrow, Hwa would contact Nu, her friend from Hanoi and now her friend in a miserable refugee camp. Nu was another formerly rich-girl who became just another destitute child from a formerly rich family. If anything, Nu was even more of a spoiled brat than Hwa. Nu was a physical copy of Hwa in the beauty of her face, but she had a fleshier body type. Nu was 13-years old – very hungry and savagely angry at her current plight - traits which made her vulnerable.

Hwa ran to Nu's tent home. She brought Nu a small box filled with portions of Vietnamese steamed banana cake plus Banh Bo, sweet steamed rice cakes. When Nu opened the box, she began to cry. Nu hugged Hwa in gratitude and began to devour the delicious desserts. Hwa told her to slow down – there are many more of these benefits to come. Hwa told Nu, I know 'an easy mark', using the street-language she had recently learned

Hwa regaled Nu with the details of the past evening. How she met a rich silly old man who had a lot of money. Hwa explained how she and Nu could play 'the easy mark' to get the food, money, and things they wanted and deserved – two rich spoiled brats, now two poor spoiled brats, becoming street-wise women – striving to live in their elegant-style again. She began to share the plan when they met the 'little sergeant'. Hwa would self-invite Nu to the dinner, a rude act of disrespect for the host of the dinner, Sergeant Pham Binh. The girls giggled as they mocked their target and talked about how they would spend his money.

The Spider thought about the dinner with Hwa that evening. She was an arrogant condescending spoiled-brat who could not hide her contempt for him, even as he paid handsomely for her food and gave her more money than she had seen for months. Instead of becoming angry, Sergeant Pham Binh, whose actual rank and true name were NVA Colonel Wang Ky operating under cover as a top-level spy in South Vietnam. He was the principal agent for the 'NVA Victory Cell' working as spies for the North Vietnamese Ministry of Defense Intelligence Department. Pham smirked as he developed his plan for Hwa.

Sergeant Pham Binh, dressed in civilian clothes, was surprised when he observed Hwa walking toward him arm-in-arm with a beautiful younger girl who was a more voluptuous version of herself. Hwa gave a supercilious haughty smirk, which she intended for the lowly sergeant to receive as a smile. Hwa casually introduced her friend Nu.

Hwa arrogantly dismissed any considerations of being overbearing to invite a person to a social event without asking the host who was paying the costs. Sergeant Pham Binh bowed and welcomed both girls, thinking all the while – perfect, two girls for the night and my plan. They will feel safety in numbers and security in their presumptuous ignorance, these spoiled young brats. Sergeant Pham Binh guided them to his car, a black four-door Citroen sedan. Both girls sucked-in air between their teeth at the shock of seeing the car. It was more luxurious than the cars their families had owned in Hanoi.

Sergeant Pham Binh explained why they needed the car, they would be visiting a different restaurant some distance away. The seating arrangement presented an awkward moment, but Pham cheerfully suggested the girls both sit in the backseat and he would be their chauffer. As the girls got into the car, both were snickering, how appropriate, the little-sergeant is our chauffer. This was better than our original plan to simply fleece the sergeant. They would humiliate him in the process.

The girls ordered the most expensive entrees on the menu, starting with birds-nest soup and finishing with a childlike choice of Keo Dua (Coconut Candy) for dessert. During the meal, the three engaged in a stilted conversation as Hwa and Nu smirked when they made several comments which were obvious condescending slights to their host.

As the main entrees were cleared from the table, each girl having consumed an amazing amount of food, Pham ordered a bottle of French wine after asking the girls if they would enjoy this foreign drink. The girls replied with a smug:

"We have enjoyed such wines many times before, thank you".

Hwa took pleasure in eating the coconut candy in a sexually suggestive manner, which was quite arousing for the North Vietnamese Colonel. Completing dessert and finishing the bottle of wine, the little sergeant said he would take them home in his car, but first he must stop at his apartment as he had forgotten to bring a gift he had for Hwa. The girls were slightly tipsy from the wine, not paying attention that Sergeant Pham Binh had split the bottle between them eschewing any of the alcohol for himself. The girls talked in muffled tones as they rode in the backseat to Pham's apartment. Part of their discussion was how they would avoid being dropped off at the refugee camp and giggling how well they had maneuvered 'the little sergeant' that evening – and now to receive a gift – then we go for some of his money!

Sergeant Pham Binh parked at the back of a three-story apartment building, his spy radio communications building. Pham asked the girls if they would like to see his apartment. Without hesitation, the girls' curiosity overcame any sense of prudence they might have had, flinging the car doors open as they said "yes" to visiting his apartment.

Pham opened the apartment building back-door and led the girls up the stairs to his second-floor apartment. The girls looked around and were simultaneously surprised at the nice condition of the building and the lack of the repugnant odious smells so common in the refugee camp. It was like 'the old days in Hanoi'. The girls carefully examined the surroundings, four doors on the first and second floor landings, suggested four apartments on each floor. As Pham unlocked his door, Nu asked how many apartments are on each floor. He confirmed that there were four apartments on each floor – a fact that impressed and confused the girls – who is this ARVN sergeant?

As they entered his apartment, the relative opulence further disoriented them. Examining the expensive furniture and seeing large rooms, it was obviously the apartment of a rich man. Pham asked them to please sit down on the western-style upholstered chairs. He left the room to return with what he called an after-dinner "health-drink"– orange juice with a substantial amount of vodka. It was a drink the girls would later come to know by its Western name, a Screwdriver. The girls tentatively tasted the potent "health drink' and found the beverage pleasant and tasty. They each took a second larger sip. Pham invited them to see the apartments across the landing, adding, bring your drinks.

The girls followed as he opened the door to one of the apartments across the second floor landing. It was unlocked causing Hwa to ask why it was not locked. Pham replied, in a humble voice, that it was because he owned the building and kept the building entrances locked. The girls again were stunned, there seemed to be so many contradictions – an ARVN sergeant who owns a whole apartment building – impossible!

As they entered the apartment their confusion escalated. The décor was stylish and definitely feminine, reminding them of the better times in Hanoi. Pham showed them the bedroom where he asked them to feel the sheets. An exquisite weave of the purest silk, as good or better than the sheets they used to sleep on in Hanoi. Pham encouraged them to drink more of the health drink and they would visit another apartment. Both girls chugged their drinks as a curious awe overcame them. Entering the second apartment, the girls found a similar feminine atmosphere employing a different interior design, the furnishings were different, but as expensive as those in the first apartment. Again. Pham insisted they look at the bedroom in this apartment, as his lust was raging.

Returning to Pham's apartment, Hwa asked who lived in the fourth apartment on that floor, the one they had not inspected. He said it was empty, for now, observing that the girls were a bit unsteady on their feet. Neither girl was used to the substantial volume of alcohol they were imbibing. Back in the living room of his apartment, Pham prepared a second more-potent "health drink" for each of them and exhorted them to enjoy more of the orange beverage. The girls had forgotten their plan to dominate and humiliate Sergeant Pham Binh. They were becoming more pliable to his suggestions with each sip of the orange juice and vodka. Pham excused himself for a moment going into his bedroom. He returned with a tray with two more 'health drinks and a small box. Apologizing profusely, he explained, he had a gift for Hwa but did not expect Nu to be at the dinner. If he had known she was coming, he would have had a gift for her as well.

Pham said,

"Please finish your drinks and we will open the gift"

The girls were now past pliable, eagerly responsive to his suggestions, suggestions which were becoming more like orders. The girls dutifully drained their glasses as Pham proactively returned from the kitchen with refills and a drink for himself. The girls giggled as he gave them fresh drinks. Smiling, Pham suggested they all sit on the large couch to see the gift. Each girl had difficulty standing, so he rushed to their aid, putting his arm around each girl's waist, in succession, to support them on the trip to the couch from the soft chairs.

Pham raised his glass of the 'health drink", offering a toast to Hwa's receiving a present. The girls responded with more giggles, followed by each girl taking a large swill of the seemly endless flow of 'health-drinks'. Pham opened the small box to display a gold necklace made from thick-links of pure 24-carat gold. The girls gasped at this expensive piece of jewelry, which was so casually offered to Hwa. At that moment, Nu felt an intense jealousy toward Hwa.

Pham asked Hwa if he could put the necklace around her neck. In a slurred voice, Hwa responded,

"Peesch, put it on my neck".

She clumsily lifted her long black hair to give Pham access to her neck. He slowly latched the necklace as he examined Hwa's flawless skin. Hwa placed her hair back, somehow artfully draping her long black hair over her shoulders.

Pham took Nu's hands in his hands. He spoke softly with compassion, promising Nu a gold necklace the next time they would meet. Nu was mollified and acted on an impulse. She kissed Pham on the mouth and held that kiss, in part to irritate Hwa.

Totally embarrassed by this compulsive physical act, Nu lowered her head in shame, but Pham put his hand under her chin, lifting her face to look at him and he smiled at Nu. Now Hwa was jealous. Noticing the girls' glasses were empty, Pham said they would have a final 'health drink' to mark a most pleasant evening.

The girls did not resist the suggestion of one more drink. Both girls lost their sensibilities under the heavy influence of all the alcohol plus the potent subtle influence of 'the little-sergeant'. The girl's inhibitions disappeared as they slid into their individual alcoholic hazes.

Both girls' heads were nodding when Pham returned with yet another

249

'health drink'. This mix was more vodka than orange juice. He proposed one more toast, this toast to the three of them and future gifts. The girls unsteadily hefted their glasses, each taking a large drink, oblivious of the strong flavor of the vodka. As they girls finished less than half of this 'last drink', Pham smiled. The young women were in a state that the crude Americans called 'shit-faced drunk'. Pham told them he could not return them to their parents in this condition, adding they should sleep a little before he took them home – the idea of sleeping vaguely registered with Hwa as she set her drink on the table in front of the couch. Nu was semi-conscious, laying back on the couch with her eyes closed and her drink spilled onto the floor. He took Nu's empty glass, setting it on the table.

He offered his hand to assist Hwa to stand and told her he would help her to the apartment across the landing. Nothing was registering in Hwa's brain now, except she thought that getting into a bed to sleep was a very good idea. Pham guided and supported Hwa across the landing and into the first bedroom they visited earlier. Hwa struggled to stand as the alcoholic daze made her motor-functions problematic and her inhibitions non-existent. Hwa had an awareness that 'the little sergeant' was undressing her. In her inebriated-state, she felt she was an actress in some pornographic movie - like those 'dirty movies', which she had viewed at one of the wild-parties of the rich spoiled-elite children of the privileged in Hanoi.

Once Pham had Hwa naked, he helped her onto the bed. He undressed and began molesting Hwa, his excitement growing as the fondled the young girl. Hwa made no attempt to stop him or even to talk. Hwa felt Pham get on top of her as he raped her. Pham smiled as he raped Hwa, silently mouthing his thoughts, you thought you were so superior, how is your plan working now? Utterly drunk, Hwa passed out. Pham thought, my plan is perfect, and this is just the beginning. Finished with Hwa, for now, he covered her with the silk sheets and walked naked back to his apartment.

Nu was still on the couch, her head lolling on the couch armrest, snoring loudly in her alcoholic stupor. Pham knew she could not walk in her condition, so he picked her up and carried her to the second bedroom across the landing, laying her on the bed. Pham deftly undressed her, overcoming the ao dai snaps and tight fit. Once he had Nu naked, he got into bed and begin to molest the girl. As he abused her, he determined that Nu was still a virgin, his lust peaked as he mounted Nu and raped her.

The next morning, with roaring headaches, two young girls rued the day they had conspired against this savage, they thought, this 'very rich savage'. Pham greeted them warmly as he led them to his apartment for a lot of green tea and toast. By mid-morning, the girls felt better and wondered – what next? Neither was fully lucid trying to deal with extreme pain from their hangovers. They each tried to remember the details from the previous night, Hwa touched her gold necklace and Nu felt a great deal of abdominal pain as Pham told them they had a bit too much to drink during the nice party the three enjoyed together.

Pham said he had a remembrance gift for each of them and looked forward to seeing them again, very soon. Pham handed each of them an envelope. Fully aware that neither girl wanted him to know they lived in the squalor of the refugee camp, he offered them a ride home in his car, or, if they preferred, he would pay for a taxi. The girls clutched their envelopes as they responded in unison, the taxi would be fine as they did not want to place a burden on him. He smiled and said, he would go to his room to get taxi fare for them. As soon as he left the room the impatient adolescents peeked into the two envelopes. Gasping at the contents, each envelope contained two-hundred US dollars in twenty-dollar bills. Pham returned to the living room and gave each girl a wad of South Vietnamese piasters for the taxi, each girl receiving an amount about ten-times more than any taxi fare back to the camp

As the girls returned to the refugee camp in the taxi, Sergeant Pham Binh drove the Citroen to pick-up Colonel Trần Quan. Concurrently, the previous-evening 'party-goers', Pham, Hwa, and Nu, reflected about their personal perspectives on the past evening and this morning. Sergeant Pham Binh concluded his plan had far exceeded his wildest dreams and these two girls would become his mistresses.

Hwa conceded that the events of the last evening had not followed the script she had developed, but smiling, she concluded the results exceeded her highest expectations, as she felt the cash-filled envelope in her pocket, touched the gold chain around her neck, and started to count the days until the next time she could manipulate Pham. Of course, the latter thought was an exercise in denial. A jealous Hwa now saw Nu as a competitor for Number One Girl. Hwa pledged to herself to do whatever it took to be Pham's favorite.

Nu was lost in thought and confused. The night before seemed like two dreams, one good and one unclear, maybe not so good. The good dream was documented by the fat envelope full of more money than she had ever seen in her thirteen-year old life. Furthermore, there was every reason to believe she could refill that envelope many times. The 'unclear dream' related to the lingering pain in her abdomen and the recognition that her relationship with Hwa as a friend had ended last night. Now, Nu was a competitor to be the favorite of Pham. The fact of the matter was, the three had entered into what would become sexual symbiotic relationship as Hwa and Nu competed for the affection and money of Sergeant Pham Binh.

Pham smiled, all this fun and the party was totally paid for with black money from the North Vietnamese Ministry of Defense Intelligence Department and the KGB. The Spider thoughtfully reviewed his situation, giving himself maximum credit in the process for every success, all the while, smiling about the black money he used to lavish envelopes of money and gifts on the girls.

He thought about increasing the security for the building. The building had 12-apartments, four on each floor. The top floor housed the radio equipment in one of the third-floor apartments. The 'radio apartment' used the former living area as the setup for the radio equipment. The rest of that apartment included a bedroom converted into a conference room, plus a room for files, spare equipment, and weapons. Two of the other apartments on the third floor were assigned to the three radio operators for sleeping, each worked an eight-hour shift so two of the operators would be off duty each shift. The fourth apartment on the third floor was used for additional file and equipment storage.

Spider lived on the second floor; the other three second-floor apartments were available and would be assigned respectively, one to each mistress. The cook lived in the fourth apartment as Pham had 'lied to the girls' that it was empty. Spider decided that installing more technical security devices would conflict with the low-profile he believed the building enjoyed. Thus, the "smart thing" was to do nothing. Spider's vain egotistical self-importance led him to sloppy security, poor tradecraft, and over-confidence.

He smirked as he thought how the black money he received from the Ministry of Defense Intelligence Department helped him to achieve great things for the Democratic Republic of Vietnam and had given him the lifestyle he deserved in Saigon. He had purchased the apartment building

252

with the black money, the Saigon deed recorded in one of his aliases. He had previously entertained mistresses and now would have a new set of mistresses living in the building. Above all, he was successfully accomplishing his mission for North Vietnam. He had power – he deserved this 'Good Life' and more.

The "deserved more" thought created a caustic resentment he felt every day. Despite all the fame he had attributed to himself, Spider was extremely bitter about several matters. His cover as an ARVN sergeant irritated him as he had to salute the ARVN officers on a daily basis, puppets of the US – those ARVN traitor-puppets. He had received no awards from Hanoi for his heroic service; and most of all, in his view, the condescending treatment he endured from the Ministry of Defense Intelligence Department was an insult equal to the "loss of face".

He bristled thinking how he was humiliated a month ago. He had a clandestine meeting in Saigon with an officer sent from Hanoi, a mere Major in the Ministry of Defense Intelligence Department. The major was to provide guidance and updating on financial regulations and procedures for his operation – "his clandestine operation!" – a major, giving guidance to me - totally outrageous and unacceptable – I am a Colonel in the Ministry of Defense Intelligence Department.

The 'mere major' was Major Hoang Tuan, young for an NVA major, 27-years old. He was 5-feet five inches tall, pudgy and soft at 165 pounds, pompous and arrogant. Altogether a very unimpressive officer and an unpleasant individual. Hoang's overbearing demeanor was the extension of his father's political position as part of Ho Chi Minh's small inner circle. The young major was quick to tell all that he was part of the NVA power structure based on his father's important position. Virtually everyone, except Tuan's girlfriend, dismissed Major Hoang Tuan as insufferable and inconsequential. But they were careful to avoid any situation which would lead him to complain to his father. Major Hoang had no serious military duties and made the most of that situation as a playboy son of a powerful communist party member.

The mission to chastise Spider was a task which had little upsides for the messenger, unless the messenger was relatively untouchable due to political connections. Major Hoang was quick to accept the mission to Saigon because his cover to enter South Vietnam would be a Vietnamese expatriate living in Hong Kong. Hoang Tuan would have the opportunity to transit Hong Kong twice during his clandestine mission. He could buy coveted goods not available in North Vietnam, engage in sleazy-sex play in the Kowloon district of Hong Kong, and demonstrate further to his girlfriend and friends what an important man he was. All paid for by the NVA.

The 'guidance and updates' were essentially a criticism of Spider's expenditures for the operation in Saigon. Spider 'lost face' being censored by a lower ranking officer adding insult to injury. The major delivered a mixed message; Spider was commended for his effective performance in his mission which had produced excellent results. At the same time, Hanoi was concerned about the excessive and often questionable expenditures Spider had made. Hanoi was demanding a better accounting of the black money the Ministry of Defense Intelligence Department sent him - money the Ministry of Defense Intelligence Department was actually receiving from the KGB.

Spider had controlled his anger and shifted the focus to a request that, given the key position he held in the North Vietnam espionage operation against the 'South'. He asserted he should know the 'true names' of the top level moles the Ministry of Defense Intelligence Department controlled in the South. The Major had the gall to answer him directly, rather than send his demand to Hanoi. The Major looked at the Spider and told him he did not have 'the need-to-know' nor clearance for the agents' true names or other information about them. The Spider remembered how fiercely he had gritted his teeth - so hard his jaw hurt for two days after the meeting with the damned 'major'. Such a gratuitous insult and loss of face! The final indignity occurred after the 'major' gave Spider a large package of cash: dollars, piasters, and French francs. The 'major', in what Spider perceived as a frivolous tone, dared to encourage him 'to keep up the good work'. The 'Major Hoang' meeting had resulted in a Spider drinking bout that produced a worse hangover than the one he just recovered from.

The Spider continued to seethe as he tried to forget his 'loss of face'. The Spider did smile as he reveled in the knowledge that he had figured out many names of the 'DRV moles' who were embedded in the South Vietnam military and government. The reports from these moles flowed through his radio center. He had identified a communist agent from the Indochina War Viet Minh days who infiltrated the Army of the Republic of Vietnam. This 'mole' had acted as an advisor to the President of the Republic of Vietnam, and amazingly was now assigned to be the Province Chief of Bến Tre Province, a major province in South Vietnam. This 'mole', Phạm Ngọc Thảo, was one of the most prolific North Vietnamese spies sending reports though Spider's radio network back to Hanoi. Phạm Ngọc Thảo had a spy's pseudonym to cover his identity in the communications – but the Spider was clever and discerned his name along with the true names and locations of other top North Vietnamese agents. The Spider suspected Vu Ngoc Nha was one of the Ministry of Defense Intelligence Department's moles using Spider's communications network. Spider, the lowly ARVN Sergeant, directly controlled the Deconfliction Department of the ARVN Joint General Staff through the insipid Colonel Trần Quan. Tran was the Spider's personal pawn – how amusing, the Sergeant-chauffer was in-charge of the ARVN Colonel.

The arrogant Spider resentful continued to fester. He was their top-spy, how could they criticize him; how could they deny him the accesses he requested. The Spider was sure he knew the answer. His enemies in the Ministry of Defense Intelligence Department were jealous of his successes and had conspired to damage his amazing career. His 'jealous competitor' excuse calmed the NVA Colonel/ARVN Sergeant as he decided he would prevail over these petty individuals who were safely in-place in Hanoi.

He diverted his thoughts to his mistresses and began to think about favoring his mistresses with a ménage à trois in the near future.

His egotistical focus had damning security consequences. He was ignorant of the Peregrine surveillance of his radio-building. He also was unaware he was unwittingly being used by the KGB, facilitating two KGB deception operations, one against North Vietnam and one against the Americans. He was ignorant of the fact that NSA was now reading a great proportion of the messages his Saigon radio transmission sent to the A Shau radio site. He was 'in the dark' that the KGB encryption method used by his network was now compromised, even as the Spider's radio operators sent supposedly secure messages every day. The truth be told, Spider should be addressing his security needs rather than lusting after his mistresses.

CHAPTER 19 TARGET AND AGENT ASSESSMENT

The assessment phase of vetting, examining, and evaluating a target is a continuous process. The assessment can be defined by two axioms: "Never Fall in Love with Your Source" (which means, there are instances where the case officer and the spy become good friends, but the case officer cannot let such a friendship cloud his judgment, so the case officer loses objectivity to see any problems with the agent, this axiom is not directed at the classic idea of romantic love). The second axiom is a variation of the first, "Never Trust Your Agent". It is often easy to form a friendship with a highly successful agent. Basking in this success can lead the case officer to rely on the agent to a point the case officer is no longer skeptical of the agent. The ensuing results are security disasters such as responding improperly to deceptive information planted by a double agent. Trust in an agent must be unidirectional; the case officer leads the agent to trust the case officer, but the case officer only appears to reciprocate in the trust relationship and must never fully trust the agent.

Captain Williams briefed the team on his ARVN Joint General Staff agent:

"CIA came through, they giving us spotting information on an ARVN lieutenant in the Joint General Staff personnel office. The target is poorly paid, a slacker trying to avoid combat duty, and has access to the ARVN personnel files. Using my civilian cover as Jason Carter, I had a target assessment-meeting with ARVN Second Lieutenant Lê Minh. Minh is from a wealthy family, but they lost most all their money when the Lê family fled to the south. As Catholics and capitalists, his father was on the North Vietnamese Police arrest list."

"Once in the South with little money, the impoverished family's political connections seemed to evaporate. After a while, a family friend in the South, did Minh's father a favor. To get Minh into the ARVN and was assigned a staff job with Joint General Staff personnel. Minh is perceived as a coward trying to avoid combat duty. Minh is continually angry about the low pay the Vietnamese military officers and enlisted-men receive. Junior officers typically received less than $50 dollars per month. The fact many senior officers collected large amounts of money, in bribes, from soldiers' families to protect a family member from being

257

assigned to a combat unit, further incensed Minh. Minh knew that his protected status would not last long as his father could not afford the required bribes to keep him out of combat."

"Under cover as Jason Carter, a US Department of Defense civilian working for the Adjunct Inspector General Team #4 in Saigon, I called Second Lieutenant Lê Minh at Joint General Staff headquarters. Lê Minh was totally taken back when an American called him. I told Minh that I was given Lieutenant Lê's name as a contact to participate in a joint Vietnamese-American study on personnel policies. I asked him to have dinner with me to discuss the project. He replied immediately, "yes; it would be an honor to be part of the project". I told him to meet at the My Canh floating restaurant, off Tu Do street, at 1800 hours for the meal. I cautioned Lê that this joint-government study would be confidential, he should not mention the call or the project to anyone".

Minh sat back in wonderment at this strange call, a mysterious project, and what his prospects might be participating in the 'study'.

Carter/Williams stood by the short gangway connecting the My Canh floating restaurant to the Saigon River bank.

"I had seen a picture of Lê Minh in the CIA spotting file and identified him as he approached, a slight young man in an ARVN Second Lieutenant uniform. Lê Minh is a willowy youth at five feet 5 inches weighing 130 pounds on a good day".

"As he reached the gangway, I smiled and extended my hand delivering a welcoming greeting, I am Jason Carter, thank you for coming; Lê tentatively took my hand but with a firmer grip than I expected. He smiled and responded, I am Lieutenant Lê Minh. I gave him my Adjunct Inspector General Team #4 business card and suggested we board the restaurant."

Carter had reserved a table on the river-side away from the eyes of passing pedestrians and any potential surveillance. In a relaxed measured voice,

"Thank you Lieutenant Lê for meeting me, I look forward to a pleasant meal together and an interesting conversation".

Lê replied in excellent English:

"I am thankful for this invitation; this is a nice restaurant; I must say I am very surprised why you invited me to be here".

258

Carter's first impression was, there is more substance to this target than what was indicated in the spotting file. Lê Minh looked directly at Carter as he spoke, showing a sharp-intelligence in his bright gaze. Carter decided to shift his planned script to a more sophisticated dialog:

"I expected you would be surprised by my call and perhaps concerned by my rather mysterious reference that this work would be confidential."

"Minh nodded his head in agreement but made no comment. I made a mental note, the target has a certain street-wise demeanor".

I needed to be careful, as in all spotting reports, the information was incomplete and contained inaccuracies – some discrepancies in the spotting are evident. I explained that my remark about being "confidential" was correct but represented a temporary situation. The project could have political implications and needed to be guarded initially to keep the information from being used inappropriately for political interests.

A waiter appeared before Carter could continue, Carter asked Minh if he would order for both of them, adding that Minh was his guest for this meal. Without hesitating, Lê Minh ordered Banh Khot (Mini Shrimp Pancakes), Banh Cuon Chay (Vegetarian Steamed Rice Rolls), Bo Luc Lac ('Shaken' Beef Bowl with Hoisin Sauce), and Banh Cam (Sesame Balls) for dessert with green tea to drink. After the waiter departed, Carter continued to describe the confidential project, the focus of the project was to do a comparative study of Vietnamese and American personnel processes to assign officers to senior staff-officer positions.

Carter unsubtly launched his test for this meeting;

"I understand you have full-time duties at the Joint General Staff personnel office, thus, your work on the personnel project would involve working on your personal time. The Adjunct Inspector General Team #4 has allocated funds to pay you for your support of the joint project, if you would accept a role in the project."

Carter detected a gleam of greed in Lê Minh's eye; a 'tell' that betrayed a vulnerability. Lê Minh was silent for a few moments, forcing himself to restrain from immediately asking Carter, how much will you pay? Minh said:

"I would be honored to participate in the project and understand the initial need for confidentiality."

Carter reached across the table to shake Lê Minh's hand and congratulate him on joining the 'project team'. Carter delivered a coup de theatre, he told Minh that he brought a 'signing bonus' for him in the event Minh agreed to join the project team. The look on Minh's face signaled 'the hook was set'.

During the rest of the dinner they talked about the food Minh had ordered, Vietnamese culture, and, of course, the war; the conversation was relaxed. Minh was comfortable with this American and was eager to know about this 'signing bonus'. Towards the end of the meal, Minh was getting apprehensive about the promised 'signing bonus', Carter sensed this concern and let Lê Minh's anxiety build to give Carter more leverage as he delivered the 'signing bonus' money. By giving Minh the money, Carter would satisfy a compulsive need ingrained in the target psychic, a need for money. As they enjoyed the Banh Cam dessert, Carter asked Minh if he would like an after-dinner drink such as cognac – extending Minh's suspense about the 'signing bonus'. Minh wanted a drink at this point, he was worrying when, or if, he would receive the signing bonus. A film of sweat coalesced on his brow as he accepted the proposal for an after dinner drink. Carter had played the target well to evaluate his greed as a vulnerability. Carter ordered two snifters of Remy Martin cognac.

As they sipped the cognac, Carter suggested they meet again in three days to discuss specific tasks for the project. Lê Minh tried to appear cool but the film of sweat on his forehead had already betrayed him, answering too quickly, he agreed to the proposed meeting. Carter took a sip of his cognac, calculating it was time to deliver on the 'signing bonus' promise. Carter pulled an envelope from his pocket and very discretely slid the envelope across the table to Minh, thanking him for joining the team and emphasizing the signing bonus was a down-payment for his future work on the project. Lê Minh's greed overcame his sense he should be cool, Lê Minh almost knocked over his snifter of cognac as he reached for the envelope.

Saying good evening at the end of the gangway, both men departed thinking it was a successful night. Minh could hardly wait to open the envelope and Carter knew the hook was swallowed; he owned Lê Minh. When Minh was back in his apartment, he opened the envelope and gasped, there were 25 US $20 dollar bills, $500 US dollars for his 'signing bonus', he counted the bills three-times, carefully handling each bill. His monthly military-pay as an ARVN Second Lieutenant was equivalent to about $40 US dollars.

As Jason Carter prepared for the second meeting with ARVN Second Lieutenant Lê Minh, Carter reviewed the initial Contact Report (CR), prepared after the first meeting. He determined that Lê Minh was avaricious, the target's prime vulnerability. At the same time, Lê Minh appeared more intelligent than suggested in the CIA spotting report, Lê Minh was reasonably 'street-wise'. There were no indications of any ideology, except avoid combat duty, a personal trait which likely would drive much of the target's behavior. Carter/Williams would press forward with the target, using money as the motivation. He thought Lê Minh had bought into the Adjunct Inspector General Team #4 'confidential report' cover story. Carter decided to end public meetings and shift to a safe house rented by Sergeant James. Carter sent a message by a Nung courier, to avoid anyone listening in on the Joint General Staff telephone system. The Nung hand-delivered the message to Lê Minh, giving the time and location of the safe house for the next meeting.

Minh knocked on the safe house door at the appointed time and was greeted warmly as Carter opened the door. Once inside, Minh noticed the table set with American snacks and American beer. Carter indicated Minh should sit at the table and help himself to a Budweiser beer, and try the American style snacks: potato chips, summer sausage, beef jerky, and various cheeses. After the expected social pleasantries, Carter guided the discussion to the 'confidential report'.

Carter repeated selected background information from their first meeting about the project. Getting more specific, He explained that the study would do a comparative examination of the personnel 'assignment polices' for the US and the ARVN to assign officers in a general staff organization, specifically, the American Joint Chiefs of Staff and the ARVN Joint General Staff. Carter reinforced the political reasons the initial phase of the study had to remain absolutely confidential. Minh nodded his head at the proper points in Carter's monolog. Carter asked if Minh had any questions.

Minh said he understood the basic aspects of the project and need for confidentiality. Carter smiled inwardly when the target went directly to the issue of what he must do to earn more money:

"What are the next actions I should do?"

261

Carter thought, 'your greed showing', as Minh was openly 'too eager' to get paid more. Carter was equally direct, setting out what he wanted from Minh in the next tranche of information. Carter explained further, The Adjunct Inspector General Team #4 confidential report 'terms of reference', would examine selected small departments initially to keep the volume of data at a manageable level. The two units in the ARVN Joint General Staff of initial interest were the Operations History Archive and the Deconfliction Division. He asked Minh if he was familiar with those organizations. Minh thought for a moment, answering he was aware of them but knew few details, adding quickly that he could find any needed information on both.

Carter nodded, digressing to ask if Minh liked the American snacks. Minh answered the snacks were good and they were similar to some foods Vietnamese ate. Back to business, Carter explained that the study needed to have the current list of officers assigned to the Operations History Archive and the Deconfliction Division: when were they assigned and what were the assigned billets in the organizations. Carter also wanted an updated organizational chart for the Joint General Staff.

"When can you deliver the Operations History Archive and the Deconfliction Division information and the organization chart for the study?"

Carter had barely concluded his questions before Minh stated:

"I can have all the information in two days or less."

Carter shook Lê Minh's hand bowing his head slightly in the Vietnamese culture style. With an amiable comment, he handed Minh an envelope:

"I almost forgot to give you the payment due for your support of the project so far."

Pleasantly stunned by the unexpected payment, Minh thanked Carter and placed the envelope in his trouser pocket. He finished his American beer, eager to open the envelope. He told Carter he needed to return to headquarters. Carter thanked him and said we will meet here two days from now at the same time. Minh departed, first, in a hurry to open the envelope and then, hurry to start gathering the information for Carter and receive another envelope full of money.

In a corollary HUMINT operation, the three Sergeants, assigned the 'hard-labor' task using bar girls in a deception operation, received an avalanche of abuse from everyone in the team-room, as they tried to brief the team on their progress so far. They had selected three bar girls to use as information conduits in the deception scheme. The Sergeants recognized that it was a challenge to trick these jaded, cloying, female predators who preyed on lonely GIs. After bilking the GIs out of money for watered-downed drinks, many of the bar girls accrued more money selling the information they gleaned from drunk GIs to the VC - to support VC killing more GIs.

Each bar girl target was picked during an objective assessment how the Sergeants could effectively exploit the bar girls to bring the Spider to 'Peregrine Justice'. The intent was not to formally recruit the bar girls as US spies, but to gain their confidence by spending a lot of money on them and dropping tidbits of information along the way. Then the sergeants would use the girls as unwitting channels to pass 'deceptive information' to the VC.

Gunnery Sergeant Risner selected Lolita from Mimi's bar on Boulevard Nguyen Hue. Mimi's is the high-end brothel-club in wartime Saigon. Lolita was an attractive slightly-built young woman, who sadly would age rapidly in the hard-life of a bar-girl/prostitute. Lolita affected the role of a vulnerable naïve young woman who was trapped against her will in this shady profession – and she was good at it – good at separating GI fools from their money – all of their money – she was so good that the impoverished GIs would return after borrowing more money from their friends.

Master Sergeant Wilson worked the Florida Bar on Tu Do Street, he developed a very friendly relationship with Myrna. Myrna was attractive, but her features were starting to show how the bar girl life quickly grinds a woman emotionally and physically. Myrna had migrated from the harsh life of rural village rice-paddies to the big city to seek a better life; instead she found the big city became a hellhole for her, an inescapable hellhole – in less than one-year, she was transformed from a gentle rural girl to a dangerous prostitute and thief, lost to the vicissitudes of a miserable life in the shadows.

Sergeant First Class Podowski elected to work the Sporting Bar where 'Sweet Susie' wanted him to be her 'best friend' – as long as his money held out. "Sweet" was a major misnomer as Susie had become a hard-core street-smart prostitute who was tough and dangerous. Susie, or whatever her real-name was, came as a refugee from the North and slipped into the prostitute-trade as a quick way to make money.

If the money was right, virtually all Saigon bar girls would serve as prostitutes. Given the free spending by the Sergeants, these jaded women were likely to fall for the planned deception operation. In each bar, the Sergeant would focus on a cover theme. Risner was a US advisor to an ARVN infantry battalion. Wilson was a member of SOG, a mysterious US military organization. Podowski was seconded to some secret group in the US Embassy – which his target believed was CIA. Through these covers, the Sergeant Trio would exploit the bar girls assumed access to the VC – and in turn, deceive VC intelligence.

Of course, the 'American names' selected by the bar girls became a source of derision at every subsequent Peregrine staff meeting.

The sergeants became bar regulars, meeting the target bar girls almost every night, buying expensive drinks instead of Saigon Tea; plus, giving each girl a large tip each night, sometimes in US dollars and sometimes in MPC, the US military currency which was used in the US commissary and PX, as well as used illegally on the Vietnamese economy. Each Sergeant vowed to sacrifice his evenings for the mission; the sergeants bided their time 'to set the trap'.

As the Americans unwittingly were being misdirected away from Operation Red, Kie^ decided to wear a long-flowing ao dai for the next meeting with "Win". The ao dai was the national dress of urban Vietnamese women. The ao dai was perfectly suited for the slender young Vietnamese women; each ao dai was specially tailored for the wearer, as the top, in particular, was form-fitting and rather tight. The ao dai had a rather ephemeral appearance as the gown-style garment was split down the sides, which actually revealed nothing as the ao dai included full-length leggings. Most GIs found the ao dai a sensual piece of clothing as they gawked at the young women walking along the sidewalks and byways of Saigon.

Kie^ found her shapely Eurasian body was more suited for a brief bikini than an ao dai, as her top and the ao dai tailored top were a mismatch – her breasts were too big or the ao dai style was too tight. Regardless, she had the tailor prepare a form-fitted ao dai for her; she thought this would work well on Win.

264

In many spy operations, the case officer will dislike the agent but has to constantly fake respect and friendship for the agent. Calthrop was an individual whom any case officer would dislike, extremely dislike. As part of the continuing subliminal 'influence' process to develop 'control' over the future spy, Kie^ took the initiative to suggest the restaurant for their next dinner.

Originally, she thought about the 'Saigon Rooftop Bar' on the ninth floor of the Caravelle Hotel, the restaurant had an uninterrupted view across the Saigon River, one could watch air strikes, the colored tracer-bullets, and fire-fights far across the river. She quickly discarded the 'Caravelle rooftop bar' option; it would be awkward because "Win" would strongly press to go to her room for a drink, or for something more intimate. Instead, she opted for the Nha Hang Vua Cua, a rather expensive restaurant. She would have her driver take her to meet "Win" at the restaurant. Having her own transportation would minimize any later insistence by "Win" to call a cab to transport them to her hotel (and try to get her in bed).

"Win" enjoyed the Nha Hang Vua Cua restaurant and seemed unaware that Kie^ was cleverly directing the conversation all evening. Kie^ told her cover story, again, about her family in 'Haiphong' and how difficult her childhood had been, smoothly shifting to her current quest in Saigon to find her missing parents and how lonely her life in Saigon. Kie^ was. She was playing Calthrop in an artful manner; she knew he wanted, needed, to be the center of any conversation. By monopolizing the conversation early, she knew Calthrop would start to force the talk to place himself at the center of attention.

She also applied the principle of reciprocity, using the normal human reaction to reply in-kind to a shared confidence. Kie^ knew Win would respond with self-serving lies, half-truths, plus an occasional dash of truth. She had watched Win closely in the past two meetings, looking for 'physical tells' which indicated when the subject was lying. Win was loaded with 'tells'. He tended to shift his eyes up to the right while dissembling; he would raise his right hand to scratch his head when lying; he would look you in the face during the few instances he was being forthright.

She sensed when Win was fully primed and ready to launch into his expected self-inflating monolog; she say back and tracked the content and matching his torrent of words with the 'tells' for truth or not. She thought as he droned on, this will be a difficult source to control if I can recruit him. He is unstable. What is the vulnerability I can identify to ensure secure control over this poor excuse for a human-being?

As Win droned-on with his boring, but revealing, self-congratulatory speech, laced with many sexual inferences and 'come on' lines, Kie^ patiently listened and mentally recorded the substance and the 'tells'.

He continued to drink heavily during pauses in his loquacious dialog, becoming very drunk in the process. Kie^ decided she needed to intervene to redirect the conversation. First, she interrupted Win to remind him, she urgently needed to get a US permanent resident visa to enter America, emphasizing how grateful she would be to the powerful and influential man who could deliver that visa. A grossly inebriated Win glibly replied,

"I can do that for you"

He returned to continue promoting himself. By now, Win was noticeably slurring his words, unsteady in his chair, and making loud sexual inferences laced by explicit crude double entendre remarks. Kie^ decided she had to get Calthrop out of the restaurant before he caused a major scene. She told him how pleasurable the meal had been and how she enjoyed listening to him – emphasizing, she wanted to be with him again – be together soon. The seriously inebriated Simmons struggled to process what she was saying to him; his reply was unintelligible as he mumbled something about wanting to be together in private somewhere.

Kie^ summoned the waiter for the 'overpriced meal and booze' bill. When she paid in US dollars the waiter smiled, increasing to a broad smile and a bow when Nyugen gave him two twenty dollar bills, one for the waiter and one for a second staff member to help take the nodding drunk American out to her car. Ensconced in the back seat of her car, the drunk Calthrop tried feebly to assert himself, calling for a cab. Kie^ calmly and sweetly told him it would be her utmost pleasure to ride with him back to the US Embassy. Giving no response as his head slumped forward, Kie^ ordered the driver to take them to the US Embassy.

Arriving at the closely-guarded embassy compound, the driver was stopped by an outer ring of Vietnamese police dressed in their white uniforms – uniforms which caused many GIs to call the police, White Mice. Kie^ got out of the car and began explaining, in Vietnamese, to the police officer that she had a high-level Embassy official in the car who was quite drunk – the police officer heard most of what she was saying, but not all, because his attention was focused on the voluptuous Eurasian woman in the form-fitting ao dai.

Three, weapons-ready, US Marines stood at the embassy gate. After hearing something about a drunk Embassy official, the young Marine sergeant, with his weapon at port arms, approached the policeman and the woman. Hearing her story, in English now, and recognizing the snoring drunk in the back seat, he signaled for help to haul 'this loser' into Embassy compound. Calthrop Simmons was not a favorite of the Marines guarding the Embassy – he was pompous and condescending – the young sergeant smiled as he entered the incident into the gate-guard logbook.

The next morning, a hungover Calthrop Simmons was disturbed by a US Marine Corporal knocking on his Embassy compound apartment door. The young Marine, suppressing a smile, announced,

"The Charge d'Affaires, requires your presence in his office now"

Shaving and dressing quickly, a rather disheveled Calthrop Winston Simmons reported to an angry Charge d'Affaires, Mason Aldershot, the number-two man in the Embassy.

Mason Aldershot was part of the lineage of 'old money' public servants who favored the State Department as a platform 'to do their duty'. He was serious about every aspect of his job and was an effective bureaucrat. He demanded efficiency from his subordinates and brooked no misconduct. Mason was highly respected within the State Department for his personal integrity and the fact he was an 'old school' gentleman with a quiet grace and was a superb diplomat. If the State Department used recruiting posters, which of course they did not as posters were beneath them, Mason would be a candidate for such a poster. Tall at six feet one inch, 180 pounds, aristocratic facial features, impeccably well-tailored suits, as Charge d'Affaires for the United States Embassy in the Republic of Vietnam, Mason represented the US in a most positive manner.

The Charge d'Affaires did not offer Simmons a chair as he launched into a scathing scolding regarding Calthrop's scandalous public conduct the previous evening – adding more remarks concerning the generally piss-poor performance by Calthrop since he arrived in Saigon.

Calthrop begin to defend himself, only to be silenced by Mason

Aldershot's raised hand, effectively telling him to shut up. The Charge d'Affaires was exceptionally blunt in this closed-door exchange. He told Calthrop the only reason he would not insert a disciplinary report in Calthrop's personnel file was the fact the Ambassador was well aware of the influence his father-in-law had in DC. However, even that level of influence had its limits to cover up incompetence and grossly inappropriate public behavior. The Charge d'Affaires returning to the paperwork on his desk, dismissing Simmons with a wave of his hand.

Rather than being properly chastised, Calthrop was furious at the berating Mason Aldershot dared to give him. All these pretentious petty bureaucrats did not appreciate him – Calthrop's anger was palpable and intense – he was slipping into a vulnerability category which case officers loved to exploit – the "disaffected", those individuals who became violently angry at their situation and wanted revenge on 'the system'. Calthrop mused, only Kie^ seemed to appreciate and respect him.

Five case officers, four American and one KGB, were moving into the development phase of the respective recruitment processes. The case officer uses the development phase to solidify a rapport with the target and ultimately establish the conditions where the target had a psychological dependence on the case officer. The case officer exploits this dependence by causing the target to identify the case officer as the one-person who can satisfy the target's most deep-seated needs. These compulsive needs become the foundation of the target-case officer establishing control over the agent. A case officer is an emotional chameleon who adapts to be what the target needs.

CHAPTER 20   NSA DF VANS

The "International Export and Import Company Ltd" charter 707 unloaded the DF Vans as the four NSA DF teams deplaned. A two-man Saigon-NSA advance-team greeted them. The four DF cover-vans, with their teams inside, drove off the tarmac avoiding a convoy appearance as they took separate routes to the NSA safehouses on the outskirts of Saigon. The direction finding technology to locate a radio transmitter, existed prior to World War II and was used extensively during that conflict. In particular, the Nazi security services used DF systems to locate radios operated by resistance groups in urban and rural locations. The basic physics of direction finding were constant, but the DF equipment evolved qualitatively with new and upgraded electronics. The increased sensitivity of current DF receivers helped the DF operators locate the elusive short-burst transmissions spies used to avoid detection.

The DF van-drivers were all Asian NSA employees to avoid undue attention. The drivers and equipment operators used the first few days to familiarize themselves with Saigon streets, traffic patterns, and what might be the optimal routes to conduct the DF operation. While the drivers prepared the covert search routes, the DF equipment operators fired-up their equipment and thoroughly checked out functionality and performance. The technicians used known US Embassy signals to calibrate the equipment. The operators had detailed data on the enemy frequencies, callsigns, and message formats gathered in earlier NSA operations in the Saigon area. Now, NSA would begin an intensified search for 'the Spider radio site'.

One of the problems for the Saigon operation was the enemy target signals were not confined to a set schedule. The brief target-signal transmission windows resulted in ambiguities to identify the transmitter's specific location. The DF collection process produced azimuth bearings (directions), but the target range was always uncertain. The second problem was the fact the target signal beam-width was a narrow-lobed beam, such a narrow beam signal was problematic to detect. Thus, the DF collection vans had to be very near to, or in the beam lobe, to determine the azimuth of the transmitted signal with needed accuracy. The theoretical solution to pinpoint a target was a combination of technology, positioning, and scheduling. The practical solution was more difficult as the DF team had limited personnel and equipment resources needed to provide 24-hour coverage. Plan A was to position all four collection vans at fixed locations along the previously roughly determined azimuths. This first-step of DF operation would be highly stressful on the teams because of the 24-hour coverage requirement. If the Plan A teams did not detect the target signal within seven-days, they would have to go to Plan B which would ensure at least one van continuously on the street for 24-hour coverage.

Four days went by with no positive intercepts, the equipment operators and drivers were approaching exhaustion. On day five the vans finally detected the target signal, at the same time, there was a surprise – a second enemy signal was detected transmitting from Saigon using a high-level KGB encryption system. The new signal was sent from a second site on a different bearing toward the A Shau radio site. Other NSA assets recorded, after the A Shau receiver received this new transmission, the new signal was forwarded from the A Shau base to Moscow, without the usual parallel-signal being sent to Hanoi as was the practice with the old encryption signals.

Fortunately, the NSA analysts had an additional intelligence input from the listening devices planted during the Peregrine recon patrol into the A Shau. While Russian technicians did not decipher and read the encrypted new signal, their conversations recorded by the 'listening devices' betrayed the existence of a new KGB operation in Saigon. The distinction helped the NSA analysts segregate the new signal operational purpose from the signals associated with ambush attacks on US advisors embedded with the ARVN.

After the Peregrine recon patrol definitively located the A Shau radio site, NSA set up three additional DF sites in US Army Special Forces camps outside the A Shau valley. These DF sites were compact automated signal collection systems, now recalibrated to look for both the old and new Saigon signals identified by NSA, one definitely associated with the threat to the US advisors. The data from the automated devices supplemented a wealth of 'take' from the two listening devices implanted by the Peregrine recon patrol. The voice recordings of Russian radio operators at the A Shau camp gave background on how incoming and outgoing messages were processed.

One important point noted from the Peregrine 'walk in the woods' was confirmed, it was obvious the Russians are in-charge of the A Shau comm operation, not the Vietnamese. The conclusion the KGB was in control intensified the mystery – why use the obsolete encryption? Moreover, the old signals could be correlated with follow-on transmissions from the A Shau comm station to Hanoi and back to South Vietnam locations. These follow-on messages all used the obsolete KGB encryption system. NSA, with the information from the code clerk defector and the increased number of intercepted messages, began the successful decryption of the content of the obsolete encryption system messages. The NSA analysts found it interesting there was no 'static' in the messages transmitted back into South Vietnam.

The new signal intercepted in Saigon reinforced the theory that the Russians had more than one agenda and more than one Russian operation ongoing in Saigon. What was this new signal using a KGB high-level encryption? The new signal also uses a different format. Another anomaly is the new signal is processed differently at the A Shau comm facility. The new signal is sent directly to Moscow – no copies to Hanoi and no transmissions back to South Vietnam.

On the sixth day, the NSA Saigon contingent redeployed the Plan A team. The new locations resulted in the prize of the day, an intercept which captured three sequential signals from the original Saigon transmitter, a serious security blunder by the Spider radio operators. This multi-message sequence required the transmitter to stay on the air for an extended period, a lack of good tradecraft and breach of communications security discipline by the enemy. Two of the three signals contained the steganography "static" to hide additional embedded messages.

The extended intercept-time allowed the analysts to refine the accuracy of Saigon radio broadcast site azimuth. Two of the four deployed DF vans had detected the multiple message transmission. Starting their engines, DF vans moved along the streets following the azimuths toward the target transmitter. For the first time, NSA had two time-synchronized azimuths cross one another. The target location was now narrowed to a three-block area northeast of the Phu Tho racetrack. The new azimuths would support a more efficient DF search pattern using multiple trucks to simultaneously determine the precise location of the enemy radio transmitter to a single building.

The DF team activated an additional resource. Military helicopter flights were constantly crossing the Saigon airspace generating a rotor thump-thumping background noise in the daytime traffic noise. These flights were accepted as part of the unpleasant daily decibel-din of the city. NSA sent a chopper up the next day to take detailed photographs of the suspect three-block area. The analysts scoured the photos for a building with an antenna array on the roof. The photos from the helicopter mission identified a single building with an antenna array for the frequency range of the target signals. This building matched the general location of the signals identified by the DF search. This building is the Spider radio transmission site!

The four vans now deployed in 12-hour shifts with two-vans per shift for continuous coverage of the transmission site building. The vans deployed to act in tandem; one van would 'sit' on the primary azimuth, as previously identified. The revised search strategy covered a limited area based on the photos. The renewed DF search produced success on the second day, reconfirming that the antenna location from the photos exactly matched the DF location for the targeted signals.

The aggregate information from the DF success, the decrypting of the 'obsolete encryption' messages, along with updated analyses reached Annie's desk as a series of reports. Annie, with a big smile, consolidated the reports and took a concise summary to Dr. Slade. She also provided a draft message for the team in Saigon with the location of the Spider radio communication site. Dr. Slade recognized the breakthrough for the intelligence side of the Peregrine problem. With a few edits to the draft message, Dr. Williams authorized transmission to CIA Station Saigon, after coordination and approval by Major-General Wojcik. Annie hand-carried the message to the Pentagon. She was warmly greeted by a smiling Bull Wojcik and the General's smile broadened after Annie briefed him on the NSA breakthrough. He immediately signed-off and ordered transmission forthwith to the Saigon Peregrine team through the CIA comm system.

CIA Saigon sent a courier to the Peregrine compound advising Williams he was needed immediately at the embassy for consultation. Thanking the courier, Williams dressed in civilian clothes and called for his Nung driver/bodyguard. As Williams walked to the jeep, he remembered the Rex roof-top dinner and the surreptitious 'intuition' photos he took, photos of the beautiful mystery woman. Williams went back to the office to grab the prints to share with his Agency contact.

Williams and his CIA Station contact went directly to the SCIF where the CIA officer gave Williams the JCS/NSA TS code-word message. After reading, the CIA guy laughed along with Williams and they high-fived:" Outstanding news!" They could nail the Spider at his home! Williams discussed the Peregrine plan to exploit the enemy transmitter location, a plan to takedown the enemy site, and the plan to eliminate the Spider. Shaking hands, Williams stood up to leave, eager to get back to the compound. Before he left the SCIF, he remembered the photos. He told the CIA contact he had one more matter, 'a wild-ass matter' to discuss.

Williams set the background, explaining the Rex steak/beer/ entertainment night and the appearance of 'the mystery woman' incident enhancing the dinner – commenting, this is probably more a brain-fart than intuition – regardless, he knew his CIA contact would seriously appreciate the photos of one 'very hot woman'. Placing the pictures on the conference table, Williams received a dual response – first, the CIA guy blurted out:

"Wow she is beautiful - and yep, sexy - very hot"

Before Williams could make his additional inappropriate crude comments, the CIA man drew a deep breath,

"I know this son-of-a-bitch with her. He recently arrived at the Embassy and is already considered a real shit. His name is, wait a minute, Throp or what, something Simmons – wants people to call him "Win" – wait, the name is Calthrop Simmons. His father-in-law is a major player behind the scenes in DC. This might not be good – who is the 'sex dreamboat'? "Win" has access to some of the most sensitive classified information available here on the war – stuff from the US and all the critical local info. Probably nothing, as "Calthrop" thinks he is God's gift to everyone, especially women."

Captain Williams mused:

"The 'mystery woman thing, very thin coincidence – sort-of just reaching, very thin, and no one likes intuition except the intuitive person. But there is the TS/SCI issue. Simmons has big-time clearances and access. Baumgartner did have the two followed by the Nungs after the Rex dinner. She went back to the Caravelle hotel and he returned to the Embassy. Well, this is not a smoking gun and is not in the Peregrine operational province. You can keep the pictures and have more of your 'dirty-mind thoughts' regarding the 'mystery woman'."

273

Shaking hands, with mutual smirks about the pictures, Captain Williams returned to the compound to issue orders based on the great new information locating the Spider transmitter location.

Williams called the team together to update them and assign new tasks. When he announced NSA fixing the location of the Saigon transmitter, the information was greeted with fist-pumps and HOOYAHs. The tasks followed directly:

"Sergeant Jones, the transmitter is located at Nguyen Ngoc Loc street, number 3, east of the Pho Tho racetrack. The building is a three-story apartment house. Check it out today to see if we can set-up a clandestine site to keep the transmitter building under surveillance 24/7".

"Sergeant James, acquire, I do not care how, camera equipment to photograph the comings and goings at the target building. Check on listening devices like we emplaced at the A Shau camp to see what might work for the urban situation. Need yesterday."

"We need to accelerate the General Staff agent inputs to support exploiting the NSA data on the transmitter location and update our analytic data base. There are 'tells' and 'indicators' here about the "Spider" – find them – Carl you have the lead on this."

"I want initial reports tonight - after chow this evening."

"LT Baumgartner, I need to see you on a separate matter."

Moving aside for a private conference,

"Gary, I gave the 'green dress hot mystery woman' photo prints to Jake, our CIA guy. I am sure you remember, photos of the showstopper from the Rex the other night – so after the CIA guy got his tongue back in his mouth, from lusting over the green dress sex goddess – he recognized the guy with her. He is a loser recently assigned to the Embassy, but a guy who sees a lot of high-level sensitive classified stuff about the war. I let Jake Reynolds, our CIA guy, keep the pictures. It is not our problem, but something still sticks in the back of my mind about this, there is more to it."

"Jake was an officer in the 75th Ranger Regiment (Airborne) before signing up with CIA, he is the real deal, taciturn, cool blue eyes, short blond hair, six-feet tall and 200 pounds, a ready smile for friends, and a personal presence for the rest, he was not a man to cross. Jake was recruited by the CIA after he made his jungle bones during the Malayan

Emergency. He was serving as a Ranger exchange-officer with the 22 SAS Regiment, British Special Air Service. Deployed to Malaya, Jake and the 22 SAS Regiment hunted Communist Terrorists (CT) in the South Swamp region of Malaya. Jake's exploits there earned him the nickname, "CT-Slayer", from his SAS buddies. CIA persuaded him to resign from the Army and join the Agency to run CIA cross border operations into North Vietnam and Laos".

"Hell Bobby, fess-up, you are just lusting after that babe who started your heavy breathing at the Rex. No sweat, we have more prints".

The team had a steak, eggs and beer evening meal with the usual juke box background blasting out some serious country music from home – Hey Good Looking; Your Cheating Heart; Sixteen Tons; Great Balls of Fire – good warmups for the evening status meeting, and good old US country music enjoyment during the meal to aid digestion.

With the juke box temporarily silent, the team settled down for the respective status briefings. Captain Williams kicked it off:

"Sergeant Jones, what have you got?"

"It was a good day Boss. We checked-out the apartment building with the radio transmitter. Three stories, two entrances, semi-quiet neighborhood. Good news is there are two apartment buildings across the street with vacancies that overlook the target building front entrance – and an apartment building that overlooks the rear entrance. There is an apartment building up the street that would be ideal for a SIGINT collection site – right along the transmitter 'send' azimuth."

"Excellent, rent the best one tomorrow, Hell, rent all three if appropriate for the observation of the front and back entrances plus an additional SIGINT collection site.".

"Sergeant James, what about the camera equipment? "

"Boss, you ask, I deliver. The camera equipment is here in the compound now and checked-out for effective operation. Yes, I had to do a little 'don't ask' on the acquisition."

"Carl?"

"Did a thorough review of where we are, identifying additional intelligence requirements to help fill gaps and connect the dots. The NSA stuff is powerful helpful."

"The message traffic to and from the radio comm building remains at a relatively high level compared to the intercept history."

"For the surveillance teams, I distributed the documents CIA gave us, the official Vietnamese police special branch IDs for the teams to use, as needed, in the surveillance jobs – with the caveat, do not flash these docs unless absolutely necessary."

"In summary, we have a 'suspect', Colonel Tran is likely the Spider. I stress 'suspect'. We should be able to confirm that assessment within a few days after we initiate the 24/7 surveillance of the radio comm building. Whoever Spider is, he will be visiting the radio comm building, or if he uses couriers, give us leads to follow back to him. The bar girl deception operation could give us confirmation, possibly within seven days after we execute the specific deception scenarios." (The last utterance gave way to raucous cat calls from the team as they berated the three 'bar girl' sergeants.)

Captain Williams brought the update session to a close:

"Good work all. Break out the beer and fire up the juke box."

CHAPTER 21   PEREGRINE WORKS THE STREETS

Captain Williams directed the team members to provide detailed progress reports for their current tasks at the morning 'action planning' meeting – the phrase "staff meeting" is out, no staff wienies here, just shooters. In addition, the team and the Nungs entered into a high-intensity physical training regimen every morning. The team would be in action soon, the physical and mental abilities of every shooter needed to be honed to a combat-ready razor edge. Captain Williams decided generating some internal competition would be a morale builder as well as pushing the troops to the maximum. Integrating the Nungs into the PT broadened the competition along with rotating the leaders of the morning PT – with the challenge to each PT leader – 'can you make this workout tougher than yesterday'. The workout that morning was led by a Nung and was brutal, brutal like yesterday morning, when Sergeant Jones led the PT.

After PT, quick showers, and breakfast – for the Americans, breakfast was orange juice, eggs and NY cut steaks cooked to order. Sergeant James was legendary for his abilities to get anything, anytime – name the cut of steak you want - fried potatoes, toast, fresh fruit - bananas, mangos, papaya, jackfruit – and plenty of coffee. All the food was devoured with a blaring juke box blasting out Ring of Fire by Johnny Cash, the Isley brothers rocking with Twist and Shout, and Dave (Baby) Cortez pounding the organ with 'Rinky Dink' – laughing, happy warriors taking needed sustenance – Captain Williams smiled – lean and mean – they are ready.

The team took their places around the conference table, coffees in-hand, the juke box silent, for now.

Williams gave the team a stern look –

"Which one of you rowdies thinks 'Ring of Fire' is a suitable patriotic song to start the day?"

Every man put up his hand and shouted – HOOYAH – Williams nodded his head and thought – I am confident, we are ready to rain Hell on those enemy-bastards when I turn this bunch loose on them.

"OK, team updates. LT Baumgartner lead-off":

"I had the task along with Captain Williams to select targets for recruitment in the ARVN General Staff to give closure on identifying the mole. The rationale for this task was the high probability that the North Vietnamese mole behind the attacks on US advisors would need access to data only available in the ARVN Joint General Staff. Among the ARVN Joint General Staff officers, many are there to avoid combat duty These coward slackers have potential for recruitment as agents. Warrant Officer Renner is studying the org charts to see if there is an obvious choke point for information used to target and kill American advisors, information which likely would point to the mole and how his network is organized."

"The Spider take down operation follows the essential process: collect information, evaluate the information, make a decision on when and how, and execute the decision as an operation to end the targeted killing American advisors. The plan depends on three critical elements. The enemy information has to flow from various sources to a central point for evaluation and a decision. The information for a potential ambush had to be absolutely precise as to the location and time for the ambush. The enemy decision has to be provided in time for the ambush force to assemble at the ambush site. The 'choke point' was always clear. That choke point is the Spider radio site in Saigon where the information is evaluated, and a decision made. Exploit the choke point to end the VC operation 'killing American advisors'. Take out the Saigon radio site and kill the Spider".

"We are confident that a cross-correlation in time, information flow, and most important, the assignments of personnel to the Joint General Staff will lock down the identity of the mole behind the advisor ambush attacks. You all are aware of the source in the General Staff recruited by Captain Williams. This source is delivering high-value intel."

"Sergeant Jones, brief the team on your progress."

"My initial task was to organize and train four 'prisoner snatch teams.' I had to identify and obtain the proper equipment for a prisoner snatch operation. My second task was to select a cadre of Nungs for training to conduct covert surveillance. Everyone is familiar with the PT program as part of these tasks" – which evoked a loud HOOYAH from those around the table. Sergeant Jones gave them the appropriate Master Sergeant stare-down and continued. Sergeant Clayton and I have selected four 'prisoner snatch' teams plus a back-up team, 20-grab men and five drivers. Each snatch-team will have an assigned Peregrine NCO as the leader."

"We are practicing daily using different scenarios: off-the street, out of an apartment, night grabs, and set-ups. That 'infamous thief, rascal, and Ladies Man', Sergeant James, has done it again. We have the initial equipment needs fulfilled – gags, handcuffs, rope, plastic ties, blindfolds, two types of incapacitating chemicals from CIA with syringes, black clothing and hoods, first-aid kits, silenced weapons, knock-knocks, (the 50-pound handheld battering rams to shatter doors), everything a good kidnapper wants to have in his kit bag. We are ready for snatch-time. The surveillance training is proceeding with street exercises. The surveillance sneaky-petes, the 'invisible watcher teams', are ready to go. Sergeant Clayton, Gunnery Sergeant Risner, and Warrant Officer Renner are continuing to refine the Nungs' surveillance and tradecraft skills. Warrant Officer Renner, you have the podium."

"As LT Baumgartner briefed, we are in the analyzing mode, examining the information flows within the ARVN Joint General Staff looking for nodes and information choke-points. This analysis is straight-forward but 'the gems' are difficult to filter out regarding the official staff relationships and the unofficial relationships; the latter is the way business is really done. We need to get a better handle on how the VC agents insert their inputs into the flow of information to the 'mole', these inputs are transformed into ambush actions against US advisors and cross-border insertions. We need more from NSA to help with the timeline analysis."

As Renner took his seat, Sergeant Risner interjected:

"We have made progress with the bar girl network – (to the hoots and avalanche of vulgar jeers from the rest of the team)

Captain Williams, with actual curiosity, asked Risner,

"can you expand, in detail, just what 'progress with bar girls' meant, reminding him the three sergeants were using team black money"

more hoots and jeers from the team, as Risner's reputation with women cast deep suspicion as just how Risner was interacting with the bar girls. All eyes and ears now focused on Risner. Looking properly offended, Risner reminded the team,

"This bar girl thing was an 'assigned duty'."

more jeers – Captain Williams intervened to bring order back to the assembly.

Clearing his throat, Gunnery Sergeant Risner began with the trip he and Sergeant Wilson made to SOG: Gunnery Sergeant Risner, USMC, ignoring the loud vocal abuse, he stated with a straight face,

"SOG had tried the 'bar girl' informant network, partially in desperation, to find a possible security-leak in the bars frequented by SOG members. SOG found the bar girl exercise was a 'bust'."

More groans and rude comments from the team –,

Williams was about to intervene again, when Risner explained how the Peregrine notion to use bar girls held promise, going a different direction from the SOG failed adventure. SOG found the bar girls included a significant percentage of VC sympathizers. In addition, the non-political bar girls had learned that they could sell information to the VC, information which loose-lips GIs told them to impress them or simply because the soldier was skunk-drunk. SOG found that information they received from any bar girl was nearly 100% fabrication to get money from SOG."

Risner could not restrain himself, he had to repeat:

"The SOG bar girl informant operation was a real bust."

Risner quickly shouted over the din of abuse,

"But there is an opportunity for Peregrine to exploit a bar girl network to deceive the enemy".

The team was quiet now and the officers noted this serious response. Risner proceeded to lay out a deception plan using an unwitting bar girl network.

"SOG has shut down their operation, so we can easily move-in as the next American suckers for the bar girls to exploit. It's very easy, we have the lay of the land, we will use our bar girl network to insert false information as a deception to smoke out the Spider. We will be able to use this deception insertion only once."

Williams nodded his head adding,

"Go for it".

"The 'mole' accessing data for the ambushes has to be an ARVN Joint General Staff insider". I am working a Joint General Staff source who has access to much of the background information we need. These data will be available in a few days because this guy's code name should be 'Avarice". He provides the information as fast as he can to get more envelops full of money".

Bringing the meeting to a close, Williams admonished the team,

"We are close to cleaning weapons and 'cleaning house'. Complete your tasks and we will get to killing these sons-a-bitches".

The resulting HOOYAH rocked the room and told Williams the team was ready to 'lock-and load'.

That evening two of the sergeants visited, respectively, Mimi's Club on Boulevard Nguyen Hue and the Florida Bar on Tu Do Street, dropping a significant amount of cash on Saigon Teas, water-downed whiskey, and generous tips for the bar girls.

On the way back to the compound, Sergeant Wilson commented:

"You know how much envy-shit we are going to get from the team on this!"

Sergeant Podowski just smiled, and said,

"Who gives a shit. Tomorrow we will hit the bars again. all with bar girls and lame whiskey. Have we died and gone to heaven?"

Sergeant James had two Nungs rent apartments for the 24/7 surveillance of the Spider radio building. One apartment covered the front entrance while the second apartment overlooked the rear entrance. Every person entering or leaving the apartment was photographed and time-stamped as to arrival and departure.

CHAPTER 22   DEVELOP THOSE HUMINT TARGETS

Development of a target is similar to 'dating'; a process where each partner tries to make a positive impression on the other partner. Case officers seek ways to establish a 'connection' such as shared interests or dislikes, assisting the target to achieve a personal goal, and generally being helpful in any number of ways to assist the target, all the while keeping a low public profile for their relationship. The driving objective is for the target to see the case officer as the one-person who can fulfill the target's strong personal needs. The case officer does this in a combination of conscious and subliminal ways. The case officer builds a rapport with the target to get the target to trust him. During this phase of the recruitment process, the case officer takes no actions or makes no moves that would disclose he is an intelligence operative. The case officer uses the development process to shape the environment and psychology for a future recruitment pitch.

Each development phase is different to fit the particular target. The case officer has to creatively and intuitively apply the right principles to fit the target. Kie^ has a target who is manifestly flawed with many potential motivations for a recruitment pitch. At the same time, Calthrop is unpredictable and potentially unstable. The KGB intends to recruit Calthrop Winston Simmons in the classic sense, a witting agent, a spy who is aware he is working for a foreign intelligence service.

Team Peregrine is using a different approach for the two human intelligence operations the team is working in Saigon. Williams/Carter is using Second Lieutenant Lê Minh as an unwitting paid informant to provide documents and information. Team Peregrine intends to use three bar girls as unwitting channels to pass deceptive information to the VC. The bar girls will believe they are sending useful intelligence to the VC about upcoming ARVN/US operations. The Peregrine case officers "develop" the unwitting bar girls by spending extravagant amount for drinks and personal tips, plus 'leaking' tidbits of information about the ARVN/US operations. The 'tidbits' of information about American

283

operations would be accurate, giving the bar girls credibility with the VC, but the information would always be provided too late for the VC to exploit on a battlefield.

Williams/Carter contacted Lê Minh for an urgent meeting at the safe house. Lê Minh was delighted with the request, another meeting, another envelope with money for him. He responded immediately and they met at the safe house the next day after lunch time, a time many Vietnamese used as a form of siesta, often a time spent in bed with a mistress rather than siesta nap. Carter thanked Minh for his quick response adding how valuable his inputs have been for drafting the confidential report.

Carter said he needed additional data, a comment which sparked a strong glimmer of greed in Minh's eyes – a 'glimmer of greed' that did not escape Carter. Carter told him the report drafting process needed the complete personnel files for the twelve officers and 18 enlisted men assigned to the Deconfliction Division. Before Minh could comment – Carter added, he was prepared to pay a significant bonus for this information - when could the information be available? Minh hesitated for a moment, copying all the personnel files would be time-consuming and dangerous. Furthermore, he could not steal the files with impunity. Lieutenant Lê explained his concerns to Carter.

Carter appeared to studiously think about Lê's concerns. Of course, Carter already had the 'solution in-place', set in motion during his preparation for this meeting. After an appropriate period of contemplation, Carter suggested that there might be a way to earn the bonus while eliminating the risk. During the siesta-time, Lê Minh could 'borrow' the files temporarily and return the files after Carter quickly reviewed the files. No one would know that the files were ever gone. As backup protection, Carter will give Lê Minh a letter which authorize him to take the files to another government office for review.

Minh allowed his greed to dominate his fears, suggesting they meet tomorrow at the same time when security is lax at the Joint Staff headquarters building. He asked, how long would it take to review the files. Carter responded asking how many pages comprised a typical personnel file. Lê answered, approximately five pages. Carter thought, 'a piece of cake', we can copy the files in an hour or less. Carter told Lê the review would take less than an hour. Lê gave a smile of relief and anticipation of the bonus.

Carter gave Lê yet another envelope which he eagerly accepted. He left the safe house, unobtrusively followed by Han Li, the Nung on countersurveillance duty outside the safe house. Han Li trailed, him to confirm that he was not being followed by any other parties.. He had already confirmed the young officer was not followed on his arrival.

Minh could hardly contain himself as he raced to the safety of his apartment so he could check the contents of the envelope. He was amazed on opening, this envelope contained $3000, a huge sum for a junior officer with no supplemental income from the common criminal-corruption that was rampant in the South Vietnamese government and the ARVN. Skipping any thought of gratitude toward Carter, the young officer wondered how much the bonus would be tomorrow.

Carter waited a half-hour before he departed and using a preset surveillance detection route for his return to the compound. At the compound, Williams summoned Sergeants Risner and James to the team room. Williams had to suppress a smile, as he walked into the room and heard the juke box fired up to play Rachmaninoff Concerto #2 in C Minor. The team had classical-music ambushed him. He just shook his head – what a great bunch of hoods!

He explained the task for tomorrow. Risner and James would photograph the personnel files Lê was bringing to the safe house. Williams ordered them to get the equipment together and checked-out for functionality. Wear civilian clothes, the Nung on countersurveillance duty would transport them to be there at 1000 hours to set up the copy-equipment in the kitchen and be on standby for the informant arrival around 1200 hours.

The next day, Lieutenant Lê arrived a few minutes before 1200 with a brief case in his hand. He looked about furtively before tentatively stepping inside the safe house. Carter greeted him warmly and ushered him into the living room where some snacks and drinks were on a side table. Lê handed the brief case to Carter with a quizzical look – what now? Carter took the brief case smiling and told Minh that he brought some colleagues along to expedite the review. Carter pointed to the side-table telling Minh to help himself to the food and drinks.

Carter left the living room and was back in less than five minutes. Minh had a few snacks on a plate and a Coca Cola. Carter joined him for snacks and a Coca Cola.

"Thank you very much for your prompt support of this project. You have been invaluable in providing the research materials necessary for the draft report."

Minh smiled, though his stomach was knotted from the stress and fear for his pilfering the personal files. If there was a problem, he knew he would be sent into combat immediately or sent to prison. Carter casually talked to Minh about life in Saigon during the war with the communists. He mentioned that before the war, Saigon had been renowned as a beautiful city, often called the Paris of the Far East. Carter asked about Minh's family. The small talk helped fill the time for Minh, but the spurious conversation did little to quell his anxiety. He began to wonder, what are they doing with the files, what if they spill a drink on them or mark them in some way. He had a light sheen of sweat on his forehead. About 30 minutes into the meeting, a tall Caucasian man walked into the living room with the brief case in hand. He smiled at Minh, saying 'thank you' as he returned the satchel to Minh.

Carter immediately stood, taking a large envelope from his pocket. He handed the envelope to Minh who felt his heart jump as he hefted the weight of the envelope. Carter shook Minh's hand, suggesting that he return the files now. Carter told him he would contact him for the next meeting.

Minh tried to put the envelope in his pocket, but it was too thick, so he put the envelop in the brief case with the files. Carter said in a kind voice,

"You should transfer the envelope to a safe location before you return to the Joint General Staff building".

The team packed up the gear and returned to the compound to develop the pictures of the Deconfliction Division personnel files.

Han Li provided countersurveillance, as before, to ensure that Lê Minh was clean. Minh took a cab to his home following the suggestion from Carter. Once in his room, he opened the envelope and almost passed out – there must be $10,000 in the envelope. He would count it later but now he had to take the cab back to headquarters and return the files before anyone noticed they were gone.

The 'take' from the Deconfliction Directorate personnel files was extremely useful to sharpen the team focus to identify Spider. The 30 personnel files each contained a photo of the officer or enlisted man, home addresses, a list of previous assignments with the dates of the assignments, and any awards earned during their ARVN service. The files were concise, 3-5 pages each.

The team had photographed the personnel files using a dual-process as insurance that at least one copy would be legible. Clandestinely photographing documents under a time constraint is a problematic endeavor for quality results. The team used two cameras, a 35 mm Pentax and the subminiature Minox with a close-focusing lens. Sergeant Wilson had constructed rigid wire frames designed to photograph documents quickly and reliably. The frames held the cameras at the optimal focal length and avoided any camera movement during the shutter action. Wilson provided built-in lighting so the best-resolution film could be used for sharp readable images.

Ban Lan, the wife of the clan chief, Ban Chen, could read and speak Chinese, Vietnamese, and English. She was the obvious person to assist in translating the Joint General Staff personnel files. After she reviewed the document photo prints with Captain Williams, Williams congratulated Sergeants Risner, James, Wilson, and Ban Lan on a job well done. The personnel data files allowed Warrant Officer Renner to eliminate most of the Deconfliction staff as likely suspects for the role of Spider. The dates for assignment to the Deconfliction Division tended to exclude all of the enlisted personnel, except one, a Sergeant Pham Binh. Three officers fit the "Spider suspect" assignment profile.

Williams told Sergeant Jones to assign a two-man surveillance team to each of the four suspects.

"Maintain the surveillance for the next five days, look for patterns of travel, photograph the suspects' homes, watch for any tradecraft, such as countersurveillance".

Williams/Carter decided to ask Minh for additional information on another General Staff organization to divert Lê Minh's attention from being solely on the Deconfliction group.

The bar girl operation was naturally of interest, great interest, for the whole team. The three sergeants were impervious to the avalanche of crude comments regarding the trio's 'devotion' to the bar girl 'duty' – and, in particular, the sergeants' commitments to their bar girl targets. The bar girl objective was to condition and manipulate the girls to be channels to insert deceptive information into the VC networks targeting US advisors, plus the SOG, and CIA 'over the fence' operations. In turn, when the deceptive information reported back through the NVA networks, it would compromise Spider's identity.

The team had studied the failed SOG attempt to use bar girls as informants. Each sergeant from the trio would portray the type GI which the bar girls loved to prey on: drinks too much, gets mouthy and loosed-lipped when drunk, often giving away sensitive US military information, and, of course, the GI the bar girl preyed on had to have money to spend, the more money the more close-personal rapport action! The conversations with the bar girls were dominated by, possibly the most used phrases in Vietnam:

"You numbha-one GI, I show you a good time", "Buy me another drink"

So, the hands-on bar girl operation continued: Gunnery Sergeant Risner and Lolita from Mimi's bar. Master Sergeant Wilson and Myrna from the Florida Bar, and Sergeant First Class Podowski with Sweet Susie as the Sporting Bar target. All three girls were suspected to be sympathetic to the VC and possibly under the control of the VC.

The trio had been visiting the bars three to five times per week. Each time the sergeants feigning getting skunk-drunk, blabbering about their connections, and US military actions – buying the girls a lot of Saigon tea while giving the girls lavish tips for the pleasure of their company. After a couple meetings, the girls identified these three GIs as easy marks with money. When one of the sergeants entered a respective bar, the target bar girl would abandon any GI mark they were fleecing to move to the arriving Peregrine sergeant.

The trio judged the bar girls were now conditioned to pass the "deceptive information" to the VC and then onward to the Spider's network. The three sergeants constantly complained to the team about the sacrifices 'they made in their arduous duty', the difficulties of their bar girl assignments and how hard the duty was. Williams duly thanked them for their sacrifices and directed the trio to get with Warrant Officer Renner to construct the respective "deception information" stories to tell the girls when instructed.

As the Peregrine team planned to destroy the NVA network targeting US Army advisors, the KGB aggressively pressed forward with Operation

Red. The KGB recruitment effort in Saigon was proceeding well in one sense and problematic in another. Calthrop was certainly captivated by Kie^. At the same time, he was a security concern for the KGB due to his latent emotional instability. Such emotional instability often exists in recruitment operations, presenting security challenges for the case officer. Kie^ had reached a point in the operation where she needed further 'guidance' from her controller – at least, that was her rationalization to have an immediate meeting with her Operations Officer/Controller – who was, by the way Sasha, her lover.

The two KGB officers knew their lovers' relationship was a violation of KGB rules and violated the principles of tradecraft and security. Their relationship would have dire consequences if revealed to the KGB

Kie^ used the telephone code, five rings and a hang up, to schedule a meet at the safe house the following day. If received, the Operations Officer would call back responding with five rings and a hang up. Kie^ received the confirmation call from Sasha and prepared for the meeting to update him on her target.

She would use a new surveillance detection route as replicating the previous SDR route could raise her driver's suspicions. She called the concierge to schedule her driver to depart the next morning at 1100 hours.

Sasha had time to think in the enforced solitude of the Saigon safe house. He had given much thought to the method to recruit Calthrop. Sasha also had given much thought to Kie^ and their relationship and the profound impact it had for both of them. Their relationship was initially driven by Operation Red – but that professional relationship had morphed into intimate loving ties between the two of them.

During the time in Saigon, Sasha had been introspective about his life, past and future. Captain Alexandr Mikailovich Petrov was a "True Believer" in the historic destiny of Russia. He saw Russian history going back centuries, not just beginning in 1917. He thoroughly understood the concept of "Mother Russia" and how this sacred concept was suppressed by the Communists until the Great Patriotic War, known in the West as World War II. Stalin resurrected the idea of 'Mother Russia' to touch the Russian soul and emotionally motivate Russians to fight and save Russia from the Nazi onslaught. After 'Russia had won The Great Patriotic War', Stalin again trashed the Orthodox Church and disparaged a Russian identity, a historic identity to be replaced, again, by the Soviet brand of communism, using the Communist slogan, "The New Soviet Man". A subset of all this was an official government core policy of atheism; one example being, you could not be a KGB officer and publicly believe in God.

He knew that millions of Russians publicly went through the motions of Soviet communism, most just seeking the advantages of joining the CPSU for a variety of perks. Every citizen held a personal fear of the secret police, the KGB Second Directorate where his General Officer father was a very powerful man. Sasha believed that millions secretly held to their Russian identity above all else, that identity was composed of Mother Russia, the Land, the Orthodox Church, and God. All of which were integral to the true Russian soul. Sasha reflected, he must have a soul, because he was a Russian. In his heart, Sasha was a KGB Captain to serve Russia, not to serve the Soviet Union. Treasonous thoughts which would earn him a permanent vacation in a Siberian hard-labor camp or worse if discovered by the secret police.

He was not sure where he was on the belief in God thing, he would sort that out later. Even so, there was no element of self-doubt on his professional situation. Sasha knew exactly who he was: a KGB Spetsnaz trained killer, a Russian patriot; and a man dedicated to fighting the "Main Enemy", the United States of America. He was a man who had been in many relationships with women during his life and, until now, he had never been truly 'in love' with any of those women.

He was brutally rigorous in this objective analysis of himself. As he was examining who he was, he understood that his life now was in a great part defined by his relationship with Kie^. He found great amusement in the fact, no one truly knew him and the secret new factor in his life, he was truly in love with Nyugen Kie^.

Kie^ stopped to talk to the concierge as the driver waited. The concierge offered a brief rumor about which generals were vying to assume the Presidency and received a modest gratuity for the information. She told the driver to take her to the Central Market. Once there she dismissed the driver and told him she would take a taxi later. Kie^ walked slowly through the market, stopping frequently, ostensibly to examine the wares, but in fact, to surreptitiously check her back-trail. She came out the opposite side of the market and immediately engaged a taxi to take her to the south side of the Cholon business district and the many restaurants in that area. Continuing her circuitous meandering, she checked the menus posted in restaurant windows, using the window reflections to check for any surveillance. She entered a previously reconnoitered restaurant, with front and back entrances, for lunch. She determined there was no surveillance and could proceed to the safe house after lunch to see 'her Sasha'.

She was correct, no one on the Peregrine team or other counterintelligence service had an interest to follow her. The Peregrine Team was totally focused on collecting information on the potential targets for an upcoming prisoner snatch. The mystery woman was not a priority for the team.

Kie^ gave the agreed knock on the door. Sasha's 'Russian heart' jumped as he heard the knock on the door. Kie^ was here. Her excitement peaked, she heard footsteps coming to the door, to her great joy "Sasha" opened the door but stepped back. He had a very stern look on his face. Kie^ immediately entered the safe house. Before she could speak or act after Sasha closed the door, Captain Petrov stated in a very official voice,

"You know I am your Operations Officer and your handler, proceed immediately to the bedroom so I can handle you."

His little joke made her smile, but it was a relief as one never knows when or how the wrath of the KGB will descend on you. They embraced, holding each other tightly as they kissed. Walking hand-in-hand to the bedroom there was a quiet comfortable ambiance in their relationship, inside the bedroom they quickly removed their clothes and Sasha began his duties to handle her and she dutifully responded, as his operative, showing him she had some of her own "tradecraft".

After the joyous and vigorous time together in bed, Sasha and Kie^ were hungry. Instead of Vietnamese food, they had a French style picnic. Sasha had prepared an elegant selection of food to celebrate their brief time together. The menu included thinly-sliced pieces of ham, a roast chicken, herbed goat cheese, plus chunks of cheddar, Gruyere, and Gouda cheeses, a hard crust fresh baguette, a Beaujolais slightly chilled, and sliced apples. Altogether a very romantic meal, for lovers, and in this situation, between an operations officer reviewing the case officer's recruitment operation. They enjoyed the clandestine picnic talking and often, just gazing in silence into each other's eyes as they ate.

Both wanted to prolong the intimacy of the moment. Clearing the table together, they reluctantly adjourned to the living room to conduct their obligatory business – the recruitment of Calthrop Winston Simmons to make him a KGB spy.

Kie^ went into meticulous detail to memorialize the meetings with Calthrop, or "Win" as he liked to be called. Kie^ had learned about Win's humiliation from Charge d'Affaires dressing-down. An embassy wife who was a regular at the Cercle Sportif pool revealed the incident to her. The woman despised Calthrop and enjoyed providing each salacious tidbit of gossip about him, Kie^ was a very good listener. Kie^ presented her evaluation of the status, problems, and recommendations for this case. Sasha asked several questions as he wanted to fully understand every subtlety and nuance from each of her meetings with the target.

Kie^'s comments about the meeting between Calthrop and the Chargé d'Affaires the day after Calthrop's drunken return to the Embassy were of special interest to Sasha. Calthrop was humiliated by the Chargé d'Affaires' reprimand, however the greatest humiliation came from the follow-on rumors circulating throughout the Embassy staff as details from the Chargé d'Affaires comments leaked out, the scorn and laughing at him behind his back were abjectly mortifying.

Sasha asked:

"In the aftermath, were Calthrop's rage and rantings a one-time outburst or had Calthrop actually become 'disaffected with the US'? Did "Win" hold the US guilty, given his perception the US continued to mistreat and undervalue him?"

Disaffection is one of the most powerful target motivations for the case officer to exploit in the recruitment process. Could Kie^ reinforce any Calthrop leanings toward being disaffected toward the US Government?

Kie^ responded:

"It is too soon to determine if Win is "disaffected". I will watch for a vulnerability on this point."

Based on Calthrop's history from the spotting report and all the impressions in the meetings between Kie^ and Calthrop, a sexual relationship or promise of an ongoing sex affair between Kie^ and "Win" would likely be a key part of the recruitment motivation for the target. In addition, such a sexual relationship would be a factor to boost the target's ego, reinforcing Win's belief he was irresistible to women. Seemingly, this recruitment opportunity would be rather elemental: use sex to build and exploit his ego. All these issues would be woven into a single pattern with the objective for Kie^ to develop 'control' over a witting recruited target.

The remaining questions were not elemental. The target was volatile, drank too much, and was emotionally unstable. A continuing concern was the issue whether Calthrop/Win would follow 'direction', from Kie^ as her case officer. That is, could Kie^ effectively control Calthrop? Could the KGB be assured that, after recruitment, the new spy would function in a manner that preserved the security of the operation. The assurance guarantee was moot in the sense, only time could tell. The KGB, and every other intelligence service that ran HUMINT operations faced these security risks every day. Risks which reflect the reality that humans are flawed and humans who agree to be a clandestine spy against their own country are some of the most flawed of them all.

The optimal 'spy' was a person who identified with the political ideology of the country running the spy operation. Calthrop had no commitment to any ideology, except the gratuitous needs of his narcistic vanity, which include the constant recognition of his personal importance and the continuous satisfaction of his hedonistic wants'.

Kie^ and Sasha, sitting in a comfortable safe house in Saigon, agreed this was a very challenging and a high-risk operation. Agreeing further, that they should 'sleep on it' until tomorrow when they would determine how to precisely and successfully resolve all the problems. They prepared dinner, enjoyed some after-dinner vodka before they went to bed - to immensely enjoy their own hedonistic shared-pleasures.

Breakfast the next morning was simple, nourishment needed to restore the energy expended the night before: coffee, hard-crust baguette with butter, cheese, and three-minute soft-boiled eggs. Once the table was cleared, Kie^ made green tea to drink during the crucial planning session to set the approach for the "pitch" to Calthrop . Sasha was a strong supporter of the leadership principle that argued, the individual in the field conducting the daily on-the-ground tasks and dealing with the risks knows best regarding all the nuances of the case. The field operative should have the most influential voice in planning risky operations. Sasha listened closely as Kie^ presented two options for closure of the Calthrop recruitment.

The original KGB recruitment plan was a straight-forward initial sexual-compromise and follow-on sex to control the agent. All plans must fit the test, is the initial plan compatible with 'existing situation' on the ground. The actual situation on the ground at the time the plan is executed seldom matched the original assumptions. In virtually every instance, the original plan is modified, or in some cases abandoned and a revised plan set in-place. The case officer always has to be ready to improvise.

This recruitment was unusual as compared to most clandestine agent recruitments. In most recruitments, the challenge is to find a compelling motivation that leads the target to agree to become a spy against his own country. In the case of Calthrop, finding a viable motivation was quite the opposite. Calthrop was so flawed there was a plethora of motivations, any one of which would likely work to recruit him. Sasha and Kie^ had to decide, how do we prioritize the viability of his various vulnerabilities? Disaffection with the US Government and America, revenge for perceived slights and mistreatment by the US government; compulsive need for sex; a need to control women; a massive ego, narcissist, and a potential to be blackmailed stood out as part of the list they had to consider. But in every situation, the instability of Calthrop made any single motivation or combination of vulnerabilities problematic. The many Calthrop vulnerabilities for the recruitment had a concerning downside.

One of the most serious handling problems a case officer faces is 'unpredictability'. Will the agent follow instructions and direction from the case officer? Further, can the agent control his mouth; will the agent observe security protocols and tradecraft procedures; does the agent drink too much? Calthrop was an attractive target due to his access to sensitive information and he was vulnerable due to the personal flaws in his character. But, his flaws were earthquake-like emotional faults, too many fissures in his character, the constant risk of a major calamity. This was the nature of the spy business, all targets are flawed to some degree. Otherwise, the individuals would not be candidates for recruitment by an enemy to spy on their own country

The subjective question was," do his flaws create an unacceptable risk for success of the operation"? The subjectivity issue is defined, in

294

part, by the culture of the major spy institutions: CIA, DIA, KGB, GRU, MI-6. A core problem for the KGB was an institutional rigidity which set a ruthless policy to punish failure or any deviation from doctrinaire policies. Thus, one of the optimal paths for KGB promotion was an ability to avoid risk or shift blame to others. This recruitment of a high-level mole in the US government was officially-preordained by powerful general officers in the KGB. The KGB case officers facing in-the-field problems would understate their operational problems, or more often hide problems from the senior KGB officers. At the same time promotion opportunities could be enhanced by 'informing' on a colleague. And so goes the treacherous cycle of life for all in the KGB.

Sasha and Kie^ examined several scenarios to construct this "Pitch" as a compelling and persuasive action to overcome inhibitions by the target to serve as a spy. The Pitch was the moment of truth – the point in time when the case officer converts the target into a willingly spy who betrays his country. Or, if the "Pitch" fails, the KGB case officer faces a career-ending, possibly life-ending, event.

The obvious recruitment motivation for Calthrop vis-à-vis Kie^ is a sexual relationship. Even so, sex had different potential implementations in the recruitment process: dependence on the case officer to satisfy physical and emotional sexual needs; sexual compromise as a basis for blackmail; a natural human need to be intimate. Sex, or the promise of sex, could be the precursor of a persuasive message for Calthrop. Other motivations would be selectively interwoven with sex to sell the "Pitch". An elemental principle is to make the target believe psychologically that the case officer is the source of satisfaction for the target's vital needs. Without question, Kie^ had the physical and intellectual capabilities to use sex to successfully recruit this flawed target.

An alternative strategy involved how Kie^ would complete the development process by luring Calthrop into a serious security violation. Then she would go for the coup de grâce using blackmail to coerce Calthrop to become a KGB spy. Kie^ could coyly request that "Win" get her an illegal visa to the United States, a permanent-resident visa.

Alternatively, she could tell Win that a person at the Cercle Sportif, who had deep-connections inside the Vietnamese government, told her that her father had been in contact with some secret US organization, about a year ago. This contact talked about a US secret organization having to do with intelligence things in the North – operations by some military group in MACV, according to the contact, the group had a three letter-acronym – the person passing on the rumor to Kie^ said the three-letter acronym could begin with a C or an S. She would ask Calthrop to help find the name of this secret organization, telling him this was the only lead she had, so far, to find her father.

In either strategy, she would suggest that she would be his mistress in the US, or they could even get married. Once Calthrop is compromised by one or more security breaches, Kie^ will give him the Pitch. The Pitch would include money, sex, and the shock factor that, 'she is a KGB operative', but she fell in love with him when she came to know him. She will tell him they will work together; and Calthrop will have access to a lot of money. She would close the "Pitch deal" by giving him an initial spying assignment and a financial bonus. Calthrop then is "witting", he understands he is a spy for an enemy power and accepts, consciously or unconsciously, he is under some-degree of case officer control".

As Sasha listened intently, Kie^ saw a look on his face she had not seen before. He asked Kie^,

"Please tell me the truth. How do you feel about having sex with the target in order to recruit him?"

Kie^ did not know how to answer. Was this a KGB test? But the look on Sasha's face told her, he meant it on a personal basis when he asked for the truth.

Trying to suppress tears, she studied Sasha's face to try to read any hidden-meaning in his expression – was there a 'tell' which reflected his intent by this question. Kie^ decided, in so many words, 'screw the KGB, I am a person, not a flesh-and-blood tool for the KGB'. A wave of relief swept through her mind and body, even as a residual fear remained buried in the back of her mind. How will Sasha react? He is a KGB officer and Operation Red is his ticket to a bright future with all the perks and power that the KGB can offer.

Kie^ bowed her head slightly and transfixed Sasha with her eyes, as two tears rolled down her cheeks:

"Sasha, I love you. I hate Calthrop and do not want to have sex with him, ever. I want to be with you and you alone".

Sasha took Kie^'s hands in his, smiling in a tender way, before he said,

"Kie^, I love you. I planned to tell you that today – but I was not sure quite how to say it. I have never 'honestly' told a woman that I loved her. I had prepared a long explanation for you, but I think the short version is better – I love you Kie^".

They sat in silence for a few moments. Each letting their deep feelings of love and mutual respect flow through their minds giving them comfort and joy.

Sasha broke the moment to say,

"I have a plan to deceive the KGB and keep you with me always. You did well to adroitly hold back the 'sex card' during the development phase of the recruitment. You will never have to yield sexually to Calthrop".

They looked into each other's eyes and silently communicated a resignation that doing the mission can carry painful consequences. The mission was to recruit this target. Kie^ and Sasha would do the mission and bear whatever the consequences and emotional costs might be.

"I think we can talk about the new plan later – right now I have some ice-cold vodka for us, I suggest we drink a toast 'to us' in the bedroom and make this toast to us as – "together now and forever" - Na Zdorovie – good health" - in their personal intimate-context, the last phrase of the toast, 'good health', was a sort of mystical totem to protect them from the KGB.

The next morning, they had a simple breakfast of coffee, buttered hard rolls, and bananas - eaten mostly in silence as each mulled over what the next contact between Kie^ and Calthrop would bring. Kie^ kissed Sasha at the door with a kiss that communicated – do not worry, whatever happens, I love you. She found a cab and returned to the hotel, planning to call Calthrop.

Calthrop had not called Kie^ for five days which was unusual and concerning. The reason for his lapse in contact would change Kie^'s life and the course of Operation Red.

CHAPTER 23   SETTING THE TRAP

Warrant Officer Renner knocked on Captain Williams' door, receiving an authoritative response

"Enter!"

"Morning Boss, Gunny Risner and I have something in the intelligence shack that you and LT Baumgartner need to see".

"Sounds good, Tell Baumgartner to get cleaned up and meet us there in 20-minutes. He is in the gym practicing hand-to-hand combat with Podowski".

"On my way Boss". Renner turned his head as he exited the room – "hand-to-hand with Podowski, does the Lieutenant have a death wish?"

"Come-on Carl – we both know Baumgartner is crazy – he is a damned sailor".

Arriving at the gym, Warrant Officer Renner found a cheering bunch of Nungs watching Baumgartner and Podowski go at it. Both were soaked with sweat and breathing hard, but it was obvious that LT Baumgartner had gotten the worst of it, so far. Baumgartner had a deep-cut over his right eye and the blood was flowing freely into his eye and down his face. Half-blinded, Baumgartner held a rubber training knife as he circled Podowski. Renner watched as the Lieutenant faked a slashing move and rolled onto his side to deliver a kicking move against the side of Podowski's knee. If delivered with full force, the kick would dislocate Podowski's knee. Baumgartner restrained the kick to be a symbolic 'gotcha' message rather than physically damaging, but a 'clear message' none the less. Both men laughed as Sergeant Podowski offered his hand to Baumgartner to help him up.

"Good move Lieutenant".

Baumgartner looked like some bloody apparition as he told Podowski,

"Look, Jake, when you mess with the bull, sometimes you get the horns".

Renner was laughing as he told Baumgartner, Captain Williams wanted to see the bloody Navy LT in the intelligence shack forthwith, but after a shower.

"I'm on my way – and, give Sergeant Podowski a follow-up message from me – he needs to thank me for the ass-kicking I gave him, I let him survive – tell him the message is from 'the raging bull from Indiana'."

Renner ran to the infirmary in the team living quarters building to advise Doc that the Lieutenant needed some stiches and needed them now.

Nine stitches and a hot shower later, Baumgartner reported to the intel shack to see most of the team, including Sergeant Podowski, standing around the conference table examining an assortment of documents Risner and Renner had placed on the table. Captain Williams turned and saw the swollen cut above Baumgartner's right eye, now fiery-red with nine-stiches, suppressing a laugh, Williams simply commented,

"Glad you could join us after you kicked Podowski's ass again" – the obligatory round of hoots and jeers followed until Williams raised his hand.

Warrant Office Renner began the intelligence briefing.

"We got a shit load of good stuff in the last few days. This stuff is telling a multi-dimensional story. We meshed the info from the Joint Staff Deconfliction Division personnel files with the surveillance photos of the radio building and crossed-referenced that with NSA translations of the old KGB encryption messages. We built a new timeline that more accurately depicts the movements and likely roles of the current bad-guys and the Spider network. Some surprises and some confirmations."

"The big surprise is the identity of the Spider – he is not the guy we originally fingered. The radio building surveillance photos showed the ARVN sergeant as the individual who most often enters and departs the building. The sergeant parks a black Citroen sedan behind the building and spends each night in the building – I mean, this guy lives in the building. When we compared the surveillance photos with the personnel file photos – voila – the ARVN sergeant is Sergeant Pham Binh assigned to the Deconfliction Division as the chauffeur for Colonel Trần Quan. The surveillance reports from Sergeant Jones's teams show Sergeant Pham is a pretty shitty chauffer. Colonel Trần often has to use taxis when Sergeant Pham is otherwise occupied. Pham is often occupied by feminine company at the building, during the day and at night. Moreover, there is a clear correlation of Pham's movements with the arrival of individuals who appear to be couriers and Pham's presence when incoming radio-message traffic arrives from enemy radios in the South Vietnamese provinces. There is another tell, he is there when some sort of consolidated out-going message traffic is forwarded to the A Shau comm site.

We originally thought Colonel Trần was the Spider, given his position as Division Chief for the Deconfliction Division. We knew Trần was corrupt so all was consistent with his shady background falsifying logistics records to set higher costs as Tran skims the excess money. There is evidence that Tran has dropped his criminal activities since Pham came on the scene. This makes sense from a security standpoint and the timing suggests Pham ordered Tran to cease actions which would draw attention to the treasonous Saigon clandestine radio operation. All the indicators now suggest the Spider is Sergeant Pham Binh".

"Pham has a brilliant cover and an even shadier background than Colonel Trần. We think Colonel Trần is part of the Spider network but he is a node rather than the decision maker. Other 'tells' come from the surveillance work by the Nungs, Duan Ho and Chu Zhu, watching Pham and Trần. When it is just the two of them, Colonel Trần seems to be very deferential to Pham. Colonel Trần visits the radio building infrequently, appearing as if Colonel Trần was summoned by Pham."

"Pham is sloppy with his tradecraft and security matters, for example, he does not conduct countersurveillance. Pham has definite patterns, and brings non-operational persons to the radio building, two young Vietnamese girls, in particular. The girls appear to be living there".

"We believe there are six to seven people living in the building based on the foot traffic observed over an extended period of time. Our estimate is: three radio operators which is consistent with three-shift 24/7 coverage of the radio net. The assumed radio operators only leave the building on what appears to be personal tasks, eating lunch, going to a movie, meeting prostitutes, and so forth. They, like Pham, are full-time residents".

"The two young women who previously visited frequently now seem to have moved into the building. We tracked them to a refugee camp before they moved into the building. They are likely refugees who have become hookers to earn money to help their families. There are some interesting specifics on these two girls. Early on, each of them wore an expensive, but well-worn, ao dai, their clothes showed wear consistent with the refugee situation. Our estimate is, they are from upper-class Hanoi families who fled the commies while leaving the family-money behind. Since they moved into the radio building, they are wearing new clothes."

"There is a middle-aged woman living in the building who appears to be the cook based on her shopping habits. She is absent on Tuesday afternoons and evenings, apparently visiting her family in Cholon. Chu Zhu followed the cook to Cholon and observed her interaction with her family and confirmed she spends Tuesday nights in Cholon."

"There are frequent comings-and-goings of individuals who appear to be couriers as the visits correlate with outgoing radio traffic. There are frequent visits by obvious prostitutes, probably for hook-ups with off-duty radio operators."

"We do not see a technical-device security system for the building. As far as we can tell looking in first-floor windows, all the ground-floor apartments are vacant. The front and back door locks are old-style skeleton key types and can be easily picked."

"Outstanding work Gunny and Carl. Did anyone check the Agency about this Pham guy?"

"We checked but they have nothing on him."

"We talked about inserting a listening device in the radio building. Sergeant Wilson could install such a device, but we are not comfortable that the Nungs are properly trained for that 'sneaky install' mission. We have never seen a Caucasian enter the building, so we decided the risk was too great at this point in the operation. We thought about asking the CIA Saigon station for help with a black bag job."

Captain Williams interrupted,

"No black bag job by anyone – no listening devices – at this phase of the operation we must be opaque to everyone except General Wojcik. When I say opaque – what I mean is, when we grab and snatch all the Spider network targets – any folks looking for our prisoners will think aliens from outer-space abducted them."

"There will be collateral damage. This is a complex operation in timing and execution. So, Sergeant Jones, I want training stepped-up and then train some more. I want to see your plan to take down the radio building occupants in 30-seconds, or less, once the grab and snatch "Go signal" is given. One four-man team per occupied room. The leader of each team will be an American. Three silenced High Standard pistols per team. Hollow-point ammo. Start the coordinated multiple-team training using the team quarters building as a surrogate for the radio building. Give me a report at the end of each training-day".

"The rules of engagement are:

Grab persons on the snatch list, or anyone who happens to be there – if anyone makes a noise that would draw attention, kill that person immediately with the silenced-pistols, make sure they are dead, two taps, one to the head and one to the heart. A knife is a better option if the problem is close enough to silently dispatch him or her with a blade.

Leave no bodies, no fingerprints, no smell of deodorant, no forensic evidence - nothing! You were never there".

"There will be an NSA team standing by to process technical evidence and operate the radios until we decide to shut the radios down. The NSA team will enter the building on my order."

"We need materials available to torch the building after we exit. I mean a pile of ashes within 30-minutes, or less, after we trigger the ignitors."

"Doc, you need to be on standby, ready for casualties. If an American is seriously wounded and needs more treatment than you can give, get him to the 3rd Field Hospital as fast as possible – tell them a VC on a motorcycle shot the patient. Take any Nung casualties back to the compound."

"Any questions? Get on it– there is a lot riding on Peregrine – there is no do-over. As always – we get it right the first time. Be ready to execute three-weeks from now".

Captain Williams sent a message to Major-General Wojcik at Special Projects, Office of the Chairman, Joint Chiefs of Staff.

```
Adjunct Inspector General Team #4

Priority

EYES ONLY: Major-General Stanislaw Wojcik


To: JCS Deputy for Special Projects

From: Adjunct Inspector General Team #4


Ready to execute in three weeks from 'approval'.
Discovered new dots.

Can you visit compound for brief and "Go" plan?

Standing by for instructions


Robert Williams GS-15

Adjunct Inspector General Team #4
```

General 'Bull' General Wojcik replied in 30 minutes. Will arrive at compound in three days.

Captain Williams and LT Baumgartner had developed a 'basic plan' several days prior to the new inputs from Gunnery Sergeant Risner and Warrant Officer Renner. During the afternoon Williams and Baumgartner made changes and updates to the draft plan to incorporate the new information. They would be ready for the General Wojcik visit in three days.

They decided to take the night off for steaks and beer at the Rex rooftop restaurant – who knows, maybe that 'beautiful mystery babe' will show again. Besides the next three days are going to be intense. We need steak and beer – which, of course, they had at the compound – the break seemed more intended to see if the mystery woman shows up.

Williams and Baumgartner got into the jeep back seat. The Nung driver and accompanying Nung bodyguard, Han Li and Chu Zhu, had been waiting, as if they had read the Americans minds. The Rex rooftop was always crowded, as good American-style food, American beer, and a pleasant environment were a rare combination in Saigon. They found a table near the back wall so they could watch the door and entertainment plus have as much privacy as possible amidst a rowdy crowd of US officers. They ordered large T-bones and beer and retrieved some salad and bread from the salad bar. The Peregrine team leaders quietly discussed the issues they needed to resolve in the morning: how to minimize any collateral damage casualties during the raid, particularly the women expected to be there; the urgent need to torch the building after the NSA crew removed the radio equipment and documents which may have intelligence value – and the 'Intel Prize' – 'the encryption and cypher keys'. A separate issue was complex 'prisoner snatch' problems for the three targets not living in the building – both agreed, no sweat, our guys can do it - they looked at each other, tapped the long-neck beers together and Gary mused,

"a lot of shit for the next two days. Bull is a hard task-master for details and no loose ends."

At that point, the entertainment for the night walked onto the small stage – this time a Filipino rock-and-roll band with the obligatory 'cute girl singer' and teenager musicians, who on their best night were not very good – but the standards for GI entertainment in wartime Vietnam presented a very low bar. The steaks and more beer arrived at the table. The Peregrine officers enjoyed the steaks and even enjoyed the music, relaxing before the coming storm. They sat there with their individual thoughts about the mission and the promise of going home soon. The droning background of dinner conversations changed for a moment when a beguiling woman entered the roof-top dining area. Baumgartner mumbled and muttered - "oh shit" Most of the diners turned their heads to see Gabriella Mueller do her queenly entrance routine, to the band's background blaring of a barely recognizable rendition of Bill Haley's, 'Rock Around the Clock'.

Bobby looked at Gary with a quizzical look,

"What's with the 'oh shit', are you referring to the 'walking sex machine' who just walked in? Have you been conducting some 'under the covers' operation not authorized by me?"

Gary gave Bobby his well-practiced faux-innocent look,

"Bobby, you have a dirtier mind than all the dirty talk about you

305

from the team. The reason for the 'oh shit' is legit. Sergeant Matthews from SOG, you know Jones' buddy, told Jones a story about this women correspondent from some European newspaper and how she did in a SOG Colonel. The Colonel went from 'hot shit leader of men' to bagging groceries in some 'shithole town no one ever heard of', USA. The short version is this, the Colonel was humping Gabriella while she was pumping him for inside information. As Matthews tells it, she was a better pumper than he was a humper, hey don't blame me. It's Matthews' story".

"Anyway, the Colonel's indiscretions were found out when some classified information that only two or three folks in SOG knew was leaked in a press article. The Colonel was given a choice. Retire and save the embarrassment to the Army and your family or just go for the court martial and a long vacation in Leavenworth. According to Matthews, this is the modus operandi for this female correspondent. He said she is still screwing information out of several MACV REMF senior officers. Damn, watch her work the room now."

Basking in the attention, the Saigon Reuters correspondent, Gabriella Mueller, looked around the room for her journalistic prey that evening. Gabriella Mueller ranked as a European top-tier American hater, whose disdain for the US was only surpassed by her antipathy for the US military. Intelligent and mean-spirited, but very attractive, Gabriella Mueller was a person all US military should avoid. Gabriella Mueller's attractive physical appearance masked her malevolent character. Men and women who saw Gabriella were taken by her striking five-foot eight-inch, 165 pound extremely well formed body, her long dark-brown hair, hazel eyes, and, in particular, her face which appeared to be sculpted as a copy of a beautiful Valkyrian from Teutonic mythology. Males tended to immediately obsess over Gabriella's physical allure, women were filled with envy and an immediate dislike. Beyond the allure of her physical appearance, Gabriella was a dangerous-woman to all she encountered.

Gabriella Mueller was the 'legend name' she used in her role as a clandestine agent for the East German Intelligence service, the Ministry for State Security - in German: Ministerium für Staatssicherheit, MfS. Her true name is Hanna Freya Berger, a fanatic communist and nationalistic East German. Hanna is as well-endowed intellectually as she was well-endowed physically. Her fanaticism gave her intellect a sharp edge and she tends to extend a callous persona toward the people with whom she interacted. She played this sharp edge aspect of her character as an essential part of her legend as a hard-nose journalist.

Hanna was recruited by Marcus Wolf, a living MfS legend,. Unlike the KGB, the MfS had few inhibitions about office romances. Hanna and Marcus became lovers for a brief, highly-erotic affair, that delighted and amused all MfS spooks as the stories circulated of their sexual escapades, stories which were as prized for MfS internal consumption as much as the intelligence successes over the despised West German government and the hated Americans.

The MfS produced a superb legend for Gabriella with extensive backstops which would defy most counterespionage investigations. The legend had Gabriella entering West Germany as a refugee journalist fleeing arrest by the East German police. She obtained a job as a foreign correspondent for Reuters, her first posting was to Saigon to report on the Vietnam War. All her articles to date show a positive bias toward the VC and a negative slant on all matters associated with South Vietnamese and the Americans.

Gabriella walked about, stopping at several tables to acknowledge officers she knew, accepting their homage, as a reasonable response based on her ability to destroy military careers at will. Baumgartner observed that she was using the adulation-tour to wind her to a destination at their table. Gary caught Bobby in the middle of a large bite of medium-rare T-bone and muttered,

"big oh shit, she is coming this way"

Bobby immediately replied though his mouth was full of steak:

"We are civilians working logistics at Tan Son Nhut – you are Johnson and I am Brown"

At that point, Gabriella Mueller walked, brazenly uninvited, to their table. She was sporting a smile that would make a saltwater crocodile envious, the just before the kill smile.

"Hi boys, I don't think we have met. I am Gabriella Mueller."

Shifting to a southern accent, Captain Bobby Williams smiled back, offering his hand,

"No Ma'am, I do not think we have met before, I am Bobby Brown, proud to make your acquaintance. My friend here is Clyde Johnson".

Clyde offered his hand. (Gabriella continued her reptilian smile while thinking, two more ignorant uncouth Americans; but something is not quite right here with this 'hick' act).

Bobby continued,

"What are you doing in Nam, Ma'am?"

Keeping her external cool while furious on the inside, these two are idiots, everybody that matters in Saigon knows me,

"I am a reporter for Reuters."

Bobby nodded his head in the affirmative,

"That's one of them European newspapers isn't it?"

Gritting her teeth, Gabriella held her creepy reptilian smile,

"No, Reuters is a major international news service. What are you boys doing here in Vietnam? You look like military officers."

Clyde just looked at Bobby, indicating Bobby had the floor for the 'two American hicks'.

"We work at Tan Son Nhut as civilian logistics consultants." (Keeping all his comments succinct.)

Gabriella, holding her predator smile, replied,

"Why Bobby, that sounds like some bullshit cover-thing. Are you boys spooks?"

"No ma'am, we are just 'good-old boys' in a foreign country for now – waiting to go home."

"Thank you, boys, it was good to meet you. I'm very sure our paths will cross again soon".

– sounding like the threat it was.

As Gabriella stood there fuming, the tension was broken as Kie^ and Calthrop walked into the dining area – all attention switched to the stunning Eurasian woman with 'some guy' – nobody cared about the guy. The room shifted their interest from Gabriella to the Eurasian woman.

Bobby latched onto the distraction, telling Gabriella,

"Now there is somebody who is a lot more interesting than us. You ought to talk to them, whoever they are."

Gabriella made a mistake, driven by her anger at the smirking evasions she got from the 'hicks' and her displeased how quickly she was being displaced as the center of attention on the Rex rooftop:

"I am not interested in talking to them. The guy is a loser working in some sensitive intelligence job in the Embassy. His father-in-law is a very rich powerful guy in Washington. The woman is just a high-priced hooker. No, you boys are much more interesting for me."

Gabriella gave a very condescending nod, offering her hand in a regal gesture. The Peregrine officers shook her hand and reverted back to their beers. Gabriella silently raged as she walked away, those simple bastards, did they think they fooled me for one-second. I am going to get the story on them and destroy them.

Gabriella almost stomped her feet, as a spoiled three-year old would do when frustrated. Using her always present camera, Gabriella began her spiteful campaign to expose 'Bobby and Clyde'. An action which would threaten the overall security of Peregrine Operation. Gabriella was able to take two quick pictures of "Bobby and Clyde" before they departed the Rex rooftop for the last time in the Peregrine Operation. She stopped at a table across the restaurant where she angrily berated an REMF colonel, asking who the two clowns across the room were. Gabriella was on the hunt with a grudge and two pictures.

Williams watched Gabriella take their pictures:

"We got real bad news 'Bobby', very bad. She is a threat to the mission. She knows how to work the system and has cultivated a number of high-level sources. We need to advance the timetable to execute the 'prisoner-grab operation'."

Before departing, 'Bobby and Clyde' finished the now cold steaks and warm beer as the band played on – the cute girl singer belted-out a loud high-pitched version of 'Twist and Shout", with an enthusiastic but untalented band in lyrical and instrumental support. Gary checked out the Eurasian woman and the man with her,

"Why did Gabriella know so much about the guy with our mystery babe?"

"I don't know 'the why' on the Eurasian beauty and the Embassy guy. But I know Gabriella was big-time pissed and did not buy our clever 'good ol' boy' story. I think this is our last time at the Rex for this Nam visit. We need to do a solid SDR to get back to the compound."

'Bobby and Clyde' took a two-hour SDR to return to the compound to ensure they were not being followed as a result of the confrontation with Gabriella. Several of the team members were sitting in the team room drinking beer and listening to an eclectic assortment of music on the juke box. As the officers passed through the team room on the way to the conference room – Williams shouted,

"accelerate training – we are moving up the Execute date. More in the morning."

CHAPTER 24   THE PLAN
ELIMINATE SPIDER AND HIS WEB

The team had some serious wake-up music for PT and breakfast starting with the rollicking version of 'Shout' by the Isley Brothers and the good old country twang of Hank Williams delivering 'Kaw-Liga' – memories of home 'all way round'. The team members were fired-up to hear what changes were in the works to execute the 'Take-Down'.

Captain Williams had a serious look on his face as he began the briefing,

"Good morning Gentlemen" – (All thought, are you serious!)"Gentlemen" –

The very suggestion 'gentleman' broke the tension inciting the team to hoots and several pithy comments. Once the raucous remarks subsided – Williams said with a smile,

"Listen carefully or you will miss the train"

"Major-General Wojcik is due to arrive in two days. We originally planned to be ready to execute on Tuesday, 17 November 1964. The 17 November date is moved up seven days. The execute day is now '10 November'."

Before anyone could ask, Captain Williams stated:

"The reason to advance the date is a security concern."

He did not specify the security concern, all knew they would be informed if they needed to know.

"There are changes to the original plan. We present the new plan to General Wojcik for approval in two days"

"First, based on some good work by Carl, we have additional information which should help reduce collateral damage during the take-down. Carl noted the 'cook' takes every Tuesday off to visit her family in Cholon. That is the reason for the Tuesday hit date."

"Second, we have no way to predict if any hookers will visit the building 10 November. We will have two Nungs in White Mice uniforms standing-by. The Nungs will intercept any visiting hookers before they can enter the building. Beyond that, we still expect at least two women will be in the building on the second floor. Treat these women as the enemy during the take-down."

"The Rules of Engagement remain the same. 'No noise is our credo'. If any of the building occupants resist, try to raise an alarm, or otherwise make noise which would draw outside attention – these individuals are to be dispatched immediately using silenced automatics or a knife. Use silenced High Standard HDM 22-automatics with hollow-point loads. As a contingency, each take-down team will have one member carrying an M-16. This brings us to another change in plan."

"No witnesses, anyone making noise is to be killed. All others are to be given the knockout drug and taken prisoner. Leave dead bodies in-place; we will torch the building once the NSA team removes all the intel materials of interest. The NSA team will enter on my command after the prisoners are removed. The command post is located in the surveillance apartment across the street from the front entrance to the radio building."

"Doc will be with me, ready if needed for medical issues – US critical-care casualties will go to the Third Field Hospital in Saigon. Less serious US casualties and any Nung casualties will go to the compound."

"After grabbing the 'intel take', the NSA team will proceed directly to Tan Son Nhut, an Import-Export charter aircraft will be waiting with engines running."

"Remove the 'Adjunct Inspector General Team #4' sign from the compound gate. Do it today and leave the compound unmarked. Double the gate guard and make sure no one but the team and our Nungs enter after today".

"Any questions so far? OK, get more coffee. We are going to review the revised plan and go over details for General Wojcik's arrival. The General will hand-carry any new information from NSA. No decision has been made yet on what we will, or will not, tell CIA Do not discuss anything with them until that 'sharing' decision is made."

There was no need to remind the team of the Peregrine mission: "find the person or persons responsible for the attacks on US Army advisors in Vietnam; neutralize such person or persons". The mission is clear and indelibly etched in each team member's mind. However, the corollary constraints on the mission made successful execution exquisitely difficult. The mission must be done from start to finish in 'the dark', absolutely clandestine. In particular, there can be no glimmer of knowledge by the South Vietnamese government before or after the take-down. Infringement on South Vietnamese sovereignty is inevitable, but no one can know or even sense that such infringement happened, thus, the mission actions and results must appear as invisible, none of this ever happened – the mission must be accomplished with absolutely no traces of the US involvement. No residual evidence of any sort of the Peregrine operation."

"Further complicating the constraints we face, we discovered that the person responsible for the attacks on US Army advisors was the tip of a 'threat iceberg'. We found evidence of involvement of many threat entities: the KGB, the North Vietnamese Ministry of Defense Intelligence Department and the Public Security Directorate, multiple enemy networks in South Vietnam, SOG and CIA cross-border operational disasters due to "moles", and a mystery new radio signals using various KGB high-level encryption systems, even as the Spider network uses an obsolete system. Our challenge is to build a revised plan consistent with mission requirements and deals with the constraints. We have two days."

"Now it's time to kick ass and take names. General Wojcik will give us guidance on any other issues. But, I suspect we will just grab prisoners and intel, immediately torch the building – and get the Hell out of Dodge."

"A 1Es will take out the A Shau radio site just before the radio building 'prisoner snatches' are executed in Saigon. Yards will install beacons for the A 1Es a few days prior the air strike. Taking out the A Shau site before we strike in Saigon prevents any alerts that might be attempted during the take-down".

"We will be 'ghosts' before and after the take-down."

"We go 10 November, detailed execution-timelines to follow. Review the pictures of the front and back door locks to be picked – six teams, shoot to kill if any noise – transport secured-prisoners directly to the compound – full-black outfits, war paint, silenced weapons, hoods for the prisoners, plastic ties to secure the prisoners, syringes to inject prisoners with knock-out drugs".

"Finally, interrogations conducted in the compound – and disposal of all the evidence including tying up 'loose ends."

The General is Here

The "International Export and Import Company Ltd" charter 707 received landing clearance for Tan Son Nhut International Airport, Saigon, Vietnam. On landing, the 'Follow Me" truck led the 707 to a parking spot on the alternate runway which was surrounded on three-sides by a massive Vietnamese cemetery. The charter 707 was configured for a combination passenger/cargo manifest. The passenger section provided top-line comfortable-recliner seating for 30 people plus galley service; The passenger list was short, five individuals: Major-General Bull Wojcik and a four-man NSA 'black bag' team. The NSA 'black bag' team would exploit the Saigon radio site as soon as the prisoners were removed from the building. They had two air cargo containers with equipment for technical exploitation of the site, plus an empty cargo container for the return to NSA, hopefully, full of enemy communications equipment and documents from the site.

Five vehicles and a forklift were waiting near the 707 parking spot. A specially modified-jeep with extra seats and a 50-caliber pedestal mounted machine gun was "shotgun" for the vehicle convoy. Master Sergeant Wilber James used his consummate wheeler-dealer skills to have the Jeep modified as a bodyguard-vehicle. James told Captain Williams he got a deal – only three cases of booze.

The modified-jeep had two extra-seats welded onto the back of the Jeep so guards could cover the rear of the Jeep from these positions. On either side, the modified-jeep had a step and hand grip welded to allow for an additional two guards, one on either side. The body-guard Jeep could carry five guards, a driver, and a gunner for the 50-caliber, a formidable capability to lay-down a wall of firepower, as needed. Two deuce-and-half trucks and a 40-foot flatbed truck completed the heavy-lift portion for the convoy. One truck was for the NSA black bag team and the flatbed for their 'black bag equipment'. The second deuce-and-half contained a heavily armed 10-man Nung combat team. A second Jeep, with a canvass canopy would hide the 'visitor' from prying eyes.

The 'welcome' party deployed and was waiting before the crew shut-down the 707 engines. The Nung combat team formed a secure perimeter. Three Americans waited in unmarked tiger-stripe jungle fatigues, wearing

45-caliber Model 1911, side arms. All drivers remained in their respective vehicles. Four-heavily armed Nung bodyguards stood behind the Americans on the runway ramp.

As soon as the engines were shut down, a forklift pushed stairs to the 707 front passenger-door. LT Baumgartner saluted the General at the bottom of the stairs, the General returned the salute and extended his hand to shake Baumgartner's hand. Looking around, Bull commented,

"You have some serious firepower here. Lieutenant".

Baumgartner nodded his head 'yes', General Wojcik thought silently – this guy is a chip off this old block.

Moving toward the vehicles Bull returned the salutes from Sergeants Jones and James; stopping briefly to inspect the four Nung bodyguards, who all stood at attention. He nodded at each Nung which evoked broad grins from each man. Turning to Baumgartner, the General remarked, "tough-looking bunch" – the Lieutenant replied, "everyman a shooter". He accompanied the General to the enclosed Jeep, a Nung bodyguard following closely.

All equipment loaded and personnel in their respective vehicles, the convey departed in less than 15-minutes after engines shutdown. As the convey moved through Tan Son Nhut gates, the General said he understood the team had some good things to tell him, and he had a couple good things in return. Continuing,

"Since we can't talk here, I will give you one of the good things to review".

The General retrieved an envelope from his pocket and gave it to Baumgartner. You can study this on the ride to the compound. It's from Annie:

315

Dear Gary,

The General advised me you are well and offered to deliver this letter to you. Not being able to communicate on a personal basis these many months has been the most depressing thing since you departed last December for 'that place'. I take some solace remembering how you delivered your 'oh so lame' pick-up line in the conference room after my initial briefing to you and the team. I must admit it now – I guess the line was not too lame as I came to love you. You can forget that line now, you do not need such lines anymore! I do love you Gary and pray every day for your safety and the safety of your team.

You have seen the 'official' side of our relationship in the various reports sent through other channels. We are part of a good team professionally – and a better team privately, as "us".

The NSA sense of security is everywhere, as it should be. I have endured many awkward moments when asked why and how I was driving such a grand (and expensive) car. Between blushing and stammering, I delivered a litany of my own 'lame responses'. Those friends at work, who know you or know about you, took every opportunity to make their own lame comments like – you know, he is a sailor; or, do you get to keep the car, and worse.

While only the Peregrine insiders know we have a 'relationship, some busy bodies seem to resent 'the car'. To that end, one of the 'very security-minded', whom I will not further characterize in an effort to be charitable, could not wait to race to the security office to report a possible enemy agent within NSA, a woman living beyond her means with "that car" on display. The 'beyond her means' evidence was the Corvette. Well, you know this workplace – no behavior is beyond some suspicion. The next day, I was summoned to the internal-security office to explain why I had such an expensive vehicle. I could not give the security inquisitor any information about our relationship because the project "security rules" do not allow such based on that strict 'need to know' rule. What a mess – the security department was about to launch a formal investigation until Dr. Slade intervened, instructing the security mavens to cease and desist, stop on the order of the Director. By the way, I love your car – but wait, what do they say about possession and the law – I guess it is my car now.

I asked the General if you and the team might be home for Christmas. The General said it was definitely a possibility. The General and his wife have been very kind to me. They invited me to visit them in their quarters at Fort McNair – the house is historic and so grand – if this house were in Indiana, it would be called a palace, I suppose you did not know about the Army Fort McNair since you are a sailor – but the history of the base goes back to 1791. The General and his wife live in quarters dating around 1895 but with many updates, given decades of necessary renovations. They had me to dinner, 'twice', the General's wife is such a gracious and sweet person. She made me feel more like a daughter coming home than an outsider-visitor. Did you know they have two sons? Both are in the Army. One is a Ranger and the other is a paratrooper. I do not know if I should tell you this or not, but it was not told to me in confidence, just privately by the General's wife. She told me that the General liked you and said you reminded him of the days when he was a young officer. Since the General has a reputation for being wild in his early days, I am not sure exactly what that means! – regardless, I am glad that he likes you.

As for Christmas, I do hope you will be back here. I talk to my parents at least once every week. My Dad always asks if you will be visiting soon. He tries to be funny saying he needs help with the chores. Another one of those things I probably should not tell you, talking to my mother a week ago, she referred to you as Robert, my brother's name, realizing what she said, she started crying. I can't write more about that now or I will cry. My parents really like you and want to see you, and, by the way so do I. Please accept their invitation for Christmas. My dad needs help with the chores.

I have to get this letter to the General as he leaves tomorrow for, as he says, a brief tropical vacation.

I love you and will continue to hold you in my prayers every day and try not to be too distracted from my work responsibilities as I think about you while I am at the office. I need another Annapolis date after Christmas.

I love you

Annie

Gary read the letter looking stoical, but his heart smiled as he read.

After the convoy parked inside the Peregrine Team compound, LT Baumgartner escorted the General to the team building where the team SCIF was located. As they entered the building door, the General heard loud clapping and raucous shouts, some might call it 'singing'. Turning to

Baumgartner he angrily asked,

"Are these men drunk?"

"No sir, they are just 'getting ready' – we have serious killing to do! This is the best team I have ever worked with Thank you for the opportunity to work with these consummate professionals. I have never seen a team coalesce so fast and demonstrate a team cohesion that would make Clausewitz proud."

General Wojcik just nodded, but his face showed he was pleased with Baumgartner's answer.

As they walked up the stairs listening to the most enthusiastic singing and clapping you have ever heard – the singing continued to shake the building:

C-130 Rolling down the strip.

Airborne daddy on a one-way trip.

Mission unspoken, destination unknown.

They don't even know if they'll ever come home.

Stand up hook up, shuffle to the door.

Jump right out and count to four.

If my main don't open wide.

I've got a reserve by my side.

If that one don't fail me too.

Look out ground, I'm a comin through

Pin my medals upon my chest,

and bury me in the leaning rest.

When I get to heaven.

St. Peter's gonna say.

How'd you earn your livin?

How'd you earn your pay?

And I will reply with a little bit of anger:

Earned my pay as an Recon Ranger

The General walked into the Team room just as the C-130 rhythmic cadence and clapping ended. Master Sergeant Woodrow Clayton saw the

General and shouted – ATTENTION! – Every team member jumped to his feet and saluted; the General saluted back and held his salute until he had looked every man in the eye. The General completed his salute. He stood there, making the silence tangible, until he thundered,

"Is that the best you can do?"

The General began to clap his hands, he burst out in a deep baritone to lead the next military marching cadence:

When I get to heaven

Saint Peter's gonna say

"How'd you earn your livin' boy?

How'd you earn your pay?"

I'll reply with a whole lot of anger,

"I made my living as an Airborne Ranger!

Blood, guts, sex, and danger

That's the life of an Airborne Ranger!"

At the end of the cadence the room continued to rock as the Team members yelled

HOOYAH   HOOYAH   HOOYAH

On the third HOOYAH – the General raised his hand and gave the order,

"Lets get to work. There are some bastards out there we need to kill".

The team gathered around the conference table hosting the planning documents and the necessary coffee and donuts. Captain Williams walked in and saluted, although he was wearing civilian clothes. The General returned the salute with a raised eyebrow. Captain Williams understood the implied-question,

"I was meeting with an agent who had time-sensitive information relative to this meeting".

Baumgartner passed folders to each man around the table with the caveat,

"Return these folders along with any notes you make. Nothing written goes out of this room except on the order of the General".

After reading the draft agenda the General said – "looks good". The General began with item one: 'updates from the CONUS' and a combination warning and admonition:

"I want to emphasize the great political sensitivity of the Peregrine operation. There is a direct path to the White House and the President. What we are doing executing this mission violates the Status of Forces agreement between the US and South Vietnam; violates South Vietnamese sovereignty; and the politicians and lawyers will have a field day finding more problems if the operation is compromised in any way, including the fact there was such an operation. The shit will hit the fan all the way to the President. I chose each of you because you will do this mission and do it, so that – no one, except a chosen few read-ins will ever know there was a Peregrine operation."

After an off-agenda spontaneous HOOYAH, the General proceeded.

"The enhanced NSA collection effort in Saigon identified additional problems for the prisoner-snatch time-line. First, the Saigon radio operators send a check-in message within the first three minutes of the change in operator duty-shifts. The Peregrine grab-snatch time-line needs to compensate to negate any Saigon radio-network alert which would tip-off the KGB and NVA that we are kicking their asses and taking names in Saigon."

"Captain Williams advised me that he and Baumgartner, the chick-magnets they are, attracted the attention of Gabriella Mueller. That woman is very bad news and has high-level contacts in left-wing political circles and in the anti-war groups around the world, including the US. She has promised our intrepid team leaders that she is going to do some investigating to find out who the Captain and Lieutenant are. (Looking at the LT and the Captain) 'Bobby and Clyde' – really? Gabriella is insidious and politically dangerous. We will "GO" - one week from tomorrow, 10 November 1964 to chop-off at-the-knees any investigation she has started and give closure to other security and political considerations."

A murmur went around the room, 'shit hot', we are going next week! The murmur instantly terminated with the look on General Wojcik's face.

"I want to know this morning – what do you need to finish this job next week and get out of Dodge?"

Captain Williams continued the updating for the team.

"Thank you General, we will be ready to execute 10 November. We have some updates as well. We have identified the Spider as an ARVN sergeant, Pham Binh, the driver for a Colonel Trần Quan, Tran is the officer-in-charge of the Deconfliction Division, ARVN Joint General Staff headquarters. The Deconfliction Division sees information about all planned US and ARVN operations. The Deconfliction Division is supposed to ensure there are no friendly-fire or other problems between planned operations. Pham has access to the perfect set of information needed to ambush US Army advisors."

"Phan Binh is a cover name for an operative who most certainly is an NVA officer in the Ministry of Defense Intelligence Department. From an estimate of his age on the basis of the surveillance photos we took and his apparent level of authority, 'Pham' is a senior officer in the NVA."

Captain Williams continued:

"General, I did not meet you at Tan Son Nhut because I was getting confirmation that Pham Binh is a major player beyond the NVA scheme to kill American advisors. Pham and Trần made a phony trip to An Loc to "officially coordinate" how the deconfliction process is conducted for the Bình Phước Province."

"Big mistake by Pham on several levels. Our agent in the General Staff alerted us before the An Loc trip. We placed a tracker on Pham's vehicle and sent a surveillance team ahead by air, two Nungs and Gunny Risner. They tracked the vehicle to the location of the meeting site in An Loc. The Nungs took pictures of the various participants' comings-and-goings, boo coo interesting pictures."

Bull listened carefully, taking notes on a ruled yellow legal-sized pad and did not interrupt the update-briefing.

"This contact and the whole trip by Pham and Trần was an unbelievable breach of security and tradecraft. We can only speculate the great success Pham has had killing American advisors has resulted in him becoming arrogant and security sloppy. First, Pham and Trần drove to An Loc through VC controlled territory without any problems. Second, there was little effort to mask who attended the An Loc meeting. Third, Pham was clearly the top guy at the meeting, given the obsequious greetings

321

he received from some high-level VC guys attending that gathering. Downside for us, this An Loc event has drawn Central Intelligence Office, the South Vietnamese equivalent of CIA, attention. Another reason to move up our end-game to next week".

"We have not shared the An Loc pictures, yet, with our Agency contact here in the CIA Station. Based on newspaper reports, one of our Nungs recognized a guy in the photos. This guy, Phạm Ngọc Thảo, is a high-level wheeler-dealer in the South Vietnamese government. We could not ID any of the others at the An Loc meeting. We intend to give the photo array and background to the Agency as one-piece of our 'sayonara Saigon' going-away presents."

"We produced an 'updated wiring diagram' showing 'our understanding' of the overall connectivity of the enemy penetration operations, moles, US players, the KGB, and the Peregrine operation. We will provide this chart to you today. If you approve, we would like to give a copy to our CIA working-level contact – he is one of the good guys – we believe giving our CIA local buddy the chart is good IC politics for the future. What our results show – this Vietnam mess is just that – a real mess – a strategic mess."

"General, do you have questions so far?"

"I have several questions, but I will hold all for now, except for one: Give me one sentence defining what you called 'a mess'."

Pausing for a moment, Captain Williams responded,

"This damned country is so infiltrated by communist spies, agents and sympathizers at every level from the villages to top-levels of every government institution – the commies will win in the long-run, unless North Vietnam is conquered and occupied, by force. By long-run, I mean, three years or less."

There was silence in the room, the General did not comment but nodded his head for Williams to continue.

"As for our mission, we have a draft plan for the 10 November Execute. I'll walk through that draft now:"

"We developed travel patterns for all of the targets and pictures of the radio transmission building front and back door hinges and locks. Breach and snatch training is essentially completed though we will continue training until two days before the 10 November breach action. Plan milestones include:

Execute, minus 8 days, 2 November 1964, approval by Major-General Wojcik. Coordinate with Wild Man Johnson for Yards to emplace target-beacons at A Shau radio camp for the Air Commando A1-E strike aircraft.

Execute, minus 7 days, days, 3 November 1964, Sergeant Jones visits the Minh Thanh Special Forces Camp to share a deception story that tracks with story delivered by Sergeant Podowski to a targeted bar girl. Sergeant Podowski feeds the SOG deception-story to Sweet Susie at the Sporting Bar. Sergeant Wilson feeds the deceptive story for a CIA cross border operation to Myrna at the Florida Bar. Sergeant Wilson coordinates an A1-E squadron strike on the A Shau radio site and camp.

Execute, minus 6 days, 4 November 1964, Sergeant Risner feeds the ARVN/ advisor patrol deception story to Lolita at Mimi's Club (the team was not aware of the message the General had previously received regarding the annihilation of an ARVN Ranger/US advisor training patrol).

The General made a note on his yellow pad.

Execute, minus 3-5 days, 5-7 November 1964, rehearse radio building snatch operation using the team compound quarters building. The grab-teams for the radio building are:

Team Baumgartner – second floor, grab Spider

Team Risner – second floor, grab one of the refugee camp girls

Team James – second floor, grab the other refugee camp girl

Team Clayton – third floor, grab radio operator on duty

Team Jones – third floor, grab off-duty radio operator #1

Team Podowski – third floor, grab off-duty radio operator #2

Execute, minus 4 days, 4 November 1964, Yards emplace beacons to guide the air strike on the A Shau radio site

Execute, minus one day, 9 November 1964. Packing equipment to close the DoD Adjunct Inspector General Team #4 compound. Destroy all classified materials and other records.

Execute, minus six hours to minus five minutes:

Nung three-man team in ARVN Military Police uniforms with official documents, grab respectively, Captain Bùi Duc (minus 6-hours), First Lieutenant Ngô Hau (minus 5-hours): Colonel Trần Quan (minus one-hour), all using the cover story of an emergency meeting at the office, MPs to provide transportation)

Execute, minus one hour, check equipment, teams mount-up in snatch vehicles

Execute, minus 30 minutes: A1-E air strike on A Shau radio site

Execute, minus five-minutes: radio building snatch teams in-place

Execute, 10 November 1964, 0045 hours, Zero Hour, radio building snatch teams execute on command: Sergeant Wilson, Sergeant 'Doc' von Eisenberg, and Ban Chen are with me in the command center

Enter building for prisoner snatch, the six snatch teams will stealthily move into the building. Four teams entering from the back door and two teams from the front door. The hinges sprayed with graphite and locks picked.

Forced-breach entries to apartments on Baumgartner execute signal – take prisoners, use syringes to inject anesthesia, secure prisoners with gags, hoods and plastic ties. Rule of engagement: enemy occupants who attempt to make noise will be silenced immediately, using knives or silenced weapons.

E + 15 minutes – all prisoners en route to compound. NSA team standing-by to work the site

E + 20 minutes – NSA black bag team enter building and exploit site.

E + 50 minutes – NSA team out of building

E + 60 minutes – torch the building.

E + one day, 11 November 1964 – interrogate high-priority prisoners

E + two days, 12 November 1964, cleanup 'loose ends'; Air America helicopters support

E + plus three days, 13 November 1964, – close down compound, pay Nungs – to Tan Son Nhut for Import-Export charter flight home

General Wojcik nodded in the affirmative, adding:

"The basic plan looks good. I'll approve it after I understand the details for several points in the plan – and – I want to hear what you have thought about regrading Murphy and his Law."

The General and the team spent the next three hours delving into the details for every aspect of the execution plan. There was a bit of fine tuning but no major changes.

The General repeated,

"What about Murphy on this mission?"

Captain Williams looked at the General and said simply –

"We have Murphy covered".

The General raised his eyebrows signaling, that answer does not cut it. No slouch on reading a General Officer's non-verbal commands, Captain Williams added:

"General you know personally from your years on-the ground in combat and clandestine operations, Murphy goes with us on every mission – and Murphy is boo-coo weird. We deal with Murphy by team cohesion, training – and more training – plus being the toughest, meanest bastards in the valley".

General Wojcik nodded in the affirmative – more non-verbal communication as in 'right answer Captain'.

Steak, beer, and country music were the order of the evening. The General loved to be out of the Pentagon with the troops. He joined in the hearty repartee including the colorful dialect fondly used by warriors – rough language, which is always clear in its meaning, but language which would not be uttered in the presence of your mother or children. As the evening drew to a close, the General thanked the team for their professionalism and good work – adding, continue doing what you do best and take these sons-bitches down a week from tomorrow. All the team stood to attention as the General left the room.

Beckoning LT Baumgartner to follow him, once outside the team room, he asked if Baumgartner had a response to Miss Hoffman's letter? Both smiled at the "Miss Hoffman" bit. Baumgartner said

"Yes sir, and I would appreciate it if the General would courier the letter to Miss Hoffman."

Still smiling, Bull stated,

"Of course, I'll perform the assigned courier mission. Let me add one thing. The team will be back in the CONUS before Thanksgiving. My wife and I are inviting you and Annie to have Thanksgiving with us at Fort McNair. Annie has visited us twice for meals and she has been a delight for my wife. Annie contributed feminine decorum to support my wife after three rowdy adult boys, my sons and me, and now the addition of grandsons. Plus, I expect my wife would like to see what a sailor is like after all the West Point men."

"Thank you General, I appreciate the invitation and will be there. Annie wrote in her letter how kind you and your wife have been to her during this Peregrine sojourn."

Bull and Gary shook hands. Gary retired to write a note to Annie.

The next morning, a heavily-armed convoy left for Tan Son Nhut after breakfast; the body-guard jeep; the covered jeep with the General, a Nung bodyguard and Captain Williams; and a deuce-and-a-half loaded with ten armed-to-the-teeth Nungs. The General was impressed with the morning PT and the esprit of the team and Nungs. He had Gary's letter for Annie in his pocket.

Dear Annie,

Thank you for your letter and the announcement that I no longer have a car. The only thing saving you from felony theft-auto charges is the "I love you" factor.

It looks good to be home for Christmas and to be at your family farm in Indiana. An additional planning point, in case you have not heard, the General and his wife have invited you and me for Thanksgiving dinner. I accepted for both of us. You'll have to drive, as I have no car. I think the invite was primarily because the General and his wife really like you. I am invited as a Navy sailor person to be observed as a strange alien-species. Sounds like fun as, at least one of his sons and family will be there – USMA type, Woo Poo is the real name of their school, they use West Point as a cover.

The General will tell you and your team about his visit and what is going down here. I will make this brief as General Wojcik is leaving early tomorrow and the old "loose lips sink ships" warning applies – to verify this axiom, I will check your lips soon and use some very lame line – you know like – sink my ship before I sink yours – OK, I will work on that.

See you soon – I love you

Gary

The General advised; the Peregrine Team is 'On Alert to Execute': The Plan is approved!

All Hands on Deck – General Quarters – Man your Battle Stations

The Team was in the chow hall, but the cooking smells and food aromas were gone. The savory meal fragrances were replaced by the smells of Hoppes gun solvent and gun oil, smells that were familiar and enjoyed by the Team members. Plates and cups are replaced by disassembled weapons, cleaning rags, bore cleaning-rods, and cleaning-cloth wads. Weapons were cleaned, reassembled, and checked. Knives were sharpened and checked for a razor sharp cutting edge. Jokes were told all way around in a group of men who had coalesced into a precision killing machine to 'do the Peregrine mission'.

Sergeant James walked to the juke box – "Any requests?"

Podowski yelled – "How about a dedication to the bad guys we are going to grab – try "Come Go with Me".

Risner added – "The bad guys can sing along – how about "Last Date" or "Endless Sleep".

Jones contributed – "Have some mercy on these poor bastards – I think "Lets Have a Party" is not threatening - and remember, our dancing-shoes for the 'prisoner grab dance' are sneaky "black converse gym shoes". It is always better if they don't know you are coming."

A rousing HOOYAH and some pounding on the table. A weapon cleaning and knife sharpening ritual that will continue each night until the team goes into action to take-down Spider and his friends.

CHAPTER 25   CALTHROP GOES "MORE BAD"

Calthrop sat alone in his apartment just off Lei Loi street. He rented this apartment to get out from under the cloying eyes in the Embassy compound. His plan was to use the apartment as 'Calthrop's love-nest'. Sitting alone on the bed, soaked in his own sweat, he was paralyzed with fear. His life was in shambles and he felt like a vortex of doom was about to suck him into an abyss which had no return. His only competing emotion the fear was an all-encompassing self-pity.

He agonized, how could things have gone so wrong! Why was he even here in this oriental hellhole? He thought back to his days in Washington where he could always find a way-out from his bad decisions. He could avoid the consequences as the potent political patronage of his father-in-law resolved issues of his poor performance in his State Department job, brushes with the law such as the DWI, leaving the scene of an accident, and rest of the long litany of his misconduct. His wife's money enabled him to live a lifestyle well beyond his civil servant salary. And best of all was his position at the State Department. His supervisors catered to him out of fear of potential retribution from political mavens who were in his father-in-law's pocket.

But he especially relished the aspect of his position at the State Department which leveraged his maniacal predisposition as a sexual predator. There were hundreds of young women who had come to Washington from all over the country. Most of these young women were working in administrative and secretarial positions, in which, unfortunately, they were underpaid and underappreciated. In this difficult circumstance, they tended to be very lonely, missing their families, boyfriends, friends, and the 'belonging' inherent in the small-town cultures they left behind. In DC, Calthrop could devote most of his time at the office to identify and stalk vulnerable young women as his sexual prey. He used his GS-15 position, his glib but facile complimentary come-hither lines, and a lavish use of his wife's money to lure vulnerable young women into 'the clutches of an evil emotional extortionist' – to be 'in Calthrop's clutches'. He devoted about four-to-six months per young woman, before he moved on to another vulnerable 'girl' to reinforce his self-image as being irresistible to all women. Calthrop had absolutely no remorse leaving behind the emotionally-scared young victims. The women could not file a complaint because Calthrop was clever to make the women complicit in the office affair and most of the time, make them appear to be the instigators of the affairs, as he became the 'smirking victim'.

Calthrop thought with as much humor as he was capable of at that self-pity moment, now, I know what the cliché 'good old days' means. I am stuck here in this shit hole country and nothing, that is absolutely nothing, goes right. He had tried the prostitute scene on Tu Do street and found the hookers there to be generally unattractive, avaricious money-grubbing, ignorant harpies – he had no clue the Tu Do working girls held him in an equal contempt for his insipid superior attitude toward them.

When he met Nyugen Kie^ he thought she would be an easy mark. She would be one of those vulnerable women; away from her Paris home, alone in a strange city, and she seemed to be attracted to him. His lascivious needs would be well served by this Eurasian beauty. She seemed to respond to his self-promoting claims and his bragging. She was classy, not like the whores on To Do street, and she had vulnerabilities he could exploit such as promises to help her get a visa to the US, plus promises to assist in her search to find her parents. Of course, he had no intention to help with a visa or in the search for her parents. He just wanted to get her in bed and sexually dominate her.

Kie^ was classically beautiful and she possessed an exceptional intelligence along with a superb social presence. She had all the traits that a woman Calthrop fantasized about as a devoted sex slave. She certainly would succumb to the virile charm of "Win" Simmons and the potent charisma he projected. But that was all in his mind. The relationship with Kie^ took an unexpected twist. Kie^ was miles ahead of him at every turn. She adroitly and graciously misdirected each of his sexual entreaties, all the while remaining like a Greek mythology 'siren', luring men on with a promise of sexual nirvana.

His frustrated relationship with Kie^ gave rise to the drunken incident at the Embassy gate. He raged further about the incident which brought down a humiliating condemnation from Mason Aldershot, the pompous ass Charge d'Affaires, who dared to deliver the rude dressing-down to Calthrop; a matter which became a humiliating 'prime topic' for the Embassy gossip circuit for weeks after the incident.

When he tried to reprise to his DC sexual predator modus operandi, which was so successful in the Washington DC State Department offices, Calthrop found his bullshit 'come-hither' lines no longer worked in Saigon – this was a new game in Vietnam. The women who worked in the Embassy were either wives of the diplomats or young Caucasian women who could pick and choose from the hundreds of men who eagerly sought the company of a 'round-eye' girl. Calthrop tried his old routine several times only to suffer across-the-board humiliating rejections. As a sexual predator, he was determined, if at first you do not succeed, find a more vulnerable target.

Evelyn Smith was easy to describe as a nice person who was the average American girl and would become the average American woman. Evelyn was the middle child with an older sister and a younger brother, from a middle-class family with loving parents, living in Cedar Rapids, Iowa. At five feet five inches tall, 150 pounds, attractive, but not a singular beauty, Evelyn would not stand out in any crowd. She was a good student and finished fourth in the competition to be her class valedictorian. Nobody, except the family, remembers who finishes fourth to the class valedictorian competition. Her older sister was a cheerleader and ran with the 'in-crowd' in high school. Two-years younger, Evelyn had several 'not-in-crowd' girlfriends and she dated infrequently. She felt she never knew what to say to the boys who asked her out. In the deep shadow cast by her sister, Evelyn became mildly introverted and turned to books for comfort: romance novels and adventure books set in exotic parts of the world. She fantasized she was the heroine in the romances as the mysterious feminine adventurer who transverses the world.

Approaching high school graduation, she realized there were few opportunities for adventure in Cedar Rapids, Iowa. She could work as a retail clerk, a secretary, a receptionist in one of the local businesses, or she could work for her Dad in his State Farm Insurance office. During a visit to the library, she found a State Department notice, they were hiring for the position of 'administrative assistant'. She applied the same day. Two weeks later she received a bus ticket to Washington D.C. to be interviewed. After the interview, she was hired on the spot as a humble GS-3 'administrative assistant'. She stayed in Washington to begin her great adventure, until reality intervened. Her pay was so low she had to share an apartment with two other women. Her daily great adventure was the bus ride to work. Her roommates loved the Washington night life scene, but the bar hopping scene did not fit Evelyn's personality or her emotional needs. The administrative assistant job was boring to the point of drudgery. And then, she saw the notice on the office bulletin board, Human Resources was looking for volunteers for the Embassy in Saigon: benefits included a promotion, foreign duty pay, war zone pay, all in addition to her base pay. Evelyn saw this opportunity as her first adventure in an exotic place. She volunteered and was accepted that same day. She thought, this will change my life, and it did.

Evelyn arrived at Tan Son Nhut airport feeling great trepidation; What had she done! – What was she thinking when she volunteered to work in the Saigon Embassy. Had she been temporarily out of her mind? Yes, the allure of extra pay for the foreign posting, the movie imagery of living in an exotic foreign country, and the promotion to GS-5. Saigon was a war zone, a real war zone with VC bombings and assassinations. Now, the thought of the term, 'war zone', was a frightening realization. Evelyn was feeling scared and lonely before the aircraft engines were shut-down and the passenger-doors opened.

Calthrop monitored all the new arriving people, that is new arriving women, who were assigned to the Embassy. For the most part, the potential prey were few in number. As Calthrop perused Evelyn's personnel file, including her photo, his elitist smirk reflected his plan to change how he stalked and abused women.

He bided his time until late in Evelyn's first day at work after her arrival. She was still weary from jet lag and overwhelmed by her new environment. Calthrop welcomed her warmly, more so than any other individual at the Embassy she had met so far. His apparent 'genuine' kindness was the tonic Evelyn urgently needed. He suggested she get extra rest to combat the jet lag, adding, he had a welcome gift, but he would wait until tomorrow for that. Laughing, as he held her hand, he said she would be fully awake tomorrow to see the gift. Evelyn profusely thanked him for his gracious welcome and said she would look forward to seeing him tomorrow. That night, Evelyn cried herself to sleep thinking – what have I done, I want to be home.

The next day, Evelyn began a formal orientation for her role as an Embassy file clerk. She was disappointed that 'the man from yesterday' had not greeted her today. During a break in the orientation, Evelyn stood by herself when 'that man', appeared all smiles. He greeted her and asked how she slept. Evelyn gave the expected pro forma reply, "I slept well", not revealing the emotional pain she experienced last night in her lonely room.

332

Calthrop reached in his coat pocket, while reminding Evelyn of the promised 'welcome gift'. He handed her a package wrapped in simple white tissue paper. Evelyn asked if she should open it. Calthrop responded, smiling, "Please open it now". Peeling back the tissue, Evelyn saw a beautiful, and expensive, carved jade dragon. Taken back, Evelyn did not know what to say. Calthrop took the initiative to ease the awkwardness, "I will be happy to show you around Saigon once you get settled". The instructor called out before Evelyn could reply as the orientation was ready to reconvene.

Two days later, Calthrop visited Evelyn in the dingy basement-room where the Embassy files were kept. Evelyn was very remorseful that she had ever submitted an application for this foreign assignment, this foreign nightmare. Tears were her companion each night in her room. Calthrop had the predator sense to strike. He invited her out for the weekend to see the sights. Evelyn was extremely grateful. So far most of the employees at the Embassy had treated her like a piece of furniture.

Calthrop went all-out to impress Evelyn as they toured Saigon in a rented cab. Among the many sights that day, they visited an up-scale market where he bought her a small but very expensive, exquisitely carved jade pagoda. For dinner that evening at the My Canh floating restaurant, they enjoyed a delicious dinner of various Vietnamese dishes. Calthrop intended the dinner and the after-dinner drinks would be the bridge leading Evelyn into bed in Calthrop's apartment. She was relaxed for the first time since she arrived in-country and owed Calthrop for the emotional release. Evelyn had fallen under Calthrop's malicious spell. He invited her to his apartment for a drink, the drink and the spell did provide the bridge for Calthrop taking Evelyn to bed and a vigorous sexual experience for both. The following day, they went to the Saigon racetrack as one of several sights they had on their agenda. Calthrop could not have imagined how profoundly fateful the racetrack visit would be –

Calthrop had lost all perspective as he tried to satisfy his ego and demonstrate an aura to Evelyn that he was 'The Man'. He was trying to totally captivate Evelyn, just because he could. At the racetrack, to further impress Evelyn, he made several exorbitant bets, unaware the bets actually were held by a powerful Saigon criminal gang who controlled gambling at the racetrack. Calthrop lost every bet and now was deeply in debt, over $3000 dollars, to the most vicious gangsters in Saigon. $3000 was equivalent to several months pay for Calthrop.

At the end of the racing-day, pulling him aside, a gang member demanded payment, Calthrop gave a reasonable response to a gang member. He did not carry $3000 in cash around the city. As this was not the first rodeo for these gangsters, they demanded to see his passport. The gangster conducting the discussion sucked air in between his teeth when Calthrop produced a black US diplomatic passport. The gangster jerked his head to the right, a wiry scar-faced intimidating man, who appeared to be the gang leader, joined them. After seeing the passport, the gang leader motioned to a sinister tough who was obviously one of the gangsters' 'collection men'.

Scar-face made an entry in a small notebook. Handing the diplomatic passport back to Calthrop, Scar-face gave Calthrop the type-leer a saltwater-crocodile might display before closing its powerful jaws on a victim. The gangster said in a quiet voice,

"You have five days to pay us. After that, that man will kill you".

Calthrop's knees almost buckled as he heard his death sentence. He did not have the $3,000. Evelyn was standing beyond earshot and could not follow what appeared to have been an extremely unpleasant exchange between her new friend and three frightening-looking Vietnamese men.

He walked back to her, his face deathly pale; his voice was shaky and strained as he explained he was suddenly hit with what seemed to be some type of flu, so very common to afflict foreigners in Vietnam. He asked if she would mind if he took her back to the Embassy – then with gravity and faux sincerity, Calthrop told her he did not want her to catch this flu-bug from him. He promised they would pick-up again next weekend for more fun, and he winked in a way Evelyn thought was cute.

Back in his apartment, a desperate Calthrop tried to think how he might find $3000 quickly to avoid what likely would be a lingering painful death five days hence. He could not ask his wife or his father-in-law for such a large sum just out of the blue and could not explain why he needed the money immediately. He had to find another source.

The phone rang. Answering, he heard the voice, it was Nyugen Kie^. He thought, to his great relief, 'the Kie^ of the trust fund'; 'the Kie^ of many contacts with wealthy individuals in Saigon'.

He composed himself to respond in a pleasant voice,

"Kie^, I was just thinking about you. I have missed you"

Smiling as she listened to the phony remarks and insincerity always present in whatever Calthrop had to say, she responded with her own insincerity, delivered in a tone that Calthrop fantasized as a life ring for a drowning man,

"I have missed you too Win. I was hoping we could have lunch together, soon if that fits your schedule, I know you are very busy at the Embassy:

Calthrop/Win answered far too quickly,

"Why, yes how about tomorrow?"

Alarm bells began to ring for Kie^. Something is wrong, gone seriously wrong for this loser. She replied in a very sexy voice,

"Win, that would be perfect, I really would like to see you. Can you meet me at the Cercle Sportif pool, say 1100 hours?"

Again, responding too quickly, Calthrop gave Kie^ another 'tell',

"Yes, I will be there. Lunch is my treat. It will be so good to be together again."

Kie^ thought, this call may change everything for the recruitment strategy. For now, I will wait to hear what "Win" has to say tomorrow as she schemed how to exploit his obvious but unknown problem. Calthrop thought as he schemed, this could change everything if I can find a way to get $3000 dollars from her tomorrow, I can save my ass from those gangster animals.

Kie^ mused that evening about the ironies in the spy business. Standard operating procedure for the case officer is planning with the focus on details and more planning and more details. The 'irony aspect' was when the case officer went into the field to meet a target or meet a recruited spy, the situation on the ground, at that instance in time, could be totally different than the situations she covered in the planning. In the end, the actual standard operating procedure was – always be ready to improvise! She went to bed early to be fresh for the uncertainties in the meeting the next day.

About 0400 the next morning, Kie^ woke as an epiphany surged from her unconscious mind; she would use a "false flag" recruitment on Calthrop. The Israeli Mossad were past-masters in the "false flag" technique. In the false flag approach, the case officer represents himself as being from a different country than the nationality of the true intelligence agency. For example, an Israeli case officer would convince the target that he or she was from an Arab intelligence service. After successfully recruiting the Arab target who had no idea who the Israeli case officer actually was, the Arab 'spy' would unwittingly 'spy for Israel' while believing he was spying for an Arab intelligence service.

Kie^ decided the false flag approach would decidedly reduce the risks to recruit Calthrop. When the time came, she would pose as an agent working for the French intelligence service, SDECE, Service de documentation extérieure et de contre-espionnage. Of course, she would need approval from Sasha, but she was confident he would buy into the "false flag" recruitment. She went back to sleep for two more hours.

The next morning, she ate a hearty breakfast to fortify her for the meeting with her target: two soft-boiled eggs, a hard crust roll with butter, prosciutto ham, Gruyere cheese, and papaya. She decided to low-key the sex aspect which had worked so well on Calthrop, she could turn the 'seduction' back-on at any time she wanted. For the meeting today, Kie^ wanted to focus on whatever apparent crisis Calthrop was facing.

She selected a modest sun-dress and flat heels, arriving at the Cercle Sportif at 1030 hours. A waiter immediately ushered her to the table she had reserved. Among the many tables packed at pool-side, this was one of two tables around the pool which offered a modicum of privacy for their conversation. The other tables allowed the shrewish gossip-elites a better opportunity to overhear neighboring conversations, which would become gossip to retell later. Kie^ ordered a vodka and tonic – and waited.

She did not have to wait long. After just one sip of her vodka and tonic, Calthrop arrived twenty-minutes early. She watched him as he navigated across the pool area to join her. While dressed in an expensive sports shirt, sharply-creased grey slacks, and well-shined black loafers, the rest of his appearance was like some bum who had made a failed attempt to comb his hair. Calthrop's red-rimmed eyes, patchy shave, his skin pallor the color of dirty wash-water, and, very telling as he approached, dilated pupils said there was a story to be told. All together his personal appearance gave clear physical evidence of a person consumed by fear.

The snarky arrogance and the smug superiority were gone. This target was indeed more vulnerable than she expected. But what is the source of the new vulnerability? Condescending looks from the elite and self-anointed-elite around the pool disapprovingly tracked Calthrop's unsteady walk toward the elegant Eurasian woman in a modest French sun-dress.

Kie^ greeted Calthrop warmly, holding one of his hands in both of hers for an extended moment. The waiter asked to take Calthrop's drink order – he indicted the same as the lady, another vodka and tonic. She wanted to control the conversation for her two objectives: first she needed to know what had happened in Calthrop's life to cause this dramatic change; second, did she need to change the original plan to manipulate "Win" psychologically and exploit this new situation. What was the best path to lead Calthrop to buy into her "recruitment pitch" at the next meeting?

Calthrop was adrift in his mind, except for his singular urgency – how do I get $3000 from her today.?

Kie^ took the initiative to focus the conversation. Using the reciprocity ploy, Kie^ revealed a problem she faced intending to entice Calthrop to respond with a problem of his own.

"I am so glad we could meet today; I have missed you."

"Win, I have a problem and need your guidance on what to do. I urgently need to obtain a visa, preferably a permanent residence visa, to enter the US. I have heard rumors that there are ways to obtain such a visa. One of the ways to get the visa is to provide adequate funds upfront to facilitate expediting the process. I know you are not involved in the visa process, but you are an important person in the Embassy senior staff. Can you advise me if the rumors I heard about 'back door' visas are true?"

Calthrop sat up in his chair. He placed his vodka and tonic on the table and his mind began to scheme, is this the opening I hoped for to get the money needed to cancel my death warrant from those murderous gangsters?

Feeling rejuvenated, the Calthrop 'con-man persona' returned, selecting his words carefully, Win looked directly into Kie^'s eyes as he told her:

"The rumor you heard is correct. There are 'alternative ways' to get a visa to the US."

Pausing for dramatic effect, he added a warning,

"I must warn you, this process is risky and very expensive".

"I am not in the visa process chain, but I do know the person quite-well who can make the 'expedited visa' a done deal. When do you need this visa?"

"I need the visa sometime in the next ten days. If that is even possible, how much would it cost?"

Calthrop put on a phony contemplative expression as he plotted how to relieve Nyugen of $3000 and do it now! His greed kicked in, why not $4000 or $5000? With his most disingenuous smile, he took one of Kie^'s hands into both of his. He confided in a conspirator-voice,

"I have heard rumors that the usual cost is around $3000 to go through the "alternative process"; but to expedite the process could cost as much as $5000 US dollars in cash, up-front."

Kie^ employed her phony contemplative expression as she appeared to consider what Win had told her, which she knew was total garbage. The KGB had done their homework, a fraudulently obtained visa could be had for $500-$1000 dollars. After a few moments, Kie^ gave a theatrical sigh of relief; she added her free hand to the now tight mutual grasp of their hands:

"That is wonderful, thank you so much for the information. I cannot thank you enough. That cost is very reasonable."

adding her own dissembling comment –

"I thought it would be more. How do I contact this "alternative way" person?"

Calthrop had regained his smugness,

"I can help as I know this visa person well. I would be glad to be the go-between, which reduces the risk for you."

The visa process in US embassies has always been problematic and varied from embassy to embassy despite the basic guidelines were the same worldwide. Exceptions were routine as local political demands would drive special considerations being made for privileged individuals. This ad hoc visa approval reality was ripe for abuse in the chaotic political environment in Saigon.

Willis Carhart, chief of the Visa Section, was a career State Department employee and a savvy bureaucrat - a savvy corrupt bureaucrat. Willis knew how to cover his tracks while he illegally 'sold visas' and collected a tidy sum each month from the bribes he demanded. The primary protection Willis used to hide his criminal activity was limiting the number of illegal visas each month to a few elite cliental who could pay well. Willis had a second layer of protection not of his doing. The Visa Sections were routinely used worldwide by the CIA to give an "official cover" position for the CIA operatives in an embassy. In addition, the Agency could use the visa staff position to acquire genuine visas for agents. Willis had a wide latitude to muddy the paperwork trail when he needed to produce a visa for one of his 'customers'.

It was not surprising that Willis was one of the very few employees in the Saigon Embassy who Calthrop could call a friend. Calthrop was aware of the illegal enterprise Willis conducted under the radar of the State Department Inspector General oversight. Calthrop's offer of $1000 dollars for the Kie^ visa would be an immediate 'done deal' between the unscrupulous pair.

As the gang's threat to kill him flashed back into his mind, Calthrop, with desperation in his voice, asked,

"When can you have the $5000 dollars in cash?"

Kie^ smiled,

"I told you this was urgent. I have that amount in cash in my hotel security lock-box now."

Calthrop gave a louder than intended sigh of relief. My miracle just happened. At the same time, he realized he had less than 48 hours to get the money in the gang's hands. Unintentionally displaying the panic he felt, Win spoke with a husky edge in his voice,

"Can you get me the money this afternoon?"

Continuing to smile as she registered all the tells in Calthrop's behavior, she squeezed Calthrop's hands before turning to a waiter for the check. She paid the bill along with a large tip. Kie^ and Win immediately departed in her chauffer driven car for transit to the Caravelle Hotel. In an appreciative voice, she suggested Win wait in the car while she 'took care of some 'things'. She returned in about 15 minutes with an envelope containing fifty US $100 dollar bills and her French passport.

Calthrop carefully controlled his emotions to avoid disclosing his profound relief and hide his smug thought how he had conned Kie^. Mentally, he was doing emotional cartwheels of joy, the gangsters would not kill him. With a broad smile, he said with an irritating false humility,

"I will do everything possible to help you".

She offered to have her driver take him to the Embassy, but he declined with an explanation it would look better if he took a cab. Calthrop waved as he got into the taxi, instructing the driver to take him to an address in Cholon. There he would pay off his gambling-debt and live another day to seduce and con women.

Kie^ went to her hotel room to send Sasha a telephone code message based on a preset number of rings; "We need to meet tomorrow."

Recruitment Plan Revised - The New Pitch

Kie^ was glad to see the arrival of 'tomorrow'. She would see Sasha today. She completed the SDR and met Sasha at the safe house. After very affectionate kisses and hugs, they went directly to business. Kie^ briefed Sasha about the target having some unknown serious problem, or serious problems, and related how the target 'extorted' money from her. Win, under his guise of an inflated cost for a visa, had pleaded for the $5000 immediately. It was clear he was in some desperate strait for the money. Her false flag proposal to recruit the Calthrop would resonate with his greed motivation to resolve his current problem as well as having a flow of money in the future. The sex-trap approach was moved to be Plan B.

Plan A was the false flag recruitment, Kie^ would use France as the false flag, representing herself as an operative of the French intelligence service, SDECE. It all made sense. France had a strong interest in southeast Asia. She had a French passport. If things went badly, the KGB had total deniability and the recruitment risk was mitigated. Kie^ would use the friendly-power idea to persuade the target to work with France as an ally to confront and combat international communism.

Sasha agreed to the new approach and complemented Kie^ on the creative modification for the mission. They agreed she must return to the hotel in case the target called. Sasha gave Kie^ $5000 dollars to replace the amount she had given Calthrop. At the door, he said,

"The $5000 bait is taken - 'Win the Fish' is hooked. Now, get 'Win the Fish' into the boat".

They held a lingering kiss before Kie^ returned to the hotel.

The gambling debt paid, Calthrop was emotionally restored to his usual smug arrogant self. Fleecing Kie^ out of $5000 was clear evidence of his skills to impress and control women. He contacted Kie^ to report he had her visa. He expected a gushing flow of gratitude, along the lines of thank you, that is wonderful, and 'how did you do it so fast'. Instead, Kie^ thanked him in a perfunctory manner before she suggested:

"Can we meet at the hotel in two days? Would 1100 hours work for you?"

Calthrop did not handle 'off his plan things' well. When 'the things' were off his intended script, he became flustered. His first reaction was, she is like the rest, she does not appreciate what I do. As his immediate anger surged, he decided he would fleece more money from this snobbish woman who continues to play the elite virgin-queen. Choking back his anger, the tone of his voice changed to a brusque tenor, as Calthrop was never quite fully in control of his emotions. He said, in his best effort to use a neutral tone:

"Two days, at the hotel, 1100 hours – that will be fine".

Gritting his teeth as he waited for her confirmation. She shifted to her Kie^ 'come-hither' voice, telling Win,

"I have missed you so very much. I want to properly thank you for your kind help solving the visa problem for me".

Calthrop smirked, reassured he had her in his control. Kie^ smirked, at the same time, things are going according to plan. Now, I go for the jugular with "the Pitch".

The Pitch

Kie^ was waiting at the hotel entrance for Calthrop. To fill-in the time, she queried the concierge for any new rumors. She wore a low-cut blue French dress that showed plenty of her ample cleavage. Calthrop arrived by taxi, on time. He was very smug inwardly. When he got out of the cab the smugness elevated to reinforce his vain self-image. Look at that dress, he thought, "today would be the day. Kie^ waved in a pleasant and subtle suggestive manner. Win and Kie^ briefly embraced in the French-way with the kisses on the cheeks. She announced they would take a cab to a place where they would have privacy. Calthrop could not suppress an obvious leer as he imagined a sexual tryst with this beautiful Eurasian woman – now, today.

Kie^ planned to take Calthrop to the second safe house, an apartment near the racetrack – where she would administer the coup de grâce. In Vietnamese, she directed the cab driver to take them to the Câu cá restaurant, which was located about one block from the safe house. Arriving at the restaurant, she paid the driver and told Calthrop they would walk around the corner to an apartment where they could 'talk in private'.

The safe house was carefully prepared to host this 'strategic' rendezvous. Two bottles of expensive French wine and snacks were on a side-table in the living room. The KGB radio operator, who lived in the safe apartment, had removed all evidence of his presence from the living room and kitchen. The radio-operator, Ivan Perlinkov, though unimposing in physical stature was a KGB thug trained in the deadly KGB Spetsnaz martial arts. Ivan could kill a man with a few strokes of his hands and feet. He would wait in one of the two bedrooms, behind a locked door to provide 'KGB muscle', in the event Calthrop might try to assault Kie^. The radio-man would monitor the listening devices and cameras installed in the safe-apartment to record all the incriminating, compromising, damning evidence from Calthrop's meeting with a KGB agent.

The safe apartment was on the fourth floor to gain an antenna advantage for the Operation Red radio transmissions. Climbing the stairs, Calthrop was thinking how he would have prolonged and lascivious sex with Kie^ in just a few minutes. Kie^ opened the door, allowing him to enter first. As soon as both were inside, Win tried to kiss her. She rebuffed his advance in a stern voice,

"We have things to talk about first. May I get you some wine?"

Calthrop was furious, thinking, who does this bitch think she is, some damned oriental princess! I just did a great favor for her with the visa. She does not get out of here until I screw her. Hooray for privacy, she cannot stop me! Although Calthrop tried to mask his fury, Kie^ picked up on his attempt to hide his anger. She smiled inwardly – right on script so far.

Handing Win a glass of French wine, Kie^ motioned for him to take a seat on the couch and she sat opposite him in a chair. Calthrop took a deep gulp of the wine, too angry to talk. Calthrop looked at his glass, trying to be 'cool', but his anger betrayed him in the words he delivered in a gruff voice,

"This wine is excellent, but I am not here to drink wine!"

Kie^ asked if he had her passport with the US visa. Win grudgingly pulled her passport from his pocket and handed it to her. He tried to take the offense with an accusing tone,

"Getting that visa for you was very difficult and risky for me".

Kie^ replied in a measured and authoritative voice,

"Thank you very much Win. You will be rewarded. I know getting this visa caused you to violate several American laws. How many dollars did it cost to bribe the visa clerk?"

Alarm bells went off in Calthrop's head. He sensed an unstated threat. Trying to deflect her question, he gave an indirect response,

"Why do you ask, this sort of thing happens routinely at the Embassy, bribing to get a visa".

As soon as he blurted out his response, Calthrop knew he impeached his prior comments about the high risk and difficulty to get an illegal US entry visa.

"But Win, you told me getting the visa was risky for you – maybe not so much because of your senior position at the Embassy, yes? You did not answer me, how much did the illegal entry visa cost?"

Now flustered, he said,

"It cost $5,000 as I told your when you asked me to help you get the visa."

Kie^ sat back in her chair, placing her wine glass on the table. Continuing in her authoritative voice, she chided Calthrop.

"Win, Win, - we both know such a visa bribe costs about $500-$1000 US dollars".

She relaxed back in her chair, waiting for a response from Calthrop. A good case officer knows that silence, at the right time in a conversation, can be more powerful than talking.

A wave of conflicting emotions swept over Calthrop, but anger was still the dominant emotion. Who does she think she is, to talk to me that way? Fear followed closely behind the anger, who is the "we" she spoke about? How does she know the actual costs to bribe the visa clerk? Believing he should take the offense as his best protection, Calthrop responded brusquely,

"How dare you insult me after I have done a great service for you and you have given nothing back to me in return!"

"Please be calm Win, you will receive a great deal for your services. Now, how much did the bribe cost and what did you do with the rest of the $5000?"

Calthrop suddenly realized this woman was a danger to him. Perhaps he should cut his losses and leave now. As he started to stand, Kie^ ordered him,

"Sit down, for your own good".

Calthrop hesitated, he could not make the choice between flight-or-fight. He waited as typical with prey faced with a lethal threat, frozen in-place as the predator readies to strike. She is dominant, he had to listen, in order to understand just how bad this situation is for him. Kie^ knew Calthrop was unaware the KGB thug had unlocked the bedroom door and was poised, 'to help Calthrop do the right thing'.

"Win, we are friends and will be even closer friends in the future. For your information, I really do not care what you did with the rest of the $5000. I have access to more money than your wife has – even more money than your rich father-in-law has. We can go forward together in a very comfortable life. I just need to know certain things which will open the door to more money than you can imagine, providing exotic comforts that dreams are made of. "

Panic set in, how does she know about my wife and father-in-law? Calthrop tried to conceive a way out of this new hell he faced.

Kie^ was relentless with quiet implied-promises of sex and money for Win even as she continued questions about the money she gave him. Each time he gave her an evasive answer, she became more explicit in clear yet unspecified threats to him. Though unspoken, Kie^ leveraged the fact that he was a moral and physical coward, plus he was an intellectually weak person.

Calthrop's defenses collapsed into a rush of self-pity. He began pleading with Kie^ for help, a standard Calthrop behavior, get in trouble and assume someone will rescue him from the crisis he had caused. He resorted to his standard, whining technique,

"Please help me. None of this is my fault. I have been 'treated unfairly' by the US government. I just want to be your friend and tried to help you.".

After listening to his sniveling as expected from this wretched pathetic man, Kie^ saw it was time to strike. She would position herself as the one-person who could protect and save him. The more Calthrop talked, the more wine he drank. Kie^, refilled his glass twice, as he slobbered his standard pleas for, 'how do I get out of this situation'? She listened, displaying a comforting smile for Calthrop, as he tried to excuse and expiate his misdeeds.

As Calthrop paused from emotional exhaustion, Kie^ began the elegant, but lethal process, similar to that of a matador as he artistically kills the bull.

"Don't worry Win. I am your friend. I can fix all your problems and make your life better."

Calthrop raised his bowed head, with the look of a drowning man who sees his rescuer reaching out to pull him from swirling waters, Calthrop spoke in a quiet shaky voice

"Thank you".

Kie^ knew Calthrop was totally vulnerable at this point.

"Win, I am a French intelligence officer. I was sent to South Vietnam to protect the continuing security interests of France. I track political matters in our continuing war against international communism".

"It was fateful that you and I should meet at the 'doing business in South Vietnam' dinner. I instantly liked you as a person, and as I got to know you better, I came to the realization that you and I could work together against international communism - and possibly have a very close personal relationship, at the same time."

Kie^ paused to observe the immediate reaction from her target. Classically, as taught in her KGB case officer training, a target responds in one of four ways: the target is indignant, the target is curious, the target begins the psychological rationalization to accept the 'pitch' to become a spy, or the target is in shock and confusion.

In his whole life Calthrop had never found a 'wrong path' that he did not embrace and enthusiastically follow. Calthrop inevitably chose 'the wrong path' again, as an expedient but erroneous solution to his current problem. Rationalization for his wrong-doings was a well-developed art-form that Calthrop lived-by. Calthrop simply nodded, implying, go ahead. The die was cast.

Kie^ continued to guide Calthrop's slide to become a traitor to his country, the United States of America.

"So, you agree that you and I will work closely, (and with a wink), very closely, to support our mutual interests?"

Calthrop smiled, thinking he could slither out of this current trouble. He would deal with this woman later, a woman he now feared.

"Yes, I agree, the communist threat is a threat to France and the western world, not just the US."

"Fine, I want to see our new professional relationship include a close personal dimension. But we do need to take care of one or two immediate problems. I have to account to my superiors for the excess $4000 dollars I advanced you. We can easily cover this money, which I am sure you have already spent. You will give me information about the SOG organization here in South Vietnam. I can use that information as a cover for the $4000."

Calthrop continued his rationalization, hell, we are allies with France. We both are fighting the commies around the world - and I need to make this visa bribe problem go away. Calthrop proceeded to tell Kie^, and the hidden voice recorder, everything he knew about SOG – his knowledge was extensive as he compromised individuals and SOG operations.

Kie^, now established as the dominant party in this relationship, reminded Calthrop their relationship was one of absolute secrecy. Calthrop shall not divulge anything about their relationship to anyone. No one, whether US or French! Calthrop nodded in the affirmative and said,

"I understand".

Kie^ suppressed a smile, thinking – Simmons, you have no clue.

"Win, I need additional information on this fight against communism here in South Vietnam. I know you are the senior officer at the US Embassy coordinating intelligence matters between the US and the South Vietnamese. One of your responsibilities specifically involves the CIA and the South Vietnamese Central Intelligence Office. I want to know the progress by CIA and the Central Intelligence Office have made identifying Soviet and North Vietnamese intelligence operations in South Vietnam."

Before Calthrop could react, Nyugen placed $4000 on the table. She said, "This is to help you in any matters needed to get this information. What you do not spend from this $4,000 to get the information, you may keep. When do you think you can provide this information"?

Calthrop took the money off the table and stuffed it into his pocket.

"It will take a few days. I will call you."

To further establish her 'control', Nyugen told her new false-flag spy,

"Please have the information no later than next Wednesday".

Kie^ suggested they leave separately for operational security and he should go now. His mind in turmoil, Win simply departed after Kie^ gave him an enticing kiss. Calthrop Winston Simmons had chosen the path of treason.

CHAPTER 26   EXECUTE – GOODBYE SPIDER

General Wojcik ordered all communications between the CONUS (JCS, CIA, NSA) and the in-country Peregrine team cease from 3 November to 11 November 1964. The only exception, situations deemed a security crisis. If a 'crisis' status determination is made by Captain Robert Williams or his Deputy, LT Gary Baumgartner, the team would use the CIA Saigon station communications system.. The use of CIA for out-of-country comms is to avoid any Peregrine electronic fingerprints which could be collected by the Soviet COMINT collection-ships sailing offshore. The General's additional guidance was straight forward: bad guys dead – no traces – this mission never happened.

EXECUTE

2 November 1964, Spider Take Down Plan approval by Major-General Wojcik

4 November 1964, Master Sergeant Jones enjoyed a SOG 'Otter' aircraft ride to the Minh Thanh Special Forces Camp. The Minh Thanh camp is located on the 31,000 acre Michelin rubber plantation near the Cambodian border. The Michelin plantation had been a strategic asset for France and became an early target of the Viet Minh, now called the VC. A large house for the French plantation manger and his family was sited next to a 3,100 foot laterite airstrip. The Viet Minh assassinated the plantation manager and his family in the late-1950s; the house had been vacant since then. The Minh Thanh Special Forces A-Team often used the house to have a beer and get a daytime-break outside the camp, a few team members at a time, all armed to the teeth. The plantation area was known for a strong VC presence with a correlated problem that many of the mercenaries working for the Special Forces team were sympathetic to the VC or being paid by the VC – and ready to betray the Americans in the camp.

The Minh Thanh camp, situated on a small rise, was constructed in irregular concentric rings; the innermost ring was off-limits to all personnel except the American Special Forces A-team personnel. Sergeant Jones was at the Minh Thanh camp to plant deceptive

349

information as part of the Peregrine bar girl deception operation. Jones told the Special Forces A-team commander to be ready to support a SOG mission into Cambodia, 11 November. The SOG patrol would need LLDB, (South Vietnam Special Forces, Luc Luong Dac Biet), guides from the LLDB troops assigned to the Minh Thanh camp.

This deceptive information was one component of a ruse to smoke out any moles in the Minh Thanh camp, and substantiate similar false information planted with a bar girl.

Sergeant Jones followed the need-to-know rule and did not reveal to the A-team commander that the SOG patrol information was false.

Sergeant Podowski told the same deceptive story to Sweet Susie at the Sporting Bar. Podowski told her about a SOG patrol into Cambodia from the Minh Thanh camp. Podowski gave Sweet Susie the 11 November date but did not tell Sweet Susie the patrol details as to recon targets and the patrol composition.

While talking to Sweet Susie, Podowski acted very drunk and complained he was scheduled to go on the damned SOG mission 11 November and he will not see her for one week. He gave the bar girl $200 USD, asking Sporting Bar 'Sweet Susie' to wait for him while he was gone. Podowski got the expected response,

"You numbah 1 – I wait for you for sure – I love you too much"

(inwardly, Sweet Susie is thinking, I tell my VC boyfriend – maybe he kill you).

Sergeant Wilson fed the second deception story a CIA cross-border operation, to Myrna at the Florida Bar. He related that a cross-border mission is going into Laos. A combined American and Hmong patrol would depart from the Special Forces Camp, Thừa Thiên Province 2 kilometers east of the Laos border – Wilson shook his head slowly and mumbled he would be on the patrol – boo-coo VC – very bad – will miss Myrna – at that point Wilson gave Myrna a wad of dollars - $250 in crumpled-up US bills – Wilson's head was lolling to the right and he was drooling slightly – Myrna thought, in disgust, another gross-drunk GI, but good money – Myrna said,

"I miss you too much – when you come back – we do boom-boom"

Ever so innocently, Myrna reassured Wilson and asked,

"I not talk otha GIs while you gone, when you go?"

Wilson shook his head as if to clear his alcohol befuddled mind, mumbling, –

"We do boom-boom when I get back, I go next Reusday – I mean Tuesday"

Wilson slurred something about not feeling well and he should go – Myrna rubbed his leg as she promised, again,

"We do big sexy boom-boom when you back - we do hot boom-boom – I need money for cab – you have more money?"

After two tries, Wilson got his hand into his pocket, fumbling to pull out a wad of piasters which he handed to Myrna – stumbling out of the bar, he nearly fell into the cab as the door was opened for him by the driver. In a very slurred voice, Wilson gave the driver an address near the compound – arriving at the address, Wilson handed the driver a bunch of piasters – far more than the actual fare – smiling, the driver kept all the money and drove away – once the taxi was out of sight, Wilson was miraculously sober and smiling, Florida Bar mission complete.

Mimi's bar filled a sex-trade business niche in wartime Saigon as the high-end bordello-club, in-between the expensive private clubs and the sleazy rip-off bars on the seedy Tu Do strip. The bar girls in Mimi's were no less street-wise or jaded than the bar girls and street-walkers of the Tu Do district; however, the bar girls in Mimi's were better actresses, more subtle, less crude as they relieved the customers of large sums of money for the same goods available at cheaper prices on Tu Do Street. Mimi's bar girls, typically from urban lives, were more attractive than the rough women on Tu Do who were transitioning from working in rice paddies to working the streets.

As Gunnery Sergeant Risner entered Mimi's, he noted how the atmosphere set a comfortable aura with muted lighting, private booths, and the melodious sounds of a Mantovani and Ray Conniff orchestra versus the Tu Do ear-shattering latest US rock and roll background music, as the girls aggressively probed new arrivals for 'you buy me Saigon tea', 'I love you GI, love you too much'.

Mimi's girls, like Lolita, conveyed the same phony message but in a more sophisticated manner. The Mimi phony message was, at Mimi's, the GI was a welcome visitor, not a walking wallet, yeah right. Gunny

Risner arrived early to miss the usual male traffic. Lolita saw Risner enter the club and gave him the sweetest fake-smile she could conjure. Risner, was a trained intelligence operative and a natural 'smooth talker'. Risner returned an equally fake smile. Lolita walked over and took his arm to lead him to an upholstered private booth, a booth they had frequented often in the past days when Risner showered her with money.

Gunny and Lolita each thought how they would use that night to satisfy their objectives. For Lolita, extract lots of money from Risner. For Risner, exploit Lolita's greed, using Lolita as the conduit to insert deceptive information to the VC intelligence collectors. Unlike his two partners in the Peregrine Trio, Gunnery Sergeant Risner did not play the drunk buffoon.

Putting on a serious sad-face, Risner quickly came to the point, he would not be able to see Lolita for a few days as he was going on a training exercise next Tuesday to give a new group of American advisors in-the-field experience. Though a good actress, try as she may, Lolita could not generate even a token tear to show how she would miss Gunny, instead, she came directly to her point:

"I am boo coo sad not see you some time; you give bar man $50 US and we go upstairs for hot sex."

Risner touched her hand gently, explaining he could not stay this evening as his unit was preparing for the US Advisor training exercise; ironically, appropriate background music was playing "Perfidia", by the Ray Conniff orchestra, completing the deception stage setting.

Risner continued,

"I look forward to coming back to be-in-bed with you, Lolita, for big fun."

Lolita's eyes betrayed her with a flash of anger as she thought, I am wasting my time tonight; Risner did not miss her reaction; he spoke quickly,

"I know we are both disappointed, I want to give you, just for you, not the bar man, some money while you wait for me to come back."

Lolita gave Gunny a toothy smile, asking where he would go on this training thing. Risner gave her the false information, as he let her watch him semi-surreptitiously peel ten twenty dollar bills off his wad of cash. I will be on patrol from Dong Xoxi to Phuoc Vinh, starting next

Tuesday. Lolita moved closer to Risner, their legs touching as her anger was displaced by the delightful satisfaction of her avarice and important information she would sell to the VC.

Gunny discretely handed Lolita the money under the table, taking the opportunity to fondle Lolita's legs. Both gave the other their best 'sad faces'. Risner stood to depart, Lolita thinking it was a good night for her, lots of money for me and something 'big' to tell the VC. Risner thought, bar girl deception mission accomplished, and Lolita has great legs.

The deception mission using the bar girls as conduits to the VC was a total success. The next day, three couriers arrived at the Saigon radio site; simultaneously a radio message to the Spider radio building was received from somewhere in the Minh Thanh region. Three messages using the KGB obsolete encryption system were sent from the Spider site to the A Shau radio site. NSA was able to quickly decipher the old encryption format to confirm each bar girl had given the Peregrine 'deceptive intelligence' to the VC. The NSA analysts agreed with the Peregrine team, the Spider network was more expansive and more real-time reactive than originally perceived.

For the next three days, it was rehearsing the snatch operation and then rehearse more, using the Team compound quarters building as the surrogate target building. The "Vietnamese MP" snatch-teams (three Nungs dressed in ARVN Military Police unfirms with the appropriate official documents) practiced the 'go-as-planned 'grabs, including the 'gag, bag, truss' drill.

Contingency drill practices were problematic as there were too many possibilities to work all possible contingencies. The MP teams practiced one 'standard' prisoner-snatch from the target homes and a contingency for the cases where the target did not cooperate. This latter snatch involved tranquilizing the target at the spot-of-contact versus in the car.

The radio building snatch-teams practiced at night to have the same conditions of darkness as the actual operation. The radio building snatch teams followed a practice-plan for 'going-according-to-plan prisoner grab' and several contingencies for targets resisting capture. Captain Williams restructured the radio building snatch-teams: each team still had an American leader, three Nungs, each team had one member with an M-16, the other three team members carried the silenced High-Standard semi-automatics with hollow-point ammunition. All members carried commando-type daggers; the uniform for the prisoner grab was black combat smocks and black Converse All-Star gym shoes. Each team carried three syringes filled with a powerful tranquilizer provided by CIA. Each team member carried a gag, black hood, and plastic ties to further secure the unconscious prisoners for transport to the Peregrine compound.

7 November 1964, Wild Man and his Yards emplaced four beacons along the ridge to guide the air strike on the A Shau radio. The beacons were set equidistance along the trail from the patrol emergency extraction site to the A Shau radio camp, a line of bearing 270 degrees. The beacons were set to turn on automatically 10 November at 0015. The beacons had a back-up mode that allowed interrogation by the A-1E strike aircraft if the hot humid weather conditions impaired the beacon automatic mode.

1845 hours (6:45 pm) 9 November 1964, A black Citroen sedan, with two passengers and a driver pulled up in front of the Ngô villa, all the occupants dressed smartly in pressed ARVN military police uniforms. A military police sergeant and a corporal, both with holstered silenced High Standard pistols, walked to the villa front door and .the Sergeant knocked A maid opened the door, the MP Sergeant spoke politely, but authoritatively, we would like to speak to First Lieutenant Ngô. Immediately concerned and intimidated, the maid bowed and said she would speak to First Lieutenant Ngô Hau, please wait, as she started to close the door, the MP sergeant put his hand against the door and stepped inside with the comment, "we will wait here". The maid turned, running to report to Ngô Lu, Ngô Hau's father. Ngô Lu was very wealthy and had used his influence to have his son put into a non-combat assignment for his military service. Ngô Lu received the maid's report with a combination of anger and a lurking anxiety, going to the door where he greeted the military police imperiously, asking what they wanted, adding angrily, they were disturbing his family. Both MPs bowed slightly in deference to Ngô Lu. The MP sergeant explained briefly that Colonel Trần Quan had sent the MPs to drive First Lieutenant Ngô Hau to an urgent unscheduled meeting.

Relieved there was no serious problem, Ngô instructed the maid to advise his son that his military duty calls him, come to the front door immediately. First Lieutenant Ngô Hau walked in about three minutes later, in civilian clothes, the MPs both saluted. When told about the meeting and the formal escort, Hau said he would dress in his uniform. Both MPs nodded their heads in affirmation.

The MP sergeant opened the back door of the Citroen for the Lieutenant, under the approving gaze of Ngô Lu watching out a window. The MP sergeant got in the back with First Lieutenant Ngô, the other MP got into the front seat, the driver departed without comment. As soon as the car was out of sight of the villa, the MP corporal in the front seat told Ngô that he needed to sign a form acknowledging the military pick-up for the meeting. The corporal held up a clipboard, as Hau leaned forward to sign, the MP Sergeant concurrently slapped a hand over Hau's mouth and jabbed the syringe needle into his neck. The slender Hau was rendered unconscious in less-than five seconds. The "MP" Nung released Hau and pushed the limp body onto the floorboard for the rest of the trip to the Peregrine compound. The MP with the clipboard handed the MP sergeant a gag, a black hood, and two plastic ties. The MP sergeant quickly gagged the prisoner; placed the black hood over the prisoner's head; used the plastic ties to secure the prisoner's hands behind his back. 'Gag, Bag, Truss'

1945 hours (7:45 pm) 9 November 1964, In a virtual repeat, the black Citroen sedan, with two passengers and a driver pulled up one-hour later in front of the apartment building where Captain Bùi Duc lived. Bùi was a playboy bachelor, a draft-dodger son of another wealthy influential father. Bùi was arrogant, living off his father's largesse and he was safe from ARVN combat duty. Bùi Duc was smartly dressed for an evening on the town, admiring himself in a mirror when he was disturbed by a knock on his apartment door. Opening the door, Bùi saw two MPs, before Bùi could speak, the MP sergeant saluted and announced they were there on the order of Colonel Trần Quan, to escort him to an unscheduled meeting.

Bùi demanded to see such orders from Colonel Trần, explaining further, that he had plans for the evening and would not be available for the meeting. As the MP corporal made a show of retrieving the order from his pocket, the MP sergeant drew his weapon. Bùi's eyes dilated in fear; though arrogant, Bùi was a coward. The MP sergeant said politely, "Colonel Trần authorized the use of force if Bùi did not comply immediately to attend the meeting". The MP sergeant added, "You may attend the meeting in civilian clothes. The meeting was expected to last only an hour, or less. After the meeting, we will drive you wherever you need to go for your evening engagement".

Bùi decided that 'discretion was the better part of valor', he stepped out the door, locking it behind him, and accompanied the MPs to the car.

Once Bùi was in the car, the MPs used the same ruse as before, 'the old' requesting the passenger to sign a form on the clipboard. The result was the same, an unconscious Bùi lay on the backseat floorboard, on the way to the Peregrine compound. Smiling, the MP sergeant repeated the 'Gag, Bag, Truss' on this second prisoner.

The ARVN was formed 30 December 1955; Trần Quan joined the new organization because he saw an opportunity to enrich himself as involved in the acquisition side of equipment and supplies for the army. A position that would insulate him from combat duty as well as opportunities to line his pockets with money from bribes and other corrupt schemes. College-educated, Trần Quan began his embezzlement scheme from his first days as a Second Lieutenant. Trần was very clever to ensure various senior officers benefitted at each step of his criminal enterprises. As a result, his promotions were rapid and his authority and opportunities for graft escalated with each promotion.

In 1961, Lieutenant Colonel Trần received a visitor in his elegant apartment. The individual was quite open, representing himself as an agent from the North Vietnamese Ministry of Defense Intelligence Department. The agent showed a stunned Lieutenant Colonel Trần a thick well-documented file exposing his criminal pursuits over the last six-years. A documentation that likely would bring Trần before an ARVN firing squad. The North Vietnamese agent explained, Lieutenant Colonel Trần had two, and only two, choices. Trần could opt to become an agent for the North Vietnamese Ministry of Defense Intelligence Department or he could take his chances with the South Vietnamese ARVN justice system.

In the first case, Trần would be paid more than he was currently making from his theft of government money and receipt of bribes. In the second case, Trần would either go to prison or be shot by firing squad. A no-brainer, Trần chose the first option to change his corruption side-business from theft to treason.

Trần's first task as a North Vietnamese spy was to request a transfer to the newly formed Deconfliction Directorate in the Joint General Staff. Leveraging his connections, he was transferred and promoted to Colonel. Trần was now the commander of the Deconfliction Directorate. Colonel Trần's second task was to have a Sergeant Pham Binh assigned to the Deconfliction Directorate as his personal driver and bodyguard. Sergeant Pham Binh was actually NVA Colonel Wang Ky, North Vietnamese

Ministry of Defense Intelligence Department, operating as a Principal Agent in South Vietnam. Although appearing as a subordinate, Sergeant Pham Binh would be Colonel Trần's controller and Colonel Trần would obey Pham in all matters.

Colonel Trần Quan lived each day in terror that his life was in jeopardy from his criminal past or possible exposure of his current treason as a spy for North Vietnam. Even the substantial monies his North Vietnamese controller gave him did not quell his fears or preclude his worries about being caught by South Vietnamese counterintelligence services. Regardless, his new source of wealth, did enable Trần Quan to live the high life with his girlfriend Li.

2345 hours (11:45 pm) 9 November 1964. Trần was in-bed with Li when a heavy knock on the door roused them both. Trần checked the bedside clock, it was 2345 hours. A paralyzing fear briefly immobilized him; had he been exposed? Is this the police to arrest him? A second banging on the door pushed Trần close to the fight-or-flight acute-stress behavior. Not much of a fighter and nowhere to flee. He stepped out of the bedroom to tell whoever was at the door, "just a moment". He quickly dressed, his trepidation increasing. Opening the door, Colonel Trần was greeted by two military police who smartly saluted him, the MP sergeant apologized for disturbing the Colonel. Apparently, they were not here to arrest him, Trần grasped the door to keep himself steady as relief rolled over him.

The MP sergeant explained, Sergeant Pham had an emergency directive from the Joint General Staff that needed immediate attention. Pham sent the MPs to chauffer Colonel Trần to the meeting. Sergeant Pham was concurrently making preparations for the meeting.

Trần quickly donned his uniform and followed the MPs to the black Citroen. The clipboard ruse was repeated for the third time. Trần leaned forward to sign the form on the clipboard, the result was the same, an unconscious gagged, bagged, and trussed Colonel Trần lay on the backseat floorboard on the way to the Peregrine compound.

2330 hours (11:30 PM), 9 November 1964, Eight A-1E 1st Air Commando Wing aircraft loaded with 250-lb Mk-81 Snakeye bombs, 500-lb. M-47 napalm canisters, and full ammo loads of high-explosive 20 millimeter shells orbit southeast of the target area. The lead aircraft, Shadow One, gives the order to attack:

357

"Shadow Flight this is Shadow One: Follow me in target run 270 degrees, line up on beacons."

Shadow One switched on the 'interrogate target beacon' system and smiled when, after five seconds warm-up, the first beacon responded to the electronic interrogation. Shadow One adjusted his 270 degree course to match the four beacons in a target line-of-bearing direction.

"Shadow Flight this is Shadow One: Follow me, 270 degrees, I will lite-um-up with 'nap'. Hit the radio shack and the camp 50 meters to the south. We will make two runs"

As Shadow One passed the fourth beacon he dropped two canisters of napalm. Both canisters illuminated the area in a flash of fire and following sustained fires. The canisters hit some 25 meters north of the radio hooch, clearly evident in the light of the burning napalm. Shadow Two adjusted his aim point and delivered two canisters of napalm - resultant fireballs enveloped the radio hooch. The next six A-1Es shifted to target the camp, now well-lit by the napalm fireballs incinerating the radio hooch. Some NVA and Russians were moving outside the camp buildings and tents. The total camp quickly became one massive fireball as the six aircraft dropped a total of 12 napalm canisters on the camp. The A-1E flight turned into a flight path to return for the second-strike, aircraft in-trail.

"Shadow Flight this is Shadow One: second pass on target will be 'snake-eye'. Shadow One and Shadow Two, hit the radio hooch. Other Shadow aircraft, hit the camp."

The 250-lb Mk-81 Snakeye bombs delivered the coup de grâce to the radio site and camp. The bomb blasts actually extinguishing parts of the napalm fireballs at the same time leveling all the NVA and KGB hoochs, killing the rest of the personnel in the camp who might have survived the napalm hell.

Shadow One this is Shadow Five: "Wahoo! – crispy critters and urban renewal"

Shadow Five this is Shadow One: Good nights work! Target fire reflecting off the clouds shows another camp about 500 meters to the southwest. Follow-me, we will make a neighborly pass. Drop all residual ordinance and give them a 20 mike-mike wake-up call. And back to Bien Hua for beer."

The A Shau radio site and camp smoldered for three hours. Twenty dead KGB and 140 dead NVA. Radio A Shau no longer transmitting due to technical problems.

The command element of the radio building snatch operation used the previous two-days to perfect secure time-sequencing for individual entrances to the surveillance apartment building. Dressed in civilian clothes, carrying non-descript bags, the command element personnel entered separately in irregularly time-spaced arrivals to avoid notice by the locals of unusual activity. The command element included Captain Williams, "doc" von Eisenberg, Ban Chen – head of the Nung 'Li clan', plus three Nung bodyguards. M-16 rifles and other weapons had been smuggled into the surveillance apartment a few at a time, over the past six days.

Stealth was the essence for the snatch mission success. The Saigon curfew worked in favor of the prisoner-snatch operation. Military vehicles could move about the city but there was virtually no civilian traffic after 2300 hours (11 PM). There were few checkpoints in the city and the snatch team route to the target and exiting the target was planned to avoid any checkpoints. Furthermore, the lead jeep in the small convoy had an American officer with official documents that prohibited any interference by US troops or any interference by South Vietnamese troops or police.

The in-bound convoy was comprised of a lead jeep with three large US Army personnel vans completing the procession. The jeep and vans had recently tuned-engines and installed new mufflers to minimize vehicle noise. The exit convoy would add two deuce-and-a half trucks, parked, under guard, in an empty lot near the radio building. Saigon residents typically ignore the ubiquitous military traffic during the nights and early mornings. There were contingency plans to abort the mission if an unexpected unacceptable risk emerged.

0040 hours (1240 AM), 10 November 1964, the jeep turned up the alley followed by two vans; the third van parked briefly at the front door and two teams exited to silently hug the shadows near the front door. Gunnery Sergeant Risner readied to pick the lock. In the back parking lot, four teams dismounted and hid in the shadows while Master Sergeant Clayton readied to pick the back-door lock.

0045 hours (1245 AM), 10 November 1964, LT Baumgartner and Master Sergeant Clayton each radioed the command center reporting:

"In-place ready to enter the building; no locals appear aware of the teams' presence."

Captain Williams ordered the front and back door teams to silently breach the front and back entrances.

"GO for entry, front and back"

The front and rear door 'old-style' skeleton-key locks were picked in less than 10-seconds. Both doors opened inward, the lock-pickers opened each door, just enough, for a Nung to spray the hinges with a silicon lubricant to suppress any noise from hinges squeaking. The six teams silently filed into the first floor landing, lining the walls, waiting and listening. Unintelligible muffled sounds came from an upper floor, but no sounds of alarm. The team carried red-lens flashlights which preserved their night vision in the dark interior

The rehearsed plan was for the teams to move to the second floor landing, third floor snatch teams in the lead. All the teams would stand-by on the second floor landing to listen before proceeding.

LT Baumgartner turned his flashlight toward his face, raising a fist to make the hand-signal to move to the second floor landing. The teams hugged the walls as they climbed the stairs, stepping near the outside surface of each tread to minimize potential squeaky-tread noises. Even so, there was one loud creak, all team members froze in place, silenced weapons at the ready. When no alarm was raised, the third floor snatch teams moved silently up the stairs to take positions against the right-hand wall of the second floor landing.

The second floor snatch-teams followed in the same stealthy manner taking positions on the left-hand wall of the landing. It was of utmost importance that the teams breach the second and third floor apartments simultaneously to avoid giving any apartment occupants a chance to sound an alarm.

All teams would move into individual apartment breach positions on the second and third floors to await the Breach Order from LT Baumgartner. The third-floor teams readied to climb the next set of stairs to the third floor landing.

The muffled sounds had continued, becoming louder, but still unintelligible, as they ascended the stairs. The source of the muffled noises was pinpointed coming from an apartment on the left-side of the landing, in addition, there was a light shining under the door. Baumgartner put his ear to the door and then moved away with a quizzical look – Vietnamese chatter mixed with giggles and laughter. Baumgartner motioned for all teams to stand in-place to allow a Nung approach and listen at the door.

As the Nung continued listening to the 'now entertaining sounds' from inside the room, he broke into a huge grin, the Nung make a charade-type gesture indicating large female breasts, he held up two fingers,' two women in the room'. The Nung was slower on the next hand-signal as he pondered the best obscene gesture to depict a man, so many choices and so little time to describe what he was hearing. Finally, the Nung grabbed his crotch and made a hip-thrusting motion before he held up one finger; 'one man'. Holstering his pistol temporarily, the Nung made a circle with his thumb and forefinger, trying not to laugh, the Nung raised his other hand to shove an extended forefinger in and out of the circle, the universal sign for fucking. All the shooters ducked their heads away to suppress guffaws and laughter. With a big smile, Baumgartner thought, yes General, Murphey is always with us, they had not practiced this 'particular' contingency option.

Baumgartner moved his red-lens flashlight so the teams could see the hand-signal for the third-floor breach teams to continue up the next flight of stairs to take ready-positions. At that moment, a door opened on the third floor, someone turned on a low-wattage light illuminated the third floor landing, they heard the door close. After the door closed, the team heard footsteps, someone was the crossing the third-floor landing to the stairs. Then the footsteps began down the stairsteps, the old steps creaking from the movement down to the second-floor landing.

The sparse light emitting from the third floor landing was enough for Baumgartner to hand-signal Jones and Podowski – the improvised signal was clear – grab the son-of-a-bitch when he steps onto the second-floor landing! Sergeants Podowski and Jones positioned themselves on either side of the stairway from the third-floor.

In the dim light emanating from the third floor bulb, Podowski made a sticking-gesture; Jones nodded and pulled out his syringe.

361

The footsteps resonated as the individual casually reached the bottom step and reached for the second-floor landing light-switch.

Podowski slammed his massive hand over the individual's mouth aa he encircled the victim's arms with his powerful other arm, lifting the small Vietnamese man off the floor. Jones stepped forward stabbing the syringe into the victim's neck, emptying the paralyzing liquid into the man's neck.

In less than three seconds, the man stopped struggling and went limp. The team brought surveillance pictures of all the known occupants of the radio building. Checking the pictures in the dim light from the third floor, Jones confirmed the man lived in the building and was likely one of the radio operators. Baumgartner signaled for two Nungs to silently move the unconscious prisoner to the first floor back door and wait – indicating the 'gag-bag-truss' process be used when at the back door.

With the first prisoner-snatch completed, Baumgartner gave the hand-signal for the third-floor breach teams to proceed up the stairs to third-floor apartment breach positions.

When the three grab teams reached the third floor, they observed a light under one of the apartment doors, assumed to be the radio room. Jones gave one squelch on his radio when the third-floor breach teams were in-place.

Baumgartner held-off on the order to breach. He wanted to gather more intelligence before the breach team enters the 'party-apartment' with continuing talking, laughing, and giggling. Baumgartner motioned for Sergeant Risner to pick the lock, another old skeleton-key type, Risner picked the lock without noise.

The unlocked, party-apartment door was slowly opened a crack, to check if the hinges might squeak. The hinges worked smoothly without a sound. Peeking inside a darkened entryway, connecting to a hallway. Baumgartner could see a light and hear the mirthful reveling coming from a room down the hall.

Motioning for his team to follow, Baumgartner moved down the hall, thankful for the silent treading of the Converse All-Star gym shoes. He signaled Risner and the Nungs to follow him, ready for 'the grab'. The team trailed closely behind him, silenced pistols at the ready. Baumgartner and Risner stealthily slipped along the hall to check the situation in the room with the noise.

They moved silently, a few inches at a time, to position themselves to see around the doorway into the lighted room. Still in the shadows, Baumgartner could now see the whole room. Smiling, he motioned for Risner to join him for a look-see. And what a look-see it was. Gary thought, we need Bobby here with his camera. They were greeted by a sight that could be the center-piece of a high-quality porn movie and will be a legendary story for the team.

The Spider and his mistresses were in the midst of an energetic ménage à trois orgy, caught 'in flagrante delicto'!

Baumgartner gave two squelches on his radio to signal the team leaders, standby – each team leader gave his team a hand signal, Standby – every team member was poised, muscles tense, adrenalin flowing - five seconds after the Standby signal, Baumgartner gave the order –

"GO - All Teams Breach!"

Game On! All teams moved simultaneously to breach the second and third floor apartments and execute the prisoner-snatches.

The Baumgartner and Risner teams charged into the party-room simultaneously with the crash of a knock-knocks pulverizing door frames on the third-floor. Shocking the sex-tower players into a terrorized awareness. Baumgartner and Risner crossed the room, followed closely by three Nungs, all with silenced pistols pointed at the naked targets,

The giggling and moaning was suddenly replaced by the non-verbal awareness of the three Vietnamese, they sensed, something is terribly wrong!

The joyous noise prior to the breach turned to silent terror with the sudden macabre appearance of men with black-striped faces, brandishing weapons – a horrific intrusion by monsters.

Before the bloodcurdling interruption, Pham, Nu, and Hwa were looking at an illustrated book of Kamasutra; laughing as they remarked about the various pictures – joking, could they improve on some of the advanced positions for sex play? Giggling as they consumed copious amounts of vodka and orange juice and played sex games

The reason for the moaning was now clear; viewing the scene, Baumgartner's first-thought - this is amazing, maybe not his first-thought, but in the top three. The prisoner snatch team beheld the naked bodies, two women and a man, the Spider, all intertwined in a spiral tower of the nude bodies, as they had been performed sex acts on each other simultaneously. Risner smirked, how can they contort their bodies like that and – do that wild sex stuff and not have at least two of them topple over in the ongoing action?

Pham and Nu could not speak or scream, given the nature of the sexual acts they each were performing, as integrated into the tower; Hwa's position and current sexual ministrations allowed her to partially disengage.

Hwa's eyes were wide-open in terror, she tried to draw a deep breath to scream - before she could expel that deep-breath as a scream, four loud pops from the silenced pistols quietly echoed in the 'party-room'. Hwa was hit twice in the forehead and twice in the heart. She toppled back, dead before she hit the floor.

As the tower collapsed, Risner and one of the Nungs moved to slam their hands over the mouths of Nu and Pham. Two other Nungs quickly reacted to drive Syringe needles into the necks of Nu and Pham. Nu was unconscious within three seconds; Pham, with burning hatred in his eyes, lasted five seconds before he succumbed.

Risner, with suppressed-laughing, said in a whisper – "the team ain't going to believe this".

Turning to race up the stairs to the fourth floor, Baumgartner ordered the Nungs to do the 'gag, bag, truss' for the surviving prisoners, and then wrap them in bedsheets before moving the naked prisoners to the ground floor back-door - the ominous sound of two pistols firing one shot each, followed by many loud pops, did not bode well for the mission.

Running up the stairs, he did a quick calculation, one radio-operator already had been captured descending from the third-floor, the cook was verified as absent. The other two second-floor apartments, used by Nu and Hwa, were empty. Two more radio operators were expected to be on the third floor, but it was uncertain which rooms they occupied.

When Jones received the order to breach, he signaled the third-floor teams to "GO!". The Americans swung the heavy knock-knock battering rams to shatter the old doors on three of the four apartments. The fourth apartment door was unlocked and open, presumably the captured radio operator's apartment, actually the unlocked room turned out to be a file-room.

364

They smashed the door of the apartment with a light showing under the door plus a faint sound of music playing, the team expected to find an occupant fully awake and likely armed. The doors were narrow for large-Americans to enter quickly with the three Nungs right behind the team leader.

Sergeant Clayton swung the knock-knock shattering the wooden door and the door frame – as wood splinters flew –Clayton lead the charge into the radio room, followed closely by his team. At the crashing and splintering of the door, the on-duty radio operator reached for a Makarov 9-mm pistol on the table beside the radio set. Swirling around the radio operator got off one shot which hit Sergeant Clayton in the chest.

Six loud pops followed before the sound of the Makarov discharge echo had ceased. The radio operator lay dead on the floor with four holes in his forehead and two in his heart; Clayton lay on the floor bleeding with a life-threatening chest wound.

Sergeant Jones pulled out his field medical packet and applied a dressing to stop the air leaking into Clayton's chest cavity and staunch the blood flow from the dangerous 'sucking chest wound'; holding the compress in-place with one hand, Jones directed a Nung to hold a second compress on the exit wound in Clayton's back, Jones used his radio to contact the command center across the street, giving a terse message:

"We have a man down, send the doc to the third floor – now".

As Jones ministered to Clayton's wound, the other three teams rushed into the remaining three third-floor apartments. One apartment was empty; a second was a file storage-room with no occupant. The last apartment held the sleeping off-duty third radio operator. The sleeping radio operator was roused from his sleep by the sound of the radio-room door disintegrating and his apartment door shattering, the formally sleeping radio man woke with an alertness typical to trained military personnel. As the door to his apartment disintegrated, the radio operator rolled over to retrieve his Makarov pistol from the nightstand next to his bed.

Flipping the safety off, the radio man turned toward the door as two men pushed into the bedroom darkness. Pointing at the nearest shadow, the radio man got off one-shot before he was hit three times by 22-caliber hollow-point bullets. The Makarov bullet hit Han Li in the heart killing the Nung instantly. Hearing the second shot from a Makarov pistol,

Sergeant Podowski and two Nungs joined the assault in the bedroom. Seeing their tribesman dead on the floor, the Nungs in the room unleashed a series of ten shots into the radio-operator's body. Podowski stopped the furious revenge firing with the associated loud-popping from each weapon discharge, Podowski contacted the command center to report "a man-down, send a medic now, third floor!"

Two radio operators dead and one mistress dead; Pham, Nu, and the third radio operator trussed and ready for transport, Baumgartner sent his message to the command center:

"Send in the exploitation team now"

Captain Williams responded, ordering,

"Exploitation team – Execute now!"

The NSA exploitation team moved immediately to 'work the site' for all intelligence documents and equipment of interest to NSA. The four-man NSA team, carrying heavy canvas bags and a tool kit ran up the stairs to the radio room and the file room. Four Nungs stood by to assist the NSA team, the Nungs would carry the canvas bags filled with documents and NVA radios down the stairs and out the back door to load 'the take' into a van.

Other Nungs were bringing cans of gasoline laced with Magnesium powder to torch the building. The stairs were a fast-moving assembly-line process – incendiaries going-up on the right-side of the stairs and intelligence-take coming down on the left side. The rest of the 'breach and grab' team members searched each apartment for materials of potential intelligence interest. The building was searched quickly and efficiently, all items of interest removed, and readied for torching which would eradicate any and all evidence the Peregrine team had ever been there.

The great prize sought by NSA were any encryption keys present at the radio building site. A small safe beside the radios was open, three documents in the safe were KGB encryption keys - suppressing a cheer, the NSA guys gave fist pumps and broad smiles. In less than ten minutes, the radios were disassembled and placed into the canvas bags; all documents from the file room, were secured in canvas bags. The precious encryption keys from the safe were held separately and tightly in the hands of the NSA team leader.

A small van was parked at the building back door; all the bags of NSA 'goodies' were loaded into the van; the NSA team boarded, hand-carrying three KGB 'encryption crown jewels' for exploitation at Fort Meade. The NSA team, three heavily-armed Nungs, and Master Sergeant Risner got in the van for immediate departure to Tan Son Nhat – where the International Export and Import Company Ltd 707 charter, engines running, was waiting to launch for the US with the NSA team and the "take".

Doc raced up the stairs pushing through the Nung traffic carrying intelligence materials out of the building and combustible materials into the building. Reaching Clayton, Doc recognized the wound-type and pulled two air-impervious compresses from his medical bag, applying one compress to the back and one to the front of the through-and-through wound. After giving Clayton a syrette of morphine, he ordered the Nungs to place Clayton in a bedsheet and carry him to the ground floor back-door. Moving to Han Li, Doc determined Han Li was dead; he directed Nungs to carry Han Li's body to the back door. Four Nungs tenderly lifted their clansman's body and carried him to the back door.

The unconscious-prisoners, the grievously wounded Clayton, Han Li's body, two Nung guards, and Doc were loaded in the van nearest the back door and departed for the Peregrine compound. Doc monitored Clayton, he decided to give Clayton the necessary additional trauma treatment at the compound and not take him to the Saigon field hospital for security reasons.

Two deuce-and-a-half trucks departed the vacant lot with a low rumble spewing black diesel-exhaust, stopping near the building front-door. Additional bags of intelligence materials from the apartments were loaded, the command center personnel boarded, the rest of the breach team personnel boarded the trucks and the convoy departed for the compound.

The radio building ceased to be an anthill of activity; each room had been searched for intelligence materials; containers of combustible liquids and fire-accelerants in-place for each apartment. The apartment windows and doors opened.

Sergeant Podowski, starting on the third-floor, inserted time-pencil igniters into the cans of gasoline and accelerants in each apartment. The igniters were time-sequenced to ignite simultaneously in 15-minutes. The open apartment doors and windows would give the fire a wind-tunnel supercharge effect as the flames shot up the stairwell to the roof. The unidentified female and the two enemy radio operator bodies were left in-place. Podowski exited by the back door and got into a covered Jeep with three armed Nungs.

The 12-synchronized ignitions generated a horrendous 4,000 degree contagion fire-storm of flames shooting out the windows with a volcano like-effect, the fire-storm rapidly consuming the interior of the building. By the time the first elements of the Saigon fire brigade arrived, all that was left was for the firefighters was to watch the collapse of the building walls in flaming chunks; the intense inferno left no evidence of the Peregrine raid in the smoldering residue. The radio building prisoner snatch and intel exploitation was accomplished in 19 minutes – the fire-storm did the rest leaving no trace who the perps were, or if there even were perps.

All Peregrine and Nung personnel, prisoners, and vehicles were back in the secure Peregrine compound 15 minutes after loading the trucks to depart the radio building area.

The top priority was for Doc to stabilize Sergeant Clayton. Doc cleaned the entry and exit wounds, applied new dressings, administered antibiotics, started a saline drip, and gave Clayton plasma. Another morphine syrette would be administered later. Doc told the team that Clayton would fully recover.

Doc then checked each of the still-unconscious prisoners; all the prisoners were stable. Some were in the early stages of emerging from the potent effects of the paralyzing drug. Each prisoner was sequestered alone in a room, tied to a chair, still blindfolded and gagged.

The body of Han Li was received by his clan with the Nung ceremony for a fallen warrior. The Peregrine team would honor Han Li, their faithful companion and warrior comrade, as soon as the immediate mission needs were satisfied.

The Interrogations

The team had to complete the interrogations in less than two days, posing a daunting problem. Interrogations tend to use different technique as fits the prisoner. Build a compatible relationship with the prisoner in a relatively-relaxed atmosphere, while eliciting the desired information from the detainee. This option required an interrogator who was highly-skilled and patient – plus a lot of time. A contrasting option was intimidation, including physical punishment to force the detainee to give up the information. This approach was problematic as it works on some prisoners and not so well others. For the prisoners who try to resist, this coercive path can take a significant time period including good-guy/bad-guy interrogations which combine elements of coercion and rapport.

The problem was, they simply had 'no time' for the traditional interrogation methods. They decided to run simultaneous interrogations for one day and focus on the most vulnerable targets on the second day. The mission time-line would dictate how much information the team could extract from the prisoners before the team 'cleaned up loose-ends'.

First Lieutenant Ngô Hau

First Lieutenant Ngô Hau was disoriented, confused, and afraid. He did not know where he was and why he was in this situation. The sensory deprivation of visual references and the inability to talk exacerbated his growing terror. Ngô was relieved when he heard the door open and the voices of at least two persons who entered. He hoped this was just a mistake and he would be freed. His relief was short-lived. When the blindfold was removed, Ngô saw a burly American and a fierce-looking Nung standing in front of him. He tried to speak but the gag allowed only a pathetic mumbling. The Nung roughly removed the gag and told him to talk when giving an answer to a question he was asked. Ngô was so terrified he started to blurt out a question of his own, only to be struck by the Nung who delivered a vicious blow to the side of Ngô's head– the Nung spoke in a threatening voice, "no talking, just answer questions" – Ngô Hau was dazed, the hearing in his left-ear damaged by the blow.

The questioning began, with the basics, what is your name; suddenly, before Ngô could answer, the Nung shouted,

"How long have you been a spy for North Vietnam?"

Ngô cried out, "I am not a spy!"

Continuing in a quiet voice, the Nung asked,

"Who is Pham Binh?"

Ngô answered,

"He is the chauffer for Colonel Trần Quan".

369

After about an hour of questioning, the American gave Ngô a drink from a bottle of water. The Nung replaced the gag and they left the room. Sergeant Jones and the Nung agreed; this guy is an unwitting dupe – just an admin 'go-for' doing menial tasks and not a witting part of the Pham spy network. Unfortunately for Ngô, like Hwa, he would be a collateral damage casualty when the 'loose-ends' are tied up.

Captain Bùi Duc

Captain Bùi Duc's arrogance was gone in a tsunami of anxiety and self-pity. He heard the door open and two men speaking English, which Bùi Duc understood. His blindfold was roughly removed by a physically intimidating American. Sergeant Podowski asked if Bùi understood English? Bùi answered,

"Yes I understand English"

Bùi turned his head to look at the Nung standing beside the massive American; his head was violently snapped back as Podowski delivered a powerful slap to his face with the admonition,

"Look at me when I talk to you".

Podowski and the Nung alternated asking questions, following the same line of questioning used on Ngô Hau. Then he faced the 'ultimate question', was he a spy for North Vietnam.

The physical 'tell' of a delayed response and dropping his eyes to the right betrayed Bùi Duc as he attempted to avoid answering the question truthfully. The Nung stuffed the gag back into Bùi's mouth and left the room along with Podowski. Out of Bùi's hearing, the interrogators agreed; we have a live one.

Returning to resume the questioning, a smiling Sergeant Podowski told Bùi the Nung would slice him up with the razor-edged knife as the Nung pressed the tip of the blade against Bùi's lower left-eyelid, drawing a small amount of blood and a delivering lot of pain. Bùi broke down, sniveling that he would give up all the information the interrogators wanted. The Nung pulled the knife blade back as a small trickle of blood continued to run down Bùi's cheek. Continuing to smile, which impacted Bùi as a terrifying grimace , Podowski gave Bùi a bottle of water – after drinking half the bottle, Bùi began the avalanche of information from a desperate prisoner hoping to avoid more pain. He 'gave up' the Spider network – and an extensive revelation about the network operations and personnel. Though Bùi knew he was part of a North Vietnamese spy operation, he knew Pham only as the leader. Bùi did not know Pham's true name.

Colonel Trần Quan

The team targeted Colonel Trần Quan as the weakest link in the 'chain' of prisoners. The Trần interrogation was delayed until evening as the interrogators developed a comprehensive plan to pressure Trần. Surreptitiously opening the door slightly, LT Baumgartner observed a man involuntarily shaking and sweating, a man in the process of a mental and emotional collapse. To exacerbate the process, the haunting strains of "Ride of the Valkyries" were pumped into the room where Colonel Trần trembled and tried to hold on to his sanity.

After several loops of "Ride of the Valkyries" further disoriented this prisoner, Baumgartner and two Nungs quietly entered the room. Leaving the prisoner blindfolded, the two Nungs began a conversation in Vietnamese about possible means to extract information from 'this prisoner'.

One Nung spoke in a rather frivolous tone:

"It was good that we soundproofed the other rooms; the screams of that traitor Bùi Duc would have scared the children. When Bùi kissed the dragon breath, he decided to tell everything – but he died before we could get all the information. The American said his propane torch flame was 3000 degrees hot; that 3000 degree 'dragon breath' burns flesh to the bone in seconds. Do you think the American will use 'kiss the dragon' to make this traitor talk?"

The second Nung commented:

"Maybe, but the American said he does not like the smell of burning flesh, he said the stink lingers in his nose."

Continuing the remarks which terrified Trần, the first Nung gave his opinion in a detached voice,

"The American knows this piece of shit traitor has the information we want. The American will use the torch to get all we want, despite the stink."

Both of the Nungs laughed heartily.

Trần felt he would pass out as he listened to this horrible fate if he did

371

not talk. Suddenly, he felt desperately hot and wet as he lost control of his bowels and bladder. Even as he thought things could not be worse, now, he had 'lost face' in front of the two men talking in the room - he was nauseous – if he vomited, he would choke to death because of the gag – even so, that seemed better than having his lips and face burned to chunks of ash as these devils cremated his living-face. He was on the verge of insanity.

Baumgartner silently motioned for the Nungs to follow him out of the room, noisily shutting the door behind them.

"Good job prepping him, he is ready to talk now!"

The Nungs had suppressed an urge to break into raucous laughter while in the room with Trần. The opaque hood, plus the blindfold totally denied Tran any visual sensory clues. Tran could not see the two Nung guards biting their lips and pinching their arms to avoid breaking into gales of laughter at the pathetic travails of the captive.

Clearly, the Kiss the Dragon with the 3,000 degree breath ruse had gotten the attention of the traitorous Colonel Trần Quan – who was shaking and whimpering in a gag-muted voice. The Nungs could not talk for a few moments as they had to curtail their amusement and reestablish a threatening demeanor to 'persuade' the 'traitor' to talk.

Colonel Trần did not know they were Nungs, but it did not matter, in any event, Tran would be totally oblivious of the discrete Nung sexual custom called 'Kiss the Dragon'. The Nung custom was an erotic-stylized sex play practiced by a few of the Nung clans. The Nung women in those clans favored a Dragon tattoo in the middle of their backs. The Nung men would kiss the dragon tattoo as they fondled the woman – all this provocative play created a high state of sexual arousal and led to additional carnal sexual intimacies between the Kiss the Dragon players.

Trần heard the door open again, which caused him to quake involuntarily. The three interrogators noted Trần's loss of control of his bodily functions - a humiliation on top of the debilitating terror ravaging the prisoner's mind.

Yes, they were sure, he was ready to talk.

A muscular intimidating American removed the hood, blindfold, and gag. As Trần's eyes adjusted to the light, his first vision was the American, who Tran accepted to be his 'angel of death'. The American

372

was looking at him as if Tran were prey for a large carnivore. The Nungs were equally frightening as they gazed at Tran with an intense burning hatred in their eyes. – Tran begin to cry and scream – I will tell you anything you want to know – please do not make me Kiss the Dragon!

Navy LT Baumgartner, Duan Ho, and Chee Chen immediately turned their heads smiling, enjoying how the Kiss the Dragon ploy had prepared the subject for interrogation. They all suppressed an overwhelming desire to laugh – Duan Ho, and Chee Chen thought, I really want to do some Nung Kiss the Dragon after this interrogation

Baumgartner told the Nungs to allow Trần to shower and clean-up, give him clean clothes, and food. We will meet with him in about an hour. And, let him know, Kiss the Dragon is still on the table if we need to move him along.

After the kinder treatment from his captors, Trần began an obsequious verbal torrent of information. Trần 'spilled his guts' on every aspect of what he knew about the Spider Network, which he called the Pham Network. Colonel Trần Quan was a traitor and a coward, but a traitor with a very good memory.

During the encyclopedia of information provided on the Spider network, his disclosures on the ill-conceived An Loc meeting carried profound implications. From the Peregrine clandestine photos, Trần identified most of the high-level moles North Vietnam had in the South Vietnamese government. Of that group, Phạm Ngọc Thảo stood tall as an important North Vietnamese spy. Phạm Ngọc Thảo had been a senior adviser to President Diem and was now a Province Chief.

Sergeant Pham Binh

Sergeant Pham Binh was identified as the leader of the spy ring by his subordinates, confirming the Peregrine analysis. The information from Trần Quan and Bùi Duc documented many of the conclusions the team made about a more expansive network than just a single network targeting American advisors. Captain Williams and Lieutenant Baumgartner agreed that Pham Binh was hard-core and would be able to resist a brief interrogation, no matter what threats or positive inducements. They decided to take a quick shot at Pham Binh and then 'tie up loose-ends'.

The Peregrine Team still did not know Pham's real name; and Pham's spy co-conspirators did not know his real name. During the 'one-pass' at Pham Binh, the interrogators would attempt to read his body language as they expected no verbal admissions from him. Since Colonel Trần had identified many of the faces from the breach of security at the An Loc meeting and the Team now understood how the Pham American advisor assassination network was organized and functioned, the interrogators could formulate a series of traps for Pham. Captain Williams, Lieutenant Baumgartner and one Nung interpreter would present portions of the intelligence evidence and watch Pham's reaction.

The Nung removed Pham's gag, blindfold, and handcuffs before offering Pham water. Pham's eyes radiated hatred, but Pham was smart enough to drink the water offered him.

The Nung asked if Pham understood English? Pham stared ahead ignoring the question. The die was set; watch for non-verbal 'tells'. A series of standard interrogation questions in Vietnamese followed, including asking what Pham's true name was.

The Nung told Pham they would exchange him for a South Vietnamese prisoner held in North Vietnam and Pham would be repatriated home to the North. That generated an unintentional 'tell' with a movement of Pham's head and his eyes shifting toward the Nung interrogator, no verbal response, but still 'an unintentional response'.

The Nung said they were going to show him a series of documents and pictures. The photo ploy was intended as a combination 'tell' calibration and a provocation. The first document they displayed to Pham was the lavishly illustrated book of Kamasutra retrieved from his apartment. Pham looked at the various pictures and looked at the Americans and smiled. Pham understood the game.

When the Nung showed Pham pictures from the Pham organized An Loc meeting NVA moles meeting, Pham flashed a look that is reserved in oriental cultures for − 'losing face'. Pham knew he had made a grave security blunder organizing that meeting. When asked if the person in one of the pictures with Pham was Phạm Ngọc Thảo, Pham noticeably winced. Captain Williams said, we are done here; this man obviously does not want to go home. The Nung re-tied Pham to the chair, blindfolded him, and the three interrogators left Pham alone to think about his fate.

The NVA radio operator was given a lengthy interrogation by Technical Sergeant Wilson and a Nung. The radio operator gave up a copious deposition of the technical procedures and the functional nodes in the Pham espionage communications network. The operator knew nothing about a second radio operation in Saigon. After the information was recorded for NSA, the prisoner was given a good meal of Vietnamese delicacies before being tied to his chair for the night.

Nu

While unconscious from the tranquilizer drug, two Nung women dressed her in a pair of black cotton pajamas, common to rural Vietnamese, and a pair of sandals. The women removed her blindfold, gag, and handcuffs. There was water, cold green tea, and sliced bananas on a plate available when she woke. As she emerged into consciousness, she was frightened and cried, pondering what had happened. Her memory was clear of the ménage à trois up to the time when threatening terrible armed-men invaded Pham's apartment. Everything after that terror-filled moment became hazy. Now, fear and consternation dominated her mind.

According to the rules of engagement, the team should dispatch Nu as collateral damage to hermetically protect the security of the operation. The situation in Pham's apartment when Hwa was shot was an unavoidable tactical event. Yet, killing this young woman, while sound security, it did not set well with the team.

Captain Williams had to decide her fate and do so now. The Spider crew would experience justice tomorrow. One enduring saying among the special operations folks is: "it is better to ask forgiveness than ask permission". Shooters had to make crucial judgments on the spot and then live with the result. Williams knew this could not be an emotional decision, he had to weigh what was necessary to preserve the security of the mission – and what was the morally correct thing as a second priority consideration. What was the morally correct thing in this situation, risk operational security or save this unfortunate refugee girl from being 'collateral damage'?

Weighing the obligation to follow the 'rules of engagement' order, Captain Williams considered, that in the short time from the breach to the time Nu was tranquilized and her eyes blindfolded, that time span was about three seconds, and three additional seconds before she was incapacitated. In those six seconds, she had been traumatized with overwhelming terror and absolute disorientation. He reached the tentative conclusion that Nu had no solid information which could damage the mission. Furthermore, her future silence would be in her self-interest. He ordered the team to ensure she did not hear any English spoken or see an American.

After hearing the results of a brief interrogation by a Nung, Williams would decide her fate. Ban Chen, head of the Nung clan suggested that his wife, Lan, perform the interrogation versus one of the fierce Nung fighters. Williams thought, that is a smashing idea. He and Ban Chen agreed on the interrogation guidelines which focused on determining if Nu had any information which could compromise the Peregrine mission. Williams ordered the Clan chief to 'make it happen'.

Ban Lan was very maternal in her approach to the traumatized Vietnamese teenager. Lan brought a pot of hot green tea and almond cookies which are popular in the North. Lan carefully quizzed Nu about her recollections of the night of the breach operation. Nu compulsively provided Lan with more details of the three-way sex tryst than Lan wanted to hear, but those details gave Nu's response credibility. Lan explained this had been a Vietnamese government operation and must remain secret, the Vietnamese government would put Nu in jail if she talked about what happened. The fact was, Nu only remembered the sexual tryst, and everything thereafter was a blur in her mind.

Later that evening, Captain Williams reconvened the team:

He announced the teenage-girl was safely back with her parents, with a generous payment to help them move forward from Nu's unfortunate choices in her prior behavior. The team gave silent fist pumps and high-fives all around.

Continuing, Captain Williams told the team the interrogations were completed and had produced additional 'good intel'.

"We got the sons-a-bitches who have been killing American advisors. Lieutenant Baumgartner, Master Sergeant Podowski, and I will be 'transferring' the bastards tomorrow on a H-34 ride to an alternate situation",

after the HOOYAH and shoulder slapping, several hands were raised.

Williams already knew why the hands were raised, all indicating - 'I am volunteering to go along for the H-34 ride'. Smiling,

"Thanks, but there is no room on the way-out for additional bodies. There will plenty of room on the way back".

Cheers and another round of back slapping.

"Everyone get packed and finish the sanitization of the compound, we leave for the Big PX, day after tomorrow".

big grins and more celebrating.

"By the way, as edification for you Neanderthals, our Naval officer has provided some information about an ecological phenomenon where the Mekong and the South China Sea converge. The nutrients in the Mekong River flow supercharge the food chain where the river and the sea converge. This results in two unusual areas forming as the fresh and salt water mix - in those two areas, the food chain is densely populated from the bottom of the food chain to the top, the top of the food chain is a large population of seriously-big predators: Hammerhead sharks, Bull sharks, and Blacktip sharks – all maneaters."

No Loose Ends - Justice Is Served

A deuce-and-a-half pulled up to a LZ outside Saigon, an Air America H-34 helicopter was waiting, rotors turning. Ten heavily-armed Nungs disembarked from the truck to set a security perimeter. Three other Nungs and three Americans held a brief conference before herding the five blindfolded and handcuffed Vietnamese prisoners onto the H-34.

Captain Williams gave instructions to load the radioman and First Lieutenant Ngô Hau first, once these two were strapped-in, 'inject both with the tranquilizer serum'. Do not drug the other three.

The Air America crew-chief strapped-in each prisoner on the starboard side of the passenger cabin. The Peregrine 'Justice Squad' (Williams, Baumgartner, Podowski) then boarded. Each member of the 'Justice Squad' attached a safety harness with an extended strap to allow them safe movement around the cabin when airborne. The H-34 cargo door remained open. Captain Williams gave the pilot a 'thumbs-up', the pilot increased the power and the H-34 lifted off on this 'flight that never happened'.

As the H-34 flew slowly over the "unusual area" where the Mekong and the South China sea mixed their fresh and salt waters. Large sharks, eight-foot Bull sharks and 15-17 feet Hammerhead sharks, could be seen swimming in large numbers in the water below the chopper.

377

The Nung removed the blindfolds from the prisoners. Without comment, Sergeant Podowski and LT Baumgartner unstrapped the unconscious radioman; they picked the radioman up and walked to the open cargo door, summarily throwing him out the door; the same action was repeated for still-blotto First Lieutenant Ngô Hau.

Colonel Trần's body was shaking in terror from the sight he had just witnessed. Trần had betrayed everyone, on both sides of this conflict, he would do anything to survive – Trần began to cry.

Captain Bùi Duc's eyes were dilated by his fear, it was obvious he was frightened though he maintained semblance of control over his emotions and body.

Pham Binh sat stoically, showing little emotion for the moment.

A Nung spoke to Captain Bùi Duc, yelling to be heard over the engine noise and the roar of air from the open door. He offered Bùi a chance to survive if he would give up more information, including the true identity of Pham Binh. As his answer, Bùi spit in the Nung's face. Baumgartner and Podowski unsnapped Captain Bùi's seatbelt; stood him up, ripped off his shirt, and used their razor-sharp knives to make shallow cuts on Bùi's back and chest – the old 'blood in the water' thing to expedite attention from the sharks. Captain Bùi Duc, met his deserved-end for killing the American advisors. 'Assisted' out the door, he took a very ungainly dive into the sea to swim with thrashing maneaters.

The Nung moved toward Colonel Trần Quan to make the same offer a 'chance to survive'. Baumgartner waved-off the Nung from any contact with Colonel Trần Quan. Trần was despised by the Peregrine team as a man who betrayed his country; a man who was easily 'flipped' to betray his spy cohorts – the team called Trần, 'Colonel Piece of Shit'. The Americans roughly unsnapped Trần's seatbelt and dragged him to the open helicopter door. Trần was kicking, screaming, and pleading for his life, Baumgartner and Podowski held , 'Colonel Piece of Shit's head so Trần could see the great predators below the chopper; Podowski ripped Trần's shirt off, making deeper cuts to produce a heavy flow of blood - Trần received his just-deserts, and the sharks received their dessert.

The Americans moved to unsnap Pham Binh. His stoic arrogance was now replaced by abject fear. His face was drained of color and he was quivering. Pham Binh 'lost face' to the Americans and Nung as he pissed his pants.

Pham screamed loudly to be heard over the cabin and engine noise. He shouted in shrill unaccented English.

"I am Colonel Wang Ky, officer in North Vietnamese Ministry of Defense Intelligence Department. I can help you, please don't kill me. I can help you, I do not want to die, please, please don't kill me. I will tell you everything you want to know – just don't kill me."

LT Baumgartner recognized the potential value of the knowledge Colonel Wang held in his head. However, the orders were clear, there was to be no evidence of the Peregrine mission, no loose ends.

Colonel Wang was sobbing in between his fervent pleas to be spared. He repeated his plaintive promises how he would serve the Americans. Wang had humiliated himself physically and emotionally. Wang was brave only when he was raping little girls and sending messages for other people to kill American soldiers.

Baumgartner and Podowski each grabbed one of Wang's feet. The Nung unsnapped the seat belt. They dragged him across the cabin floor to the open door. The roaring wind gave Wang's continuous screams a surreal echo through the cabin.

They lifted Wang so he could see the water below. Baumgartner shouted above the noise of the wind, engine, and Wang's screams,

"Do you see that dark spot in the water, that is where the sharks ate your commie bastard buddies. Now you are going to go to Hell after the sharks eat you."

With that, Baumgartner and Podowski took one of Spider's legs and arms, lifting him off the deck, Baumgartner said,

"On three".

They swung Wang out, "One", swung him back and then out again, "Two", swinging him out for the final time,

"Three",

They pitched him into the air. Wang screamed until he hit the water. At the impact several large maneaters turned to race to the splash point. In a few seconds, the water was a red froth.

The Americans and Nung shook hands all way round and sat down on the metal seats in the rear of the cabin. The Americans contemplated that The Spider's 'memorial' will be the spreading of his body across the South China Sea as shark excrement. Justice for our American advisor comrades. Loose ends cleaned up, the H-34 turned back for Saigon. The next flight leg would be a 707 for the Peregrine team trip home.

Once back in the Peregrine compound, Captain Williams announced,

"This bunch of bad-guys are now 'shark shit'."

After the cheers died down, Captain Williams amended his remark,

"Colonel Wang Ky was a sniveling simpering coward, he died crying trying to betray his country to save his ass."

The last comment generated immediate murmurs - who the hell is 'Colonel Wang Ky?'

Captain Williams smiled and provided the clarification,

"Colonel Wang Ky was the Spider. Wang was a rapist, a coward, and has been sent to Hell as he deserved. We did the mission and, in the process, terminated one of the most despicable individuals to walk the planet."

Execute plus three days, 13 November 1964) – The Team prepared to depart the compound for Tan Son Nhat airport and 'the bird that would take them home'.

The team held great respect for the loyalty and service the Nungs had given the Peregrine Team – the Team saw the Nungs as fellow warriors and loyal friends. The compound had been sanitized from a security standpoint leaving no evidence of the American presence. Captain Williams decided to resolve the legal status of compound ownership by transferring the title and deed to Ban Chen, Chief of the Nung 'Li clan'. Ban Chen was a grizzled, hardened veteran from decades of battles and hardship. Ban Chen had fought the French, the Japanese, the French again, the Viet Minh, the NVA, and always taken care of the people despite the desperate conditions they faced continuously

When Captain Williams explained that the compound now belongs to the 'Nung Li clan', Ban Chen was overwhelmed with emotion by this surprising compassionate gesture from the Americans. After Ban Chen signed the legal documents taking possession of the compound for the clan, Ban's second-in-command raced to spread the news. The Americans were engulfed by laughing Nungs: children, women, and scarred veteran fighters; all the Nungs wanted to hug the Peregrine team members.

The team did not forget the courage and heroism of Han Li on the A Shau run for life, when Han Li covered the wounded Warrant Officer Renner with his body to protect Renner from additional enemy fire, and how he escorted Renner to the safety of the 'hot extraction'. When Han Li was killed in the radio building prisoner snatch, Han Li's widow faced a difficult future. The team presented Han Li's widow a bonus of $10,000 US dollars, making her the wealthiest person in the clan. Weeping, she embraced each Peregrine team member with gratitude that her family would overcome and survive the great loss of their father. The Team members thought, this young widow, now wealthy young widow, will not be unmarried for long.

The Nungs inherited a stock of weapons, a large quantity of ammunition stored in the armament bunker, plus substantial stores of food in the second warehouse.

Captain Williams took the Peregrine 'exit' message to the CIA Station for transmission, he brought a wealth of intelligence materials with him for transfer to his Station contact, Jake, Bill, or whatever his real name was. These data included the An Loc pictures, updated with names from the Colonel Trần interrogation, the wiring diagram of enemy spy networks, and summaries of the 'Spider team' interrogations. This was a coup for the CIA station to have for the official reporting status for this profoundly important intelligence information. The Station would send DC a series of priority intelligence reports. These "CIA messages" would further conceal any existence of a Peregrine operation in Vietnam.

Sergeant James distributed the 'rather large residual stock' of booze, doing so as a true wheeler-dealer. Liquid gifts provided in appreciation for support and help for this mission (friends at SOG, the motor pool Sergeant, Air America, and the 1st Air Commando Group at Bien Hua), at the same time, collecting IOUs for future help, and bottles for old friends who James hoped to see again in better circumstances. Of course, Master Sergeant James also held-back a modest stock of booze for the long flight home.

Now, to Tan Son Nhat for Import-Export charter for the flight home – Home!

CHAPTER 27   PEREGRINE MISSION COMPLETE

Captain Williams sent the 'exit' message to Major-General Wojcik using the Saigon CIA communication channel:

```
General Wojcik:

I advise you: Mission Complete.

Packed and ready to get out of Dodge. .Please send charter
aircraft for departure from here 15 November 1964.

Request the incoming crew include a doctor and nurse. One
WIA from the team will be on-board.

Very Respectfully

Robert Williams

Captain, US Army
```

The reply arrived one hour later:

```
To: Captain Robert Williams:

From: Major-General Stanislaw Wojcik

Congratulations on mission complete.

International Export and Import Company Ltd 707 charter
to arrive Saigon 0600 hours 15 November. Doctor and Nurse
will accompany flight crew.

0800: Board Peregrine team and equipment.

0900: Wheels-up for CONUS, Eglin AFB, Florida"

Well Done

Stanislaw Wojcik

Major-General, US Army
```

Master Sergeant Wilbur James extended his master-scrounger legend. A flat-bed truck was parked in the Peregrine compound with a load of repatriated essentials packed in three air cargo containers and on two pallets. The 'repatriated essentials' included Peregrine team personal weapons, personal gear, a Wurlitzer juke box, and selected furniture for the team's future-base in the CONUS. And, for the pièce de résistance demonstrating 'the Sergeant James supply-wizardry', James 'acquired' a hospital bed from the Third Field Hospital in Saigon. He had the bed attached to an aircraft cargo pallet. US Army Master Sergeant Woodrow Clayton would ride home in the 'medical comfort and style' of a fully-functional hospital bed.

15 November, Tan Son Nhut airport Vietnam, the 707 Import Export charter was refueled and the two CIA air crews on-board. A forklift picked up a pallet with Woodrow Clayton in a hospital bed. Sergeant James and 'Doc' von Eisenberg were standing on the pallet, holding on to the bed as a forklift raised the pallet to the aircraft cargo door. As the aircraft loadmaster strapped-down the hospital bed pallet, 'Doc' von Eisenberg briefed the doctor and nurse regarding the status of the seriously wounded Clayton. The doctor and nurse would examine Clayton once airborne and treat, as needed, from the comprehensive set of medical supplies they brought with them. As soon as Clayton was safely in-place, the Peregrine team boarded the aircraft, the three pallets of cargo were loaded, engines started. Aircraft liftoff was on-time, 0900 local time.

The doctor and nurse checked Master Sergeant Clayton's wound and overall condition. He was in serious condition, but stable. After the check-up, the nurse changed the wound dressing. Always thinking about his men, General Wojcik had ordered the doctor to bring a young, very attractive female nurse to attend the Peregrine patient. The doctor congratulated 'Doc' von Eisenberg for his excellent work dealing with the trauma condition from the gunshot wound. Clayton would live, with the burden how to explain two gunshot scars, classified scars, to his children and grandchildren.

The flight steward was prepared for this rowdy bunch, having been on the first flight in-country so many months ago, a rowdy-bunch now fewer in number, one killed in action and two recovering from combat wounds. The steward prepared a spread of Porterhouse steaks, rare and medium-rare, cold beer, fried potatoes with onions - and some token vegetables.

384

For 'later eats' after the steak feast, Sergeant James again exploited the JCS priority for the return flight as he contacted base operations at Kadena air base in Okinawa and Elmendorf air base in Alaska to order VIP meals and cold beer for the team and aircrews during the aircraft refueling.

Touchdown at Eglin Air Force Base, some 25 hours later, was a happy but subdued arrival. Major-General 'Bull' Wojcik was waiting as the 707 engines were shut-down and the stairs moved into place. General Wojcik literally bounded up the stairs as the aircraft door was opened. Entering the 707 passenger compartment, "Bull' greeted each man with a powerful hand-shake, pats on the back, congratulations on the success of a difficult mission, a mission that was 'exquisitely completed'. The General moved to the cargo area to spend time with Master Sergeant Clayton, to thank the doctor and nurse, and to commend Master Sergeant 'Doc' von Eisenberg for his professional treatment of Master Sergeant Clayton and Warrant Officer Renner. Master Sergeant Clayton, the doctor, and nurse were transferred to a medevac jet to move Clayton to the Walter Reed National Military Medical Center in Bethesda, Maryland.

The rest of the team and General Wojcik boarded a bus for the ride back-home to Field #3, air cargo containers and the cargo pallets were loaded on a flatbed truck which followed in the two-vehicle convoy.

CHAPTER 28   THE NEW KGB AGENT

Calthrop Winston Simmons, newly recruited KGB spy, has access to the highest levels of US Top Secret/Sensitive Compartmented Information. He is amoral, greedy, and has no remorse for his treachery and his treason, all vile characteristics a case officer can manipulate and exploit. The reality is, Calthrop is a psychopath which accounts for his having no moral compass, and no remorse for evil he does. Calthrop manifests virtually all the classic symptoms of a psychopath in his routine daily behavior, including an ability to seem normal and even charming at times. One essential competency for a good case officer is the ability to read subtle and not-so-subtle aspects of the spy's personality and leverage these behavior traits to maintain control over the agent. A manipulation not so easily done when the spy's mental processes are driven by a psychopathic personality.

Calthrop took a taxi back to his apartment, his pocket bulging with 150 US $20 dollar greenbacks, and the promise of much more money.

Calthrop was unsettled in his mind. He had just given a foreign power, albeit an ally, highly classified information. Furthermore, the last tranche of information had little to do with fighting international communism. On top of that, he accepted a monetary payment for his treason. He fully understood the French intelligence service had compromising evidence of his wrongdoing in bribing an embassy employee to purchase an illegal visa. Beyond that and more damning was the transfer of sensitive classified information to a foreign power. His warped mind dismissed any concerns as he patted the envelope full of money – this is great – what can I do now to get more money and show these US government assholes that I am smarter than all of them.

Consistent with his usual behavior, he reasoned none of the problems he faced over the years were his fault. The US government had treated him unfairly denying promotions and not respecting his labors. He was helping a friendly ally fight communism. The woman he once fantasized as his next conquest had become a brutal, threatening individual leading him into misdeeds. Misdeeds he would not have committed otherwise.

His lust for Kie^ waned as he felt two new emotions for her. First, he feared her because she had the power to destroy him. Second, he hated Kie^ because she had rejected his sexual advances and disrespected him.

Calthrop always created mental imagery to rationalize his behavior, no matter how egregious his conduct was. He was helping fight communism and was a hero. He could outwit Kie^ and he would receive a great deal of money in the process. He mused how he would spend his newfound riches: high-priced hookers, better yet, spend the money on classy high-priced courtesans and sexy geisha-type girls. Now, only the best for Win, it was a win-win for him. His mental prowess would help him be a 'good spy', an effective spy for the greater-good in the 'fight against Communism'.

Returning to work the next day, the embassy folks stared and wondered about him. He looked like 'the old Simmons', but he was actually working diligently. The rumors began to circulate, actually rumors more in the form of questions. What happened to this guy? Why isn't he hitting on all the young women? Did the Chargé d'Affaires actually straighten him out? What is the back story here? And so on.

Only three people knew the back-story: KGB Lieutenant Nyugen Kie^, KGB Captain Alexandre Petrov, and the spy-traitor, Calthrop Winston Simmons. The irony and reality were that each individual had a different view of a Calthrop 'reality'. The most amusing part of all this, in Calthrop's twisted mind, he convinced himself that he was working for French intelligence and fighting international communism.

Back in the Embassy, Calthrop was carrying-out his duties efficiently, even enthusiastically. He was setting up meetings with the various organizations he was responsible to coordinate: CIA, SOG, the various US military intelligence units, the Vietnamese Special Branch police and the South Vietnamese Central Intelligence Office. He made his first visit to the Central Intelligence Office since he had been in Saigon. Calthrop diligently wrote reports but no one noticed that the 'new Calthrop' made an extra copy of the most important reports. Calthrop expanded his duties, on his own initiative, to include counterintelligence information. This was a curious and unwarranted addition to his official responsibilities.

The change in Calthrop's behavior were remarkable, even radical in comparison to what all had witnessed since he arrived in Saigon. When a person holding a high-level clearance demonstrates a radical change in behavior, the altered behavior should attract the attention of internal security and counterintelligence agents. The US Saigon Embassy was so overtasked and overworked, no one investigated the former 'Embassy joke' when he began his radical change in behavior, especially his new interest in counterintelligence matters. The latter which was beyond his assigned job purview and violation of the 'need to know' principle. Most coworkers simply accepted that Calthrop was reformed into a 'shining example of the diligent employee'. He had reacted in a positive manner to his 'counseling' from the Charge d'Affaires. As a result, the standard security alarm bells did not ring and the appropriate security alerts simply fell through the crack in what would become a catastrophic oversight.

Win met with his case officer in the safe apartment once a week, staggering the days and times for operational security. Win even stopped his previous tendency to hit-on Kie^ at every opportunity. He rationalized that he had to save his energy for his live-in Vietnamese girlfriend, a beauty who served his many deviant needs. He even tried opium once, prepared by his girlfriend, his very mercenary girlfriend. But for the most part he and the girlfriend just did the sex and booze thing - and like filming a movie production, a porn movie – it was for them – scene one, take-one; do over, take-two until Calthrop could take no more takes. The new girlfriend was very well-paid by Calthrop, thanks to the 'French' black money he received.

At the meetings with Kie^, his 'French' case officer, Win would deliver piles of documents, give verbal reports, and receive new intelligence requirements for him to collect a wide-range of information. Win was enthralled to collect his 'spy fees' and secretly demonstrate he was smarter than everyone at the Embassy. He even had persuaded Kie^ to give him a bonus for the most important reports. Win was unaware that his every act of his treason was being recorded by the KGB goon in the safe house bedroom. As the thousands of dollars rolled in, Win never stopped to think, Why would SDECE want 'this or that' particular piece of information?

Sasha and Kie^ were amazed by the productivity and quality of the material from their new agent. KGB Chairman Semichastny and General Sakharovsky were ecstatic. Operation Red had worked beyond all expectations. General Sakharovsky signaled Captain Petrov by encrypted message,

"Keep throwing money at this 'spook jewel', adding as humor, the KGB 'is good for it'. Standby for further orders".

One of Calthrop's reports on CIA and Vietnamese Central Intelligence Office provided information on two parallel investigations conducted respectively by CIA and the Central Intelligence Office counter-intelligence officers. CI agents from both organizations were perplexed; a group of Joint General Staff officers disappeared without a trace. In the same time frame, a separate report noted that a NVA radio-relay camp in the A Shau had been bombed into oblivion but there were no flight records as to who had conducted the airstrike.

These investigative events caused little concern for the KGB. A basic rule for intelligence services is, "there are no coincidences". While the KGB was concerned where these investigations could go, the fact was, the Americans had taken the bait and believed they had eliminated the threat to the US advisors. The KGB Chairman and the Head of the First Chief Directorate knew the Operation Red objective had been accomplished. They had inserted a high-level mole into the US intelligence community. The loss of 'the Pham Network' was just sacrificing a pawn to create checkmate.

They expected NSA had intercepted the radio traffic from the Operation Red radio site in Saigon. But the KGB was confident the high-level encryption used would stymie the NSA analysts.

The success of Operation Red was a cause for celebration. KGB Chairman Semichastny and General Sakharovsky shared an ice-cold vodka toast – now, on to Operation Pravda, the new name for Operation Red after relocation of the KGB mole to the US.

CHAPTER 29
OPERATION RED - MISSION COMPLETE

The Operation Red radio operator in the Saigon safe house was having difficulty keeping up with the high volume of intelligence materials from the new KGB spy, Pravda, the KGB code-for Calthrop. Long on-air times transmitting the lengthy reports from "Pravda" posed a serious security threat as the signals were almost certainly being intercepted by the NSA.

When the A Shau valley radio site mysteriously went off the air, the Operation Red radio operator had to modify his antenna to transmit directly to Moscow. NSA continued to intercept the new signal from Saigon to Moscow. The high volume of intercepted transmissions drew the NSA analysts' attention. The KGB encryption was the same high-level cypher as before, and still unbreakable by NSA. The NSA collection group sent Annie a copy of the new-signal collection report in case it might have a relationship to the Operation Peregrine. Annie duly noted how the new signal changes related in timing to the take-down of the Spider network and the A Shau radio site.

The old KGB encryption system was not intercepted again after the takedown of the Spider network and the air strike obliterating the A Shau radio site. This fact further tweaked the interest from some NSA analysts who believed the old KGB encryption system was part of a KGB deception operation.

In Moscow, KGB Chairman Vladimir Semichastny consulted General Aleksandr Sakharovsky on the next steps in Operation Red. The success of Operation Red, up to now, was virtually perfect. The 'virtually perfect' appearance caused General Sakharovsky to reflexively recall the generic intelligence maxim – 'when things are too perfect, something is wrong'. Sakharovsky sent a message to Captain Petrov to increase the rigor of his tradecraft and countersurveillance security for the Saigon Pravda operation. While Sakharovsky had security concerns, Semichastny was a politician, not an intelligence field-operative, Semichastny simply reveled in the success, oblivious of the possible professionalism of US counterintelligence and the Russian version of "Murphy's Law".

In the Chairman's view, the Americans had swallowed the bait and the KGB recruited their high-level mole, Agent Pravda, right under the noses of US counterintelligence forces. The destruction of the North Vietnamese Spider intelligence networks went as expected as collateral damage in Operation Red. The Americans were fooled by the use of an obsolete KGB encryption system and the 'providential' defection of a KGB code clerk which 'gave them' the NVA assassination network as a throw-away in the KGB deception plan.

It was time to shift Agent Pravda into the heart of the US intelligence community in Washington. The next step would be to accelerate agent Pravda's early return from Saigon back to a high-level position in the State Department Bureau of Intelligence and Research as an insider, privy to some of the most highly-classified intelligence materials in the US. At the same time, the INR wielded much less influence in the IC than the heavy-weights: CIA, DIA, NSA, and the military intelligence services in the Pentagon. Thus, the INR had a relatively low profile, giving Pravda wide access but affording him a lower visibility to escape FBI counterintelligence scrutiny. An important added security consideration insulated agent Pravda. Unlike the other senior players in the IC, the State Department did not use the polygraph to examine candidates for TS/SCI clearances or periodically vet employees who held TS/SCI clearances.

The first two orders issued for Operation Pravda were: initiate a process to have agent Pravda return to the US as soon as possible for duty in the INR; second, Captain Petrov and Junior Lieutenant Nguyen would be recalled to Moscow for consultation.

When the two orders arrived at the Saigon safe house radio site, the second order spiked Sasha's concerns for himself and Kie^. Since the 1930s to the present, a recall to Moscow was a dreaded demand received by any KGB operative. During the Stalin times and his rampant paranoia, 'the recall to Moscow' was usually a death sentence, carried out in the Lubyanka basement. Sasha knew he had many enemies at KGB headquarters, career-competitors who were jealous of his protected-position, his influence as a junior officer, and envious when they heard the whispered rumors of his successes.

Such recall orders resulted in many KGB officers defecting to the West during the 1930s and 1940s. For security reasons, Sasha and Kie^

had minimized the frequency of their meetings in Saigon. For the most part, they now worked separately. Kie^ worked Pravda out of the safe house near the racetrack and Sasha worked from the original safe house in Cholon. Kie^'s time was absorbed running the enthusiastic greedy agent Pravda. Now, with the looming threat of the Moscow recall, it was urgent for Sasha and Kie^ to talk. Sasha used the phone code to summon Kie^ to his safe house.

Kie^ followed her SDR to arrive on-time at the safe house. Quickly stepping inside, she was greeted with an embrace and kiss from Sasha. He immediately led her to the living room to discuss the Moscow orders. The order for Agent Pravda to return to the US at the earliest possible date was dealt with in less than five minutes. Kie^ would instruct Pravda to request a transfer back to the US. The order for the two of them to 'return to Moscow for consultation' was the next item on the agenda. Both were aware of the potential dire consequences of a 'Moscow consultation'. Despite the stressful nature of the recall situation, they calmly sipped French wine and enjoyed being in each other's presence.

Sasha had made his personal determination the prior evening. He was dedicated to serving Mother Russia and would comply with the KGB order to return to Moscow. Sasha wanted Kie^ to feel free to make her own decision regarding a return to Moscow. He thought how he would present his personal decision in an effort to generate minimal pressure and allow her to freely decide what she thought was in her best interests. When Kie^ heard about the order to return to Moscow for consultation, her face went pale, and she took Sasha's hands into hers. She sat in silence for about three minutes as she processed the possible consequences and scenarios for a return to Moscow. The historic antidotal information indicated a bad ending was more likely than a good result from returning to Moscow for 'consultation'.

Kie^ made her decision during the first 30 seconds of those contemplative three minutes Her conclusion was, she would go and do whatever Sasha decided. The remaining time was used to professionally analyze the other possible scenarios.

She broke the silence asking Sasha, "What are you going to do?"

There was no talk of defecting or the potential for horrific consequences from a Moscow consultation. Sasha did not philosophize. He looked Kie^ in the eye,

"I am going to return to Moscow as ordered".

Kie^ hugged Sasha and whispered into his ear,

"I go where you go".

The decision was made. They would stay together and they will take whatever fate might await them on the return to Moscow.

After an additional brief discussion about Pravda, their potential super-spy, the spy business was finished. They decided to switch to vodka and moved to the 'fun' part of their meeting agenda.

Kie^ met with agent Pravda three days later. She instructed Pravda to initiate a request to return to Washington at the earliest possible date, citing a family emergency or some other urgent reason. When Pravda asked the 'why' for this rather extreme request as it would disrupt his gathering information on the war. Kie^ explained there were broader French concerns about the communist international threat which could be best served by his presence in DC, adding, before Pravda could comment further, the payments for his services will be much higher in Washington. The deal was closed as soon as the higher pay promise was put on the table – and, Calthrop thought with relief, he would be out of the daily dangers in the Saigon hellhole war zone. At this point, Pravda did not give a rat's-ass about geopolitics or patriotism, he just wanted more money, plus, like many spies, Calthrop was becoming addicted to the adrenalin highs of his espionage activities.

KGB Headquarters – The Moscow Consultation

For security, Sasha and Kie^ flew back to Paris on separate planes, using the respective legends from their American and French passports. They checked into different hotels in Paris where they were individually contacted by a Soviet courier to provide different passports for the travel to Moscow. Sasha left early the next day and Kie^ followed one day later.

Arriving in Moscow Sheremetyevo Airport, Captain Petrov was greeted by Ivan, his former driver. Bypassing customs and passport-control they proceeded to the car. The driver gave Petrov an unexpected message, the driver had been instructed to take him directly to apartment 21. Tomorrow morning, the driver would pick-up Captain Petrov, drive back to Sheremetyevo to meet Lieutenant Nyugen. Petrov asked his driver about the latest rumors at KGB Headquarters. The driver gleefully related how two salacious office-affairs were exposed, a KGB senior-officer arrested for improper use of funds, and the sudden organization of a mysterious new group in the First Chief Directorate. There were whispered rumblings about a new super-secret agent being run by General Sakharovsky. Sasha internalized the last rumor, thinking, this is not good and may represent a danger to him and Kie^. It could be the reason for the recall for 'consultation'.

Early the next morning, the driver and Petrov departed apartment 21 to meet Lieutenant Nyugen arriving from Paris. Captain Petrov greeted Junior Lieutenant Nyugen in a most proper manner, shaking hands. She did not salute as both were in civilian clothes. The trip to their Moscow designation, the Lubyanka, passed in silence. Once inside KGB headquarters, Captain Petrov and Lieutenant Nyugen were escorted directly to the KGB Chairman's office. The Saigon Operation Red team was greeted in an enthusiastic manner by Chairman Vladimir Semichastny and General Aleksandr Sakharovsky. They embraced and greeted Captain Petrov and Junior Lieutenant Nyugen with hearty hand-shakes and Russia style hugs, followed by a vodka toast, actually several toasts – the toasts emphasized, now forward with Operation Pravda – in the United States!

Kie^'s knees were shaky but she felt relief. Petrov thought in the standard Russian suspicion paradigm, this is either very good or very bad – but it appears to be very good – hopefully, Kie^ and I are on the way to Washington together to handle Pravda.

Chairman Semichastny gestured toward a couch and the upholstered chairs in his spacious office,

"Please sit down, Major Petrov and Captain Nyugen". Semichastny and Sakharovsky laughed at the looks on the two KGB officers' faces; Chairman Semichastny continuing jokingly,

"I am the Chairman of the KGB. I cannot be wrong – I got your ranks correct – your new ranks. You have served the Party in an exceptional manner and the success of Operation Red exceeds all our expectations."

Sasha relaxed, finally, even though as a true Russian, in the back-recesses of his mind, he wondered if there was a 'next shoe' to drop, and it did immediately.

General Sakharovsky announced,

"I understand agent Pravda should be back in the United States before the New Year. Therefore, we are reshaping part of the operation to address evolving security needs. We think agent Pravda may become our most important mole since Kim Philby in British MI-6 and Richard Sorge in Japan during the Great Patriotic War.

"You and Captain Nyugen will proceed directly to the US after you study your new legends for travel and the details for your residence in the US as illegals. You will surreptitiously enter the US from Tijuana, Mexico as a married couple, US citizens John and Lisa Carmichael".

Sasha and Kie^ dared not look at one another, a 'married couple!' They had to suppress any and all emotions, like laughing and cheering.

"You will use a circuitous route to avoid leaving any record of your entry into the US. In the process you will employ two throw-away legends. You will receive your final US legend documentation just before entry into the US from Tijuana, Mexico. The security procedures for US citizens returning as day-tourists from Mexico to the US are notoriously lax, virtually non-existent from a CI perspective".

"The first leg of your infiltration route is from Moscow to Vienna, Austria. As you both know, Vienna is a seething hotbed of competing intelligence agencies: kidnappings, assassinations, bribery, black-bag work, our 'wet-work', you name it, all the subterfuges and treacheries in espionage are active in Vienna. The KGB has a strong effective presence in Vienna. More important, there is a large number of Russians in the city for various pursuits".

"Two Russians arriving in Vienna from Moscow is not big news. You will travel to Vienna as a married Russian couple, Petr and Galina Ivanov. The legend for your travel to Vienna is a combination of tourism and evaluating a business opportunity to open a Russian-language bookstore in Vienna. After checking into the Grand Hotel and seeing the Vienna sights for two-days, a Vienna Rezidentura operative will contact you with new identity documents for travel to Madrid, Spain and onward to Mexico City. For that travel you will be Canadian citizens, William and Katherine Clausen. These short-term legends will ensure that your US identity documents do not show any foreign travel such as visas and entry-departure stamps".

"Arriving in Mexico, you will check into the Gran Hotel Ciudad de México in Mexico City using your prepaid reservation, staying for two-days. At the end of the two days, you will fly to Tijuana, Mexico still using your Canadian documents. Check into the La Villa de Zaragoza hotel under your Canadian identities. During your second day in Tijuana, an operative from the Mexico Rezidentura will contact you with the American legend documents you will use to enter the US and continue to use during the operation in Washington DC. The Rezidentura operative will have US currency for you and provide you a car registered in the state of Virginia. You will cross the border by car using your US identities and drive to the Washington DC area. This cross-country travel will help orient you to the US social practices and give you geographic knowledge for a large portion of the US. You will operate in Washington DC as John and Lisa Carmichael. There is an existing bank account in a Springfield, Virginia bank in your names with $30,000 deposited for you".

"John and Lisa Carmichael will buy or rent a house in the Washington DC area. You will set-up an engineering research business cover as a means to create a cash flow of income for living and operational expenses including initial payments to agent Pravda. The customers for the consulting business will be KGB front organizations. Any questions?"

"Yes, Comrade General, one question please. What will be our relationship with the Washington Rezidentura?"

"I will advise the Rezident you are on a secret mission, directly under the order of the Chairman of the KGB. The Rezident will know nothing of your mission objectives. You will use the Rezidentura for selected communications support, but the passing of any information to the Rezidentura will be handled through dead drops. Your KGB contact in Washington DC will brief you on the dead drop procedure and dead drop locations. John Carmichael's legend will be an independent consultant for engineering research. Lisa Carmichael. will be his administrative assistant for the consultant business. Operationally, nothing will change, Major Petrov will continue to serve as the Operations Officer and Captain Nyugen as the case officer for agent Pravda. A decision has not been made yet whether to provide you with a dedicated radio operator in America. If Pravda is as productive as expected, you will have a radio operator added to the operation as a part of your cover business staff. Did you give agent Pravda instructions how to make recontact once in Washington DC?"

"Yes, Comrade General, Pravda has been instructed how I will contact him. I will use a rather standard procedure placing a preset coded advertisement in the Washington Post personal ads section".

"Major Petrov and Captain Nyugen, I will remind you, no one in the KGB, except the four people in this room, is cleared fully for Operation Pravda, support individuals only have limited knowledge for the specific duties they will fulfill – beyond that, no one outside this room has a need-to-know about Operation Pravda. Any further questions?"

Petrov and Nyugen answered in unison.

"No, Comrade General".

The KGB Chairman and the Head of the First Chief Directorate both stood, indicating the end of the meeting, Major Petrov and Captain Nyugen both jumped to their feet to stand at attention. The Chairman and General thanked their officers for their dedication, shaking hands and returning the salutes from the newly promoted officers: Major Alexandr Mikailovich Petrov and Captain Nyugen Kie^.

Walking back to the car and the waiting driver, Sasha put his finger to his lips signaling, be careful with what you say, adding,

"We should take a walk later to enjoy the fresh Moscow air".

Later, during the walk, Sasha reminded Kie^ that the cook and driver will be spying on them for any breach of security - such as discussing Operation Pravda matters in apartment 21. Nothing had changed regarding the KGB security paranoia.

Five days later, Sasha and Kie^ departed for Vienna using the false Russian passports and identities. The travel process to the US went smoothly with the various identity changes and the appropriate documents to backstop the identities. As Sasha and Kie^ crossed the Mexico-US border at Ciudad Juárez, Chihuahua, Mexico, they smiled – crossed as a 'married couple', 'for them, they were beyond operationally married'. For Sasha and Kie^, this 'marriage' was the "real deal".

CHAPTER 30 BACK IN THE USA

As the two-vehicle convoy entered Eglin Field #3, the team noticed many changes since the they departed almost a year ago. There was a US Navy Construction Battalion (Seabees) diligently refurbishing the infrastructure of Field #3 with new buildings and training facilities. The bus stopped at a new barracks while the flatbed proceeded to a large storage building. General Wojcik told the team to stow their personal gear and be ready for a team meeting in one hour.

Bull motioned for Captain Williams and LT Baumgartner to follow him to the new conference room. There were Krispy Kreme donuts and fresh coffee waiting, evoking smiles from the Peregrine officers. General Wojcik voiced his immediate concern,

"Just how hermetically-sealed was Peregrine security with the shut-down of the operation in Vietnam?"

Captain Williams answered, prefacing his comments with a basic caveat,

"General, one thing you know, and we learned in the counterintelligence course at The Farm, there is no such thing as a perfect crime or total security. The is always evidence no matter how obscure, there is evidence. To answer your question specifically, we believe the residual security issues are very minimal risk, from our perspective, virtually non-existent. The only in-country organization that knew the mission and details is the CIA station. A couple of SOG contacts knew we were running an undercover black operation, but no details beyond the A Shau recon patrol were shared with these individuals. The Nungs have the cover story that we were bodyguards for the "Adjunct Judge Advocate General Team #4". The Nungs, in fact, performed duties as our bodyguards. I think the Nungs actually accepted and believe our bodyguard cover stories. Frankly, they didn't give a shit; they were well paid and treated respectfully by these 'Adjunct-something' Americans. The Nungs and Yards are the only indigenous groups in Vietnam who are truly loyal and faithful to the Americans. Our conclusion is the Peregrine security situation is excellent – our mission never happened."

General Wojcik did not comment. He just nodded his head in the affirmative.

The team meeting gave all hands a view to the future:

First the General announced, each team member had been promoted one-rank effective immediately. Warrant Officer Carl Renner would be medically retired from the US Army but hired on as a civilian contractor to support the Peregrine team. This information was exceptionally well received with loud HOOYAH, high fives, slaps on the back by all team members

Second, Field #3 was being upgraded to serve as the base for an expanded Peregrine program. Two additional teams would be selected and trained starting February 1965. The expanded Peregrine group would work closely with the Special Air Warfare Center at nearby Field #9, Hurlburt Field.

Third, the existing veteran Peregrine team members would all be assigned to the JCS Special Projects Office at the Pentagon. After the groans subsided, General Wojcik added, most of the time the team would be TDY to Field #3, of course, with TDY pay in addition to their base pay. General Wojcik suggested the team members might want to find housing quarters on the Fort Walton, Florida civilian economy. With the TDY pay, they could afford nice living arrangements for their families. The Washington assignment location was basically eyewash as part of the continuing cover for the team.

Fourth, the team would have 45 days leave, starting two days before Thanksgiving. There will be special assignments for certain individuals which will be handled after this meeting.

A very happy Peregrine team filed out of the conference room. General Wojcik said the newly minted US Navy Lieutenant Commander, should remain.

"Gary you are assigned to attend MIT to earn a Master's degree in Aeronautics and Astronautics. The orders say 18 months, I want you to complete your degree in a year or less. You are slated for a special assignment in Europe after graduation."

Thanksgiving 1964

Holidays are particularly important for military families to be together, given the deployments and distant postings which often leave an

400

empty chair when the family gathers for the holiday. The Thanksgiving gathering at the Major-General Stanislaw Wojcik quarters, Fort McNair, was exemplary of the military family holiday-time together – especially with the war clouds growing as US troops continued to pour into Vietnam and the continuing nuclear first-strike threat from the Soviet Union.

Participants in this joyous 1964 Thanksgiving Day assembly included Captain Paul Wojcik, USMA Class of 1959, stationed with the 75th Ranger Regiment at Fort Benning, Georgia. Paul's family was there, all smiles, as his wife, Mary let the men fawn over her two-year old son, Stanislaw II – another soldier in the making - and see these hulking men melt before her very sweet little tousle-hair three-year old, daughter, Julie. Little-Julie was the darling for all at these celebrations. LT Gary Baumgartner, USNA Class of 1961, who had rather mysteriously disappeared from the Navy rosters, some said he went to spook-land. Gary was accompanied by his girlfriend, Annie Hoffman, who worked somewhere in the intelligence community. Annie was highly regarded and loved by the hostess, Ruth, the General's wife.

Captain Peter Wojcik, USMA class of 1961, was not there, but his wife, Amanda with his, just had-his-birthday now three-year old son, smiled as James added another voice to the five 'boys' noisily playing - Grandfather Bull, Uncle Paul, Gary, Stanislaw II, and James. Peter was a paratrooper with the 82nd Airborne Division at Fort Bragg and was in the process of being transferred to a new unit being formed within the 101st Airborne Division at Fort Campbell. The new unit, 1st Battalion, 7th Cavalry Regiment, was formed to test a new concept, 'air calvary' using helicopters as modern horses. Peter was transferred at the request of LTC Hal Moore, also from the 82nd who was to be the commander of the new 'air mobile' unit. LTC Moore held Peter in high-esteem as an officer and leader.

The afternoon before dinner was filled with the shouts, laughs, and the running around of three-generations of boys and men 'who remained boys at heart'. Little Julie was near tears several times, as she tried to exert a maternal influence on the out-of-control 'boy' marauders. She was being ignored as she raised her three-year old girl-voice to chastise the boisterous horde 'to behave'. Resigned that boys are naughty, she retreated in tears to help her grandmother, mother, and aunt prepare dinner.

Part of the boys' play was punctuated by friendly jabs, as Gary reminded Paul of the recent dominance by the Navy football team lead by Roger Staubach over the 'Woo-Poo on the Hudson River' football team, Paul retorted with unflattering commentary about the 'Boat School on the Severn River'. Pausing for breath after chasing the two little-boys around the house, Paul tapped his right-eye socket-bone, and then pointed at the cut above Gary's right eye, closed with nine-stitches, still deep-red as a scar formed.

He asked Gary,

"How does the other guy look?"

Gary replied,

"Well, he successfully completed his 'screen test' to star in the movie, "Sucker Punch".

General Wojcik interrupted the subsequent laughing,

"Let me tell you what really happened", stifling his own laughter,

Bull began the story.

"You see, our sailor here picked the biggest bad-ass on the team for hand-to-hand combat practice – and Podowski is serious big. Anyway, Podowski whips-up on the sailor with a slashing elbow and busts the sailor's forehead open. Blood is gushing and running into the sailor's right eye – he can't see but has this rubber knife – got it so far. The smaller of the two combatants looks like a bloody Cyclops holding a now bloody rubber knife – but the sailor has a plan. The sailor makes a stabbing move at Podowski's stomach. The stabbing move was a feint so the sailor could drop to his side to deliver a kick to Podowski's knee, which at that point was solidly implanted bearing Podowski's ponderous weight. The sailor made the kick, but held back on the force – otherwise Podowski would have been permanently crippled. Then the sailor was off to improve his sorry-looks with the nine-stitch embroidery."

The adult-boys laughter was interrupted by two' ready-to-go-again' little boys and the fun continued for all. The little boys thought Gary looked like a pirate with his red scar.

Dinner brought an overall change in the decibel-level as the mood shifted to a sense of the meaning to be thankful for the blessings they all shared. General Wojcik united all in his Thanksgiving prayer of thanks:

thanks for the family which was together at this table, remembering Peter and asking for the blessing of protection for the young paratrooper captain, and thanking God that they all were blessed by being citizens of the greatest nation in history, the United States of America.

A perfect day of celebration by family and friends ended after a happy, reflective conversation in the Wojcik living room. Ruth, the wife of a soldier, mother of two soldiers, and grandmother of future soldiers had made so many good-byes over the years, but no 'good-by' was ever routine for the military family – deployments or just going back to various homes after a joyful time together – each time carried an emotional cost. Ruth did not cry, though she would have liked to cry. She hugged grandchildren, her son, her two daughters-in-law, gave a gracious hug to 'the sailor', and a special-compassionate hug for Annie. The men shook hands. Gary and Annie thanked Ruth for the pleasant day, great dinner, and for her kindness in inviting them. In the blue Corvette for the ride back to Annie's apartment, Annie tried to speak but her quivering voice and salty-tears running down her cheeks choked her from talking about how much she had appreciated this special Thanksgiving Day.

Christmas 1964

The team had 45 days leave for the holidays. Annie and Gary would depart 20 December for Christmas 1964 on the Hoffman family farm. Between the pleasant Thanksgiving dinner and the sheer happiness of being together, a symbolic action was taken. Gary sold his Corvette. Annie said he was finally maturing, Gary said the Corvette was not good in snow. Smiling at each other, they moved to the bedroom to reconcile their disagreement and mourn the loss of the Corvette. Annie hid her private concern that their conversations all seemed to drift away from any specifics for their future, beyond their respective near-term assignments to Harvard and MIT for advanced-degree studies.

Gary saved a lot of money while he was in Vietnam. In addition, he got a very good cash-deal for his Corvette, a horny Navy pilot, who wanted a chick-magnet vehicle and had plans for a sojourn over the holidays at the 'snake ranch' he and his buddies had in Norfolk.

Annie commented,

"Is there any other kind of Navy pilot than a horny one?"

They bought Annie a light-blue 1964 Ford Galaxie 500 XL. Gary purchased a pristine 1957 Chevrolet, black, two-door Bel Air for himself. They decided they would drive the Ford to Indiana as part of the break-in period. The new-car break-in rules would help Gary keep his 'need-for-speed' driving under control. Annie allowed that Gary could drive the Ford, some, but only if he promised to 'not behave' when they stopped for the night. Thinking that proposition over for about one-second, Gary agreed.

The trip to Indiana was pleasant but Annie continued to fret and be privately frustrated that Gary seemed to avoid making serious plans for their future beyond their upcoming student-time in Boston.

The ground was covered with four inches of snow and the temperature was 25 degrees when they arrived at the farm. Gary's blood was still thin from his time in the heat and humidity of Vietnam. Annie's parents had been watching and waiting – expecting the Corvette, they did not recognize the light-blue 1964 Ford Galaxie 500 XL driving up their farm lane.

When Annie got out, her mother laughed and quickly brushed away a tear. Smiling, she just muttered, "new car and new winter coats for those two." Annie ran to the door leaving the luggage to Gary and her father. Embracing her Mom, she thought how good it was to be back home in Indiana.

In some ways the 1964 visit was a replay of the 1963 Christmas: farm chores, drinking beer, and telling stories for the men, personal time together for Annie with her mother, with good food and fellowship for all. Even so, Annie was still troubled. She decided to share her concerns with her Mom. Annie confided that she did not feel Gary was serious in their relationship. Annie wanted a future with Gary, but she did not seem to be able to get Gary to commit beyond the 'here and now'. Annie's mother embraced her daughter.

"Annie, Gary just got back from the war. Please give him a little time".

Annie's mother decided not to mention that the new car Gary purchased for her held some significance.

While Annie teared-up talking to her mother, Gary was talking to her father down in the barn, his breath forming small frozen clouds as they conversed.

"Fred, I would like your permission to ask Annie to marry me".

Fred gave a hearty laugh and slapped a hard calloused hand on Gary's shoulder,

"Son, her mother and I would like to have you as a son-in-law – but you know, the only vote that counts here is Annie's "vote".

Before supper, Gary asked Annie if she wanted to walk down to the barn with him.

Without hesitating, Annie said, "No".

Annie's frustration had turned to anger. Her mother's advice to be patient, instead of being comforting, that sage maternal advice had refueled her anger toward Gary.

Gary asked Annie,

"Why can't we get some fresh air, this cold is refreshing. You could cut the hot-humid air in the Nam jungle with a knife".

Annie responded,

"It's too cold"

Now Gary was frustrated,

"I thought we bought the new coats and boots for cold weather".

Annie noticed she was getting disapproving looks from her father and her mother.

She brusquely said, "OK", and stomped out of the room to put on her new cold-weather coat and boots.

Annie and Gary walked in silence toward the barn. Gary stopped and turned to her,

"Are you mad at me?"

Annie was now embarrassed. She did not have a reasonable response to this simple question. She just hung her head wishing she had not agreed to go on this walk. Gary said in a calm voice,

"I had something important to talk to you about. If you are angry, we can do it another time."

Annie continued to walk toward the barn again as Gary stood waiting for an answer. Turning her head, she said,

"I thought you wanted to walk to the barn".

Her curiosity about Gary saying, I had something important to talk to you about, helped her gain a sense that she was overreacting to emotions of frustration and her consequent anger.

They walked into the barn with the smells of hay, straw, animals, and machinery, all fused as the familiar smell of a working-barn in Indiana. Gary was not sure how to proceed. He sat down on a bale of straw and motioned for Annie to join him.

As they sat in silence, Annie rejected her mother's advice to be patient - she asked in a strained tone –

"What is it that you wanted to talk to me about?"

Gary pondered the situation he was in. This is not the plan, but hell, this is what I do when the situation changes – I modify the plan and improvise as needed and do the mission.

"Annie, this is not how I rehearsed my plan. This setting is not the romantic aura I wanted. Here we are in a cold barn, and you pissed-off for some unknown reason. I can say that for sure, this setting will be memorable"

All of which made Annie smile, a little bit.

Thinking on the motto, 'With my shield or on it' – Gary went directly to his point, albeit, not as smoothly and movie-romantic as he had originally planned -

"Annie, I love you! Will you marry me?"

At the same time Gary was reaching in his pocket for a blue velvet box. Annie burst into tears and thought, Mom was right,

"Gary, I am sorry. I was mad at you because - because you were not asking me to marry you".

Gary took his gloves off and wiped her tears away before they could freeze. He opened the blue velvet box to reveal a simple ring set with a large solitaire-diamond, asking her,

"Are you going to answer my question or not".

Annie said,

"Yes, yes – I will marry you" – adding in jest – "I cannot believe I am going to marry a sailor".

They kissed and laughed as Gary put the ring on her finger, in the family-farm barn in Indiana.

The rest of the Christmas 1964 visit was happy and even dreamy. The gift exchange on Christmas Eve had a couple of special moments. Gary gave his future father-in-law a hand-carved jade dragon and Annie's mother an exquisite hand-woven silk scarf. Annie feigned anger and asked, "what did you get for me?"

Gary, using his most innocent look, responded,

"Well my darling, I got you me!"

This earned the sailor a hefty punch in the arm from his fiancé.

Annie's parents handed Gary a heavy flat box. When he opened the box, he saw it contained a very-used Colt 1911 model 45 caliber semi-automatic pistol. Annie's mother had tears running down her cheeks as Fred explained,

"It's Robert's gun. The Marine Corps returned it to us from Iwo Jima."

Gary could not speak, fully understanding the meaning behind their gifting this weapon to him. Annie did not know before-hand about the gift, and she began to cry along with her mother.

Gary shook hands with Fred with their mutual powerful grips. Gary leaned over to hug his future mother-in-law. Annie cleared her voice, trying to lighten the mood,

"That's a hard act to follow".

She handed Gary his present wrapped in Santa Claus wrapping paper. Annie gave him a long super-soft velveteen robe, with a note, "We need to just relax more together, Love, Annie"

So went Christmas 1964 – a proposal in a working-barn – a gift of a precious weapon that bonded the four of them in an unexpected loving-intimacy.

The Cold War raged on and intensified. The US government stumbled forward in the Vietnam War with an incredible lack of vision and virtually no viable perception of ongoing realities. The existential first-strike nuclear attack by the Soviet Union continued as a 'strategic sword of Damocles' over the US. The veteran True Believers from the Peregrine team and the Operation Red KGB operatives prepared for the next step 'into the future' – their next "MISSION".

EPILOGUE

"...there are things in this world that are more important than ourselves. Freedom. The Constitution of the United States. Our way of life. We belong to something greater than ourselves,... this idea called America, binds us together in citizenship and community and brotherhood."

USAF Lieutenant Heather Renee Penney. A True Believer F-16 Pilot, volunteered to ram a terrorist aircraft, UA flight 93 to saves lives in Washington, DC

A True Believer is a person who is totally committed and devoted to a cause and willing to give the "last full measure of devotion" for that cause.

Each member of the Peregrine Team is a True Believer fully committed and devoted to serve and protect the United States of America and its citizens from threats to their security and welfare.

The KGB adversaries, Major Alexandr Mikailovich Petrov and Captain Nyugen Kie^ are True Believers who pose a strategic threat to the United States as they continue to run the top KGB mole, agent Pravda, buried in the US government. Alexandr Petrov is fully committed to the historic idea of "Mother Russia" and the 'Russian people'. Nyugen Kie^ is a True Believer as she was equally committed and devoted to her mentor and lover, Alexandr 'Sasha' Petrov

The Peregrine Team conducted its sensitive Top Secret mission in Vietnam with exemplary professionalism and dedication. The successful completion of that mission "taking down The Spider and his network" would save countless American lives over the duration of the Vietnam War. The Team paid a high price experiencing over 30% casualties in killed and wounded in action. In addition to saving American lives the Team provided a second result. The Team demonstrated Major-General Wojcik's concept that a small team of select True Believer professionals could effectively take on a strategic threat to the country and take-out that threat.

At no time did the Vietnam War result pose an existential threat to the United States of America. The existential threat to the United

409

States during the Cold War was the Soviet Union's ability to launch a massive nuclear weapon attack on our nation. Such a Soviet attack would annihilate the United States as a viable country and society. At the same time, the Soviet leaders faced an equivalent annihilating nuclear strike from the United States nuclear forces. The resulting balance of nuclear terror created a perception and a strategy called Mutual Assured Destruction (MAD).

But MAD was based on a deeply flawed simplistic concept. The strategic principle behind MAD was the two superpowers, the US and the Soviet Union, each possessed an arsenal of nuclear weapons which could effectively annihilate the opposing superpower. The MAD argument was a first strike would generate a counterstrike and both superpowers would be mutually destroyed. Thus, rational leaders of each country would be deterred from launching a first strike nuclear attack. MAD had two inherent flaws that caused the MAD strategy to be unstable and dangerous. The primary problem was the assumption that national leaders always would 'act rationally'. Historical evidence shows this is a flawed premise, humans do not always act rationally. The second flaw was, if either side achieved a quantitative or qualitative nuclear missile advantage or one nation deployed an effective ballistic missile defense, that superpower would have a transitory strategic advantage to destroy the nuclear threat from the opposing superpower with a 'first strike'.

The leaders of the Soviet Union were aggressive and paranoid. They ruled the Warsaw Pact eastern European countries with a brutal-hand administered by the KGB and the Red Army. Furthermore, the Soviet leaders espoused spreading a Soviet-brand communism around the globe. The USSR national resources and human capital were primarily devoted to building a dominant military force to advance their strategic agenda.

The Soviet leaders understood and were afraid of the military might and industrial capacity of the United States. Furthermore, the Soviet leaders believed the United States intended to launch a first strike nuclear attack when the 'correlation of forces' was to the American advantage. A high level CIA spy in Russia with access to some of the Soviet leaders thinking reported that the Soviet leadership had just committed their nation to a massive deception program. The objective of the deception was to hide development of a strategic ballistic missile defense system. Once the USSR had an effective ballistic missile defense system deployed, the United States would face an existential asymmetry in nuclear attack survivability. In that circumstance, the USSR could destroy the US at will unless the US submitted to Soviet subjugation.

The very existence of such a destabilizing Soviet strategy would cause comprehensive political problems for the US and potentially place the existence of the US at risk. Major-General Bull Wojcik was tasked by the Chairman of the Joint Chiefs of Staff to prepare an "off-the-books" Top Secret plan to undermine and defeat the Russian deception strategy. General Wojcik convened his Peregrine True Believers to take-out the Soviet threat. A small group of clandestine operatives would execute a clandestine mission to ensure US security from the Soviet intention to conduct a nuclear first-strike attack on the US.

GLOSSARY

Acronyms, Military/Intelligence Terms & Jargon

AFB: Air Force Base

Air America: Air American was the cover name for a covert airline operated by CIA in Southeast Asia. Air America used a diverse fleet of fixed-wing aircraft: large transports, small aircraft capable of short takeoff and landing (STOL) from jungle and mountain runways, and helicopters to conduct and support 'spy missions' in all the countries in Southeast Asia, including South and North Vietnam.

AK-47: An automatic high-rate-of-fire rifle for individual infantry troops. The AK-47 fired a 7.62-mm round. This Russian weapon was widely used by the VC and NVA.

ARVN: Army of Vietnam (South Vietnam)

Black bag job: A clandestine operation to physically penetrate a target facility to plant listening devices, steal documents, photograph materials, and otherwise surreptitiously collect intelligence.

Boo-coo: GI bastardized French, from the word beaucoup, meaning "much" or "many".

Brigadier General: One-star flag officer

Case officer: A case officer is a clandestine operative working in the field to recruit and control agents (spies)

CI: Counterintelligence

CIA: Central Intelligence Agency

Clandestine: Clandestine is the term used to define the ultimate secrecy for an operation, that is the 'very existence' of the operation is to be kept secret. Done properly, the enemy concludes 'No such event ever happened'.

Clandestine agent: The in-house professional term used for the more widely used term "spy"

CONUS: Term commonly used by the Americans deployed out of the country, "continental United States", related terms were "land of the big PX" and "Home"

COMINT: Communications intelligence (radio and other message traffic intercepted and collected by technical means)

CNO: Chief of Naval Operations

Coup de grâce: Death blow, finishing stroke

Coup de maître: Masterstroke, stroke of genius

Coup de theatre: An action for sensational effect

Cover: The role played by an intelligence officer (or agent) to conceal his true purpose for living or traveling abroad. The KGB refers to 'cover' as the 'legend'.

Cover organization: An entity created specifically to support the cover of an operative and/or to support single, or multiple, clandestine operations.

Covert: Covert is used in situations where the operation is designed to conceal the identity of those conducting the operation and give an opening for plausible denial

CPSU: Communist Party of the Soviet Union

CR: The contact report (CR) is a classified document prepared after each 'contact' with a spy. The CR memorializes, in fine detail, what happened during the meeting and the case officer conclusions from the meeting

Dangle: A "dangle" is in effect 'human bait' used to entice the enemy behave in a certain manner and force an enemy into security blunders. A dangle usually has the goal to become a double agent.

Deconfliction Division ARVN headquarters: The organization in the ARVN Joint General Staff which reviews plans for ARVN and US combat operations. The objective was to avoid incidents of friendly-fire or other cross-purposes actions. This sensitive information on US and ARVN operations was used by the North Vietnamese 'moles' to kill US and ARVN troops.

DF: Direction finding, electronic equipment used to locate a radio transmitter

Double Agent: Agent in contact with two opposing intelligence services, only one of which is aware of the contact with the other agency

DRV: Democratic Republic of Vietnam (North Vietnam)

DZ: Drop zone, a clear area for agents to parachute into

False Flag: The case officer is from country A intelligence agency; the case officer deceives the target to believe the target will be working for country B intelligence service. The spy delivers information which the spy believes is for country B; but the case officer, under the' false flag', forwards the information to country A.

GCHQ: Government Communications Headquarters (UK agency similar to the US NSA), collects communications and signals intelligence

GET SMALL – the order to 'hit the ground' as a danger-close air strike or danger-close artillery barrage is incoming

GRU: Soviet 'Red Army' intelligence service. The GRU had an effective SIGINT capability among the many GRU intelligence competencies. The KGB tended to be condescending toward the GRU even though the GRU was highly effective.

HUMINT: The use of individuals to collect intelligence information (HUMINT), spies

Humping it: Carrying a full rucksack, weapons, ammo, and water during an on-foot-missions in the jungle, Mekong Delta, Central Highlands, or the rural rice paddies

IA: Immediate Action drill, the immediate reaction by a US patrol in response to an enemy contact

IC: US intelligence community composed of CIA, DIA, NSA, the military services' intelligence organizations (Army, Air Force and Navy), State Department INR, and the FBI. The separate agencies operate independently on a daily basis but collaborate at the national level on high-level intelligence products such as the National Intelligence Estimates (NIE)

Illegal: KGB term used for deep cover agents operating in a foreign country; these spies have assumed identities and false backgrounds. The 'illegals' are run by one of the most secretive parts of the KGB, Department S

In-country: Slang term used by American troops meaning, 'you are in Vietnam'

INR: Bureau of Intelligence and Research, the US State Department intelligence organization

JCS: Joint Chiefs of Staff (top military leadership of US forces, composed of the Chairman of the Joint Chiefs of Staff, Vice Chairman, Army Chief of Staff, Air Force Chief of Staff, Chief of Naval Operations, US Marine Corps Commandant)

KGB: Soviet intelligence service (similar to the CIA)

Liaison Directorate: DRV super-secret Liaison Directorate dealing with running North Vietnamese spies in South Vietnam

LLDB: South Vietnam special forces (Luc Luong Dac Biet)

LTC – Lieutenant Colonel

Lt General: Lieutenant General (three-star rank flag officer)

LZ: Landing zone for helicopters

MACV: Military Assistance Command Vietnam

MACV-SOG: Military Assistance Command Studies and Observation Group (SOG was a top-secret unit carrying out covert missions in Cambodia, Laos, North and South Vietnam)

Major General: Two-star flag rank officer

Maskirovka: Russian term meaning deception or disguising truth.

MfS: East German counterpart to CIA, Ministry for State Security - in German: Ministerium für Staatssicherheit

MI-6: British intelligence agency, similar to CIA

mike-mike: Millimeter size of a weapon projectile/bullets, the A1-E had 20-millimeter cannons; the AK-47 was a 7.62 mm weapon

Ministry of Defense Intelligence Department: North Vietnamese intelligence service, similar to the US CIA

NCO: Non-commissioned officers, corporals and sergeants in the Army and Marine Corps and Navy Petty Officers

NIE: Reports produced as a collective effort by the IC. An NIE is the highest US form of intelligence reports and are limited access to only a few 'customers' including the President, National Security Council, the intelligence committees of Congress, and others on a "need-to-know" basis.

NKVD: Soviet intelligence agency renamed as KGB after WWII

NSA: National Security Agency, top secret organization for collection of communications and signals intelligence

Number-1: Vietnam slang for 'very good'

Number-10: Vietnam slang for 'very bad'

Nungs: A minority group of ethnic Chinese descent living in South Vietnam. The Nungs had a reputation as fierce fighters. They served loyally with the U.S. Army Special Forces in a variety of roles.

NVA: North Vietnamese Army

Operations officer: The operations officer (Ops Officer) acts as the leader of a group of case officers who handle spies. The Ops Officer evaluates and approves the case officer plans to recruit and handle spies.

Public Security Directorate: North Vietnamese internal security service, similar to a combination of the US FBI and local police or the Second Chief Directorate of the KGB.

REMF: Crude GI slang for service members in headquarters 'non-combat' assignments (Rear Echelon Mother-Fuckers)

Rezidentura: KGB term for the KGB main 'station' in a foreign country, The CIA use the term, 'Station' to mean the same thing as Rezidentura. For example, CIA Moscow Station. The head of a 'CIA station' is called 'the Chief of Station'; the KGB use the term: Rezidentura to identify the primary headquarters of the KGB in a country. For example, for the KGB Rezidentura London, the head of a Rezidentura is called the 'Rezident'.

RPG: Deadly 'rocket-propelled-grenade' – used by VC and NVA

SCIF: Secure Compartmented Intelligence Facility, a controlled access area for Top Secret/Special Compartmented Intelligence activities, specially designed to negate enemy collection of COMINT, avoid enemy placing bugs, or enemy physical access. The SCIF is routinely swept for enemy listening devices; all who enter a SCIF must be on the access list and be properly badged

SDR: Surveillance detection route, a preplanned route, either on foot or in a vehicle, that is designed to expose any surveillance of an operative or agent

SIGINT: Signals Intelligence, information gleaned from the collection and analysis of electronic signals. SIGINT includes the COMINT and ELINT technical disciplines

Sitrep: Situation report, a report on the current status

Slicks: UH-1 'Huey' helicopters to move troops on the battlefield, the term Slick distinguished the cargo and personnel models from Huey gunships; the Slicks did have door gunners who manned M-62 machine guns

Snake and Nape: "snake", 250-lb Mk-81 Snakeye bombs: nape, 500-lb. M-47 napalm filled canisters.

Spy: "spy" is a generic term used in literature to designate a person acting illegally to collect information for a foreign power. In the HUMINT profession, the terms agent, source, and asset are the professional terminology for a recruited "spy". In this book, the term "spy" is interchangeable with agent, asset, source.

TDY: Temporary duty at a specified location, personnel on TDY received an allowance for food and housing at the TDY destination

The Farm: A CIA classified training facility located on the grounds of Camp Peary Virginia

TS/SCI: Top Secret/Special Compartmented Intelligence, a high-level security clearance, the access to compartmented SCI programs is on a strict 'need-to-know' basis – all TS/SCI programs are limited-access. Just having a top secret clearance does not give direct access to SCI compartmented programs – there must be a "need to know".

VC: Viet Cong, also known as The National Liberation Front. VC were the local communist forces in South Vietnam. The VC were of varying fighting quality, some units were of high combat effectiveness. The VC and battle hardened NVA troops worked together during the war against the South Vietnamese and Americans

Willie Pete: White phosphorus, a deadly burning material when released from a bomb, grenade, mortar round, or artillery shell

Xin Loi: Vietnamese term causally used by this meaning "sorry"

Yards: A term used for the disenfranchised Montagnards of Vietnam's Central Highlands who were recruited by the U.S. Army Special Forces to fight Vietnamese communists during the Vietnam War.

ABOUT THE AUTHOR

Gary F. Bowser has dedicated over 60 years of his life to the national security of the United States of America. He is a retired military officer (USAF, LTC retired) with 60+ years' experience in the areas of intelligence and national security.

He served two years in Special Operations during the Vietnam conflict. After that, he served overseas as a HUMINT Case Officer and directed a clandestine HUMINT organization as Operations Officer for over six years. He had extensive experience in Washington D.C. as a DIA Directorate of Estimates, Branch Chief. In that role, he was involved in drafting and coordinating National Intelligence Estimates (NIE) and NATO Military Committee documents.

After retiring from the USAF, he lived in Riyadh, Saudi Arabia, for three-years as an advisor to the Chief of Intelligence, Royal Saudi Air Force. He has been involved with intelligence and business operations internationally in more than 40 countries.

Professor. Bowser taught courses on intelligence principles, intelligence analysis, clandestine operations, HUMINT field procedures, and counterterrorism for Henley-Putnam University and the Henley-Putnam School of Strategic Security, National American University for 14 years.

Professor Bowser holds a Bachelor of Science degree from the US Naval Academy; a Master of Science degree in Aeronautics and Astronautics from the Massachusetts Institute of Technology; a Master of Science in Political Science from Auburn University Montgomery.

Lieutenant Colonel Bowser was an instructor at the Air War College and co-authored (with Colonel Paul Nikula, USAF, and Paul Cherry, CIA) the AWC Soviet Studies Course and related curriculum. Professor Bowser instructed a graduate course in Advanced Guidance and Control Theory for Florida State University. He is a graduate of the Executive Program, School of Business, University of Michigan; the USAF Command and Staff College; the Counterinsurgency Course; and the US Army Airborne School (qualified military parachutist). He is the author of various monographs, articles, studies, and holds a number of patents in the area of x-ray security inspection devices.

PRINCIPAL CHARACTERS

US

Major-General Stanislaw "Bull" Wójcik - Advisor to the Chairman of the JCS as the JCS Deputy for Special Projects. Bull was an OSS veteran who operated behind German lines in France during WWII.

US Army Captain Robert Williams, USMA Class of 1959; 6 feet 2 inches, 215 pounds, brown hair cut short, classic features, played linebacker for the West Point football team, effective in negotiations and coordinating with other organizations such as CIA. Combat experience during a tour in Vietnam as an advisor to an ARVN paratroop battalion

US Navy Lieutenant Gary Baumgartner, USNA Class of 1961; 6 feet 2 inches, 205 pounds, light brown hair cut short, ruggedly handsome, expert in Krav Maga (hand-to-hand combat taught to Israeli special forces), tour in Vietnam with CIA on a protype mission to find and assassinate senior Viet Cong leaders (a prelude to the CIA Phoenix Program), relaxed with a sense of humor.

NSA Analyst: Annie Hoffman: brilliant young analyst and was described as every America man's "Dream Lover". Her fervent patriotism drives her to go the second-mile to identify and mitigate any threats to the US and American citizens.

Soviet/Russians

KGB Captain: Captain Alexandr Mikailovich Petrov (known to his friends as "Sasha"), his father is a KGB General in the Second Chief Directorate. Captain Petrov is rising star in the KGB.

The Swallow – Nyugen Kie^, a KGB female seductress. Kie^ is a beautiful French-Vietnamese Eurasian woman. The KGB uses the "swallows" as a type 'intelligence service' prostitute to compromise targeted individuals. Kie^ is good at her job and is highly intelligent.

North Vietnam Mole in ARVN Central Joint Staff

Principal Agent controlling the North Vietnamese spy network assassinating US Army Advisors serving with the South Vietnamese army.

A Corrupt American

Calthrop Winston Simmons: US State Department employee. Heavy drinker and profligate womanizer. Ambitious, excessive ego and narcissist, a psychopath. Married to daughter of very wealthy and politically influential businessman.

THE TRUE BELIEVERS

Warriors, Agents, Villains and Other

US True Believers:

Major-General Stanislaw "Bull" Wojcik - Advisor to the Chairman of the JCS - "General Wojcik was the JCS Deputy for Special Projects. Bull was an OSS veteran operating behind German lines in France during WWII.

TEAM PEREGRINE (Cover name in Vietnam - "Adjunct Inspector General Team #4")

Commander – US Army Captain Robert Williams, USMA Class of 1959 (cover name – Jason Carter)

Deputy Commander – US Navy Lieutenant Gary Baumgartner, USNA class of 1961

Ops Officer – US Army Special Forces, Captain Reginald Denning, - two tours in Vietnam, speaks Vietnamese, German, French; former French Foreign Legion officer with experience in Vietnam – believed to be an ethnic German and is serving under a false name in the US Army

Operations Lead NCO: Master Sergeant George Washington Jones; USA, Master Sergeant, Special Forces. The only black member of team. Married with three children. Devout Christian; one prior tour in Vietnam in SOG

Operations NCO: Woodrow Clayton: USA Master Sergeant, Special Forces. Master woodsman and tracker. Devout Christian. Tall lean and wiry. Expert in hand-to-hand combat. Superb marksman with a variety of weapons. Taciturn, but speaks with authority when he talks. Married with two children.

Intelligence: Jacob Risner: USMC, Gunnery Sergeant, Force Recon. Powerfully built. Master at hand-to-hand combat. Drinks and likes the ladies. Divorced, no children. Very earthy guy.

Intelligence: US Army Warrant Officer Carl Renner – brilliant intelligence analyst, meticulous, works the details, enjoys reading and drinking with friends – known to be a bit wild at times

Weapons: Jacob Stanislaw Podowski: US Army Sergeant First Class, Special Forces. Expert in explosives, from the coal mines of West Virginia. Built like a bulldozer and probably the toughest man in a team of 'hard-cases'.

Communications: James Arthur Wilson: USAF Special Operations, Technical Sergeant, Expert in communications and electronics. From California. Surfs, drinks, chases women.

Supply & Logistics: Wilber James, US Army Master Sergeant, known as a world-class scrounger, 'I can get that for you', and, an all-around, wheeler-and-dealer known to have 'liberated' any and all equipment from other units to support his unit's mission (and comforts). Fast talking and glib – drinks and romances the ladies – a fun guy

Medical: US Army Master Sergeant Karl von Eisenberg, "doc" von Eisenberg – expert in medical matters, treatment, medications, and even has performed surgeries in the field during his previous Vietnam tour – Special Forces medic

NSA Analyst: Annie Hoffman: brilliant young analyst – and quite attractive

Soviet True Believers

KGB Captain: Captain Alexandr Mikailovich Petrov (known to his friends as "Sasha"), his father is a KGB General in the Second Chief Directorate. Captain Petrov is rising star in the KGB.

Vladimir Yefimovich Semichastny a Soviet politician, who served as Chairman of the KGB from November 1961 to May 1967

KGB General Aleksandr Michael Sakharovsky, head of The First Main Directorate (or First Chief Directorate, KGB

The Swallow – Nyugen Kie^, a KGB female seductress. The KGB uses the "swallows" as a type 'intelligence service' prostitute to compromise targeted individuals. Kie^ is good at her job and is highly intelligent.

"Illegal" KGB 'mole' in the State Department Personnel Section. James Carter (Dimitri Dimitrovitch Vasilyeva)

North Vietnam

Intelligence Agents who are Moles for North Vietnam in ARVN Central Joint Staff

Colonel Trần Quan – recruited by North Vietnam in 1957 to become the head of the Deconfliction Division in ARVN headquarters. A weak greedy man who cowardly avoids ARVN combat duty as he spies for North Vietnam

Captain Bùi Duc – NVA agent working for Colonel Trần Quan in the Deconfliction Division

First Lieutenant Ngô Hau – unwitting dupe in the Deconfliction Division who is used by Colonel Trần Quan for minor tasks – coward, seeking to avoid combat duty, playboy, rich parents

Sergeant Pham Binh – True name, NVA Colonel Wang Ky. Colonel is a Principal Agent for the North Vietnamese spy under cover as an ARVN NCO as a 'mole' in ARVN headquarters. Colonel Trần reports to Phan and takes orders from Pham. Pham's cover is chauffer for Colonel Trần

ARVN Officer recruited by Team Peregrine Second Lt Lê Minh – avoiding combat by working in South Vietnamese Army General Staff personnel section, recruited by the Adjunct JAG Team – coward, wants money

NUNGS – Ethnic Chinese who lived in Vietnam and often served as mercenaries for US Special Forces

Ban Chen – head of the Nung 'Li clan'

Chee Chen – leader of the Nung fighting men in the Li clan

Duan Ho – ferocious fighter, loyal. Was mercenary for US Special Forces

Chu Zhu – ferocious fighter, loyal. Was mercenary for US Special Forces

Han Li – ferocious fighter, loyal

Villains

A Corrupt American Calthrop Winston Simmons: State Department. Heavy drinker and profligate womanizer. Married to daughter of very wealthy and very influential businessman. Ambitious, excessive ego and narcissist. Bitter that he has not been promoted faster in the State Department. Accepted an assignment to Vietnam Embassy to avoid INR departmental punishment.

The Spider Sergeant Pham Binh – True name, NVA Colonel Wang Ky. Colonel is a Principal Agent for the North Vietnamese spy under cover as an ARVN NCO as a 'mole' in ARVN headquarters. Murderer of US Army advisors; despoiler of young girls; greedy narcissist.

OPERATION PEREGRINE
Deceit • Espionage • Seduction

- A twisted web of espionage, deceit, treachery

- The KGB has a mole in the South Vietnamese assassinating American officers

- Protagonist love affairs conflict with mission demands

- Epic tour de force bringing You inside a complex US espionage operation facing constant dangers from the North Vietnamese Army and the KGB

- Adversaries fight a deadly 'smoke and mirrors' war in the steamy jungles of Vietnam and the urban crucible of Saigon

 www.garybowser.net
Auburn, Indiana U.S.A.
ISBN 978-1-7375133-1-5

 Gary Bowser is a retired US Air Force officer and intelligence operative running clandestine operations against the Soviet Union. Warsaw Pact, North Vietnam and other communist adversaries of the USA and Free World. He also served as a Defense Intelligence Agency Branch Chief responsible for drafting National Intelligence Estimates. After retirement from the military, he served for three-years as an advisor to the Chief of Intelligence, Royal Saudi Air Force. Currently he is a Professor with the Henley-Putnam School of Strategy Security, instructing clandestine operations (the spy business), intelligence analysis, and counterterrorism. Operation Peregrine is his first venture into fiction and readers will be caught up in its realism, excitement and spell-binding action because they realize that Gary is writing with personal knowledge of a recent intense international conflict.

Made in United States
North Haven, CT
01 December 2021

11838581R00241